GENESIS II

CHARLES YANNETTE

Order this book online at www.trafford.com
or email orders@trafford.com

Most Trafford titles are also available at major online book retailers.

Edited by Ben Yannette, Illustrations by Joshua Norman

Printed in the United States of America.

ISBN: 978-1-4269-6900-3 (sc)
ISBN: 978-1-4269-6901-0 (e)

Trafford rev. 05/09/2011

www.trafford.com

North America & international
toll-free: 1 888 232 4444 (USA & Canada)
phone: 250 383 6864 ♦ fax: 812 355 4082

For Tony and Jean Yannette

FOREWORD

I only remember visiting my great-grandfather twice. Sadly, most of my knowledge about him has been secondhand. I had heard some very interesting things about him: that he was a police captain, a top marksman, a pool champion, the unlikely but much appreciated hero who took my father to all of his piano lessons, and, of course, that he liked to write. After reading and editing this epic and always surprising novel of his, I feel like I know him. Between the lines, there is a gold mine of clues about who he was.

First of all, it is now easy to see where my grandfather got his knack for mechanics and chemistry. This was a man who was aware of the physical world around him and how it worked. It struck me that for as farfetched as the story gets at times, when it comes to how his underwater city functioned, or the exact specifications and dimensions of it's layout, or the precise blood content of the squid-human hybrids—a.k.a. Octomen, fish men, human fish, squidtallum, uglies, and little bastards—or even the entire process of curing CANCER, he pushes himself to painstaking realism and detail. Nowadays Google makes research on these things somewhat easier to do, but I imagine him poring over books in his garage, late at night, creating this complex, scientific world one slow keystroke at a time

Another trait of his that becomes obvious from reading this book, and another trait obviously passed on to my grandfather, is an absolute dedication to family and friends. As mischievous as his protagonist is, he constantly reiterates his love for his mother and father and his best friend Juan. It is reminiscent of the traditional family unit, unbreakable and always dependable. That's how our family is now, the nucleus being my grandparents that hold everyone together, and I attribute part of that to his legacy.

You may notice that every single character he introduces is accompanied by a list description of their age, height, weight, build, hair and eye color. As a read, this gets a bit redundant. I wondered why he wouldn't have come up with a more subtle and interesting way to describe them. Then I realized that to a police officer, who was trained to catalogue and communicate those details about a person immediately upon sight, this must have seemed a perfectly natural way to identify them. Outside of this book, he did some very serious and thought-provoking writing on the subject of police work and his frustrations with the rising crime levels in Florida at the time, never to be published.

One thing I clearly remember from my visits with him is that even in his 80's he was still an intense and powerful guy. One could never be sure that they were safe from a hard pat on the back or being scooped up for a slightly painful bear hug. This aspect of his personality comes across clearly in his writing. His characters don't just kiss and hug, they give each other "*colossal*" hugs and "*earth-shattering*" kisses. And more. Which brings me to my next conclusion, which I did *not* know about him from my visits, which is that his libido must have been absolutely out of control!

It was interesting, to say the least, getting into the manuscript and realizing that this was not just an over-the-top science fiction story (as my grandfather had described it), but an erotic one as well. This guy must have had sex on the brain 24/7. The book is full of rounded rumps, female explosions and love-cove explorations. He even goes as far as to list many characters' scientific sexual output (notated in 'pitny grams' which, after some research, I assume to be of his own invention). Aside from the inherent humor in this, it's been fascinating to examine my great-grandfather not through the lens of his old age and familial role, but as the red-blooded Italian guy that he was. And let me stress again, he was very, *very* red-blooded.

These are just a few of the things I have learned from working on Pop's book. I undertook this project as a gift for my grandfather's 80th birthday. The manuscript already had several notes from him trying to edit it himself, but being the head of a five-child household, as well as the president of his company, he never had the time to finish it. I hope that he, and everyone who reads it, has as much fun with it as I have. Thank you to Joshua Norman, a wonderful artist and the illustrator of this book, Jana Krumholtz, who insisted on typing the whole thing out while she watched *Dexter*, and to Pop Pop, Grandmom, and the rest of my family, a rock that is as dependable and supportive as the ground beneath my feet.

Ben Yannette, Editor

PROLOGUE

The great ship, a pinpoint in the sky, came to a smooth stop, its 1,000-yard hull still fiery red. Large scopes protruded from her port side and enormous eyes peered into the small adjustable lens. With deft fingers, the being adjusted the scopes for a close scrutinizing of the landscape, which consisted of a calm body of water and level happyground bordered by a base of mountainous section. The breathtaking locale was so beautiful that it warranted another closer and deeper look.

The vehicle moved in closer to the surface. From its new vantage point the being observed small, hideous creatures strewn about the happyground. Some of the unsightly creatures were running toward an opening in the mountainous slope while others pursued. Repulsed by the sight of the slaughter, the leader of the expedition, Keemons, he of the beautiful eyes and shiny skin, backed away from the scopes.

"Throw the shield," he yelled to Sarsal, second in command. "Throw the shield! It is evil to gaze upon the taking of a life."

Immediately, an invisible shield was cast down, making a barrier at the hillside opening, leaving an escape lane for the creatures being pursued. A score of the aggressive creatures crashed against the barrier, fell to the ground, got up and walked off in the opposite direction, their dull minds failing to grasp the situation.

CHAPTER I

JIMPS
LOVER-----SCIENTIST
The 21ˢᵗ Century's not too Perfect Savior

It was the first day of school and Jimps had already become the class hero, for as he walked into the room he placed a frog on the teacher's seat. When the bespeckled old hag finally sat down, the poor animal croaked. For a moment it appeared that Mrs. Thatcher was going to join the frog in the hereafter. This would have been most satisfying to the students, especially Jimps.

After four hours of games, lunch and a nap, Jimps and Cindy Joe arrived at their homes. Jimps decided that the rear tire on his father's aerocar had too much air in it and that being flat would make it look better. That mission was accomplished. To ease his guilt feelings, he weeded the garden bed. During the process, he decided to bottle ten worms. After dinner, these worms would be ready for dissecting. *About four cuts should do it. Bet the first section will live the longest.* It always had before.

Finally it was sleep time. Along came the ever- welcome dreams of trips to strange planets, where monsters, always under Jimps' control, would try to slay and devour Cindy Joe. In the nick of time, the young hero would appear and save her.

* * * * * * * * * *

All were in a holiday mood, flags waving, drums beating, fans screaming. It was a beautiful autumn day. The score was knotted, 7 to 7, and the visiting Sover High team had the football on the 21 yard line. First and 21 yards, for a score that would rob Bate City High of its first undefeated season and the undisputed state title.

The ball was snapped to the quarterback who handed off to the left halfback who scooted to the right defensive back's territory. Before he could cross the scrimmage line he was tackled by defensive cornerback Jimps, who kneed the ball carrier as he was trying to get up from the straw-colored turf. Jimps helped the tackled gladiator to his feet giving him a pat on the back and an ear to ear smile. *Was that an intentional knee?* Hell no! Not with that smiling face, the ball carrier decided.

Second and ten. Again the ball was snapped back and once more it was shoved into the gut of the left halfback, who believed that a dash to the same flank would be unexpected. It would have been if one Mr. James Bard wasn't around. This time it was a vicious tackle that caused the ball to squirm from the halfback's hands and be justifiably recovered by the same Mr. Bard.

The noise from the drums and the shouting of the hysterical 10,000 dimmed the rumble of thunder coming from the dark clouds overhead. The unusual thunder at this time of the year and the slashing rain failed to diminish the thrill of victory. It continued to pour as a somber and cold Jimps realized that two passes and a field goal would be sufficient for a victory for dear old Bate City High. Heaven and Hell combined to agree with Jimps and the hardy, half-frozen 10,000.

That evening, an excited, tuxedoed Jimps and an equally excited Cindy Joe entered the school gymnasium for the Senior Prom and football victory celebration. Jimps, at nineteen, was quite a handsome, desirable boy; 6' 1" in height, a lean body at 165 pounds, darting blue eyes and blond crewcut hair. Yes, quite a knightly figure to an adoring Cindy Joe. A honey-haired Cindy Joe, 5'6" tall, 110 pounds, with light blue eyes and dimpled cheeks, was a picture of glorious health, the nibbs of her slightly over-developed breasts pointing majestically skyward.

Some ten dances into the night and Jimps was drifting on cloud 9, having consumed some six or seven shots of Gem Juice, a highly active body charger. Taking a momentary break from dancing, Jimps suggested to a sparkling Cindy Joe that a stroll about the grounds would be pleasant, to which Cindy Joe agreed.

Sitting on a bench isolated from peering eyes, Jimps, highly primed, started some serious lovemaking. Long choking kisses and the sensitive stroking washed away any resistance that Cindy Joe may have had. A not-too-strongly fighting Cindy Joe was gently pushed down on the damp, cool grass and a wet finger commenced to spread the cushions of her hot throbbing organ. A perspiring, hard-breathing Jimps, his brain pulsating madly, climbed upon the equally blind Cindy Joe. Easing apart her legs, she enveloped his prong of joy. After much moaning and many bursts of womanhood, Cindy Joe, spent and back to normal, tried to act coy, as though the incident was all of Jimps' doing. Jimps, not that the effects of the Gem Juice had left his system, was apologetic, even proposing marriage (that is after he finished college), knowing fully well that he was to enter the School of Biology with its ten year training program.

*　*　*　*　*　*　*　*　*

September 2, 2045, 6:00 A.M.

A cool, frost-bedded morning was suffering the break of day. Having consumed a breakfast of pancakes, sausage and eggs, the mood of a sleepless night left the three members of the Bard family. It was again the beginning of a new school career for Jimps, this time at the World College. Florence, having nursed her third cup of javaline, lovingly fondled Jimps as he donned his overcoat. Motherly advice on the dangers that may arise when living alone and the remedies for such problems fluttered from her quivering lips. Jimps, arms about his mother, bent down and planted a number of kisses on her nose and forehead. Tearful eyes, a handshake and a bearlike hug preceded a pat on his father's back. A not too steady Jimps, knowing that he was leaving his home of nineteen years, rushed from the room mumbling a, "G-d bless you both."

After two days of traveling, Jimps arrived at the World College of America. In awe, he viewed his new home and the beginnings of a new life. Silver colored domes reached hundreds of feet into the heavens. The escalating pushbutton workshops and dorms were each large enough to comfortably teach, house and feed one thousand students. These buildings, paneled with insulated, bombproof aluminum, were erected within a 25 square mile area in the confines of the Rocky Mountains. Above the entryway of each building and over many of the interior doors was engraved the Sworn Code of the Students of World College, "The mind shall be free of all bodily needs. It shall be cleared for all but the task ahead, the pursuit of knowledge and truth for all mankind."

Each building housed specific students who could be identified by the color of their uniforms: silver for the future spacemen, white with blue bands for the medical specialists, green for agriculturalists, black for the marine biologists, and on and on went the colors of tomorrow's budding scientists.

In the storerooms, floor upon floor of chemicals, tools and equipment were stacked on shelving a hundred feet high, all of which made one feel as though he were in a deep ravine with steps leading to the sky. The store rooms were maintained by the World Federation of Supply Depots. Jimps, completely awed, was thrilled upon seeing every imaginable piece of equipment that he would need in the next ten years.

To Jimps, after a day of physical and mental screening tests, it seemed as though he was in a strange world. The computer had revealed that Jimps's active sperm cells needed immediate relief to neutralize his brain cloud. Here in this complicated new setting there wasn't the outlet of a contact sport (a growing boy's key for energy output). There was, as Jimps later learned, physical, mechanized equipment, which could only be used when sanctioned by the physical therapist, governed by the Strain Computer.

There was so much to see and do that there was no time for anything else. Even thoughts of Cindy Joe did not enter Jimps' mind until the arrival of sleeping hours, midnight to 6:00 A.M..

The next day held more tests on the body and tours of the college. The highlight of the day was to be a speech in the afternoon by the Matradean, welcoming them all to the new world. The following day would bring the beginning of three months of learning: the location of equipment, its names, uses and the assigned hours for usage. Three months of memorizing numbers, weights, lows, highs, inside, outside, regular, irregular, possible, and impossible. They would be started down a path of no return. After a short break, the students would begin regular classes. For twelve hours a day they would be bombarded with books, lectures, and recorded class matter which would remain with them to the day of their demise.

Upon returning to his quarters for the regular one-hour relaxation and meditation period, Jimps was pleasantly surprised to find waiting for him a strikingly pretty olive-skinned, dark-haired and eyed girl of about 19 years. She immediately started to disrobe as she introduced herself. Slim of leg and body, she had within a five-minute span completely drained Jimps of all earth-tied memories. Eartha, all 5' of her, had a sperm output of 400 pitny grams, far exceeding the normal output of 126 pitny grams. She was the computer-selected roommate for Jimps for the next ten years at World College.

A short while later, Jimps met the other two roommates who would occupy the four bed apartment. Juan Codora, 5'2", 145 pounds of muscle, black hair and brown eyes, was a product of Costa Rica and had recently been the recipient of 9 gold medals, having broken the Olympic swimming records of a half-century. Juan's partner, 6'2" Olga Borge, with wide hips, overlarge breasts, white blonde hair, blue eyes, a straight nose and a sensuous mouth, had a mild pitny output of 106, compared to a moderate 224 for Juan.

Together the four roommates headed toward the giant auditorium and found seats near the front. After a few minutes, a hush fell over the crowd of students. The Matradean of this great school of learning stood tall and erect, scanning the one thousand students before him. The winner of two consecutive Nobel Prizes, Professor Antonio de Revisio, 6'4" and lean, resembled a hungry hawk. His brown, prematurely dried wrinkles seemed more conspicuous under the piercing eyes and the hooked nose, but his accomplishments in life were beautiful beyond one's imagination. The dark, searching eyes told a story of the love and devotion this man held for all of G-d's playthings.

"Fellow students," a smile lit his face as he spoke, "yes, fellow students. Aren't we all students? For if at any time we cease to study, all is for naught. This cannot happen to this class, for here come those dedicated to learning, not to glory and gold, which are far too important to so many. This, my friends, is the heartbreak road, the unbalanced road of a million failures for every success—*if* you are one of the fortunate." Once again his heart-searching scan swept the room.

"I have been the recipient of two Nobel Awards. Consecutively, may I add. Both were for work in the field of cancer research, one for the arrestment and the other for the cure. What earthly benefits did I receive? None! The two million dollars that came with the awards I placed in a trust fund for the development of the Bali tribe of the Great Amazon territory of South America." A glass of water and a blue energy pill were gulped.

"For nine long years, here in these halls, I worked with the late Doctor James Pling, our assistant director. Our goal was not to find a cure for cancer, for this seemed too much to ask. We wanted only to find a direction to take, a path for others later to follow. The theme of this struggle was one familiar to all researchers: failure, perseverance and maybe, by some chance, the light of success. I would like to tell you at this time about our struggle.

"I had to start somewhere. For the first year, I studied the records of the experiments by the great biologists of the past, hoping for a lead. Unfortunately, all paths led to only one possible solution—the destruction of all affected cells without damaging healthy cells, an idea which had been explored without success for 100 years. After two years of failures, with the added heartache of hundreds of premature deaths of our human guinea pigs, I thought that I was ready to give up. Somehow I found the strength to continue. I hope the students of this class and, with the help of G-d, all scientists will always find the fortitude to strive toward the impossible and the unknown." Another smile met the thunderous applause from the standing and spellbound thousand.

The voice continued. "How will we know how far to go, where it will take us, when to stop? We will not! All we know for certain is that we must continue. We will continue! It doesn't matter where we are led or what the ultimate results may be. Even knowing that they may lead to disaster, we can never stop. There is only one direction, straight ahead.

"Sometime later, I was offered the position of Assistant Director with the Cancer Research Division, sponsored by the University Medical Society. This was a much needed and satisfying job, as I had at my disposal the greatest devises conceived by human hands, together with the most complete bank in the universe, containing every known substance within the bounds of our explored galaxy.

"We worked with ten men, five physiologists and five biologists, with the belief that the path we were following was the proper one – that being the separation of live and dead cancer cells by electron charges and the added administration of pre-toned bio salts. Great strides were made in the complete demolition of the dead cells, but, as always, the live cells received corner damage, no matter how mild the charges.

"Three years, a million dollars, and what had we gained? Only patience and fortitude, which I pray will be instilled in you men…" Every man in attendance had the impression that the gaze was cast at him. "…For your patience may some day become the light we need in the quest to find a way to feed a billion people." The professor smiled again.

"I must apologize. How did I ever come to the conclusion that I could relate twenty years of living in a half hour's time? No way! But, of course, I never did have a time clock in my mind. Time, as you will later learn, is of no importance, especially when there is a goal involved.

"Where had I gone wrong? Had I, after all the years, been on the wrong trail? Could it be that the solution lay not in the destruction of the diseased cells, but possibly solely in the controlled growth of the healthy cells? Could these overly healthy cells double their productive capacity, and possibly eliminate the sick cells? Hundreds of thoughts and possible solutions cluttered my mind.

"Our research grant had reached its end. After three years of failures, setting aside that phase of the project was not an easy matter. Hence, sleep would not come to my troubled mind; that is, without an injection of Mico. But I didn't attempt to force sleep. I wished to stay awake and suffer the failures of the past years. Reaching for and grasping another old ledger alongside my bed, I unconsciously rifled through the pages and started to read a few isolated passages about the Bali Tribe of South America. These natives, about five thousand in all, resided on a one hundred mile square reservation on the banks of the Amazon River and had a life expectancy of one hundred years, twenty more than we are privileged to have.

"Dr. Felix Basuk, author of these documented writings, lived with this tribe for ten years. In his summary, one seemingly unimportant observation by him was that in all those years, he didn't find one symptom of cancer among these simple people. Sleep started to move in. Could it be? Was this the path I was to follow? The thoughts of a grander country, simple people, and the thrilling discovery of a cancer cure was the much needed sedative for my tired mind and body.

"I immediately applied for a grant from the Biological Society which would cover a limited time of five years. Needless to say, I was thrilled with the immediate grant. So, with my computer mate, Marlene, thousands of empty jars, a case of aspirin, some tools, cigmarwetts, a transradioform and toilet needs, we boarded the Helicraft plane.

"The four thousand mile trip was made in ten minutes, enough time for a hot cup of javaline. Hovering over the reservation, the three extended propellers kept the ship stationary above the trees. My day of days had arrived. Too long had I been waiting for a glimpse of my mind's paradise. With all of our possessions, Marlene and I were chuted to earth. Standing before us was a beautiful specimen of manhood. He was my height, but there the resemblance stopped.

Here was 230 pounds of solid muscle. The arms, legs and body development were such that they would be the envy of all athletic men. This chocolate-skinned man, wearing a bright red pair of shorts, a gold chain about his neck and a beautiful plumed headpiece, was an inspiring individual. Corresponding to that appearance was a deep bass voice which boomed, 'Welcome, Doctor. May you and your mate's stay here be one of enjoyment and success.' This greeting was startling as the words were spoken in a distinctly beautiful British accent.

"J.L., as I later learned, was a medical doctor, having received his degree from the medical college of Eaton, England. J.L., known as the tribe's "witch doctor" (just a title) was devoting his life to the betterment of man. The Bali Tribe's district was the place of his choosing.

"After introductions to Chief Docti, his six wives and thirty-one children (an occasion itself) we were accompanied to our quarters. Surprisingly, we had very adaptable lodgings -- a bedroom with screening, a kitchen containing gravity-flow running water, no fixtures and a slate-type stone over an open fireplace for cooking. The last section of our log cabin was a shelved storeroom built under the supervision of J.L., to whom we will be eternally indebted. The most needed facility was the godly building at the rear of our cabin, the Stately Outhouse.

"After a three day feasting period, we prepared for work: month after month of trudging through forests, always with a guard assigned by J.L., digging, clipping, netting and marking the bottled samples. Nights, when Marlene and I weren't too tired, we would record the happenings of the day, with reference to every movement made by the residents. We tape recorded their eating habits, the time they took to consume the food, their order of consumption and intake of iron, starch, protein, carbohydrates, etc. We also kept a record of their health habits. Ironically, I have never seen whiter, more cavity-free teeth in our universe, and these teeth have never been graced by a toothbrush. Extreme body cleanliness was the rule, as the populace was continuously in and out of the homesite waters.

"The tribe's nourishment was derived from fish, frogs, turtles, eggs, an occasional hedgehog or possum and corn. Also, milk and cheese from the great llamas of the area, which are occasionally used for labor and transportation, played an important role.

"Here on these grounds I would have loved to have challenged the hygienists, archeologists and other specialists and have them ascertain the ages of these people. I would have enjoyed their amazement upon finding that a person who was one hundred plus years old, appeared to be roughly sixty. These citizens of the Amazon, the one hundred plus, I dare say, had a pitny output of about 350. The old devils were continuously going to their place of funning, staying for about an hour and returning acting as though they had the greatest gift imaginable. They probably did and knew it.

"The never ending cycle of tests, the depletion of prepared molds, the sickening failures, the hope that this was the time for success and then again, the maddening stab of failure. These were the things we lived with. Only the accidental findings of other cures in other areas, not remotely tied to the project we were working on, made one feel that all was not for naught.

"Some of you may recall the findings of the salts from the mold of the blighted palm trees of the South, now the accepted blood builder for leukemia sufferers (an accidental finding, of course). This was accomplished by the unselfish work of Professor Juled Brahn, the foremost biologist in that field, and an equally dedicated staff headed by Doctors Edith Statler and George Peil. Simply, many are the times when working toward one goal achieves another."

Taking a large yellow handkerchief from his inside coat pocket, the professor wiped a wet brow, saying, "I believe this next statement needs a bit of brow dabbing.

"I not only believe, but know, that the following discovery was one of man's greatest achievement. Prepare yourselves. Thirty years of trying to find a cure for the crippler of man and beast, and what do we accidentally discover? A laxative!" Another smile guided the appreciative applause from the audience, a smile which took all of the professor's willpower to keep from becoming an outright laugh. He continued, "Always be thankful that you are the men you are, for many of your paths, seemingly at a dead end, may eventually lead to another road. Never dismay." He gave another long searching glance about the chamber.

"An everlasting thought must be embedded in your mind. What does one do when a solution seems beyond one's grasp? At your disposal are the results of millions of hours of study by the greatest minds in the universe, all in script and on tapes. Review this matter and you may find your starting point.

"Back we went to testing, sampling and eliminating. We had decided that the answer had to lay in the diet of the Bali. Thousands of food derivatives were tested to attempt to determine which food or combinations of foods contained the most balanced minerals and nutrients necessary to produce the healthiest body cells. The amount of food consumed and the time of consumption were eliminated as insignificant factors. Hundreds of pages of data, partly disassociated, led us to the dire need of computer banks for determination of any significant correlations. Our work with the Bali Tribe was nearing its ends with the prospect of likely failure. I was sure it was not a total loss, for I was certain that we would find something in their mode of living that would reveal the secret of the fast healing of their bodies. When they were cut or bruised by thorns, their bodies usually healed within a twenty-four hour period.

"Many evenings after a strenuous day, Marlene and I would relax by smoking and watching the youngsters splash and scream in the cool waters that were a few feet from doorstep. Their bodies glistened as bright as their beautiful large eyes and shiny teeth. It was an unforgettable scene.

"After almost five years of friendship with J.L., Chief Docti, his wives and family of children (which had grown to 43), it was an ordeal to say goodbye. With five thousand looking on and with a promise to return someday, we bade all our friends a tearful farewell. There in the heavens was our transportation back to civilization and the Biological Society Building.

"How much do I owe these wonderful human beings? Can I ever repay J.L., a very busy man, who spent countless hours, bedside, extracting poisonous fluids from Marlene's fevered body when it became infected after receiving a bite from the deadly green snake? This ten foot reptile, even after being cut in two, had its teeth imbedded in Marlene's leg depositing the death dealing juices into her vein. That unselfish act of J.L.'s made it possible for me to be graced with ten more years with my fellow biologist and computer mate, whose eventual death resulted from, not the bite of a visible snake, but from a snake mightier than all others, my nemesis: Cancer.

"Here at World, in this building, all of the foods that we had stored in a preservative with multiple limesalts were detemperaturized and made into pill form. They were later placed into metal containers, tagged and shelved away for future use. Review after review, test after test, the Bali findings were beginning to point to a staggering discovery. Could this simple line lead us to the answer? Could it be that we had to go back to the start of life, every life? I believed that the first builder of cells was the basic cancer resistant substance: Milk may be the answer! MILK! Also, the findings revealed that the milk from the human mother lost its salt, calcium 2 and plasma antitypes three to four months after birth and built up a water reserve, unlike some of the animal milk from the Bali Tribe which did not lose any of its mineral or blood contents.

"It is now the accepted fact that the milk needed to finalize our experiments had to be heavier with more blood contents, far greater than the amount furnished by humans or the domestic cow. Was altitude a factor? Was high temperature a link? Could this milk be obtained from the sheep of the Pitcan Islands, the llamas of Tibet or from any milk-producing animal from high altitude areas?

"I was terrified, very much afraid to articulate my thoughts. It sounded too simple. Was the cancer fight of so many heartbreaking years at our fingertips? My mind was clouded.

"Fifty specialists were assigned to the most probable milk producing animal and plant producing areas in our galaxy. We, that is, the senior biologists, believed that this latest mission could be accomplished within a six-month period. Work began immediately on the testing of milk contents taken from animals throughout the world. Four months later, almost to the day, the Board members were informed that the milk from the udder of the big horn goats of Rockamondolf, Italy met with all of the basic requirements.

"My three compatriots for the next three years, Doctors Belfast, Moore and Henderson, had planned and acquired all of the needs for this hopefully last exploration. A new, and what would become the last grant had been approved months before, allotting the money needed to carry this project through.

"A trip to my native country, the first in twenty five years! Would the changes be noticeable? Anxious to start on our project, we left with our laden ship and arrived at our destination on January 14, 2038 on a cold day that dipped the thermometer needle to twenty degrees below zero. Rockamondolf, the world almanac told us, was a village situated in the mountains of the Alps at an altitude of six thousand feet above sea level. It had temperature readings ranging from highs of eighty degrees to lows of forty degrees below zero. This village of some five hundred hearty souls had had a goat population increase of thousands during the past half century and a human increase of fourteen people during the same span. This mountainous country was blessed with fertile soil, which yielded lush green stems of grass, able to support the heavy jawed and strong limbed goats of the region. All income was derived from the goats, as the milk and cheeses were taken to Bouino, a city of fifty thousand, situated six thousand feet below Rockamondolf, part of the Principacio de Combobasso. Bouino, the city of twenty-five churches and one hundred cantinas, was known worldwide for its delicious cheeses.

"Our station, a modest three bedroom home, had been the proud possession of the village's distinguished Chief Constable. Three large garages, fully heated, were at the rear of the property. These were set up, equipped and maintained by the advance crew, who incidentally had the responsibility of seeing that a three-year supply need was on hand.

"I am not going to repeat the procedures of all the primary tests that ensued during the next year, but may I say, and it is important, that our normal work day was eighteen hours long and that was never long enough. Out of the five hundred rosy-cheeked, strong-limbed people, sixty were on the sweet side of fifty-five. These were the group that agreed to go along with our plans, after we had convinced them that these tests would not interfere with their daily routine, nor would there be any after effects from the medication. Two of our staff members were delegated to contact Bishop Angelone of the Diocese do Combobasso. We hoped that through him and the church, we would be able to draft the necessary amount of volunteers. The task was a surprisingly pleasant one, as all of the populace that was over fifty knew that if the results of the experiments were successful, it could be their savior; their release from the dread of the disease.

"We now had over three thousand benefactors and all of them, when receiving their first treatment, looked and acted as though they were martyrs. As quoted through the ages, fear can make one submit to the Devil himself. We are eternally grateful to Bishop Angelone, the people of Bouino and Rockamondolf and most of all to our work crews and the beautiful long-uddered goats.

"Rockamondolf, this little bit of heaven's kitchen, will leave a large scar on my heart. My after dinner constitutionals during the late evening hours failed to dim the sparkle of the dark aqua spindle cones of the Alpian pines, or the grey clouds that hovered chest high as they drifted through the narrow roadway. How can anyone forget the crisp, cold air that makes your nostrils bristle with the exhilaration of being alive? Never can one forget the pulsating feeling that expands your chest and then the immediate longing for a large steak, hot soup and a gallon of blistering hot javaline.

"After eighteen months of thinning, adding and omitting from certain known and unknown drugs and herb qualities, we were able to balance the total ingredients required for the injecting experiments. Ironically it took products from every corner of the Earth to gel into the one eventual destroyer of the scourge of mankind. Yes, it took the secreted fluids from the high altitude goats from Italy, the sap of the balsam tree from Bali, the hormone oils from the Australian koala, the yellow sulfur from the lava pits of the Pitcan Islands and the root from the African dustweed. Ironic, indeed. To combat the feasible threat of blood coagulation, Antiserum #501 was added to the other indispensable ingredients.

"Not one sign of the sickness had come to force in any of the people who had stayed with our program. Cancer had been put in check. Six months later, cancer was permanently put to sleep. Further work on the drug resulted in a cure for already damaged cells.

"Incidentally, those of you who require booster shots may receive them in building 402 from 7:00 A.M. to 9:00 A.M. daily. All of you who receive such booster injections or pills shall isolate themselves for a period of twelve hours, the allotted time needed to throw off the noxious odors which ensue from the body.

"May I close with the statement that my rapport with the people of the world was the one instrument which kept everything together. Without that closeness, there could not have been a cancer cure.

"You have heard it all. This was my mission in life. Yours is a very different one. You must find a way to feed the people of the world. As you know, food supplies are becoming short. Time is running out. By the end of the decade it may be too late. What will happen if you do not have the fortitude and undying desire to succeed? We will become physically monstrous-looking within a few centuries. Our bodies will shrink to about 40% of their present size. If anyone is interested, we have an artist's sketch of our future offspring in room 106. I am of the opinion that upon seeing these hideous people you will not only place your noses to the grindstone, you will insert your heads into it.

"You have two-score years to accomplish your mission and with G-d's help, you shall. Get your shoulders to the wheel!"

Professor de Rivisio, slumping, left the chamber. Complete silence followed him to his room of high office. Minutes later a somber de Rivisio leaned back in his chair, his mind drifting back to the long gone years. At that moment, an explosive sound thundered through the hallway, slapping from side to side against the walls. The hurricane sound startled the Professor for a moment and then a broad smile lit his face as he realized that the erupting sound was the echoing rumble of the one thousand madly applauding hands. PEACE HAD ARRIVED.

"*Care to take a stroll around the grounds?*"

CHAPTER II

It was December 1, 2047. Eight hundred students awaited the arrival of the Super Ship, the wingless, cigar-shaped liner that would take them to Chicago. There they would board smaller aircraft and be transported to their nearest landing lanes.

To Jimps, this was the day of all days. Thirty days of Cindy Joe, Mother, Dad, Midge, and if time warranted, some school chums. Thirty days of nothing to do but relax and enjoy each day to its utmost, rich food, Gem Juice, and most of all, being with Cindy Joe. It had better be an enjoyable vacation as the next one assigned to Jimps was January, 2049, and then February, 2050, then March, 2051, etc. There were always eighty men on leave, leaving a complement of nine hundred plus students, so as to have the necessary quota of students for the perpetual cycle of classes.

Leaning back in his seat on the liner, Jimps wondered how Eartha would get along in her own Louisiana. Could this little Creole girl fight her almost uncontrollable cravings? Eartha -- especially when stretched out on her stomach, legs spread apart as though trying to reach the sides of the bed, her head buried in her pillow, breasts peeking out from under her -- left a denting impression in one's mind. A chill enveloped Jimps. What a way to meditate! He felt a deep longing at his mental picture of the full, light brown rump, and a continuous urge to rub both hands on it to smooth away the everlasting, squirming moans of ecstasy. What a beautiful, beautiful, beautiful, godloving creature.

Leaving the shuttlecab, Jimps was thrilled to see that nothing had changed; same street, same freshly painted house, same well-kept lawn and to spice the day, the same over-bearing snow clouds. Glancing at the house next door brought on the deserved guilt complex. Their pledges to either write once a week or place a visaphone call every two weeks was partially upheld by Cindy Joe, who after writing a half dozen letters and not receiving any response, discontinued the mailings.

Cindy Joe. Would she ever understand? Would she forgive and forget? It would be a major crime to never again feel the pressure of those soft lips, tightly hold both breasts, so beautifully firm, and to forever lose the feel of those long legs wrapped around his body. Jimps, in a momentary trance as he stood on her doorway, could once more feel the entrapment, as though a thread had been spun about his brain, a soft, relaxing web.

Push the button, dummy!

The door came ajar. First the top of a head, then the eyes, then the rest of the stunning features, followed by the ever proud, still-oversized breasts that were always fighting to leave their captive lace caps. There she was, doubly attractive in her loose lounging garment.

"Oh, Jimps! Oh, Jimps!" Then a hesitating, repulsed glare. "I hate you, you conniving liar, you space monster, you viper, you no good, lousy, no good bastard!" The door slammed closed as Cindy Joe's emotions seemed to have lifted her to the treetops. A sickly Jimps headed home.

"I hope that Mom didn't see that my first stop was next door. Women! All women are sensitive, especially mothers," he grumbled to himself as he crossed the lawn.

The beautiful sound of chimes was heard throughout the house. Then there she stood, indescribable Mom.

"Hi, Mom."

Need a son say more? Florence, shocked and thrilled, was able to say, "I look a mess," before she ran into Jimps' arms, her kisses matching the falling tears of joy.

Entering the house, arm in arm, an adoring Florence all in one long breath said, "Are you hungry? Wait until Dad sees you. What a pleasant surprise! Midge is going to have a baby. Cindy Joe just got back from school. Vacation time! What do you want to eat? Sit down! Take off your shoes while I make your favorite cocomilk. It's so good to see you." She took a deep, deep breath before taking off for the kitchen.

A few moments later, his father's voice was heard booming through the house.

"Florence, Florence! Where the hell are you?

"Here, dear. In the kitchen."

"Flo, I got the O.K. to go ahead with my plans--" but the thumping of his heart interrupted him when he saw his son.

"Jimps, my boy. Jimps, come here. My my, not a boy anymore, but a full-grown man. I don't know which is more to my liking. I have lost a boy. Now I have found a man. A few inches taller, a bit heavier of body, but still those deep, searching blue eyes. Welcome home, son."

"Hi, Dad. You sure look great, getting younger every day. You sure look tip top." The customary hug and pat on the back, the signs of deep affection and love continued into the living room.

"How was it, boy? Start from the beginning. Time is what I have plenty of."

Dinner and a year's schooling and problems were all cited in two hours. Not bad considering that Jimps' thoughts were next door. He finally escaped and headed to Cindy Joe's. The trek next door, a hundred and fifty feet, seemed to be five miles to the heavy-footed young man, who's thoughts centered on the sickening belief that his life with Cindy Joe was about to come to a disastrous conclusion.

Down went the door-knocker, releasing the house chimes. The door opened slightly and an unsteady voice said, "Come on in before I shut the door with the hope that it flattens your ugly face." All this hard voice conveyed was, "Come in, dear. I love you."

"Would you like a glass of Gem Juice? Mom and Dad went shopping and they won't return until about midnight. They've gone to New London, I believe."

Two feet apart, eyes searching…then chest against chest, lips frozen together and a shattered world record in the art of clothing removal, made it possible for Cindy Joe to relieve her fevered sex urge. Thirteen months of dreaming was an eternity. Time does tell more than words, for it took six more continuous eruptions to relieve and normalize Cindy Joe's pitny grams (which had in all probability skyrocketed to at least 514). A dropping Jimps, dead tired, had erased all of Cindy Joe's distastes of the past year.

A spry, singing Cindy Joe returned from the kitchen with frostcakes and javaline. She was preparing to serve Jimps' favorite dessert when she heard snores coming from him. Believing it to be one of Jimps' poorly times jokes, she bent down and kissed him on the lips, a long, lingering kiss with the ever so slight hope that he would, well, *just that he would.*

One hour had elapsed. Frostcakes and javaline had disappeared. Jimps, planting a little peck on Cindy Joe's neck, left with, "I'll see you every day or night, O.K.?" Even though Jimps was still there, the thought of seeing him later caused a pulsation at the mouth of her bruised but satisfied love cove.

The next evening, a pleasant time was had at Cindy Joe's. Her parents were excellent hosts and a good supply of Gem Juice was obtainable (undercover of course). After dinner, Cindy Joe and Jimps excused themselves, as an after-dinner walk was necessary and their promise of a return in thirty minutes met with approval from all. They strolled silently, hand in hand, for quite a while. Jimps suddenly turned to Cindy Joe.

"Cindy Joe, can you get away for a few days? A telegram from a troubled friend should work as a good excuse. A day later I could find a reason to leave for a few days. I could say things were too boring with you gone, and it's a very good time to contact a few of my school chums. We can meet at the Hotel McCord, on Key Largo Ave., in Key West. You'll have to allow at least four hours for reservations, as the monorail only makes four trips a day and is crowded at times.

"Key West is a great place for fishing, boating, drinking, loafing, sightseeing and all the necessary requirements for a pleasant day. The night time sporting events will take care of themselves." And under his breath, "if the swelling ever goes down!"

* * * * * * * * * *

Key West, city of 25,000 with high-speed monorails, flying holiday tourist ships, jet-propelled air taxis, circular system atom auto cars and the sightseeing balloons, was a city of beauty. With all of the 21st century conveniences, Key West had never lost its 20th century lure. Narrow streets, the Hemingway home with its irreplaceable sketches, Joe's nationally known bar, the gasoline touring pram, the old navy port, and the quaint shops where one could purchase anything from a rare antique to a worthless ten cent balloon. Key West, internally, had not changed during the past one hundred years. Only the outside of the buildings were altered, now covered by the standard alumindome, the universal bomb protection metal.

The one hundred mile, one hour ride to the Key was delightful. The hop from island to island, the blue-green waters and the cruising autocars below, all aided in making the trip a relaxing one. Leaving the monorail, Jimps made the five-minute walk to the Hotel McCord in a hurried four minutes flat.

A somber looking clerk, superbly attired, addressed an uncomfortable Jimps.

"Mrs. Belaire's room number is 610. The porter will attend to your luggage. The hotel's welcoming drink is in your room. Drink it in good health, may your honeymoon stay be one of pleasure." Jimps' eyes blinked in utter disbelief. He had just heard the world's most asinine remark.

As always, a delightful-looking Cindy Joe opened the door. A large kiss preceded, "I only got here a short time ago. Let's hurry. I'm famished. I read the hotel specialty of the day is breaded kingfish and conch chowder. Sounds yummy. Shall we try it?"

Hours later, having completed all of the needed arrangements for the next day's fishing trip, Jimps and Cindy Joe retired early, knowing that 5:00 A.M. would burst on them with a cruel suddenness.

Morning seemed to arrive before sleep to Cindy Joe. Jimps, spry as a young stallion, welcomed the beginning of a hot, clear day.

The thirty foot craft waiting for them at the dock, powered by two 350 H.P. Chrysler Atommotors, was purring like an enraged kitten. Releasing the towlines, Jimps leaped upon the forward deck and eased into the operator's seat. A slight forward thrust of the throttle and the craft eased seaward, its boat rods outspread, waiting for the hopeful action of a fighting sail or blue marlin. The bait compartment contained a good supply of frozen mackerel and squid and below deck, adjoining the head, was a large basket with a variety of sandwiches and brew.

One hour later, bordering the Gulf Stream, Jimps and Cindy Joe damned their stupidity, for already the red sun, coming from the east and bouncing off the water, made it impossible for them to glance in that direction. Beautiful, circular sunray protective glasses were encased and lying on the bedroom bureau.

Four hours of trolling and not even the sight of a fish, let alone the thought of the one that got away. A disappointed Jimps was ready to throw in the towel. How could anyone combat the killing sun and the boredom of no fish action? And Cindy Joe was ready for land, her head aching. Not even the sight of a sandwich or brew could rid her of a weak feeling in the pit of her stomach, but it wasn't seasickness. Cindy Joe was a bonafide sea sprite. Even a hurricane couldn't upset her sturdy innards. Still, it was a sad looking and smelling couple that tied their boat to the dock. Entering the hotel lobby, they were greeted by the ever-proper desk clerk, who pointed his nose skyward.

The salvation of a wasted day was the thrilling takeoff of a huge aeroship from the water; a sight to behold, especially to Cindy Joe. The belief that anything so huge and weighted could take off from the water was staggering in itself. Only when hearing the roar of the water-leveled atommotors, and seeing the powerful streams of shooting vapor, did one have the feeling that possibly this man-made miracle wasn't a mirage.

After four hours of much needed sleep, the handsome couple (in matching attire of light blue) set off to try to locate a restaurant that specialized in deep fried seafood, namely large, crispy *scallops*. Mr. Perfect, the desk clerk, recommended the Fishhouse. A five-minute stroll took them to a narrow lane with a blinking light atop a small, round building advertising, 'The World's Best Deep Fried Sea Food.' The dimly lit two-room eatery carried an aroma of fried fish, a most pleasant smell to two healthy, very hungry people.

Stomachs full (but not overloaded) a hand-holding Jimps and Cindy Joe enjoyed the red setting sun disappearing on the horizon. The cool breeze and 72 degree weather were an unnecessary stimulant for these young, forever stimulated animals. A long stroll along the shoreline, a large glass of fresh orange juice, a few more lung-drawing cigmarwetts, and Jimps and Cindy Joe were ready for the motel room where they could relax, love and schedule a day for tomorrow.

Freshly showered, Cindy Joe, in a sheer, black nightgown, stimulated Jimps far more than all of the deep fried scallops in the sea. The minutes of mutual admiration left both breathing heavy with the thought of the anticipated climaxes.

Cindy Joe, already primed after two fast eruptions, was leveling off for a long satisfying session. Jimps was overjoyed and amazed that he was one of the most fortunate people in the world. Didn't he have two of the most beautiful, sexiest and lovable female things ever produced by man and woman? Possibly they were robots. The thought was laughable, even to a serious Jimps. *That would be a good project to start at World.*

Jimps, the scientists in him always trying for the unknown, said, "Cindy, honey, let me know when you are ready to blast off. Of course, I know when you are due, but I just want to hear you say it. O.K.?"

"Sure, dear, if that's what you want. I don't think it will be far off. Seems like they come one after another. Oh Jimps, here it comes."

At that moment, for reasons known only to Jimps, he jabbed a small sewing needle into Cindy Joe's soft, revolving rump. A violent scream charged past her lips, a scream that came from deep in the bowels. A terrified, shocked Cindy Joe, her pitny grams dropping to 0.0, cried out, "Oh, G-d! I think I was bitten by a snake or a poisonous spider of some kind. Oh, please help me! It's my right side. Hurry, please!"

A serious looking Jimps, seemingly stunned, shouted, "Get out of bed and fast!" After a close inspection, he pretended to discover the needle where he had placed it.

"Here it is. This is the viper, a crummy needle that had become imbedded in the mattress. Some careless guest no doubt left it there. I'd like to get my hands on him, the crumb. I'd make him damn sorry. Roll over. Maybe a kiss on the injured spot will relieve the pain."

"It's uncanny, Jimps, but now that I know what it was, the pain has left me. Just feels as though I had received an injection of some sort. Kiss the spot again, dear."

"Let's have a drink and then get some sleep. I don't believe I can appreciate any more lovemaking tonight. We'll try to make up for it in the morning."

"Thank you, hon. Thank you very much for your deep concern."

A smiling Jimps, at peace with the world, was sound asleep within seconds.

A few days later, a well-rested Jimps, luggage in hand, paid the autocar operator and started to cross the street. Midway, he stopped for a moment to admire the wide street and it's overhanging sugar maple trees, beautiful though leafless. Not even the 40% chill of the morning could dim the beauty of the New England landscape. Before the chimes completed their echo through the house, the door was opened by the ever beautifully neat Florence.

"Come in, dear. Damp, isn't it? Did you have a good time? You look so rested and good." This came in the course of many pecking kisses and not too-bruising hugs.

"Cindy Joe got back three days ago and she wanted to know when you would get here. Better call her. I just made some fresh javaline and sugar maple buns, your favorite. Bet you haven't eaten breakfast this morning. Bless you, you were always the one for running off without even a sip of juice, let alone any solid food. For the life of me, I don't understand how you ever grew up so tall and beautiful, but, after all, you are a Bard."

"Where's Pop? He doesn't work on Saturdays, does he?"

"No, he isn't working. He's just taking a walk. Exercising, he calls it. You remember his old cliché. 'A little bit of eating and a lot of walking gives you ten extra big ones to enjoy.' Silly, he does just the opposite, very little walking and a lot of eating, especially the past few years and there isn't any sign of a let up. Bless him, I love every wrinkle of fat that he has added. Promise that you will never tell him I said that."

Two cups of javaline, six sugar maple buns and the greatest Mom on Earth can sure light up a day, even a gray, chilly one.

*　　*　　*　　*　　*　　*　　*　　*　　*

Elmira and Duane Henderson were Jimps' second choice for perfect parents. Elmira, still slender and beautiful at 43, was always dressed and ready for any occasion that could arise, even at seven in the morning. Duane, 6'2", sporting a flat-bellied 190 pounds and a thin-line mustache, had a slow Southern drawl, although a life long resident of Connecticut. Duane was always easy-going and obliging. They greeted him with affection when he stopped in for Cindy Joe.

"Hi, Jimps. Did you have a nice time? So silly of me to ask. I'm sure you did. Cindy isn't here. She went shopping and should return in, oh, I'd say within an hour. Come on in for a while and tell me about your trip."

Cindy Joe finally returned from shopping.

"Guess what? It's starting to snow! How about taking a walk, Jimps? Better button up. The temperature has dropped to 15 degrees."

Cindy Joe leaned up against Jimps as they walked.

"Cold, honey?" Jimps asked.

"No, I'm not cold, not when you take my hand. In fact I feel warm all over. Do we have to wait nine more years to get married? That sure is a nutty school. Oh well, we'll have to do the best we can in thirty days a year. Promise me that there won't be an outside girl. *Promise*."

Right hand skyward, Jimps, crossing his heart, was sincere in his promise, for no one could possibly consider Eartha an outside girl. No way!

"Why the sudden smile?" Cindy Joe asked.

"I'm smiling because you sound so silly when you questions my honesty. You're more than I need. Let me change that. You're exactly how much I need."

"Jimps, just a few more weeks and then an eternity. You will write, please."

"You know I will. The past year has been a hectic one. I felt alone and lost and there were millions of things to do, so much to observe and learn, but you were always with me, especially at night when I was trying to sleep." For a few seconds, a picture of a full, rounded, dark-skinned rump and breasts flashed before Jimps' eyes, causing a chill to engulf him.

"Jimps, you're shivering. Shall we go back?"

"No, I'll be alright. I was thinking about the eighty-degree weather in Key West and it threw me for a second. Cindy Joe, whenever my mom and dad are out for the night, we can get together at my house, and the same would apply when your folks are out for the evening or day or afternoon, O.K.? That would give us at least two four or five hour sessions a week."

Cindy Joe smiled and nodded. They had arrived at her doorstep.

"See you tomorrow" preceded a long, lingering kiss.

CHAPTER III

The sight of the giant dome...

The sight of the giant dome with it's fiery eagle emblem didn't lift Jimps out of his depression. Seconds later, it was the outstretched arms of a bit of honey called Eartha that changed a day of gloom into a day of light. A change of clothes, a light lunch and the taped registration followed.

"James Bard, age 20, state of Connecticut, marine biology, #23162. January 1, shut down hour, 1:03 P.M."

Jimps turned at a hard rap on the back.

"Amigo, good to see you, my friend."

Funny, but Juan looked the same. Why shouldn't he? It was only thirty days ago, but it felt like years.

"Come on, Jimps. Let's hit it with a cold drink. Boy, sixteen free hours. I guess you've seen Eartha. Looks great, doesn't she? Olga had the flu. She received three days of grace. She should be in the day after tomorrow."

"Hey, man. Tomorrow is a big day. We find out how we've been computer-scheduled! Like Professor de Rivisio said, 'I wonder who we are, where we're going and how we will end up.'"

"Hope I make the underwater exploration team. After all, I am the great Mr. Olympian, Juan Codora. Bullshit, I'll probably end up washing beakers and lighting test tube burners!"

First thing the following morning, Jimps raced to the giant bulletin boards where the results of the computer scheduling were to be posted. Fighting his way through the crowd to the front, Jimps scanned the lists for his name. There it was! He broke out into an ear-to-ear grin when he saw the division he had been assigned to. Looking back at the lists he searched for the names of his three roommates.

Back in their room, a very flushed and perspiring foursome met and drank a toast to the gods of faith. Juan, as he had hoped, had been assigned to train as an underwater crew captain. At the end of his schooling, he would be in charge of the underwater activities of an entire outpost. Jimps was assigned to the Food Division to continue his biological studies in the hopes that someday, he would aid in the search for new and better food sources to feed the world. The girls had been assigned to train as nutritionists and experts in the management of food and its preservation. A bright and shiny Eartha and the voluptuous Olga sat on the bunks sipping Cocoa Bean Sizzlers and trying, without success, to play down the important moment. A highly excited Juan sat on the floor, doing pushups and yelling, "I'll be goddamned. I'll be goddamned." A stunned Jimps, momentarily out of this world, sat on a chair, daydreaming about the day *he* would be standing on a podium and addressing one thousand aspiring biologists.

Early the next morning, Jimps met Professor Henry (Hank) Hudson, biologist extraordinaire, the father of the Heyena Vaccine and discoverer of the laughing sickness serum. He was to be the instructor for Jimps and his nineteen classmates for the next three years.

"Men, my name is Henry Hudson. I prefer the name of Hank. You will, on every occasion, address me as either Professor or Mister Hudson.

"Before the jokes emerge, no, I wasn't the first to explore the Hudson River and yes, it was a relative, my great-great-great-great-grandfather who was the explorer. He was, I was told, a stringbean of a man who lived on raw fish and bear meat. Any questions?"

Jimps immediately liked Professor Hudson, all 5'10" and 180 pounds of him. Mostly it was the easy going, eye to eye attitude that gave one the feeling that he was a man who had the fortitude to finish whatever he started, one who would leave his mark on you.

"There is a ten-foot workbench and shelving area assigned to each of you. Your nameplates are attached at the lower right hand corner of the bench. This area will be your kingdom for the next three years. All that you see on the bench, shelves and in the bench drawers are your personal tools, the tools of your trade. Treat them with respect. If any of the equipment is damaged, report the damage to me and I will have it replaced. Sorry, I will issue an order of replacement. You will have it replaced.

"Each person is responsible for the condition of his area. All waste materials are to be disposed of with the proper care at the close of the day's session, whatever the hour.

"Later this week, you will all be fitted with underwater gear. Save the smile. It will be a long time before you use it. Classes will start 7:00 A.M. and end 7:00 P.M., Monday though Friday.

"Some of you appear a bit cloudy, so let's take a fifteen minute break. Walk about and get acquainted with your fellow classmates. The smoking light is on. At the conclusion of the break, align yourselves in front of your work benches."

When they returned, Professor Hudson leaned back against his desk and smiled at them.

"You do seem more relaxed. I'm sure you will be happy to hear that I believe that periodic smoking breaks are a necessity for one's mental attitude, if not one's health."

"This term, all eleven months, will be known as the 75-25 term. From 7:00 A.M. to 4:00 P.M. we will have our scheduled classes. From 4:00 to 7:00 P.M. is the time for your own experimenting, under my guidance. All breakfast and lunch hours are included in the time schedule. Breakfast will be served between 8:30 and 9:30, lunch between 1:00 and 2:30. Your dinner hour is from 7:00 to 9:30.

"We are going to start our schooling with simple solution tests. I trust that you are acquainted with all of your bench equipment. Let's all get started on the right foot. Always, when in doubt of any point, whether you misunderstood or failed to hear the subject matter, don't hesitate to ask for a repeat. All questions are vital, especially the seemingly simple ones.

"So, any questions? The first day of school usually turns into a get-acquainted day, sort of a sparring session, feeling each other out. Let's roll along. Yes, Mr. Bard."

"Sir, if we need certain supplies and don't have them, how do we get them?"

"Good question. Anything you need, other than what we have in this room, will come, very simply, by your written request. I will record the request and make out an order form for the item and you will take that sheet to either room 16 or 17, depending on the request. There you will give the order form to the supply technician. Your class brochure has a listing of all items available and where they can be obtained.

"While on the subject of supplies, let me carry this topic to its conclusion. Any equipment, materials, information, etc., needed from one of the other colleges here at World, will be channeled the same way as the local requests: a written request and an order form from me. Many requests for goods from other colleges will come from this department, and vice-versa, but by far the most transactions will be between the schools of Chemistry and Biology. Chemistry and biology are sisters of the universe, each devoted to the betterment of man's living conditions and to man's condition of health. The chemist's demands from the biologist will be as everlasting as the biologist's wants from the chemist, for as I've said before, we are sisters of science.

"We will complete this day with discussions. Feel free to ask questions and make suggestions. If you have a better way to learn and improve, let's hear it now.

"What is our aim? That is my question. The young man, third from the left. Mr. Pierce, is that right? Thank you. Go right ahead."

A bespeckled, pudgy, chattering Donald Pierce inhaled and exhaled at least a room's supply of oxygen and then with a short gasp, "Mr. Hudson, sir. Our aim is to find a way of multiplying the world's food sources, mainly through marine life." Two more drafts of air and with a steadier voice, Mr. Pierce continued, "so that we can feed the overpopulated world and if by some means we believe that we have found probable ways to increase the food supplies, other than through marine life, we shall immediately record our findings and turn those recordings over to our instructor, you, sir. We should leave nothing to chance. An idea or finding may be imbedded in us for only a few minutes, then lost, probably for all time."

"Thank you, Mr. Pierce. Very well done, indeed."

"Your pledge to the people of the world, our college and yourselves is one of finding a way to triple the amount of marine food and to speed up its development. We all know that there isn't any sacrifice too great when attempting something as staggering as our goal is, for if we do not succeed, the psychological catastrophe could cause far more damage than the destruction caused by the monocule bomb. We have forty years to succeed. We will not accept failure.

"This work does not have to be a burden unless we make it one. This study can develop into the most satisfying and gratifying feeling that we may ever embrace. We have, here in this building, the greatest writings on biology in the universe. Here, in these halls, are the most complete tape recordings of man's biological findings ever collected in one place. I would recommend that you get in as much reading as possible, for I am a believer in the reading system. Even though becoming obsolete, I believe it can aid in the sharpening of the mind. I place just as much emphasis on the use of subliminal recordings during the sleep hours, a timesaving, proven technique.

"Before calling this day a day not lost, I will attempt to give you a brief resume on biology and the biologist.

"Your previous teachings have told you that this Earth is populated by millions of different types of living creatures. Each has its own way of living, but all share the only known kinds of structural and chemical organization that means being alive. Whatever their dissimilarities, plants, animals and other creatures solve their big problems, those of survival, in much the same way."

"Biology is the sum of man's knowledge about life, his own and that of all other creatures. This knowledge consists not only of a collection of facts, but more importantly, of the way these facts are associated and interpreted in general theories. This may be hard to believe, but only a couple hundred years ago, scientists debated continuously on the question of whether life could rise spontaneously from nonliving matter.

"Surely a tree and a fish do not resemble one another and yet, they are similar-for both are composed of cells, as are all forms of life. Unifying theories explain isolated facts, but science is at its best when it seeks a new theory, our never-ending quest. On and on we can go, to what heights cannot be theorized. The sky is not the limit. All of the universe is our playground, and history shall record our accomplishments.

"Good afternoon, gentlemen. It has been a very enlightening day. Class will begin at 7:00 tomorrow."

CHAPTER IV

It was december 28, three days to...

It was December 28, three days to the end of the second term. Three days, followed by thirty more days to forget all they had learned. Thirty days of family and Cindy Joe. *Thirty nights of no Eartha.* Many were the nights that only her strong, unmatched love could reduce the pressures of his almost unbearably boring and repetitious days. Funny, but the last month hadn't seemed as long. Could the nearness of vacation have relieved the condition? More than likely. It was good to let it all hang for a month and enjoy what was coming, for it was a long time between work and play.

January 1, 8:30 A.M.

Standing at the doorway to their apartment, the four friends said goodbye.

"Bye, Juan. Take care. Heard that you landed a job as a diver. I keep forgetting that Costa Rica is sporting 80-degree weather. You be careful. So long, Olga. You'd better believe that a big kiss is in order. No more colds now. Better skate with your clothes on. That's a joke. See you, dear."

Taking Eartha's arm, Jimps led her towards the departure terminal.

"Come on. We have a lot of time. Let's get a warm drink and find a nice, cozy corner. I'm sure as hell going to miss you, more than last year, and I thought that was impossible."

"I know, Jimps. I feel the same way. I thought that maybe we could meet somewhere for a week, say a halfway point, maybe Virginia Beach?

Jimps didn't reply. With an anxious, sidelong glance at him, Eartha hurried on, "Forget it. It was only wishful thinking. I know it would be very cruel. After all, our parents waited a year for these days. I do get selfish, but that's the way it is where you are concerned."

An hour later, they gave one another a long lingering kiss, a kiss that would imply to a bystander that it would be their last.

* * * * * * * * *

The dirty slush and the gray, threatening snow clouds cast a downsurge of loneliness on a bundled Jimps. Pausing to take in the familiar street of his childhood home, there was a feeling in the air that something was missing. There it was, the specter of a healthy, pink-cheeked boy of eight. One moment he was laughing and rolling in the snow, and the next moment he was rushing into the house, crying for Mom to take away the pain of frostbitten ears. A shake of the head, a deep breath and the little boy was gone.

"Hi, beautiful!"

Like a painting framed in the doorway, stood the most beautiful of the beautiful, Florence, on whom, year after year, Nature bestowed her stamp of excellence. In Florence, there would always be beauty, for she was the rare possessor of eyes that could only see the good in all creatures. In her encircling arms, Jimps felt sheltered by an unbreakable barrier of peace and contentment,

"James, you look adorable! When did you start wearing that pencil mustache? Don't you ever shave it off! Wait until Dad sees it. You look exactly as your father did when we got married. The mustache makes a shocking difference. So much alike! Wait until you see our old photos. I'm sure you've seen them before, but they will seem different now. But you know what? I think you're more beautiful."

"I know, Mom. I won't tell Dad. I never do." Jimps replied with a grin and a big kiss.

"Hi, Cindy. Are you alone? They did? Good, I'll be right over."

"You know, you're putting on weight. Don't look at me like I stabbed you! It's only a bit that you put on and it's on the legs, from the knee down where you needed a wee bit. Hell, you look perfect to me. You know that. In fact, I would like to see some of the real material right now. You positive that they will be gone all evening?"

"James Bard, you talk too much. Kiss me and start shedding. Bet I can beat you."

"I wouldn't be so sure," laughed Jimps.

"Oh, Jimps. It's so good. I think I'm ready again. Not so rough. Here I go. Kiss me. Oh, Frank, kiss me. It's so good."

A shocked, ice cold Jimps leaped from the bed.

"Who the hell is Frank? My name is James. Did you forget that?"

"Damn you, Jimps. I was almost there again. Frank? I don't know any Frank."

"Hell, Cin. You don't have to lie to me. We've never lied to each other before."

Eye to eye, a soul searching Cindy Joe, head bowed, simply said, "I had a few drinks at a party given for a girl friend, and this boy that I met there offered to take me home, and with the drinks and all, it just happened. I can't explain it."

Jimps, hurt to the depths of his innards, was feeling the pain not of lost love, but of the lost belief in his self-magnitude, the pride in believing that Cindy Joe would never need another man.

This was Jimps' great moment. He would have excelled in the world of the Arts. Eyes downcast, slowly donning his clothes, he mumbled, "I can't believe it's true. Why didn't you write and tell me about it right after it happened? At least I wouldn't feel like I just took a bath in ice-cold water. All this time, like I've said many times before, I've never had an outside woman or ever thought I would desire one. Heaven help me. Good night, I'll be seeing you. This is awfully hard to swallow." Now the slowly upraising eyes fixed on a sickly, green Cindy Joe. "I don't know if we should continue. I feel sort of dirty now. I've got to have time. I've got to think it over."

A not too unhappy Jimps walked across the lawn, thrilled with the effect that his actions had on a deserving Cindy Joe and knowing that he wasn't about to give up that bundle of joy. No way! Not when he could have it for only thirty days a year. Where the hell would he find anything better to do?

Two days later, Jimps figured that Cindy Joe had suffered enough and called her.

"I'm so happy that you called," cried Cindy Joe. "I haven't had any sleep in the past forty eight hours. Fine, I'll come right over. Are you sure that you want me to?"

"Come on over. I now realize that we aren't all gifted with certain strengths, and I forgive you. I promise that I will never again question you. I double promise."

Down went the receiver and a grinning Jimps was completely enthralled the past forty eight hours' results. Now, he awaited masterfully the thrust of that ever-exploding body. There goes the doorbell.

"Hello, Cindy. Boy, do you look good."

"Jimps, just hold me for a few seconds."

The mystery of youth and passion. Time stood still.

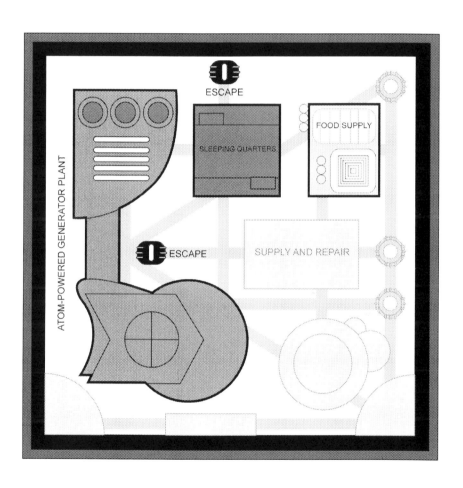

CHAPTER V

James Bard #23162...

"James Bard, #23162, state of Connecticut, age 21, check-in time, 10:41 A.M."

A shower, a change of clothes, and to the cafeteria for a light lunch. There he was. Juan and Jimps smiled at each other as they shook hands.

"Juan, you son-of-a-bitch! Hey do you look good, a tan on a tan. You look as healthy as a couple of pounds of deep fried, crispy scallops, and that's saying something. Get your chow and sit here and tell me all about your job."

"I'm hungry as the devil. First you, Jimps. How did it all go?"

Jimps blurted out the month's happenings, even the Cindy Joe episode, for lying or omitting wasn't in the makeup of these closely-knit friends.

"Now come on, Juan. I want to hear about this job."

"Well, I made good money. I had twenty-five days of diving experience, and I was fortunate enough to have one of the greatest divers in the business as my instructor, Captain Fortesque. The weather was mild, the food was tops and everything was perfect, except we didn't find a damn thing around the wrecks. The only jewel I found was located aboard: the Captain's wife. Man, what a salt and pepper woman. Now I see why the Captain spent so many hours in the water.

"Seen the girls, yet?"

"Nope. I sure miss my long-legged honey. Well, well. Turn about forty degrees to the port side and look what's coming down the lane. Bet they could smell that we were here."

Jimps, looking down at his Eartha, and Juan, looking up at his Olga, didn't waste any time in accomplishing their mission, two earth-shaking kisses which brought understanding smiles from the customers of the cafeteria.

*   *   *   *   *   *   *   *   *   *

The days of relaxation were over. It was back to work in Professor Hudson's class.

"Men, we have made great strides this past year and we shall make greater moves this term. I see a definite breakaway trend. You are drifting in different directions. You are beginning to become individuals in thought and planning. That is what I am striving for, in the hope that within the next few years, someone's direction will eventually lead us to our path of success. You can all become biologists, of that I am certain, but let's make sure that out of this class there will emerge a few super biologists.

"This is a marine school of biology. The oceans cover about seventy-one percent of the Earth's surface. They are the reservoirs of the Earth's water. We cannot drink it, nor can we use it to irrigate our crops, but it is the home of our needed food supply."

The smiling Professor Hudson suddenly sat down, unbuttoned his collar, detached his tie, wiped his sweat free brow and very casually said, "I have a statement to make which is significant to this morning's topic. Before I make the statement, I want to talk about a location that may become a second home to some of you, a location where the greatest exploits of man may come from, a location that carries the beauties of the world. I am speaking of the Gulf Stream.

"The only great current along the shores of the United States is the Gulf Stream, the mightiest of all ocean currents. The source of the Gulf Stream is the equatorial Atlantic. The trade winds drive the surface waters westward. The northeast coast of South America guides most of the water from the equatorial currents into the Caribbean Sea. Pushed on by the trade winds, surface flow is concentrated and funneled into the straits between Yucatan, Mexico and the western tip of Cuba. From there it runs into the waters of the Gulf of Mexico, which turn eastward, and which by this time are known as the Florida Current and flows up along the east coast of Florida. This current, which starts off the coast of Florida, is about five miles offshore at that point and it drifts out to about twenty miles off shore by the time it arrives at Cape Fear, at the North Carolina boundary.

"Now if I may make my statement. At 0400 today, Matradean de Rivisio was informed that the site for an underwater city will be there, at the coast of North Carolina, U.S.A. Let me elaborate for the benefit of some of you who aren't aware of the importance of this announcement.

"For five years, the food administrators of the Continents have been meeting monthly to discuss the cost and location site of an underwater laboratory. At their first meeting it was decided that cost funding would be equally divided between the Continents. The five years of monthly discussions were not a political hassle of any kind, but united with one purpose: that of finding the most productive site for the food supply experiments. Through the efforts of the world's foremost geologists, chemical, civil, electrical engineers and hundreds of other specialists, it was decided that the underwater city would be erected off the coast of North Carolina, bordering the waters of the Gulf Stream.

"A set of the plans has been statescoped to this school and there is a set for each of you. Let's take a look.

"The atom-powered and monocule-pressured ships, capable of taking off in water and circling the globe in an hour--these were accomplishments created from the combination of man's ingenuity and the elements of nature. They will be dwarfed by this immense undertaking.

"Let's start with the border. That one-inch double line around the complete project (follow my pointer) is a concrete wall fifty feet thick at the bottom and narrowing to twenty-five feet at the top. It is over three hundred fifty feet high. The depth of the water is two hundred feet. The wall rises above the water level and also goes into the soil below the water. The wall is one square mile, 1 mile along the shore, 1 mile into the Atlantic, squared off and back again. It is completely closed off from everything but the sky above. You will note that the wall will be reinforced with thick, six-inch girders running the whole length of the wall, and the concrete will be imbedded with radioactive aluminicol, to deactivate the atoms of a Monocule bomb.

"This is the atom-powered generator plant, large enough to hold machines, lights, air, fighting power, lifts, etc. Here are the sleeping quarters. The next building is the food supply area and next to that is the equipment supply and repair sections. Note that throughout the whole city there is a walkable passage from one building to another and there are two walk-up escape corridors, some three hundred stairs to the top like a stairway to the skies. A good song title.

"Right above the sleeping areas and the computer sections are two hatches for entering and decompressing.

"Wow," cried out student Pierce, "This is fantastic, I'm flabbergasted!"

"Right here," continued Hudson, is a stall for Little Mide, the Atom Sub, and smaller stalls for the underwater sleds. This large cross section is a two-section door and each section is 100' X 100'. I can't understand why they would plan to have a door on the east side, the Gulf Stream side. Wait, the dawn is breaking. Excuse me, I'm ahead of you, as I am reading the advance recommended plans and it sure is beyond all belief.

"Lunch hour has arrived and it is a good time to put something other than plans in our systems."

An hour later, everyone was back at their desks. Professor Hudson continued with his talk.

"The work on this project will start May 1, and will take approximately seven and one half years to complete. The building of the underwater city will require all of that time and after four years of that phase, work will begin on the building of the wall bordering the city. This complex work is timed so that the city and wall will be completed at the same time. Just think, this city will be completed the year of your graduation, and I am thrilled with the possibility that some of you will be a part of this once in a lifetime experience.

"I read during our lunch hour that as soon as the city is in operation another wall will be erected. This one will run parallel with the east wall and will be on the east side of the Gulf Stream. At that point the walls will be eighteen miles apart, the width of the Gulf Stream. At the north end, the flow-through end, there will be a gigantic net spanning the Stream. This net, the same depth as the wall will be constructed with the interlocking, six-inch crossbars. This will allow the continuous flow of water to travel unhindered and for fish with a girth measurement under this width to squirm through the gratings.

"Now the large gate is in its elements. The eighteen mile wide, open sky tunnel can be used as a corral. All of the millions of fish riding the Gulf Stream currents can be herded through the gateway and into the enclosure, where they can, hopefully, through our sciences, be fattened and made to breed in double time.

"The plans we have here are a set of the originals. The later plans call for an open shoreline. This land area will be enclosed by heavy gauge, electrically charged fencing and will be policed by the Department of Security. The land area will contain supply buildings, repair shops, fast freezing storage compounds, cranes, lifts and all the necessary loading and unloading equipment needed for operations.

"That seems to be about all we have pertaining to the underwater city for today. Starting tomorrow marine life specimens may be obtained, on your time, from 7:00 P.M. Take elevator 52 to the ground level and please, don't forget to sign in and out."

The first trip to the ground floor fish tank area is one of remembrance. If biology and chemistry are sisters of science, then physics and engineering are brothers. Here, housed under one roof, were some of the finest fruits of man's ingenuity, and the largest conglomeration of aquariums ever assembled. One hundred stainless steel water tanks, each fifty feet wide by one hundred feet long. The inside of each tank was divided into four sections and contained water levels of three, five, seven and ten feet for separation of fish sizes and classifications.

All the tanks were interlocked and automatically moved one tank length every three days. Tank 1 became Tank 2 and contained specimens that were six days old. Tank 2 became Tank 3 and contained specimens which had been alive for nine days and so on. Tank 100 contained life that was three hundred days old, enough time to show if there had been any development in the quality, quantity and weight of the contained fish and crustaceans. The fish supply from the one hundredth tank when emptied became part of the food source for the occupants of World College. Tank 100, having completed the cycle, reverted to the beginning and became Tank 1. Bordering the tanks was a non-magnetic runway, three feet below the top level of the tanks, making visibility into them for separation easily attained.

Ten enormous stationary tanks were lodged against the west wall of the enclosure. These tanks contained the denizens of the deep: the whale, marlin, seals, giant rays, walrus, etc. These were also fed from the never-ending food supply from Tank 100.

Adjoining the fish area, with its dozens of elevators and chain lifts, was a large cavern. Cut into the mountain, this two hundred foot-high underground compound was an awesome sight. Hundreds of computerized machines lined the walls. It was a sight similar to photos taken of the unmanned station on the Moon.

There it was, that morbid feeling…contagious to the guided twenty…the feeling that this was the city of the dead. Here, the only thing alive was the ear-piercing hum of the generators.

Waiting for class to start, a meditating Jimps reviewed the sights of a few hours ago. He knew that one day he would be an important cog in the wheel of things to come. *Man sure is a great, powerful creature…there isn't a thing beyond his grasp.*

* * * * * * * * *

February 1, 2050, 7:17 A.M.

The beginning of another greatly needed leave. Juan and Jimps woke to find letters in the box on their door.

"Hey, Juan. Get up. Here's a letter from de Rivisio. I got one too. Maybe we're going to get canned for too much screwing."

"You're wrong as hell, man. Bet we get a citation and an offer to lecture on how it should be done."

"Listen to this, my next year's schedule: 'Dear Mr. Bard, this is to inform you that your computerized schedule for the next four years is as follows: major-advanced marine biology, first minor-electronic mechanisms of organic chemistry, second minors-biophysics, advanced integral calculus and world literature.' Wow, I must be a brain. How did you do, muscleman?"

I got the same kind of letter. 'Dear Mr. Codora, this is to inform you that at 0900 March 1, 2050, you are to report on board the Marine ship "Progresso". There for the next two years, under the guidance of Dr. Franklin Moore, you will be instructed in underwater techniques, diving safety, diving equipment care, the identification of marine life, the handling and preservation of marine specimens and the use of underwater protective and destructive devices. Your assistant on this two year special course will be Olga Borge, #41613, Food Specialist, Grade 1.'"

An unhappy Juan and Jimps stood as though transfixed, neither able to utter a word. A handshake, four soul-searching eyes, another handshake and each walked off in the opposite direction simultaneously whispering, "See you in two years."

*   *   *   *   *   *   *   *   *   *

"THE FISH TANK AREA IS OUT OF BOUNDS FOR THE REMAINING PART OF THE WEEK," was the flashing notice on the electronic note pad.

Jimps, leaning over the empty #2 bench, called to William Baylor, "What do you think, Bill? That notice on the electric pad. No fishing for a while."

"I got the dope from Pierce, and you know Don. He should be a Sherlock. He said the reason is so that we would use all of our energies on our exams and finishing up our basic training. It makes a lot of sense, for as soon as we complete these tests, we will have the last four years to do nothing but screw around with fish and all the other shit swimming in those smelly tanks."

Lying in bed that night, Jimps reflected, waiting for sleep to come.

What a day. Thank god for my Eartha. She becomes more beautiful with each passing day. That haunting smile, the large white teeth, firm breasts, the well rounded legs, and the soft lips of her love cove, which brings on moans of contentment as my finger spreads and explores. That warm, sponge-like channel of mystery. How can one compare? Cindy Joe is a volcanic eruption, a tidal wave, all locked up in one body. Eartha is a swift running stream and deep clear waters. I'm so tired I could fall asleep on a school of porcupine fish.

CHAPTER VI

"Hi, Dad." The bearlike hug...

"Hi, Dad." The bearlike hug, the hand shake and the spontaneous kiss on the cheek inserted in Frank the realization of how much a father can miss his son, a son who had grown too fast. It was only yesterday that he had driven the motor carriage all about the neighborhood so that all could see and admire the occupant. Only yesterday. How true is the proverb, time waits for no one!

"Mother should be here shortly. She's next door, paying a short visit to Mrs. Henderson. I believe she has a cold and Mother felt she should cheer her up."

"Hi, Mom. You're still my best girl. No, I haven't eaten. Yes, I will have some lunch. How about you, Dad? Going to eat with us?"

"Set yourself on this stool, away from your dad. Him and his pipe smoking. Pipe tobacco may not be detrimental to the throat, but I am inclined to believe that the stench that comes out of that pipe can't possibly help our sense of smell. Not for a few hours, at least. It smells like a tannery is located in the neighborhood. Lord help us.

"Cindy Joe will be home Wednesday. Have you been writing to each other? You children have been so close and it was only natural to assume that the inevitable would happen, your getting married."

"You know that we have been seeing each other quite often when I'm home, but while I am at school, it's only an occasional letter or phone call. We like each other very much. We like to be together and we have been very close, but marriage is another story. Why marry when living together simplifies everything. I know that you and dad have had a very good marriage and hit it off real well, but what would have happened if it didn't work out? You can only be separated by death and if you lost your marriage mate and you wanted to remarry, you could only marry someone who had lost their marriage mate. No way! When living with a person, everything is simplified. When you want to split, you do it. No property settlement problems, for whoever signs for the house, car, furniture or any piece of personal property is the owner. The no-dual signing law was a good piece of legislation, the one sensible piece of legislation passed during the past twenty-five years. More important than anything is that if you want to live with someone else, you go ahead and do it.

"You know what? You and dad will be the first to know when I decide to make you grandparents and that may not be too far off. You never can tell. I may have a girl chained to the bedpost somewhere, waiting."

Cindy Joe never arrived home. She sent word to her parents that she was staying at school to work on a special project. The letter Jimps received, however told the real story.

Dear Jimps,

This is so hard to place on paper. It would be much more pleasant to tell you about my plight eye to eye, and I know that is how you would want it. First, never doubt my love for you a second, try to understand the way I am. You helped in the molding of me. I like to believe that, even though that may not be so.

I know how much you looked forward to your first summer vacation in years, and what I am about to tell you makes me feel like a person who is about to cut off the air supply of an astronaut.

A few weeks after we parted last, I became pregnant, willingly, and I gave birth to a stillborn son last month. The father was Frank Romano. You remember. He is the only other person that I have been with. Funny, you may not believe this, but every time we had some love, I would imagine it was you. Jimps, you were always on my mind, always, no matter where I was or who I was with. All was fine, that is until hands were placed on me. It didn't matter where, just the touch of hands and I would lose all control of myself. No one knows that better than you, but I only thought that it was your hands. Forgive me. The wanting urge was more than I could fight. I won't be going home for at least one year. I'm not quite up to par. Frank left this morning for Argentina and will be gone for a while.

As ever,
Cindy Joe

*   *   *   *   *   *   *   *   *

"I'm sorry, Mom, but I have to leave today. I know that two weeks wasn't very long, but I have to go to Costa Rica. My roommate has a good prospect lined up for our future. In all probability I will stay with the government, but one has to check on all other offers. Then you won't have the feeling that something spectacular may have turned up on this or that job if you had checked them out. Really, it's just as tough for me, but I'll try to make it up by calling you on the visaphone every week, I promise."

July 2, Acopendo, Costa Rica.

"Hi, Jimps! Welcome! Jimps, this is my father, Senor Juan Codora. This is my mother, Senora Estela Codora and this cute animal is my sister, Teresa, age twenty-one. She lost her husband and already is looking for a replacement, so watch out Jimps."

"Juan, behave! These modern children. I don't understand."

"I'm only joking, Father. This is not only my schoolmate, but a real brother, as close as any blood brother." A steel gaze encircled all, a gaze that let them know that this wasn't idle chatter, but a declaration for all to respect.

"Beautiful, man. It's beautiful. Is this your ranch? How much land do you have? Seems like we drove twenty-five miles since entering the gateway. The house looks like it has at least thirty rooms. Some adobe shack!"

"My father is the commandante of the countryside, sort of a major-type character. We have about fifty thousand head of cattle, house thirty men who take care of the cattle and outside work and their wives and children. Plus, Pedro and Maria Martinez, Luis and Anna Valdez, the inside help, and let me warn you, they are considered as members of the family, especially the women. They were here when my grandfather was the lord of this land."

Senor Codora took Jimps' arm and guided him toward the large parlor.

"James, my adopted son, my home and all of my possessions are at your disposal forever, my boy. Come, let's enter the living room for some brandy. I trust you are a brandy lover. If not, we will make you one. You do the honors, Juan. Keep a steady hand. Salud, to your parents' health, James."

They drank the brandy, sealing their friendship. Senor Codora's dark eyes turned to Jimps.

"Tell me about your country. I have planned many trips for a visit, but the time will not allow it. I shall have to make sacrifices and make the trip when you and this mastermind of mine receive your diplomas."

"Sir, this is so peaceful sitting here, like being in another world. Everything seems to have a yellow tint. What's that sweet smell coming in on the breeze?"

"That, my boy, is the sweet smell of sugar cane, that is the life of the island. Without them there wouldn't be the beautiful country that we have. Much of the money derived from our products have been reinvested in our school system, housing, etc. Just a few short years ago, during my father's time, the people had no say and 95% of them were illiterate, a far cry from today, as all children must have at least 10 years of schooling.

"Sometimes I believe I talk too much. I will leave you and Juan alone. There isn't any doubt that you have many things to discuss. Good night and may the Lord watch over you! Good night my sons."

"Good night sir."

"You know Juan, it sure would be something if the girls were here with us. I wonder what the yellow tint would do to Eartha, the yellow on an olive complexion. "That has to make it a golden color. I sure miss the little fireball."

"Juan, what are you going to do about Olga when you graduate? You don't have to answer, as it really is none of my business."

It was a question more directed towards himself than Juan. The ten years at World, which had seemed to be an eternity not so long ago, was coming to it's end…and something had to be decided on the matter of Eartha and Cindy Joe. *Maybe another fishing trip with Cindy Joe will do it. One more explosive session below deck should be good enough to decide, then maybe I'll just cut her loose.*

CHAPTER VII

Jimps, following cindy joe

Jimps, following Cindy Joe, reached the top deck as she was about to go below with her tray of drinks. A momentary flashback: he was again five years old. It was the first day of school and there was Cindy Joe all decked out in her Sunday best. *She looks so prim and sure of herself. I think I'll mess her up a wee bit. This should do it, grab her ankle. How's your knees? How nice you cry! Midge!*

"Watch out! That corner is sharp. Cindy Joe? Get up! For christ's sake, get up!"

She was out cold. There weren't any cuts on her forehead, only a slight bump and what looked like blood coming from her ear.

"Cindy, goddamn it! Get up. Holy Jesus, somebody help me!"

A sick, weakened Jimps staggered about for a second and then collapsed onto the deck. How long was he out? How do you measure time in darkness?

Sitting up, a cloudy-brained Jimps reached out and touched a cold Cindy Joe, but the open eyes staring skyward and green tint forming under her nose erased what little hope Jimps had that Cindy Joe wasn't seriously hurt. Another touch of the cold body revealed the startling madness that Cindy Joe was no more, for rigor mortis was starting to set in.

Oh god, why couldn't it have been a dream? I've got to think. Think. My career, my Mom and Pop, Eartha, Mr. and Mrs. Henderson and Cindy Joe! I can't think. Why Cindy Joe? That dirty f___g Romano. Curse you, you no good son-of-a-bitch!

I must have been out for hours. The sun is going down. Have I got the courage to leap overboard? That would simplify everything. G-d forgive me. I know I haven't got that kind of fortitude. Fortitude hell. It's just the right kind of guts that I lack.

I can't leave her staring at the sky. I've got to take her below deck. Forgive me. You're not Cindy Joe. You look like a wax doll. You set there and I'll see what's to be done with you.

This is one hell of a boat. No running lights, not even the required self-powered battery is on board. Too bad I'm not a predator, and then who can say I'm not. Hallelujah! Dock lights ahead.

As Jimps approached the dock, he could see the proprietor pacing up and down, stopping now and then to gaze out to sea. When he spotted Jimps, he waved his arms over his head a bit frantically and hailed him with relief.

"Mr. Bellaire. Thank goodness. I was getting on edge. I visualized you people drifting with a dead motor. I had old 'Laurie D' here all tanked and ready to go. Sure good to see you. Need any help with the ropes?"

"No, thank you. Mrs. Bellaire and I can manage. It has been a crazy day. The lack of fish action and the hot sun caused us both to doze off for a few hours. So, if you don't mind, we are going to sit on the top deck, eat our neglected sandwiches and enjoy the last few minutes of setting sun. Goodnight, sir, and thank you for your concern about our safety."

As soon as the proprietor had left the dock area, Jimps tied the boat to a piling and, leaving Cindy Joe and all the gear aboard, raced into town. His first stop was the hotel, where he packed both his and Cindy Joe's bags. Walking up to the desk, he again faced the stern face of the desk clerk whose somber eyes seemed full of accusations.

"May I have my bill, please? Mrs. Bellaire and I are checking out within a few hours."

"No motel problem, I hope."

"No, nothing serious. Just a work schedule mix up."

One problem behind him, Jimps contemplated the steps ahead.

What do I need? A transportation vehicle, a place to deposit bags, a good javaline shop and a good pair of legs, as staying in the motel room is an impossibility. Maybe I'll be picked for loitering and then shot as a spy. No such luck!

Grimly he entered an antique shop, which only the day before had been filled with Cindy Joe's laughter. There, on the highest shelf was a large trunk, *the perfect size for a...*

"Ma'am, that trunk on the top shelf, the large one. What is its cost?"

"$2500 in American coin."

"That much? Seems awfully high."

"Not so when you consider that it is the only one of its kind in existence. It will make a fine gift for a special lady."

"...She's special. Will you take a draft for the amount?"

"I will, but first I have to make a credit tally run. It will only take a moment."

Jimps leaned against the counter for support.

"Sir, your credit draft came through. Would you like to have the trunk delivered within the city or have it shipped out?"

"Neither, thank you. I'll take it with me. Seventy pounds, did you say? I can handle it. Can I have a good, sturdy lock, one that blends in with the brass couplings? I'll wait."

Depositing the travel bags at the monorails depot, Jimps, losing all track of time, walked from the west end of the island to the east shore, arriving at the boat location at daybreak. Boarding the craft, Jimps primed and started the motors. How differently they sounded. Yesterday they had purred like two kittens; today, enraged mountain lions. The same glaring sun, an occasional flying fish and the cry of a lonely seagull all contributed to the morose mood of a man whose soul had been to hell and hadn't as yet returned.

One hour had elapsed, or was it two? What difference did it make? This cemetery was large enough to accept a million bodies.

This looks like a good place. There is a lot of foliage, plants of the sea, a wonderful place for a burial.

Oh, god, Cindy. Help me! So stiff. Hope it doesn't hurt your neck, but how else can I get you in your nice casket. At least you won't get wet. Over you go. Please forgive me. Don't disappear so fast. Please!

CHAPTER VIII

"How are you, Mom?"

"Oh, Jimps. Come here. My, my, you look so drawn. Have you been worked that hard? I think that I should write to Statesman Klein. It's a shame. One would think this was the day of slavery all over again.

"James, when you cuddle like that it brings back memories, memories of a little boy who had done something wrong and would run to his mom for protection from the big lion's punishments. I often wondered how that little boy would have felt if he knew that the big bad lion was a gentle little kitten with nothing in his heart but love for a mischievous little boy."

"Thanks, Mom, and truthfully, I haven't any problem, other than one, as do thousands of other people, and that is, if you want something bad enough there isn't any sacrifice too great to make. So simply, I am making that sacrifice.

"How is Pop? Is he keeping busy?"

"He is, with lawn care, errands to do, his daily inspection of the Dome home colony and his advising the builders. Surely keeps him up. I'd go a point further and say he's too busy.

"We expected you home two days ago, and when you didn't arrive yesterday, I became worried and was going to put a call through to the school. Your father over-ruled the suggestion. He thought it would seem as though we were babysitting."

"I could have gotten here two days ago, but I would have left some unfinished work that would be piled on my associate's back, so it was easiest for me to finish it."

"I understand. Do you want to freshen up? By the time you are finished, I will have lunch prepared and your father should have completed his tour. Why a man wants to retire is beyond my comprehension. The whole system is ridiculous. A man should retire between the ages of forty and sixty. They are the foolish years. Men should work from age sixty-one to the time allotted by the Master."

Jimps, gathered up all his courage after lunch to make the expected visit next door.

"Hi, Mrs. Henderson. Hear that you have been ailing. Feeling better, I hope. How is Mr. Henderson?"

"I'm coming along just fine, James, real fine. Mr. Henderson is as usual, very busy making money. His first love is, and always has been, the money making. I have accepted the knowledge that I am the number two love in his life. I'll have to rescind that statement. I am the number three. Cindy Joe is the number two, of that I am positive."

"Have you heard from Cindy Joe? You didn't? Let me know as soon as you do."

"James, I won't have to do that. You know that as soon as she gets here, she will dash to the phone and call you.

"Sorry that you have to run off. We will see you later and I'll tell Mr. Henderson that you are home. I'll walk you to the door. Your lateness in arriving had us all worried and imagining all sorts of things that could have caused you to be late, so much so that your mother was going to contact the school. I'm responsible for implanting that fear, for who knew better than I how punctual you are and how you hated for anyone to be tardy. Gosh, how you hated waiting for Cindy Joe when she was late for the Saturday puppet show."

Later in the week, Jimps' parents called him into the living room. They looked at him with worried eyes. "Jimps, you've been home for a week and you haven't left this house. How about a good tanabath? It's great for the skin and will pep you up. Can it be that you are down because Cindy Joe isn't here? Don't you worry about that. She will show up, I promise you."

"No, Dad. That isn't the reason, not that I wouldn't like to see her. She is good company. It's just that I'm off the beam. My work pattern is such that it requires more time than I can give it, just too much. Yes, let's go get the tanabath. It can't make me feel worse than I do now. Toss you to see who pays for the rubdown."

"James, a moment, please. We know all about Cindy Joe."

The shocking statement staggered a petrified Jimps. Grasping the table's edge, a sickly Jimps would have collapsed if the follow up sentence wasn't blurted out immediately.

"Yes, we know all about that Romano fellow."

A deep breathing Jimps sat down in his chair, the color slowly returning to his cheeks.

"I'm sorry, James. I didn't think the news would effect you like that. Evidently you know the story. When and how did you find out?"

"Yes, Dad. I knew. Cindy Joe wrote to me explaining the whole mess. It does upset me. You know how close we have been, good buddies since childhood. How did you learn about it? Through Mrs. Henderson, I suspect."

"That is right. Mrs. Henderson got the facts from Cindy Joe's roommate, a Patty West, but that was only after Mrs. Henderson promised that she would never let Cindy Joe know that they knew about the baby.

"Well, Mrs. Henderson had to confide in someone, and naturally it had to be your mother. You know how close our families have been through the years, so close that we assumed that you and Cindy Joe would someday…Oh well. That is neither here nor there now. Let's go get our treatment."

Finally, the difficult days of vacation were over. With a feeling of relief welling up inside, Jimps said his goodbyes.

CHAPTER IX

"Jimps, darling, did I miss you! What in tarnation has happened? Your clothes are hanging on you. Have you been ill? Now I am positive that I am right. I've decided that there will be no more separations and that includes vacation time. That is, if you agree. I explained all to my parents and they understand and agree, but had one request. They do want to meet you. Now that I have settled that problem, let's have something to eat. You have a double order of your favorite, M.E.T. and J., mashed potatoes, eggs, toast and javaline. Did you miss me, and tell me how much and why? I do need some compliments."

"Hell, I don't have to tell you how I feel after all these years. I'm sure you know. You have always been and always will be the love of my life. How does that sound, you kept woman? Ouch! Juan, you bastard! I should have known it was you. Who the hell else could have that heavy a hand. Olga, come here, dear. Still as pretty as ever."

"Santa Maria, did you ever get thin! I should have taken you to the Pampas, That raw meat would put the meat on your bones. Momma and Poppa and Teresa send their best. Eartha, you are a fortunate woman. You've got some kind of man. My family loves him madly, especially my little sister, Teresa. There isn't a day that goes by without her mentioning Jimps."

Eartha, beaming like a queen who is proud of her possessions, whispered to Olga, "Didn't I tell you that Jimps would be great with children? I may start planning."

A few weeks later, seated in the lab, Jimps grinned at John.

"Lord, John. We are about there. All we need now is a place where we can put all our practice together, something small like the Bering Sea. I'm about fed up with the smell. Excuse me, that's too polite a word, the stink of fish, fertilizer and the preserved herbs and insects."

"Me, too. Too bad there isn't a known way to make them smell good and at the same time not lose their effectiveness. There, if I ever heard one, is a good suggestion for a project. Jimps, you may have the honor of seeing Professor Hudson and selling him the idea. His door is always open."

"Thank you. I will consider the honor, for that is a good way to rupture your sardine. Sardine, what a sickening word. That, my friend, is the main dish of the day, sardines, eggplant, hot dogs and corn. What a hell of a mixture. I'm passing mine up. Care to take a walk?"

A few weeks later, Juan approached Jimps with concern written all over his face.

"Jimps, what the hell is troubling you? You aren't the same person who left for his leave a short time ago. From a person who enjoyed company, loved to gossip and was happy with his work, you have made an unbearable change. Your sitting around on foggy ground has upset all of us who are close to you, especially Eartha, who just looks at you and dies with your crazy mood. Christ sakes, James. We're family and your problems are our problems. See you later." Only a Juan who had become unhatched would have addressed Jimps as James.

"Just a minute. I do have a problem and what a problem! How can I try to explain and hope to hold your friendship and love?"

"Try, Jimps. Just try me."

Elbows on the table, chin in hands, a voice choking Jimps stared at a blank wall and again lived the day of madness.

"The day I left here, I went directly to Key West, where I met my neighbor, Cindy Joe. You remember, I had spoken of her a number of times. We had planned a three-day holiday. We had done this same thing a few years ago and really had a wild time, food, sights, sex. All went well the first day. We started where we left off years ago, food, sightseeing and the crazy, mad sex. The following morning aboard a thirty-foot rented fishing boat, paradise turned into purgatory, all within minutes.

"The damned fish weren't biting. It's ironic, but my whole life is governed by fish. We decided that they day wasn't going to be a total loss, so we went below deck, stripped and started in our lovemaking, a hell of a lot more productive than waiting for the stupid fish to bite. If only one, just one of billions of fish would have taken our bait, I wouldn't be here repaying my debt to the devil.

"How can one describe lovemaking with Cindy Joe? One would have to be a part of it, to know the feeling of her violent eruptions and how their never-ending spasms would seep into your soul, making you a pawn in her drive of maddening desires. She was a queen bee. You were engulfed and there was only one thought in your mind, to leave part of you imbedded deep within her never satisfied gut.

"Midway through the orgy, she being in her world of ecstasy, called me Frank. Frank, she had told me was the only other man who had touched her. He was the bastard who had clicked her love box. The mere mention of his name at that sacred moment set off a fire in my brain. There was only one thought in my mind and that was to inflict a hurt onto her, a hurt that would last as long as my own. It was a few minutes later that she suggested having a drink or two and that she was to be the topless and bottomless server of the concoctions. Minutes later, I followed her to the top deck and with Satan's guidance, I reached the top deck as Cindy Joe was about to approach the turn to the stairway. At precisely that moment, I placed my foot between her feet causing her to fall to the deck. It was a moment of joy, for all I could think of was seeing the hurt that would come to her eyes as her knees scraped the deck. G-d forgive me, she came down on her knees and in trying to hold onto the tray, lost all sense of balance and struck her head against the corner of the metal bait box. There was the sickening snap of something breaking, not unlike the breaking of a dry twig. There wasn't any cut on her head, but a light green circle was forming above her nose. Believing that she was unconscious from the blow, I bent down to get her to her feet and upon seeing her eyes wide open, starting into the sun and drops of blood oozing from her ear, I froze and only the timely arrival of oblivion saved what sanity there was to save.

"Consciousness returned as the sun was starting to set. There was a distinct chill in the air and upon seeing Cindy Joe lying there, I reached over and touched her. A sign of the cross, dozens of pleadings to god for help went unanswered. Cindy Joe was beyond help, for rigor mortis was starting to set.

"I couldn't have been sane. It was all like a maddening dream. The next twelve hours were clouded hours. I do recall purchasing a trunk and taking my luggage to the monorail terminal. Then I was on board the craft, the motors were running and at my foot was the trunk. I pushed the throttle forward and directed my course eastward into the eastern sun. I went below, picked up Cindy and together with her clothes, forced her body into the trunk. I continued due east until I arrived at a location that was deep in vegetation that glided over the small swells of the ocean. There I heaved the trunk overboard, right in the midst of Nature's greenery. That's all there is. I wonder if it is true. Stupid. I know it is."

Juan, blessing himself a number of times, placed his arm on Jimps' shoulder and said, "Compadre, what's done is done. It was accidental, so you should not feel guilty. Her parents, somehow I feel that it is better for them to believe she is alive than to know that she is dead. Too much time has elapsed. Nothing can be gained now. This is too deep for me. My feelings haven't changed. If they had, I wouldn't be a worthwhile brother. You see, I still love you and you never told me anything. You spoke in English and you always said that my English is atrocious. So, Mr. Jimps, I not understanda too mucha."

CHAPTER X

Later that week, as Jimps sat brooding over a cup of javaline in the dining hall, Jane approached.

"Hello, Jane. Sit down and I'll get you a drink or some lunch if you're ready for it. Do you know if John is coming for lunch? I know that he had received a message to call his home. Hope everything is O.K."

"That's why I'm here, to tell you that the message was from his brother. Their father died during the night, an accident and the cremation will be this afternoon, so John was given a forty-eight hour leave of absence. Thank you, I'll have a mintcrock. That is a very refreshing drink. Ever try one? Has Eartha had her lunch?"

"Yes, she has, but she was only allotted a half hour. She had to get to her post at station 22. She gets upset when that two hour extra duty time arrives. You would think it was two hours a day instead of two hours a month, but it is boring."

"When is your next class?"

"You trying to pull my leg? John and I don't have classes. We are on our own. It sounds as though you are fleecing me."

"No, I'm not. It's just that I'm not thinking too clearly. I'm in dire need of company. Would you be so gracious as to walk me to my apartment?"

"I deem it a pleasure, especially when the escorted one is a female and beautiful."

"Thank you, Jimps. I feel the same way. It is the company that enhances the hour. Care to come in for a while? No one will be here for at least ninety minutes and I'll brew you some javaline."

"Thank you. I'll accept both invitations, the coming in and the javaline."

"Jimps, where and how did you possess such a name? I don't care for it. Sounds like a name for a pet of some kind." A slinky smile. "Of course, having you for a pet can't be too bad."

"My given name is James," stammered a very puzzled and searching Jimps, who detected a slight tint of pink coming to the fore on the cheeks of a Jane who was fighting and losing a battle of control. *Control of what?*

"Do you want sweets in your javaline?" sputtered a hand shaking Jane, who dropped the tray and all of its contents to the floor. Kneeling besides a helpful Jimps, Jane, quivering like a wounded deer, raised her head to find Jimps' eyes.

"James, I've never been alone with a man in eight years. There has only been John." Suddenly, lips met lips and then the feeble cry of helplessness. "Please don't be so rough. I'm very tender there, but don't stop, not even if I beg you to. Jimps, you are so wonderful, so don't stop. This may be the only time we will be together such as this, so never, never stop. Don't you dare."

"Yes, Cindy. I won't. Enjoy it."

"Wasn't that lovely. So satisfying. If only John had your staying power. Thank you, James. Who is Cindy? You don't have to answer."

"I don't mind. It's just that I thought of you as my fairy tale Cinderella."

"That is a beautiful sentiment. Thank you for the most glorious day of my life. Come kiss me before you go. Why couldn't we have had another hour. Bye, love."

When Eartha met Jimps at the door that evening, she was full of smiles. Giving Jimps a big hug, she kissed his cheek, glowing with pride.

"Jimps, I am so proud of you. Do you realize that you and John have made the bulletin board notice three consecutive months? That has never been accomplished before and not to mention your citations from the World Governors, which will be encased and placed in the Hall of Achievements.

"Jimps, you are famous. For generation, other students will read your thesis on marine life. Most important at this time is that is has made me a lady of great standing, for it is common knowledge that your computer mate is the needed pen factor in keeping your physical and mental attitude balanced."

"Agreed, honey. There isn't any doubt. Without you there is nothing."

"Jimps, it is beyond my belief or anyone else's. A doctorate before the completion of the school term. You had better call your parents. Even though they will be notified, there is nothing like the excitement of hearing their words of disbelief.

"Dr. James Bard. I even love the sound of it all. Sounds awfully important. I wonder how John is standing up to his successes. Excited, I bet. Jane will be another story. I'll wager that her nose is pointing skyward. Funny, but I feel the same way, like reaching for the heavens. I am so thrilled. Let's go to bed and celebrate."

CHAPTER XI

"Eartha, will you throw the switch on our graph machine so that we can see what's happening that's new in the world? Hold it, play that last message again."

"Graph message 121. Classes will be omitted from the schedule of Tuesday October 2, 2055. The Board of Governors will be in session throughout the twenty four hour period. At 8:45 A.M., October 3, 2055, all students will assemble in hall 111 for an announcement of vital interest to all."

*   *   *   *   *   *   *   *   *   *

One thousand students and faculty members rose as Matradean de Rivisio entered the auditorium. The director, wearing the black uniform of the marine biologist, stepped on to the podium and addressed the packed hall, consisting of one hundred phase-in students, eight hundred plus students of records and a number of officials.

"Good morning. Today is a day of vital importance to all of mankind. Today is the start of another phase of our twenty year struggle with Nature and its aquatic creatures." A hesitation. "The struggle to unbalance Nature's breeding and production.

"I believe that we are now on the right plane for a productive conclusion, that of doubling the weight of all marine food stuff and accomplishing that goal in one half the time required by Nature. I trust this will be accomplished before January 1, 2064, for that is the year that is designated by the World Congress as the start of the famine century. Let us all meditate for a moment.

"As of January 1, 2064, most of the people of the world will receive fifty percent of the food they are receiving today, and by the year 2070, they will receive only thirty percent of today's quota. Can we survive, physically and mentally under these conditions?"

Complete silence greeted this question, and prayer followed the bowed heads of the thousand.

"Three days ago, I was informed that our underwater city off the coast of North Carolina is completed and will be ready for occupation July 1, 2056. Anyone who wishes to obtain a copy of the complete plan and diagram of the city can do so by placing a request through Specialist George Dunn, room 122.

"The World Board has voted and decided that the underwater project, in its entirety, will be under the supervision of our Professor Henry Hudson." The applause continued until a smiling Professor Hudson stood up and raised both closed fists overhead.

The good Professor continued, "Assigned to work with Director Hudson," a hesitation followed the emphasized word of "Director" (and the hesitation imbedded into the one thousand) that the title of Director can only mean that Hudson would automatically become the Matradean of World College upon the retirement or demise of Professor de Rivisio. The standing ovation failed to bring a shocked Professor Hudson to his feet. The applause continued until a very unsteady Mr. Hudson rose and gave the hand raised sign.

"Working with and under the wings of our Director Hudson will be the two of our young eagles who have far exceeded our expectations with their development of the proper biological and chemical needs for marine life breeding and weight control. On the borad shoulders of these two men and their crews rests the fate of all nations. Three short years ago, we drafted fifty chemistry students to team with fifty biology students and had them work separately as teams to find the right highway to follow for success. I believe that we have found that team.

"Please, when the following names are called, these students will stand in front of their seats. We don't want them to try to walk and, truthfully, I don't believe they will be capable. We can't have them go into shock; They will have to much work ahead of them for that.

"This young man, was drafted from the School off Chemistry. He received his doctorate a few short weeks ago. Stand up and greet your friends of the past nine years, Professor John King."

As the title of "Professor" struck John, he rose, raised his fists upward and then practically collapsed onto the chair. Not even the high setting of the volume on the speaker and the voice pleading for quiet could stop the roar of the one thousand.

"Please, now may I present the other fifty percent of this successful team. Ladies and Gentlemen, Jane Halley."

Jane stood up, raised her fists and immediately sat down. At times, the saying goes, the Lord protects the innocent. The four unsuspecting students who would have drowned in Jane's tears if John hadn't handed her a mansized handkerchief would have appreciated the saying.

"Thank you. Somehow I am receiving a message, a message that this is slowly but surely becoming a day of rejoicing, so why break the trend? This day will be recorded as a specialy holiday.

"Will Dietician Specialist Eartha De Rene arise?"

Eartha, head held high, eyes smiling, teeth sparkling between opened lips, got to her feet, raised both clenched fists skyward, proudly gazed about the room and then flashed her eyes downward to rest on the face of her man.

Another blue pill, and de Rivisio continued, "Not if I may, it is a great honor to present the man of the century, Professor of Biology, James Bard."

The nearest anyone can come to describing the next thirty minutes would be to say all hell broke loose. Jimps, in a complete state of shock, well beyond the realm of reality, grasped the side of the seat, stood up, gave the hand sign, gazed in the direction of the podium, but not being able to see through the mist in his eyes, eased himself back into his seat. Not even the backslapping and the handshakes were potent enough to return him to the world of the present. Jimps, still very emotional, was led from the auditorium by a tired, but happily flushed Eartha.

That evening came the happy task of calling Jimps' parents.

"James, it is simply wonderful seeing you and hearing your voice. We are so proud. The news is flashing all over the universe and they are showing pictures of you that I don't even remember seeing. I suspect that your father had a part in discovering them, as he had been running off with some people I had thought to be acquaintances of his from the Dome home development. The newscasters are dubbing you as the savior. Gosh, I can't believe it! Your father is running about like he is trying to locate his head. James, will you move to your right a tiny bit so I can see Earth? Thank you dear. Eartha, you look adorable. James is a fortunate man."

"Thank you, Mother."

"I am insisting that you both come spend some time with Dad and me before you go to that city. Isn't it awfully dangerous to be under water for a long period of time? Eartha, you had better see to it that you and James have your vitamins, especially D for the sun replacement."

"Yes, Mother. I shall see that he receives all of his needs."

"Thank you children. I do have to run and see Florence. Poor dear, if only she would receive some news about Cindy Joe. It is slowly draining all the life from her. Today she had a visitor from the state department who believes there may have been a suicidal pact between Cindy Joe and Mr. Romano. Seems that his parents committed suicide and Romano possibly inherited something or another. Sounds awfully silly and stupid, they just don't have any clues. They both simply vanished. Oh yes, before I forget dear, they were going to talk to you about Cindy Joe because of your close friendship, but upon hearing that you are attending World College decided against it. I do pray it all comes to a conclusion for Florence's sake. This is just too much to carry. Dad and I will be home every night except Saturday, our dinner tour night. We will expect a weekly call. Night Jimps, night Eartha."

The face dimmed as a simultaneous "good night" hummed. "Jimps, your folks are so wonderful. I'm so happy that they have accepted me."

"Why shouldn't they, I got the best of the bargain. I felt the same, thrilled that your parents accepted me."

"Thank you my dear for those loving words."

"Hi Olga, Hi Juan," said Jimps as the two burst into the room. "What the hell is so funny? Why the grin? Better watch it or you will push your ears outa line."

"Have you read the bulletin news?"

"No, what news worth reading can there be on it? Eartha and I supplied all the important reading a short time ago."

"You damn gringo! You know! You saw it! Man oh man, am I going to celebrate. Let's go Olga. Happy to bed is better than rise or shine."

"Congratulations Dr. Cudoro. Juan, I am thrilled by your doctorate even more than mine."

"I know Jimps. I felt the same way. Way out! Captain of the underwater crew and assigned to underwater city, wow!"

"Jimps, did you notice that out of twenty-four couples assigned to the project, eighteen of those couples are close friends of ours. Funny isn't it?"

"Don't worry Juan. I'm sure it is not because they want us to die together. That is, unless we fail in our assignment."

"You Mr. James, are funny as hell. Ho! Ho! I'm dying with laughter."

The light dimmed. Jimps' mind wandered. *I've had my relaxer pill. So why doesn't sleep come! Funny, but as soon as they learned that I was attached to the college everything stopped. Naturally no stench can be attached to the academy. No, not at any cost. Cindy why? Why you and I? Poor Florence, poor Cindy, poor me-poor me-poor ME—*

The following morning, a sleepy-eyed Jimps wandered out of the bedroom.

"Morning, Juan. What have we got on the tapes?"

"I don't know. I'll set them. I woke up starved having dreamed about food have the night, so to the cafeteria I ran."

"Christ's sake, Juan. You know that could be serious. The cardinal rule is to set the tapes immediately upon morning call. Hell, you know that."

"Sorry Jimps. That was stupid. Here they go."

"Code 1. James Bard, contact Director Hudson this morning. Urgent. Code 1. 8:10 A.M."

A short time later, Jimps sat in Hank Hudson's office.

"Good morning, Professor Hudson."

"Good morning, Jimps. I'll make this brief. You caught me at a pressed hour. I have to meet with the Board in fifteen minutes. All of the personal assigned to the underwater city will receive a six-week leave starting in mid-April through June 30. Six weeks, and in all probability, that will be the last leave anyone will receive until the project comes to its conclusion. You and John King will report to the project site June 24, a week before the others, so as to familiarize yourselves with the layout and operations systems. I will also be there with the engineers, computer and solar people. You will note that for every specialist assigned to the underwater city, there is a replacement at the above ground station.

"The eight specialists assigned to the underwater city are people that you don't know. The other forty are close friends and good acquaintances, and I will answer your unasked question. The forty were chosen because of the close ties, for we believe that a close and friendly crew will make for a successful undertaking. Above all, they are all highly qualified to do the job at hand.

"Jimps, one other point. I would appreciate your addressing me as either Henry or Hank." A handshake and, "Good luck, Jimps. The best to you and Miss De Rene."

"Thanks, Henry. Be seeing you. The best to you and yours."

Walking back toward his lab, Jimps' thoughts took a contemplative turn.

How time does fly along! It's been less than a year since I've seen Cindy Joe. Why can't I erase it from my mind? Poor Mrs. Henderson. She sure has gotten old. How can a damn year change a person so much? Still, it has to affect her. Even I feel aged because of Cindy Joe and I know where she is. I sure as shit know! Poor Mrs. Henderson. I wonder if the male angels are chasing Cindy Joe. She sure would change Heaven.

CHAPTER XII

"Good morning. I'm Professor Bard. I'm to meet with Director Hudson."

"Enter, sir. The second building on the left, the consulting chamber. You are expected."

"Thank you."

Jimps and John had arrived just that morning at the land compound of the city. They were to meet with Henry, tour this area of the city and then go below water and begin living in the underwater area.

"Good morning, James." A sturdy handshake and, "Meet Mr. Ernest Belli. Mr. Belli is our Chief Electrical Engineer. The tall young man on your left is solar system engineer, Stanley Bender and the blond fellow is atomic reactor specialist, Mr. Chancey Hawks. Men, this is Professor James Bard, my right arm and second in command of the project." Handshakes all around and the suggestion of breakfast was acknowledged by all.

At breakfast, Jimps learned that the three men were in charge of the building housing all of the needs in their field required in the underwater city. A tremendous undertaking! All of the personnel attached to the project were under thirty-five years of age. That is, everyone except Director Hudson, who would soon be known as the "Old Man". This reference did not pertain to age, but to the leader of the ship.

"Here comes John. Where have you been? Get lost?"

"Sorry, but we were grounded in Chicago. Lost one hour."

Introductions completed, Jimps and John followed behind Hudson and the three men in charge of the tour. Entering the first building, John's "Phenomenal" described the supply station. Here, as in all the buildings, was housed a spare part for every article that was in the underwater city, from the smallest nut and bolt to the four ton reactors.

"How do you like those beauties, John?" asked Professor Hudson. "They were built to your specifications and under the supervision of Professor Borf von Stepf, at the Grupplin plant in Germania. Awesome, aren't they?"

Mr. Belli leading the tour, entered the next building.

"John, James, have either of you had any underwater exploration time? I am not referring to the skin diving time at the World training pool."

"I haven't, sir."

"Neither have I."

"You will enjoy this segment. Here every possible need of the underwater scientist is stored. This building is affectionately called the 'gas chamber.' There to your left is a spare mini-sub and here are six scooter sleds, all powered by atomic power (as is all of our equipment). In the nose of the sleds, you will note there are two spears that have the driving force to penetrate through a whale shark. Also, on the spear head is a mechanism that can be set to explode when penetrating any creature. The spear will hold its power for one hundred yards and water depth has no bearing on its performance. Quite a handy toy to have. The headlights of the sleds are equipped with seer-tubes, which will neutralize any water color-change because of depth.

"There against the west wall are the cranes, lifts, loaders, nets and all the necessary vehicles needed for loading and unloading the edible fish and sea vegetation. Left of the underwater tank are the greatest assortment of diving equipment known to man, from the uniform to minute gauges."

As the group was about to continue the tour, an attendant approached Director Hudson and informed him that there was a message of importance waiting for him in the reception room. Seating themselves in the lunchroom, the group munched sugar beans until the Director's return. Shortly thereafter, Henry returned bearing the news that he had to rush back to World and meet with Board members. Giving the raised fist sign, Henry, promising to return within three days, left the building. Arrangements were made to continue the tour the next morning under the guidance of Stanley Bender.

7:00 A.M.

"Come on, John. Hit the boards."

"Good morning, Stanley. It sure is something the way powdered taters and eggs can be prepared. It is belly filling."

"Stanley, John and I would appreciate it if you would dispense with the Professor and Sir bit while no one is around. Agreed?"

"Agreed, and thanks, Jimps.

"This compound is one half mile square and is encircled by the same type wall that borders the underwater city. At the base of this wall is a radar system that notifies the computer station when anyone or anything is approaching the wall. Then automatically, a picture of the section is flashed on the large screen over the computer south wall. On top of this two lane highway wall are four Polar Bear ships, all set to take off immediately on a given signal. Also, on the wall are eight radar eye beams, four on the north wall and four on the south wall. These beams, capable of making a complete 360-degree turn, cover a distance of one eighth of a mile in all directions, making it possible to cloak the whole compound. If and when full power is extended, these lights would be capable of injecting serious burns on anyone they contacted.

"Why the precautions? Well, even though this project is beneficial to the world, it wouldn't eliminate the irrational man, the crackpot, the offbeat character who destroys because of his warped mind. History has substantiated that fact.

"Looking about, one has to wonder what the hell a project like this costs. The amount has to be staggering."

"Believe me, Stan. Whatever the cost is, it isn't too much, for if we don't come up with the answer, there won't be any need for money," John said contemplatively.

"John, Stanley, what do you say about cutting today's tour? I'm feeling flat."

"O.K. by me, Jimps. How about you, Stan? Fine. Then let's call it a day."

"Jimps, I've got a nice room in town, two large beds. One is yours if you want it," said John as they walked away.

"Thanks, I accept."

"Pack your gear. We'll take off as soon as I warm up the fly-cub. How about hunting up a good sauna bath house and a good rubdown artist? I miss that little lady of mine. She relaxes me better than any machine will ever be able to do."

A short time later they were aboard the fly-cub and headed toward town.

"How does this little fly-cub handle?" asked Jimps. "She rides real smooth."

"Real easy. Want to take her off the ground?"

"Me? Hell, man! If I took her off, we would crash land within a second. I get sick just sitting in these things, let alone trying to learn to operate one. How much of a ride do we have?"

"About ten minutes. This thing will buzz up to about two hundred and fifty miles an hour and can land on the proverbial dime. Not bad at all."

"How's this for schedule. A shave, a shower, a good meal, a sauna bath and rub, a good quiet corner in a gin hole where we can sit and get slobbered. This will probably be the only time we will be able to think about something other than fish food and reactors."

"I'm with you all the way, Jimps. I will pick out the eating house. I found a nice little cozy steak house a few short blocks from our lodgings, "Cindy Mae's Tasty Steaks'."

Cindy Joe. Poor Cindy Joe. I can't seem to remember how she looked.

"The steak suits me fine, as long as we seal it with about a dozen glasses of Gem Juice. I believe I'm going to need help falling asleep."

The following morning at nine o'clock, Jimps and John walked into the cafeteria. They found Stanley at a table and went to join him.

"Morning, Stanley."

"Morning, Jimps. Morning, John. Sure is a beautiful morning."

"Sure is, Stanley, sure is."

"Right on time, Jimps. You look good. That is, as good as a dead man can look."

"All kidding aside, I feel so-so, but I'm sure a good breakfast will cut away the webs."

"Are you fellows ready for a tour of the inner wall? We can drive around it in one of the scamper vehicles. The road that turns toward the south fence near the entrance leads to the ramp to the wall."

"This is some sight. From below, you could never get this perspective. Kind of frightening, like driving over a skyway bridge without any protective railing," Jimps said as he gazed about him in awe.

"This wall has the same scanning lights as the outer wall and the exact same radar system. There, at the red marker is the south entrance to the underwater city, three hundred and ten steps to the main chamber. Directly across on the north wall is another entrance to the city. Why that marker is blue and this one red is beyond me. I go batty trying to find a reason.

"This roofing overhead, seeming like another road above us, is in reality our solar energy system. This covering extends the full length of this east wall, one mile in length. This system supplies all of our hot water needs, air conditioning, etc. This system, incidentally, is the largest one of its kind in the world.

"That is it, the end of the tour. This is quite a ride, and I'm more amazed after each ride. There, just over our admittance building, that hilly section That is where most of our atom cartridges and other highly contaminables are stored."

"Thanks a million, Stan. It was tops. Jimps and I will float around, seeing what we can do. No sense in tying you up anymore. Thanks again."

"It was a pleasure. See you around."

CHAPTER XIII

"Good morning, James, John. How did everything go?" asked Professor Hudson, who had just returned from World.

"Fine, Henry, and you?"

"We had a very productive meeting. One hundred percent go all the way.

"We have a choice by way of entrance to the city, either by scuba or stairway. I'm inclined to lean toward the stairway. What do you so to walking toward the entrance? It's about a mile and for our return, we can have a scamper vehicle waiting for us.

"That was quite a climb. The ramp is longer by leg than by sight, but it was worth it. What an illusion! Even at this height, I have a tendency to sway when looking down at the water. Seems as though the waves are reaching up and trying to pull you to her breasts."

"I feel that way too," said Jimps, "but there is another feeling I have, and that is the feeling of being alive and alone with god. How about you, John?"

"Ditto. That's exactly the way it strikes me. Isn't that breeze something? And smell that salt. I can never tire of this, never."

"Here we are," said Hank. "I suppose you noticed the other day that these hatches can only be opened from the inside by a button at the top of the stairs and by a release button on the computer board. We have a few minutes to wait.

"There she is. Let's go. This stairway is funneled through the center of the wall. Here at the top we have approximately twelve feet of reinforced concrete on either side of the stairway and at the base, there is double that amount. The stairway has a forty-degree pitch. A thousand feet separate the top and bottom steps, making for easier walking down than up. The airflow is mild and cool. The lighting is good. Do either of you suffer from claustrophobia? No? That's fine. This is a test run, so if you have any suggestions to improve the conditions here, voice them. John, will you please clock the time needed to reach the bottom step? Any discomfort?"

"None, sir, but I get the funny feeling of sort of like, entering hell. I'd have to say that one's imagination can run away and you have to fight that claustrophobic feeling. How about it, Jimps?"

"I feel tops. It's just a matter of thinking concrete, be a part of it. How often will we be using these stairs? For me, hopefully, it will be the scuba entrance from now on."

"This entrance and exit may be used far more than we can imagine," said Hank. "Many are the people with a fear of water, especially with so much of it overhead. But, then, it shouldn't effect the members of this body, as all have withstood the pressure chamber."

"Time is four minutes and twenty seconds," said John. "If I didn't time the walk down, I would have said it took about ten minutes. Time certainly slows when you're boxed in."

"Enter men," smiled Hank. "In a few days this will be your home. For how long, only success or failure can designate.

"This is our recovery station. The airflow here is automatically set to balance the body change needs per pound per square foot. We won't feel the change, mentally or physically. There to your right is the decompression chamber which leads directly to the exit and entrance to the water. Every occupant of this city will experience the direct water entrance to these buildings. There will be training programs set up under the guidance of Juan Codora.

"The section to your right is where the top six officials and their mates will bed. The rooms are sectioned for privacy. That hallway leads to the rooms where the other members are quartered.

"To your left is the cafeteria. There will always be an abundance of food and drinks, as all are delivered daily. That opening in the wall is the sear-burner, where all refuse is shuttered to the burner and flowed out into the water when it completes its burning process. Another food source for the residents of the sea.

"The tunnel we are entering is composed of corrugated steel fibers and a synthetic rubber mold that can far exceed the pressure limits of all other known materials.

"This, my friends, is the heart of our operation." A smile creased Hank's face as he glanced at the open-mouthed expressions of his right and left hand geniuses.

"Christ, I didn't expect this."

"You can say that again. How the hell did anyone assemble all this in the limited time and under water at that?"

"This is the most delicate computer system in the world. The banks have been compiled by the greatest international scientists alive. There stands their product of ten years' slavery. All of us attached to this undertaking are at the mercy of these machines, god love and protect them. Later, after lunch, study the board and you will be amazed at the complexity of the computers and know how that the computer specialists have attained. Here above the computer section 4-B are the starters for generators, lights, airpressure tanks, generators for the scanning lights. For these scanners, there are sixteen buttons, one for each light and whenever a section is lit, the section is shown on our large screen on the opposite wall. There in the center over section 5-B are two small screens. These are used for direct contact to our outside compound, the World College and to the World Government Headquarters. There is also direct screen contact to our mini-sub.

"To your extreme left, above 6-B, is the overall power switch and the starter for the great wall fish entrance gate on the east wall. One point that I may have overlooked is that all scanning lights here, as above, turn a full 360 degrees and their beam interlock. The only space where there is a blind spot is on the far side of the three ships which were sunk here for fish sanctuary. This was an afterthought, completed only two weeks ago.

"Tomorrow, we will inspect all of the outide, via mini-sub. I think we will skip the generator sections. There isn't much to see other than large generators like the ones at World. You two go ahead and inspect your offices and living quarters. I have some work to catch up on."

*   *   *   *   *   *   *   *   *   *

Jimps, John and Hank walked toward the entranceway to the building that housed the mini-sub.

"Captain Monta Keely, meet Professors James Bard and John King, second and third in command in this operation." A hard handshake from a short, stocky man, square jawed, who one had to assume did not receive those flattened ears outside a squared circle, gave one the impression that this was a man who guided himself by the book of regulations.

"Captain Keely and a crew of two will pilot our mini-sub. The Captain is regular Army and will be attached to this station for an indefinite period. Captain, we are in your hands."

"Thank you, sir. This way please. This is the only dry entrance to the sub, via the generator plant and tunnel hookup to the sub. This is the same type tunnel that we have leading from building to another, all but the locking device to the sub. The only simplified description that I can relate is that this is the exact looking device that we use on our interplanetary space ship docking equipment. These generators are atom powered, as all of our mechanized units.

"After you, gentlemen. Watch your step. This tunnel is composed of the same metal that is used in all of our tunnel entrances. Pound for pound, it is the strongest metal in the world, but its greatest asset is in its pliableness, giving just enough where ever it is needed. There is seating for ten men on this ship, three to my immediate right, two directly behind me and two each on the port and starboard sides. In an emergency, we can safely evacuate ever member of this underwater city, even if that safety is one thousand miles away. This ship, as you know, is atom powered. It has an automatic decompressing unit and a temperature device that is instantaneous in its settings. There are two propeller units driving this thing and in the event that one wouldn't function, which is highly improbably, the other would get us to port safely. We can from our lowest level reach topside, 250 feet, in less than two minutes. We have a forward speed of twenty knots and a reverse creeping speed of less than one knot an hour.

"In the nose of the ship are two revolving head lights and alongside the lights are two four inch tubes containing high speed powered spar guns. These spears were set in these tubes for use in this project. Primarily, they were erected so as to contain and discharge the one-fourth ton atom gun. The conversion, if needed, can be accomplished in less than one hour. There are three of the same type lights on the port and starboard sides and two on the tall section.

"We are radar beamed. This ship will swerve automatically from any solid matter while traveling forward or reverse. The overall dimensions of this ship are sixty feet by eighteen feet. Under her hull are some one hundred spikes, two inches wide and five feet long that have eliminated any possible scraping of the ship's bottom and have made it possible for the ship to attain a firm grip on anything from hard metal to plain every day sea muck.

"Sir, I would recommend your sitting up front, to my right. The outside vision is greater from that point. Overhead and focused on the operator of the ship is our screen, our visible contact with our base. The ship to base radio is always open and in contact. Make ready for takeoff, sir.

"S-U-B 1, to base. Takeoff – 6-29-54, 0900, off and out.

"Sir, I will head due south to the south wall and then proceed in a northerly direction for one quarter mile and then due north to the north wall. From that point, sir, I will proceed along the north wall. If at any point you wish me to stop, call out and I will cut the motors.

"There ahead, slightly to your port side, is our first scanner light. As the light beam makes it sweep, sections of the water seem to turn from blue to green, from green to blue and at great depths, become black. Takes a bit of getting used to.

"Right at our nose is the first of three ships that have been scuttled to make the artificial reefs. The east side of that ship and the north side of another scuttled ship are the only blind areas in this whole enclosure and that was brought about by the late scuttling of the ships. If it is permissible, sir, I will take the sub top side so that you may view the structure from inside the walls."

"Fine, Captain. Whatever you decide."

"There, sir, is the first of the giant reactors. My knowledge of their functions is limited."

"That monstrosity, Captain, is the brain child of Professor King. Care to elaborate, Professor?"

"Well, they were placed at their precise locations so that the proton shock waves from one reactor can interlock with another and hopefully, these shock waves will cause all of the marine life that is encircled by these waves to become so stimulated that they will go on an eating rampage. Now the efforts of Professor Bard come into being. James?"

"Well, I believe that I have found a food that the marine life cannot resist, nor will they tire of it. With a bit of luck, they will gorge themselves like children given all of sweets and goodies they want. I believe we have found a combined way to grow and fatten the marine life in one half the time that Mother Nature has taken. This will be accomplished if we are fortunate enough to receive a bit of cooperation from the Master above."

"Make ready for rise," the Captain said. "This lift will take less than two minutes and when come afloat, we will go to the tower where there is ample room for four. Hatch is open, sir."

"Thank you, Boats. This is an unforgettable sight, like being in an enormous swimming pool. One question, Captain. What the hell is the reason for two different colored flags at the tunnel entrances to the city? Is it a light barrier?"

"Partially. The blue is more visible when the sun is directly over the north wall. Shall we go below?"

The men reentered the sub and the hatches were secured. Looking out the viewing screen, Jimps suddenly pointed out and said, "That is some run of fish. There has to be at least ten thousand blue fish in that school."

"Yes, sir," replied the Captain. "Those fish are first cousin to the tuna and are the most ravenous fish in the ocean. They eat for twenty out of twenty four hours daily.

"Two hundred feet to our starboard are what are called the pit ledges. This ledge drops off about fifty feet and runs alongside the east wall. In reality, it is the outer west ridge of the Gulf Stream. I will stop here for a few minutes, sir, for there to your right is the great lock. I have seen this doorway a dozen times these past few weeks, and I believe that what stands there is the greatest engineering feat of all time. There is a lot of pressure coming from the door and that is meant to be. Those two inch square openings are there to relieve the pressure that builds up at that point, sort of a safety valve.

"There ahead is the second sunken sip, a light cruiser, the most beautiful of all of our fighting fleet, even though she may be obsolete." Eyes downcast, head bowed, the Captain walked off, leaving the impression that he had attended a funeral, which he, no doubt, had.

"This is our last rectangular run. Shall we start a sweep from west to east, or shall we dock?"

"Docking will be fine, Captain, thank you. This has been a very enlightening and pleasurable tour. I must confess, I was apprehensive. This was my first experience, this viewing from a submarine, and I didn't know what to expect. It is a world of fantasy."

"Thank you, Director Hudson, Professors Bard, King. I am at your service if you need me."

CHAPTER XIV

"Hi, baby. Unbelievable, you get prettier every day. It has been a long time."

"Oh, Jimps. Did I miss you! As much as I enjoyed Olga and Juan, there was that something missing." Arms wrapped about each other, lips parted, and an instantly aroused Eartha came near the collapsing stage upon feeling the pressure of the enormous growth against her stomach. Eartha, meeting the pressure was only able to utter a feeble, "Let's go and see our room."

Can one describe the havoc that two healthy bodies can inflict on each other? Can one describe the head twisting, the tormentuous body movements, the moaning of tortured guts, the grasping and the great eruptious sighs of contentment? No, no one can!

A cold shower, and a revived Eartha called out to a sluggish Jimps, "Come on, lover. Move it. I feel like I own the world and I'm hungry enough to eat all of it."

A puzzled and droopy Jimps got to his feet and pondered, "How the hell do they do it? They're all alike in one respect. One minute they are dying, that is while popping their corks, and the next minute they are charged like they have batteries in their asses, and I mean a large battery. Women! Why try to understand them. I think I'll stay with fish behaviors. It's more stable."

Jimps and Eartha walked into the cafeteria and headed toward the table where Juan and Olga were sitting.

"Hi, Juan. Hi, Olga. Let's have the news."

"It was a nice restful week. Eartha's parents are the tops. Say, I've got a letter for you from my little sister and it's marked personal. She didn't know where to reach you, so I had to be the letter carrier."

"Thanks, Juan. What are you having for breakfast? It sure looks good."

"This is my friend, powdered eggs, powdered taters, toast, javaline, orange juice and what the hell is wrong with your eyesight? I know it has been a long time, but has your vision been drained also?"

"You go to hell, you grinning ape!"

"Never mind, lover," smiled Eartha. "You sit there and I will get your breakfast."

A few minutes later, Eartha returned and handed Jimps a tray. On it alone with his breakfast was a small package.

"It's a bit early," she said, "but happy birthday!"

A stunned Jimps tore open the package and saw a beautiful chromate watch which he badly needed, having recently broken his own. After studying the watch for a moment, Jimps uttered a, "Yeezez, thirty-three! At least I made it as far as Christ. That is if there ever was one."

Juan, kissing the silver cross around his neck, gazed heavenward and whispered, "Please, dear Father, forgive my beloved brother. Sometimes he doesn't think like the rest of us."

"Juan, tomorrow is your tour day. Are you going to enter by the stairway or are you going to scuba in?" Jimps grinned. "Sorry, I know that it is a silly question, and would be very insulting to you if you took the stairway, especially after all of the specialized training that you have received. I apologize, and ask again, how are you entering the underwater city?"

"Funny, funny! You should hope to be a comedian, but for your information, Olga and I are going to swim the route. We both suffer from claustrophobia. Ha, ha."

After breakfast, Jimps left for a meeting with John and Professor Hudson. Juan, Olga and Eartha went on the tour of the above water sections of the city. The four friends did not see each other again until evening when they met in the cafeteria.

Juan, Olga and Eartha all talked at once.

"I'm still in a trance."

"It's unbelievable, beautiful beyond one's imagination."

"The sub ride has to be the ride of rides, the lights, the gate, the sunken ships. It was a dream world, so beautiful and yet so terrifying."

"For some reason I felt as though I was the last person in the world. Alone and lost: real weird."

"Weren't the schools of fish colorful? I didn't see any of the so called denizens of the deep."

"The Captain said that at that time of day, the sharks and other large scavengers were in the pits and do whatever fish had to do while in the pits. I thought that was one heck of an answer. Gruesome, but he said, unless there was spillage of blood to draw them, they wouldn't come of the pits until about 10:00 A.M. Ugh, I could almost feel my leg being bitten off."

"I would say that you have all enjoyed the tour," smiled Jimps. "That's fine. You can, if you so desire, get a rerun at a later date."

"Look here. Tomorrow is for real, so what do you say about the four of us heading to town and have our last fling? It may very possibly be a year before any of us will see dry land. That's barring illnesses or the unforeseen. What do you think about traveling by road vehicle? It is nice country and worth the effort to see it. Any votes of dissension? None? Good. Let's meet here in thirty minutes. I move that Captain Codora pilot the creeper. All in favor say aye." Five ayes and one nay were boomed thorugh the cafeteria. Needless to say, Captain Codora made a good pilot.

At 6:30 the following morning, Jimps woke up Eartha.

"There goes the buzzer. Get up, sleepy head. You sure slept soundly. How do you feel after your first night under water? Never mind the lightheadedness. That's from being under water and all will be stabilized in a day or two. I just returned from the lab and noticed that the bulletin has you scheduled for the first four hour at the screen board, from 0800 to 1200. It's a pleasant duty for while there you can screen any section of the plant that you may care to inspect, providing that you aren't tied up with other communications. Fortunately, there aren't too many messages that come through in the average day and when they do, they are for short periods of time. Therefore, you will have the whole theater for your enjoyment, you lucky woman!"

"Oh, Jimps, I'm so excited. I know that I will love it here with you and the work is going to be gratifying, so come here and kiss me."

An hour later, Jimps went into John's office for their daily meeting.

"Morning, John."

"Hello, Jimps. Hey, what do you think about my running the reactors for one hour a day and running them at their lowest power output? I'll run them for two hours next week and push the juice to the next strength. We can keep to that ratio of addition for a few months. I believe that is a good starting point. O.K. with you?"

"Good, John. It's your crutch. Whatever you decide is fine, and I will work the same system on food changes, for here, in their environment, the fish may not take to the prescribed food as readily as they did in the smaller enclosures, right?"

"All I can say is, we sure as hell will find out, and in short order. Let's go and see Henry and breeze with him."

Two weeks later Jimps and John sat again in John's office. This time they were morose, their enthusiasm drained.

"Two weeks have gone down the drain," sighed Jimps. "Can you believe that? Keeping busy erases any chance of boredom striking you, and with the days not being long enough, how can one enjoy the luxury of boredom? This whole damn setup is crappy. Not a change in their habits. Their eating time and everything else they do is so regular that you can set your timepiece by their every movement. John, how about boosting the reactors to 200 revs instead of 100 and if they get hyped too much, we can cut it back a little? I'm going to do a bit of rehashing with my formula. What the hell good is it if it isn't just a little more enticing than their dull every day food? I wish I was a fish for a few days. Then I would know what the hell they want in the way of food."

Two more weeks passed and success still eluded the two men. They met in Jimps' office.

"Hi, John. I sent for you so that you can read a message I received from World. After skidding backwards for a month, I decided to send two of my formulas back to World for a recheck with my originals. This is what I got back! Jimps handed John a sheet of paper.

0900 World College 8-3-54
Underwater City
Professor James Bard:

Sir:

Your formulas successful. Reactors set on minimum charge.
All fifty of tank occupants fought for formulated foods.
All consumed three times their normal intake.

Specialist I-X Perry
Finch, #917426

"John, it has to be the cursed size of this enclosure and the reactor setup. The fish are eating their normal every day amount so right now the tons of pulp mixture are not needed. It's pure waste unless we can get them pepped up. Let's get that reactor up another notch and if nothing comes of it we will have to start rechecking, working backwards and see where our dividing line starts. Two weeks time should be long enough for results, hopefully good."

The two weeks and more went by and still no results.

"Here we go again," sighed Jimps. "Seven weeks of pure and unadulterated shit for results. Let's go and see Henry. He may have a suggestion or two."

"Hi, Jimps, John. Bad news, I can see. You're carrying it on your faces. I can understand all of your problems, but only you men are in a position to solve them. I can only assist you with reference to your needs. There is only one aid that I can give you and that is the knowledge that you will succeed. I am as confident as were our computers which have phased both of you as the most likely to succeed in this undertaking. No one has been computerized within forty percent of either of your markings, so get with it. It is destined."

"Thank you, Henry. Thank you very much."

"I know how busy you both have been, but I would appreciate your stopping here for lunch for the next few days. It may help to relax you."

"Thank you," smiled Jimps. "See you tomorrow at lunch time."

"Jimps, I've had the reactors running on a four on and four off basis, and nothing happened," said John. "How about if I set them to run all day and see what turns up?"

"Go ahead. Fire away. What can be worse than being at a standstill? Maybe the whole goddamn plant will blow up. At least that would be a change."

September 1, 2054

"S-U-B-1 to Computer Station. Marine life unstable. Thousands acting as though fighting for oxygen. All rising topside, stomachs upwards."

"Jimps, did you receive Captain Kelly's report? The damn fish are dying like flies."

"Yes, I did. You had better cut the reactors. And John, have a few of the fish taken to my lab."

A few minutes later, Jimps sat in his lab looking down at a mess of fish.

"Did you say that they were taken out of the water fifteen minutes ago?" he asked. "They're soft and smell as though they have been out of water for hours. Look here, John. Their innards are cooked. These damned things were electrocuted, or at least a facsimile."

A few buttons were touched and land base was set in motion. Their diagnosis was that it would take three or four days to clean up the mess. Just what was needed to make a crazy house out of an asylum.

CHAPTER XV

September 3, 2054
World College
Matradean Henry Hudson

Sir:

Today at noon, Matradean Antonio De Rivisio of World College expired. As of this time and date, you will head World College as Matradean. Your presence is requested immediately. The late Matradean's ashes will be entombed here at World College tomorrow, September 4, 2054, at 10:00 A.M.
Professor James Bard will be in command of the Underwater City, and Professor John King will be second in command. Confirmations to follow, to be forwarded from the Governor's Palace.

Verbal signature-Professor Thomas A. Feeney

"Jimps, John, I must leave for World immediately. Time is of the utmost importance, so I will have to be brief. Needless to say, you know how much I think of both of you. If any problems arise and you need my assistance, don't hesitate to call me. May god love and guide you. Now, if I may, my last order to you. You and your mates are granted a 48 hour leave. This is a good time to relax for a few days while the cleanup is completed."

A handshake, a pat on the back and Jimps for a second was taken back to the farewells to his father. The droop of the shoulders and the soulful hurt expressed in the eyes told one of the enormous weight of responsibility that had been placed on Professor Hudson's back. Time, what is it? Here, within a few minutes, a man had aged ten years.

"Any suggestions, John, or shall we leave it up to the ladies? Personally, I would like to soak up all the sun I can get."

"I know just the place where we can relax and fatten up on good old honey bread and wine and that is in Bermuda. A nice short stop."

"Sounds pleasant. Even the name is relaxing, Ber-mu-da. Not bad at all."

"Let's locate the girls and after telling them about De Rivisio and our advancements we can spring the 48 hour leave on them. Truthfully, I think they need the change more than we do. Holding half a dozen jobs can be strenuous. Bless them. They aren't only beautiful, they have intelligence and that inner something special that is bred in them."

"John, it has just this moment reached me, but I am now in the same classification as the World Governors. As of this day and until the day of my demise, I will have at my disposal all of the necessities of life. Wow! That sounds terribly important. This all means that I have at my service a ten seater Beaker plane and I am doubly fortunate in having a person that can pilot the little lady." A grin was aimed at the not too unhappy John whose second love was flying.

"John, place a call for Juan. Have him meet us in the cafeteria."

A soulful Juan entered Jimps' office a short time later.

"Hi, Jimps. It is a sorrowful day. We lost a great man, but time waits for no one. Congratulations to you and John."

"Thanks, Juan. John and I are going on a 48 hour leave and I want you to open the gates and get your tank and sled crew together, so as to herd as many fish as you can into our city. This is one hell of an undertaking, let alone being the first such attempt. It's going to be one hell of a job, especially when you realize that at the mouth of the walled channel, it is 10,000 yards wide and then narrows to 500 feet. It almost seems ridiculous to imagine that a dozen men can get fish, millions of them, to travel in one direction, with almost all of them going in that direction and not attempting to scoot the wings and go back the other way. It is too damned impossible to accomplish. With a few thousand divers, it could be done. With a handful of dreamers, it is plain nuts."

*   *   *   *   *   *   *   *   *   *

"Beautiful Bermuda," sighed Jimps. "Here. Read this. This makes it more beautiful."

> *September 5, 2054*
> *Professor James Bard*
>
> *Jimps:*
>
> *Herding a huge success. Enjoy yourselves.*
>
> *Juan*

Backing at work again, Juan was ecstatic over the success of the herding.

"Jimps, the results were fantastic, just unbelievable. We had the two tanks on the bottom, the mini-sub traveling from one side to the other, east to west, three scubas were at mid depth and three were riding ten feet from the top of the water. It was crazy, like herding cattle to their corral. Millions of fish entered the walls and continued in a northerly direction, none of them trying to backtrack or even making an attempt to get around our flanks. They just kept going straight in line toward the great gates. They were so closely knitted that one would have had difficulty in penetrating their files. It seemed as though this was all a comic opera. They stood at the gates waiting for them to be opened and when they were, they fought their way in, like they were entering a promised land. I swear that they were guided by the hand of someone much stronger than I. I'm positive the Gulf Stream flow was a contributing factor. I believe they were headed to a certain point, sort of a breaking off point, and from there they would branch off to a breeding or spawning area. I only hope that I will one day be fortunate enough to see it all again." A gaze at the ceiling, a sign of the cross and Juan continued.

"There is one thing that will stay with me for all time and that was the crustaceans, those beautiful crabs and lobsters. Jimps, they walked through the gates like the infantry, in line and by the millions. It was a sight to behold. They were the armies of the underwater world, banding together to sacrifice themselves to feed the armies of another world. Jimps, we must on our next herding, have our camera crew join us so that the world can see and believe the unbelievable sight."

"Thank you, Juan. We will not only have one camera crew but two so we can catch everything from different angles. I would love to see the sight myself and I'm sure it would be very advantageous as a training film.

"John, I received a communiqué from Dean Henry. He did some experimenting on his own and he thought there was a possibility that we were going in the wrong direction in relation to the reactors. He suggested that we try reversing the reactor power. The facts showed that the salt content of the ocean was 40% heavier, contained 15% more iodine and there was 60% more pressure per square inch at its natural birthplace. As soon as the water is taken from its natural element it immediately loses its nutrient values, hence, the reactors may do their best if the reactor power and timings were reversed. Then again, there is the possibility that under certain conditions, the high voltage setting may release more voltage power when at its lowest power output. Being that all will be reversed, the continuous running of the reactor may have less effect than when it is on for an hour or two. I trust that all is plausible. What do you think, John? Does it have its merits?"

"I'd say that it is feasible, but let me sleep on it a few days. It reads very well. Three or four days will be time enough to come up with the answer. I'm going to get the Chief Engineers, Ferguson and Staples and have them assemble about one half dozen slow circuited coils, each with a different voltage capability.

John when to work immediately and a few days later everything was ready for a trial run.

"Here we are," said John. "Five days to rebuild and convert. Not bad at all. This crew is out of this world. There will never be another like them.

"Jimps, the old teacher knew something, for everything is checking out perfectly. Shall we run it through tomorrow? I've had the reactors set at top level and will run them for one hour and then keep my eyes wide open, hoping. All set, Jimps?"

"All set, John. It's your bubble. Keep it from bursting. "Juan, I've got a job for you. How long will it take to set forty traps at specific locations? These traps are made from corrobale strips and will be from two square feet to eight square feet. Each of these traps will contain two of the same species, according to size. Daily, we will whole feed them, no small pieces of food, but solid balls of our prepared food. Every other day, your crew will check their weight and size and keep a chart and have the figures on my desk by mid-afternoon."

"We should be able to place them and the designated fish and crustaceans in them in about eight hours with a crew of four."

"How about it, John? Is the time element of O.K.?"

"If Juan will have the traps loaded by noon tomorrow, we go at that time. That is the hour that they do the least amount of feeding, so that is the best time to charge their little asses. Make it, Juan?"

"No trouble at all, if I get going. See you all tomorrow."

$$* \quad * \quad * \quad * \quad * \quad * \quad * \quad * \quad * \quad *$$

"S-U-B-1 to Station: Three bell alarm. Everything going topsy, fish eating like mad and attacking each other."

"Jimps, I just intercepted a message from Captain Keely," shouted John as he ran into Jimps' office. "I think we have arrived. The bastards are eating like they are starved."

"Wonderful, John. Cut the juice and that will give us time to triple their amount of food. That should stop them from slaughtering each other. Let's see. Today is Tuesday. We will give them four days of grace, no power charge, check their weights and then give them some spark and compare the change. This should be the final test for all.

"Want to sit in, John? Juan and his crew are going to check the traps. Hope the occupants didn't grow so much that they are crammed in them. Some joke. If only they would.

"How are you doing, Juan? I'm focused on you."

"Jimps, this is the fourth trap that I have checked and every damn fish has grown three inches in length and one inch at the girth. Man, oh man. We'll have fried fish, baked fish and raw fish for dinner tonight."

December 7

"Let's have it, Juan."

"I don't believe it. I was at trap 23 and was amazed at the difference. As had the fish in the other traps, these had grown, but because they were larger when placed in the trap, they grew faster. Simply, the bigger the fish, the faster the growth. Even the small cod had added six inches in circumference."

"Beautiful, Juan. Come on in. We are going to celebrate. Cold orange juice, fish and all the trimmings. How does that strike you. By the way, are the fish firm? Bring a few of the cod in."

"You better believe it. I just checked trap 24, containing the eels, and when I grabbed the two footer and checked it for firmness, it felt like a pice of solid rubber. At that moment I wished that the Madonna had installed that firmness in me. What a pleasant thought."

Later that afternoon, Jimps called the entire crew of the underwater city together. Stepping up to the podium, he smiled at the people sitting before him.

"Friends, today is December 7. A little over a century ago, tragedy struck our country. We had the strength and fortitude to do what we had to do. History has told you what a tremendous, sacrificing undertaking it was. Today, we have won another battle, one even more important than all of the wars gone by. This, the war of survival, has come to an end for us and our neighbors of the world. This, my friends, could not have been accomplished without your complete devotion to the project. Who, better than I, would know about your many unselfish sacrifices and for that, I thank you.

"Not too many years ago, I envisioned the day that I would step onto the podium and address the students of World College as its Matradean. Great as that dream was, standing here, today, far exceeds that honor. I wouldn't trade this moment for all of the honors and wealth in the universe, and for making me feel this way, I thank you again, dear friends."

Eartha, one of the 46 who had vision problems at that moment, met Jimps as he stepped down from his perch, kissed him and loudly whispered, "I will always love you, but never will that love be as strong as it is at this moment. Kiss me and hold my hand."

CHAPTER XVI

December 12

"Codora to base—I am behind cruiser 1, scanner post 6, just inside the pit drop off. My scuba lights are picking out a shiny object below, and I am going to investigate. Cameramen, George Spade and Pete Frankfort, will stand by at the stern of the cruiser for your pickup of district vision.

"It's a broken locker of some kind, like an old time treasure chest. Hope it's full of valuables. There isn't any lock on it. Here goes…. There's another broken trunk in this trunk, a double header, and both empty, as I would expect."

"Base to Codora—can you identify? Out."

"Codora to base—Hold on. It's not too clear at this point, a bit of scraping may do it. Seems to be markings of a cross swords and a large letter 'C'. It has to be mine, 'C' for Codora! Shall I retrieve or abandon? Out."

"Base to Codora—Leave object and mark location. Out."

"Codora to base—O.K. I will skim the ridge and head in.

"Holy Christ! Where the hell did that come from? Holy Christ! Pete come forward. Look at the size of that ugly bastard." An almost hysterical Juan was yelling as though madness had struck him.

"Those tentacles are over fifteen feet long. Pete, George! Where the hell are you? Come in fast. Holy Christ!"

Having come upon the creature suddenly and being too close to back off, Juan shot the two scuba spears into the face of the monster as the tentacles reached out for him. The force of the spear impact drove the squid from his post, but not before one of the tentacles circles Juan's body and drew him toward the dark cloud.

Saint of saints. Does the Savior take one's sanity before death? Am I mad? Jesus Christ, help me! Was it my imagination, or did I see a woman's body under that thing? Was that really blonde hair that was swaying with the slow tide? Was legs that were spread apart under that creature? God almighty, was that bastard feeding on the body, or was he planting his seed in it?

Only the quick actions of Pete and George saved Juan from the crushing power of those tentacles. With four more spears in its body, the squid, ejecting heavy clouds of black ink, faded into obscurity. An unconscious Juan was rushed to hone base, received medical aid and was transported to the land base hospital.

Juan's injuries, although not too serious, required him to stay in the hospital for over a month, mostly as a precautionary measure. Jimps kept close tabs on his progress and breathed a deep sigh of relief when his adopted brother was finally able to return to the city. He met Juan in his quarters with a grin and a handshake.

"Ready for work, or are you going to play up your experience with the little squid? Incidently the carcass was found alongside scanner 8 and it was partially devoured by sharks. It's strange, Juan, but for some reason, which I'm sure we will find later, all of the squid family has multiplied twice as fast as all of the other species and has also grown at a ratio exceeding even that of the crustaceans, and that is saying something. As of this moment, you and all of your crew are to destroy all of the cephalopads which attain tentacles over four feet in length. We are not going to have any more problems with those things and they can be good food for the other marine life.

"Tomorrow we are having the start of our first fish haul. It has been assumed that it will take ten days to net and load the thousands of tons, so, while this work is in progress all but the eight man skeleton crew will have a twelve day leave. This is effective as of 8:00

A.M. tomorrow. Juan, you will be in command while I am on leave, so to plan your next herding for the day before I return.

"The day after my return, you and Olga will start a fifteen day leave. Is that sufficient time, or will you need more?"

"Fifteen days is fine, Jimps, but more important than a leave is a discussion I have to have with you about my bout with the squid."

"O.K., Juan. Let it hold until I return. I'm leaving within the hour for World College. I will be there for two days and from that time on I will be at my parents' home."

February 1, 2055

"Matradean Hudson—oh hell, Henry. It's so good to see you. How are you? Are the students driving you up a tree?"

"I'm just fine, Jimps. How are you feeling after all the success? We are all so proud of you. And Eartha, you look wonderful. I still believe that you are the most beautiful in person in both worlds, the college world and the outside one."

A hug, a kiss on the cheek and a "Thank you, Henry" erased the ten years that Hudson had inherited with the responsibility of his position. Even though it was shortlived, the transformation was amazing, even to the added spring in his walk.

"Come on you two," Henry said. Let's have a snack. We have time on our hands. I trust that John will get here."

"He should arrive within the hour. He had some last minute instructions to forward to the electrical engineers. Henry, speaking of engineers, who but you could have solved the reactor problems. Truthfully, the credit's all yours."

"Jimps, thank you for the kind words. That is my reward, and it is reward enough."

A short while later, Jimps followed Hudson into the great auditorium where he had sat during his first week at World. Weak-kneed, he gazed to his right and upon recognizing some of his old instructors and school acquaintances, nodded and sat down on one of the chairs behind the podium. There, the right, second and third seats. That is where he sat with Eartha. How long ago was it, a month, a year, ten, twenty?

"And now," came the far off words, "Professor John King."

What were Matradean De Rivisio's words?

"Patience is a virtue, for someday your patience may become the factor of light in your quest." And his following words. "Forgive me. How did I ever dream that I could relate twenty years of my life in half an hour?"

Did I have patience? Could I tell my life story is one half hour? Could I tell the story of the past two years, the days from Cindy Joe to hello success?

Once again the distant words drifted in, "…and, if I may, I would like to present my friend, a man that has been a close companion the past few years. Ladies and gentlemen, Professor James Bard."

The spontaneous eruption of voices, the sounds of pushed chairs, the applause and the shrieks and whistling all contributed to bringing Jimps back to reality. Jimps, walking through a mental fog, stepped up to the podium and addressed the faceless figures.

"Matradean Hudson, Doctors of Science, students. Thank you, thank you very much. This moment has made one of my two dreams come true. The other was to see the day that we could work with nature and succeed in doubling the food supplies of the oceans. That day is here and in the not too distant future, other plants like our underwater city, will come to life. This second dream was accomplished because of Professor King, our Doctors of Science and all of our specialists and I were taught by the greatest minds in the universe. Through their knowledge, understanding and patience we were able to grasp their directional teachings.

"Success, my friends, can only be accomplished if you give your complete attention and trust to your peers, for faith in their knowledge of things and the faith that that great knowledge will be inserted in you is your path to success."

"Jimps, turning to the group behind him, pointed to that group and then raised his closed fists and joined the noisy applause for the others as the faculty rose as one and gave the united sign.

Jimps continued, "Many were the sacrifices of the people close to the underwater project, even death didn't shy away. Two seconds separated life from death in one very dear to me. Yes, two seconds and I would have lost a friend and brother of twelve years whose battle with a giant squid didn't dim his desire to be back in the hub of things and do the work that was entrusted to him. All have given so much, not seeing their families, friends, not living a normal life and always living with the subconscious fear that all may collapse on you. Now, what is their compensation? Only that of knowing that they are in a small way helping mankind. That is it. That is their reward. Do you know what each of them would say if you told them that it didn't sound like much of a reward for so big a sacrifice? They would, as one, say, 'We were overpaid!'" Seemingly studying each and every occupant of the hushed room, Jimps, for a moment losing control of his emotions, struck the podium with his fist and whispered, "They were overpaid!"

Not giving the audience time to regroup their thoughts, Jimps continued, "Friends, I have one announcement to make. As of April 1, 2055, I will resign my commission."

For a second or two, on one was able to grasp the significance of the statement. Even Matradean Hudson and John shook their heads, wondering if they had heard what they thought they had heard. From the silence of minutes ago, there arose the whispered, "No, no, no, no!" and then the shouting of "Can't, you can't, can't!" The shouting and stamping relaxed as Jimps, fists raised, pleaded for quiet.

"Please. Thank you. The computers can carry on indefinitely, unerringly and without heart and the headaches of we mortals. I trust, dear friends, that you sympathize and will allow me this luxury which my mind and body so badly need. Someday, in the not too distant future, I may, if asked, return here to World College and teach. G-d bless you. May you always have health and succeed in your life's undertaking."

The quirks of nature. The frowns of minutes ago had turned to smiles of appreciative understanding and joy. A very composed and contented Jimps shook hands with all of the men standing behind the podium before leaving the chamber.

CHAPTER XVII

The day that Jimps returned from leave, Juan came into his office to report on the events that had taken place in Jimps' absence.

"How did it all go, Juan?"

"Everything went off as planned, especially the herding. Wait until you see the film. It has to be something else.

"Jimps, have you got a few minutes? I've got to get this off my chest."

"Go ahead. I'm listening."

"Did you hear the tapes on my encounter with the squid?"

"Only up until the time where you saw something bright near the pits. At that moment I was called away for a communication on the other line, and when I returned I was told about your main bout with the squid and with all of the excitement and worry, I never thought about getting back to the tapes. Quit your grinning, you damn ape. I was worried and glad to say I was."

"Thanks, Jimps. Well, here goes. I found this broken trunk, or should I say, I found a trunk within a trunk, identical to the one you told me about months ago. The trunk, seemingly made of brass or bronze, had cross swords and a large letter C under the lock." A paled Jimps, staring ahead, sat as though transfixed.

Juan continued, "When that stinking overgrown fish bait started to pull me to him, he was backing off because of the force of the spear gun blasts, and Jimps, unless I'm going off my perch, at that time, I saw a woman's body under it. Her light colored hair was moving about like drifting seaweed and Jimps, her legs were spread apart, real wide. That son of a bitch looked like he was," Juan stopped, wiped a sweaty brow and continued, "either planting a seed in the body or getting ready to eat it. So help me, I thought I saw all this. Everyday, while you were gone, I checked the area and never came up with anything, not one sign of the naked body. Only the trunk was there, exactly where I had marked it."

"Juan, let's go and get a drink. I feel sick right down to my toes."

"Do you want me to get the trunk?"

"No, let it remain there."

No amount of food could fill the void in Jimps' stomach. Possibly contact with the outside world would relieve the nauseous feeling. Upon returning to his quarters, Jimps called his parents.

"Mom, how are you? How is dad?"

"James, why didn't you call us? It has been months. Your father and I are fine, but the world has too many problems. Poor Elmira, she had to be taken to an asylum. The poor dear. I wonder what Duane will do now that Elmira is gone. We feel so bad."

"Had they ever received word from Cindy Joe?"

"No, dear, not a word. She has to be dead. She could never have been alive this long and not have contacted Elmira or Duane, especially her father, who she adored. No, Jimps, not a word.

"Now you call more often. Yes, I'll tell your father that you called. He does worry about you, you know. Give my regards to Eartha. Bye."

"Bye, Mother, bye."

March 12

"Captain Codora, scuba patrol to base. Come in."

"Base to Captain Codora. Standing by."

"Base, contact Director Bard, emergency."

"Base to Codora. Director Bard will meet with you in the consulting chamber."

A pale and frightened looking Juan removed his headgear and waddled through the funnels with fins still attached to his feet. Arriving at the consulting room, an exhausted Juan dropped the covered trap that he had been carrying, looked at Jimps with bulging eyes, tried to speak and failing to get the words out of his mouth, collapsed on the cushioned chair. Jimps stunned, shocked and frightened out of his wits, summoned and instantly received aid. Within minutes of that aid, a partially calmed Juan looked at Jimps and said, "I don't believe it. I know I'm possessed by the devil." A sign of the cross, a kiss on the crucifix that was attached to a chain about his neck and, "Jimps, please. Can we be alone?"
Another sign of the cross, a few deep breaths and a much more composed Juan began to speak.

"We were rounding up the heavy steel traps along the pit area near scanner22 to throw them in the pits. Pete and George were with me about fifty feet away and doing the same thing. I reached down to get trap 27 and when I started to lift it out of its bed of seaweed, I felt something around my wrist, with my finger in it's mouth was that thing." A very dramatic and emotional Juan accompanied Jimps to his lab, where he removed the cover from the trap and dumped the contents on the table.

Twelve inches long, with skin much like the skin of an eel, a round shaped head, two slits for ears and two eyes with double lids. There behind the straight opening of a mouth were two rows of teeth. Balanced arms and four-fingered hands were part of a perfectly formed torso, with an equally balanced pair of legs and partially webbed feet. Two inches below each arm was a tentacle, about one inch longer than the arms. The head was covered with a mat of hair, not unlike seaweed, but light in color. Failing to see any organs protruding or an opening in the crotch of the creature, Jimps assuming that the creature was female rolled it over on its stomach and there, with lids closed, was another set of eyes, identical to the first pair. At the base of the buttocks was an opening, either for reproductive or excretory use, or possibly both. Slowly being released from the cloud of stupor, Jimps addressed Juan, "Were there anymore of these things about? I must have another of the freaks for my own dissecting. Keep a sharp eye, but I pray that there aren't anymore." Jimps, very much the scientist, studied the thing intently, noted the findings and taped the conclusions, before placing it in a large bottle of alcohol and phenotol for shipment to World College for dissection.

"I didn't see any, but there was a lot of movement in the heavy foliage. You may get your specimen sooner than you think."

"Juan, can it be? Can I be the godfather of these things?" *Could there have been a body under the squid? Why would the condition of the body be as it was? Why wasn't it decomposed, and, why wasn't it eaten? Could the body have contained a sperm intake? And how the hell could a Squid mate with a dead body, let alone a live one? And then again, Cindy Joe's hot box would be the one to make it possible.*

Jimps, deep in thought, was silent for a few minutes and then said, "Juan, it may seem improbable, but it's the only thought that can make some kind of 'theoretical sense'.

"As you know I dropped the trunk in the area where Cindy and I fished and I recall that the whole area was radiation contaminated from materials coming from the Eldorado nuclear plant. I'll wager that the radium and the food building force from our reactors and the warm gulfstream temperatures probably strengthened and preserved some of the portions of the body, possibly even the eggs from the ovum within the body?"

After a deep sigh, a sickly and distressed Jimps mustered enough strength to cry out, "That dirty f----g, crummy, stinking Romano! May he rot in hell! I know what. I'll call this little bastard and any others 'romanos'. This creep I shall christen 'Cindy Joe Romano'!"

Juan, easing out of the lab, shook his head, kissed the cross and looking skyward, asked the Heavenly Father to look after his brother and try to reset his troubled brain.

CHAPTER XVIII

"Jimps, can I see you for a few minutes? How about in half an hour?"

"Right, Juan. In the cafeteria. John and I are having lunch. How does hot soup strike you?"

"Fine. I'm in need of about ten cups of something, as long as it's hot."

"Sit here, Juan. Before we get on to your business, listen to hid. About an hour ago, a message was received at World College and relayed here. Olga's mother has passed on, so I gave her a two week leave and Eartha will accompany her. She will need the companionship, as I understand there aren't any other members in her family."

"Thanks, Jimps."

"Now, what's your big problem?"

"A short time ago, I saw about fifty of the creatures and some of them are over two feet tall. And Jimps, they are capable of walking upright, sure a sight. That isn't all. They are also able to scoot along in a horizontal position. They place their arms and tentacles against their body and then release pressure from the tentacles, as do the squid. Four or five of them approached me and acted as most fish do, dull and looking for food. Also, there seemed to be a steady flow of bubbles coming from the side of their mouths. It was funny. If I didn't know better, I would think they were a toy of some kind. One second they would be walking upright and then, bam, they would shoot out like they were blasted from a cannon. Sure looked unreal.

"The crew members were really spooked by them at first, but now it's more of a curiosity thing. There's talk of these creatures being a missing link between man and the ocean animals."

"What else are they saying?" asked Jimps.

"Well," replied Juan, "I've heard theories that they are from outer space, but i think the majority of the men believe that they are some sort of mutation caused by the reactor discharge. At least they're over the near panic that hit at the first sightings of the creatures. I'll be glad when we get a report back from World on what they are and what to do, so we can set the men's minds at ease."

"What do you think, John?" asked Jimps.

"Not too much, other than at their present rate of growth, in two weeks or so they will be six feet plus."

March 29

John grinned as Jimps walked into the lab.

"Morning, Jimps. Too bad you weren't here about an hour earlier. You could have enjoyed the circus with me. I awoke at daybreak and having nothing but this time on my hands, I decided to do a bit of scanning. Truthfully, I haven't been appreciative enough of my surroundings, so I decided that this was the time and am I ever grateful. I stayed glued to the screen and only hunger drove me from it. Jimps, it's the damnedest thing I've ever seen. Those little monsters have to come from another planet. They are weird, to say the least. One moment they seem stupid and dull and the next, they are acting like they know what they want, very humanlike. Yep, one second they are fumbling about like a three month old, looking for food and opening their mouths and waiting for someone to pour it in, and the next second they are acting like adults, hopping on each other and screwing like mad. I tell you, if they aren't playing house, it's a damn good facsimile. First one, then the other climbs on their back and squirms around until the tip of one of their tentacles finds the slit in the buttocks, then locking their arms and tentacles around each other, they spin around like a top. They keep that up for a minute or so, and I swear, after they break apart, their dull expression seems to take on a new dimension. A few minutes later, they hop on board and start the spinning game again. They sure make it look pleasing. I know what I'm going to do. I'm going to fill the old water hole and try the system. In the butt and spin around. Should be interesting, if not for me, possible for Jane."

"You're probably right. She is so soft and who knows, thought a meditating Jimps.

"It must have been fun. At times we can learn something from our lesser beings. By the way, did I tell you? I have decided to carry on here for an extra month."

"That's great, Jimps. Why not extend it for at least one more year? You know that nothing would be the same with you gone. We all need you."

March 30

"Jimps, about two hours ago, I followed a school of the human fish. How is that for a name, human fish! Well, anyway, they propelled right up to the beach where half of them crawled right out of the water and stayed on the beach for ten or fifteen minutes. They didn't do a damn thing but stay in one place, in a group, almost like a football huddle. That was it. Then back into the water and a swim back towards the pits. And Jimps, these things were about four feet tall."

"I'm not surprised, Juan. Here's a report that I received from World. Read it."

March 30, 2055
World College to Underwater City
Report of Specimen 1431

Director James Bard

Squidtallum—Length 14", weight 21 Lbs., 6 oz. Outer skin is eelopak and nonporous. Bone structures not unlike the human frame. Cranium is solid and has a thickness of 1/16 inch. Specimen has a mental reading of +004. Heart and lungs are encased and protected by a rib cage. Two stomachs are attached. One is a digestive organ and the other is a waste container. The power receptor is also storebed for a black gas that is derived from waste materials and can be released whenever the creature is frightened, an automatic shock release organ. The body has 116 arteries and they contain a light green fluid with a content of 20% protein, 35% calcium, 2% iodide, 28% potassium and 15% chloride. Specimen, oily and tough, is not for human consumption. Professors William Elliot and Allen Crumm, Chief Biologists at World, are certain that this marine life is bisexual and can survive out of water for limited periods of time. Their lung capacity is nominal. Assuming that this mammal may be related in some way to the squid family and based on it's comparative size, we do not believe that it can be a threat to your environment. Most logical to assume that this is not a new species from this earth, but a native of another planet. Find acclaimed by the media as a new species, and is received by the public as an unimportant farce. Request another specimen for further dissection.

"Juan, it may be speculated that these things come from another planet, but we know better. Here, tack this communique on the bulletin and alongside it a request for notification to all personnel to appear at the cafeteria at 6:30 tonight."

That evening, Jimps stood before the entire crew of the underwater city.

"Good evening. I believe that you have all read the bulletin message from World. For those that haven't and should have, the following are the basics.

"A few months ago, Captain Codora caught and brought to my lab a liver and unknown specimen of the sea. This animal, about 14" in length, greatly resembled we earth beings, that is, if you did not look too closely. On the bulletin there is a good likeness. No way can this be a new earth find. In all probability, this thing came from another planet. How and why is not known at this time. The most plausible belief is that it has been transported here by one of our interplanetary vehicles.

"These are air breathing mammals and may attain a height of six feet plus. They are believed to have the same temperament as a young squid, and are not in anyway a threat to anyone. Naturally, all of us who are working inside, undercover are not too interested in that statement, but it is extremely important to Captain Codera and all of the underwater crew. Whoever may be on scanning assignment, shall if any of the creatures are seen, record the time of sight and location by scanner number. Also, the creatures size and their numbers. A copy of this information shall be delivered to me immediately and the above findings shall be recorded on tape. Thank you. Let's enjoy our dinner."

CHAPTER XIX

April 9, 1554
World College—Matradean Henry Hudson
Special Code #146-Data Computer #5
To: Director James Bard, Jr.

Dear James:

Refer to your message #146, following computer #5. It is beyond the probability of nature for any sea animal to fertilize a human body with positive results. Jimps, I am cutting off right now. Why the questioning along this line, is there anything that I should know? I believe that we have been and still are more to one another than teacher and pupil. I am free Tuesday, April 11th for one hour between 0900 and 10.00. Be here.

Regards, Henry
World College-1551

Tuesday April 11-0600

It had been a beautiful take-off. The buildings between the mountain crevices seemed to grasp the plane and ease its landing much like those of geese settling for the night. All in the mood of the moment brought back memories of the loneliness and the pleasures of days gone by…at the college, a bewildered boy, De Rivsio, Hudson, Eartha, Juan, Cindy Joe, Labs, some smelly fish, and most of all friends.

"Hello Jimps, take a seat"

"Good to see you Henry"

"Eartha is fine I pray?"

"All is tops, thank you. Codora, John and the crew send their best."

"Thank you. Now lets get to the heart of your problem, time is pressing."

"Right Henry. For what it's worth, my brother Juan is the only that had been told what I am about to disclose to you, weird and obnoxious as it is. Yes, I told you it was weird. Also, I'm not the greatest believer that there is a god; sure doesn't help one does it?"

"Jimps, that may just be your problem. Try believing, in small doses for a start, and you will be pleasantly surprised at how believing will grow on you." Henry sighed deeply and continued, "Now bear with me. It is beyond any reasonable doubt that sea animals cannot fertilize a human body, much less have an act of sex committed on that body. It is absolutely impossible. Now for the second point, a human body can be preserved or partially preserved in waters that are contaminated by radioactive materials. For how long a period of time they can be preserved is regulated by the strength of the active materials, together with the type of mixed substance. At this time science cannot substantiate why the bone structure is likely to decompose before the fibers in the body, but such as it is, facts prove the results. Where the water is not contaminated, the fiber will disappear in a short period of time. The creature is 100% fish fodder. All of this information has been compiled by the world's greatest minds with whom I met last evening.

"Now hearing your story about your misfortune and Codora's sightings while battling the squid, I believe that it is imperative that before we can go further we must have a scan of Codora's mind to separate the real and the unreal. We will not tap the subconscious, only the conscious. This is a simple matter that can take place at the underwater city by two of Professor Elliot's assistants. I will arrange for the exploration to take place tomorrow morning and will meet with you here the day after my return on Friday the 14th at 1300. I am running a bit behind my schedule so if you'll excuse me I'll take off. Give my love to Eartha and don't let yourself get down, everything somehow moderates after awhile. See you Friday, goodbye. "Thanks Henry, have a safe trip."

Friday-1300

"Good afternoon Jimps, have you lunched?"

"No thank you, I'm not quite up to it."

"Have a Java and cigarette and relax." This may take a little time. Let's get to it. On this script before me it states that Codora was an excellent subject. That isn't surprising as his superstitious and very religious background together with a high sense of trust in friends and family make him a relaxed and cooperative subject. When questioned about a body being present during the bout with the squid he answered that there wasn't any body, just the squid and a trunk. When repeated, the answer was always the same, there wasn't any body, just the squid and a trunk. That's it, no other diagnosis. Gazing at the ceiling and breathing deeply, Henry, scratching his head furiously continued, "We all know that the human mind is a delicate beautiful instrument capable of almost anything, the possible and impossible. It isn't surprising that Codora saw a body when attacked by the squid. It had been stored in the subconscious mind and brought to the fore when needed it. How and why did the body appear? How simple the solution is after listening to the tapes on Codora's history and studying the scanning report.

"After hearing your story about Cindy, starting with your first sex involvement with her, and up until her accident, Codora's mind could only accept the fact that she was responsible for all that occurred later, even her death. If she stayed faithful nothing would have happened. She was the blame for all of your discomforts. On that basis, his loathing of her grew and grew, way out of proportion. If Codora had been in a Florida swamp fighting an alligator, he would have had

Cindy come back and mate with the creature. That was his way of punishing her, bringing her to the level of the earth's most fearsome and disposed monstrosities. James, Codora's love for you exceeds all. Even if you were a blood brother you couldn't have been any closer to him, so it's with little wonder that his mind worked as it did.

"How many times have you heard the phrase, there cannot be a greater love than brother for brother. True, but much too sensitive and painful at times. That love triggered the vision's appearance. Immediately the subconscious was accepting the thought that never would Codora be able to help you if that help was needed. Not being around to help was more terrifying than death by the squid. That's it, Jimps, there isn't any more, thank god. These last few days were hectic and have taxed me terribly."

Easing out of his chair and getting to his feet, Henry's eyed downcast, and he simply asked, "Why Jimps, why didn't you report the incident to the authorities. It was an accident?"

"I don't know, Henry, I believe it was the shock of seeing Cindy Joe as she was and the fear of what it would have done to our parents."

"That wasn't reason enough, I'm afraid, and you will repent the rest of your life. Nothing can be gained by reporting the accident now. It would only bring more agony to the innocent. Let's close the books on this misfortune for all time. I'd say a bit of lunch is in order. Will you join me. I took the liberty of arranging your takeoff time for 1430, which will free us for an hour or so. Come, let's go."

0946-April 11

"Captain Keely to Base. Start of daily exploration cruise. Out— 0947."

"Captain, sir, #4-2 at starboard stern. There must be hundreds of the man fish circling about, the goddamn things. Sorry, sir. The things look like a bunch of kids playing."

"Boats, you and Seaman 1st Class Mason don your underwater gear and try to net one or two of the smaller ones. Better add an extension pole to the 24 inch hoop."

1014

"Mini-sub to Base. We are off the pits and are standing by as my crew members are trying to capture two if the fish men from a group of about two hundred which were sighted at 10:24."

"Thank you, Captain. We have you on screen. Out."

"Captain sir, this is Boats. We have two of these things netted and this is screwy as hell. These things are all around us, almost like a football huddle. They aren't making any moves to close in or move off, sort of like studying us. It sure gives you a funny feeling. The capturing of the two didn't seem to affect them one way or the other. They seem to float about. It sure is spooky. We're heading for the sub, sir."

"O.K., Boats. I can see you."

1114

"Good afternoon, professor, and begging your pardon, sir, the damned uglies have been out of the water for one half hour and they seem to be breathing without any effort. May I say. Sir, when they were taken from the nets, they didn't offer any resistance, just sort of stared at you as though wanting to know what the next move would be. Unbelievable as it might sound, sir, the eyes in front of the thing were dull, but the eyes behind the head seem to expressed intelligence. It's beyond my comprehension."

"Thank you, Captain, and many thanks to your crew. These tapes are indispensable. I hope to see you at dinner."

April 12-1410

"All channel systems open. Professor King and Captain Codora, please report to Lab #1. Professor Bard out."

"John, Juan, look here. This is the larger of the two Octimen that Captain Keely's crew captured. Look here. See this crevice at the rear. Now look from the inside. This little pron here opens this little section, a sort of trap door and it can be penetrated into the rear trap of another of the species and fluid erupts into the and the damned thing becomes fertilized. Now this same fertilized individual can also get the prong erection and penetrate into another of its brothers, which can also bear young. All of these bastards are bisexual. That is why there are so many and they grow and produce so fast. Shades of hot nuts, Cindy."

"Beg pardon, Jimps. What did you say?"

"Nothing, John. I was just thinking out loud. Well, that's it. Juan, will you send one of the girls in here? I want to have a report typewritten together with my tape report for World College."

April 27-0800

"Good morning, Juan. How are things? Hear from Olga?"

"Everything is tops, Jimps. I received a message from Olga last evening. She sends her regards to all. By the way, did you receive the message from Shore Base? Supply Officer Bender wants to talk to you. He seemed excited. He said he'll be in Section 104 up until 1200."

"Thanks, Juan. See if you can reach him for me and I'll be in my lab."

April 12-1410

"All channel systems open. Professor King and Captain Codora, please report to Lab #1. Professor Bard out."

"John, Juan, look here. This is the larger of the two Octimen that Captain Keely's crew captured. Look here. See this crevice at the year. Now look from the inside. This little pron here opens this little section, a sort of trap door and it can be penetrated into the rear trap of another of the species and fluid erupts into the trap and the damned thing becomes fertilized. Now this same fertilized individual can also get the prong erection and penetrate into another of its brothers, which can also bear young. All of these bastards are bisexual. That is why there are so many and they grow and produce so fast. Shades of hot nuts, Cindy."

"Beg pardon, Jimps. What did you say?"

"Nothing, John. I was just thinking out loud. Well, that's it. Juan, will you send one of the girls in here? I want to have a report typewritten together with my tape report for World College."

April 27-0800

"Good morning, Juan. How are things? Hear from Olga?"

"Everything is tops, Jimps. I received a message from Olga last evening. She sends her regards to all. By the way, did you receive the message from Shore Base? Supply Officer Bender wants to talk to you. He seemed excited. He said he'll be in Section 104 up until 1200."

"Thanks, Juan. See if you can reach him for me and I'll be in my lab."

"Hi, Professor. This is Bender, Supply Officer. Remember me?"

"I sure do and the name is still Jimps. What can I do for you? How are the rest of the boys? Is Belli losing any weight?"

"We're all fine and the only way Belli will lose weight is by having his mouth sealed. Jimps, I wanted to call you about a week ago but was unable to do so because of an infection in my arm and the antibiotic I received kept me on cloud six, which is all part of why I called. About ten days ago, I was walking on the beach admiring the outside of the Compound when I came very near stepping on what I at first thought to be a dead Man-o-War. On closer examination I saw the weirdest thing I've ever seen. This animal was curled up like a ball. I straightened it out with a small branch and as I did I thought I was going off my beacon. This thing had legs, arms, a couple of tentacles, a face, though octopus shaped, still had human qualities. When I got over the shock of seeing this thing, I turned it over on its stomach and damned if it didn't have another set of eyes blinking and looking at me like it was asking for help. So help me, it looked intelligent. Slowly, I bent down to pick it up, and when I did, it wrapped its legs, arms and tentacles around my arm and bit my wrist before I was able to shake it off. At that point, I bent down and placed one foot on it to get it off my arm. In my excitement and fright, I must have applied too much pressure, so much that I crushed the head section and killed the little bastard. I took the damned thing and placed it in a preservative tank, where it still lies today. Well, anyway, about an hour later my arm started to swell and shortly after I started to get double vision. I was immediately taken to the dispensary and only released this morning. Thankfully, I'm feeling back to normal. The teeth or fangs penetrated about ½ inch."

"Christ, you really had some experience and I'm afraid we may have the same. Just a while back Captain Codora was bitten on the finger by one of them, but there weren't any after effects. Presently we are being plagued by the things and believe they are a serious problem. We had assumed them to be harmless, which they were, until they reached maturity. This is as serious as all hell itself. Bender, will you please send the little biological misfit to World College to the attention of Matradean Hudson with a full report of your experience. After it arrives, I will contact the college. Thank you for calling and please alert all of the land personnel and emphasize to the fact that extreme caution is to be used when attempting to handle them. You are a testimony of the danger that exists. Thanks again for calling me. Your information is invaluable. I'll keep in touch."

World College-4 P.M.

"Jimps, I've got startling news for you. One hour ago the dissecting of the Man Thing was completed and we believe we have come up with some answers. As soon as it gets to mating age, it develops fangs in the vicinity of where our eye teeth are and behind the fangs are poisonous bags, not unlike the vipers of half century ago. How and why this happens at that particular stage of growth isn't known at this time. I have given immediate orders to our technicians to find a solution to eradicate the creature even if it involves destroying all other marine life. That in itself isn't too serious as we can always replenish our fish supply, but under no conditions can we have these things leaving the compound. Imagine what would happen if they got to our oceans of the world. Jimps, even more dreadful is the fact that we believe that these creatures have an enormous brain development that expands parallel with their body growth. Please be careful and issue orders to destroy these things by what ever needs are necessary. I will call you if and when we arrive at a definite solution to the extermination. Take care and don't be disheartened." A closed fist and a haggard Matradean Hudson faded off the screen.

1600-Bulletin Notice

As of this time and date, all underwater personnel are forbidden to dive solo. There must always be a party of at least three. Keep a sharp eye while diving and destroy all manfish regardless of size. Try to stipulate time of sight of subjects, the estimated size and location of same. When possible, capture one or two of species for dissecting. Use extreme caution. Venom extracted from creature's bite can be fatal.

Jimps sat in his lab trying to keep his mind on work. He had been plagued all morning with a strange feeling of dread. He had tried to pass it off as the leftover from some weird dream, but it still persisted. Finally, he pushed his chair back and was about to go for lunch when he noticed the light on his message board was blinking. Pushing the communicator, he was told to contact World College immediately. Jimps' heart sank. Had something happened to Henry? Was that the reason for this strange feeling of dread?

When Jimps contacted World and was told that Matradean Hudson would speak to him in a moment, he was filled with relief. At least his old friend was all right. However, upon seeing Hudson's face, Jimps was again filled with despair.

"What is it, Henry?"

"Jimps, I've received a message from Governor Chang. I'll play it back for you."

Henry reached over to the recorder and in a moment Jimps heard the Governor's voice.

"Henry, terrible news. Hang on to something. At 8:06 this morning, we here at the Palace received a distress call from the Minister of State in Australia. He reported a series of earth tremors and only one minute later, we got another call, unscreened, with a two-word message, 'All collapsing'. That was it. It was frightening beyond one's imagination. We tried to reach some of the neighboring islands and everything was negative. Within a half hour, we had our planes hovering overhead with instructions to stay above the radioactive level. Even though their sight was impaired to a certain extent because of heavy smoke and sort of a sulfurous colored haze, they were able to see that the land was leveled. There isn't any possible way to check for survivors. It will require weeks of cooling off before anyone could land on that inferno. It is so strange, especially as our quake meters registered a puny reading of 0104, below that of a stigma bomb. The poor people. I pray that this is a freak of Nature, the one in a billion happening.

"Henry, I'm sorry to be the one to have to burden you with such a ghastly message. If there is any other information I will contact you immediately."

"Jimps, that's the message I received from Governor Chang and it is even more frightening than he had expressed. The scary thing is what with all of our technical knowhow and precision equipment we failed to receive any warning whatsoever. The media here broke the story wide open, including the possibility of an occurrence here. That is all we need. Nothing like mass hysteria, but we must be a lot stronger that I imagined or we are a nation without feelings for others. There is shock, but more of a sort of disbelief and an almost 'who cares' attitude.

"Jimps, explain as well as you can to the crew. No leaves please and all are to stay below."

Jimps walked in a daze toward the main communication room. What could he say to all those under his command? He knew that above all he must avoid hysteria. They may be scientists, but they were still people. As he looked around the room and told his news he was filled with sorrow. If only Eartha weren't away on leave. He needed her now more than ever.

A horrified group listened to the unbelievable words that Jimps was speaking. All, as one, visualized the pain and the suffering that the people must have endured. The deep lines of sorrow were etched into all of their faces.

April 27-1420—Underwater City Intercom

"Dr. Bard, please come to the recreation center. Ugent."

"Yes, Tom. What's the problem?"

"Doctor, about thirty minutes ago when my relief, Marion Braun, you know the cute little blonde Australian with the wide hips, failed to show I knew that something had to be wrong for she had never been late and if something unusual had turned up detaining her I'm positive that she would have notified me.

"Well, I sent out an intercom message and not receiving any answer, I sent out a general alarm for a check throughout all of the buildings. I sent for you upon getting another blank.

"She seemed so composed when hearing about Australia and now I realize that the composure was one of shock. Ten minutes ago I learned that she had lost her mother, father, three brothers, a sister and a great number of relatives. I got to thinking of a possible suicide and that rushed my call to you. While waiting for you, I relayed the information to Captain Nelly and he said he was positive that no one had entered the outlet cove to the entrance to the water."

"Tom, give another call for her on the intercom and if she doesn't respond I'll assign a few more people to aid in the check about the city. I'll also have the Mini-Sub tour about. One other point of check, the emergency flight of stairs to the outside. You had better check the north side and have someone take the south entrance. I can imagine what this will do to Fred if we don't locate her. They were so much in love. This is just what we need with all of our other problems, an epidemic of depression."

"Jimps, this is John. I'm assisting in the checking and we haven't spotted Marion. We have covered every square inch. Rest assured she isn't here."

"Captain Neeley to base. No results. Too much time has elapsed and the way these animals are feeding it wouldn't take much time for every bit of evidence to disappear, but I am positive that this hasn't been her route. Mini-Sub out."

"Dr. Bard, this is Tom and I've located her. She was about half way up to the north exit when I approached her and she seemed to be resting in a comfortable sitting position. As I got to her I was stunned to see her sightless eyes staring straight ahead. She couldn't have been dead more than five or ten minutes. It seems as though she had run up the stairs full speed as her face was strained and lined. I can only surmise that she kept going until her heart gave out. Such a pity, such a beautiful woman. Please have someone meet me at the entrance. I should arrive within a few minutes."

"Fellows, take the body to Captain Kelley for disposal and try to get there with the least amount of display. Tom, contact Fred, no intercom, and have him come here. He'll need some talking to. I will give a full account of the happening to the crew later this afternoon.

World College to Underwater City 0800 April 30

"James, I'm leaving for Worlds Palace immediately to meet with President Chang and the other Council Members to ascertain what moves will be needed to defend ourselves from whomever the agressors are, if there are any. We also have to solve the problem of relief wherever and whenever it is needed. Not to forget the stabilization of each country, a task so major because of our own great differences in living standards. Those are just a minute part of the problems needed to be solved." His head left the screen as he bent to retrieve his attaché. An already drained Hudson returned to the screen with a weak, "I will return in 48 hours and contact you immediately with information on how to proceed."

World Palace 2020 April 30

"Gentlemen, be seated. There isn't any reason for introductions as that had been accomplished prior to our dinner of an hour ago." Only an Oriental's face could change with such suddenness, a suddenness that in one second showed a gleam that brightened the chamber and the hopes of the occupants and the next second cast a light of doom within the smoke-filled room. The eyes remained fixed, lips moved and words began to form meaningfully.

"This meeting is our most grave. The destruction of Australia." We have all reviewed the results of our flights over the area and the improbability of a landing in the near future. With little or no answers we can readily understand the public's disbelief and their attitude that this will occur again somewhere in this world. This attitude makes it doubly important that we prepare sooner than we thought was necessary for with that attitude a reoccurance would be of such a major catastrophic shock and magnitude that no power of Earth would be able to control the billions. Immediate answers are essential. What was the cause? How was it accomplished? What is it that can be so devastating and not show on our instruments? Why wasn't there any radium activity in the atmosphere? Is there a bomb or instrument powerful enough to destroy so secretly and completely? If so, where does it come from?

"There isn't any indication that the cause was by quake or volcano, that is until Nature took over after the leveling. It's imperative that we come up with some answers. Can this come from an alien people of a world we don't yet know? Is there the remote possibility that someone or a few in this fathering are Judases. I believe not, for what gain can destruction of the nature be for anyone."

"Friends, before we get deeper into this meeting let me implant one thought. Not even for second are we to lose the fact that with all of our intricate techniques and complicated instruments, we are children in this game of science and men." A gulping glass of water and the oval eyes scanned the somber faces.

"I have one closing statement and then I shall receive requests or suggestions from the floor. One hour ago, as agreed, I had sent a directive instructing all of our field scientists to stay with our problem as long as humanly possible. They must come up with some feasible answers. If necessary, they are to take stimulant #740 which, as you know, will eliminate fatigue or sleep, but will eventually cause a breakdown in the body elements and the certainty of a paralytic death.

"Yes, Mr. Hudson, you may have the floor."

"Sir, my motion is that we immediately contact all of our military heads and have them assemble their constituents for a red warning alert. They are to make ready for the use of all of our power needed to destroy our adversaries, if there are any. Our 200,000 mile Micki-6 is not to be excluded. At strategic locations throughout the world we are to set up stockpiles of food and medical supplies and draft the necessary medical specialists to administer the needs of the people. Thank you, Mr. President."

"I, Mr. Hudson, would like to second the motion and I see that all of the hands are raised and the fists closed for a unanimous vote.

"Mr. Clark, the floor is yours."

"Thank you. I believe that we should have a continuous broadcast from the world media to keep the people informed on all that is occurring about the world and especially what is being done at this meeting. Stress what will be done if tragedy strikes again. We must ask for the public's understanding and above all plead with them to try to remain calm. Insert in them that only by losing control of ourselves. We must stay strong even if that strength means turning our faces from the death of dear ones. Strong we will be even if it takes our troops to keep it that way, Heaven forbid that we may have to go to that."

"Thank you, Mr. Clark. Again I see complete agreement by the Board. I will now appoint the committees and their major functions.

May I see the sign of adjernment? Thank you all, gentlemen and god speed."

Underwater City
May 4 0830

Henry Hudson reviewed the major events of the meeting via video screen replay to an anxious Jimps.

"Jimps, that is it, all but the specified time limits to our assignment completions.

"After a few cups of javaline, I left the building and there were thousands of people milling about the square. People of all denominations, dragging their feet and occasionally nodding to someone, not from recognition but from habit. All was too quiet, too orderly. In fact, it was as though someone had lit the fuse of a bomb and was listening to the fizzle which for the moment was much more important than the noise of the bomb.

"James, the past forty hours have been the most hectic and trying experience of my life. This whole affair staggers the imagination with its magnitude. I am drained completely. Somehow while at the meeting, though our emotions were on edge, we were able to hold up and get control of these emotions and decide on problems that we had to agree to, even though they were contrary to our moral beliefs. Jimps, control is the key. We, no one, can afford to lose control. We must be strong no matter what comes about, so strong that if necessary to keep that strength we have to use our troops, even to getting rid of the chronic hysterics. We, that is the world, are going to have a tremendous fight on our hands. The people are taking to the consumption of large quantities of Bardopuates and you know what a highly explosive drug that is. I find that the people are more emotional in this part of the world, or at least in the showing of their emotions. Not that our feelings aren't just as painful, but I believe we are able to control them better.

"Just a few more seconds and you will be rid of me. At the meeting were the heads of all the major networks and we were assured that they would not froth at the mouth and overplay any news pertaining to our discussions. Now is not the time to fight for ratings. We stressed the fact that we would get 100% cooperation or we would shut down the offending network.

"I've reached my limit. I must get some rest. It is strange to say goodnight to you so early in the morning, my friend. 0845 April 4 World College-out."

May 5, 2055

"My god, Jimps! It's terrible, absolutely terrible. We received another flash from the Governors. Asia, Antarctica and all of the coastal islands have disappeared. Maybe we are all under a hypnotic spell of some kind, sort of a mass hysteria. A million people gone within seconds. It can't happen. It just can't."

"Good god, Henry. I can't believe it. What the hell is happening?" replied Jimps. "We have been taught that for every happening, there is a conclusive diagnosis of the reason. If that is so, why doesn't it hold true now?"

"There on the computer flash board is the continuous flow of the photos and descriptions of occurrences that are in process about Europe, South America and our North America. They are not pretty as you see. Murders, rapes, looting, burning, most caused by the mad intake of drugs, the public's escape route, the least of our needs at this time. Look at these photos. Parents abandoning their children and heading for high country with probably one thought in their sick minds, the animal need for survival. No power on Earth can change that sickening behavior until the fright of the unknown has left the mind."

World College to Underwater City

"James, I'm sorry about awakening you at this hour but my conscience got the better of me. Since our conversation of a few hours ago, I have been debating about whether I should or shouldn't disclose the true action of the populace since the catastrophies in the eastern hemisphere.

"I have decided to run the tapes I had received. After you see and retape them from our screen, you can decide whether you want to disclose them to your people. I believed that the seeing and hearing of them would undoubtedly add to your already taxed problems. I trust that your mental and physical being can digest what you will see and hear. To ease the anguish I recommend the taking of tablet #x-407 for body and mind stabilization. Perhaps John's presence will be helpful. The tapes are set to commence within fifteen minutes after the second buzzer sounds."

"May 4, 0220, Western Hemisphere. Filmed, narrated and recorded by chief photographer, Josh Lampish of WBC. Exposure time, 56 minutes."

Only moments into the tapes and one would assume that the viewers were in a state of suspended animation. If it weren't for a slight movement of heads and an occasional flow of tears streaming down pale cheeks, one would assume they were in the world of no return.

One hour later a drained Jimps, his face creviced from pain, headed for his quarters, bidding an equally distraught John a hollow good night. Hours later a functionless mind was unable to succumb to a much-needed rest.

How does one sleep when the mind keeps reviewing a people gone mad? A madness that travels from one extreme to another. How can the mind conceive the many rapings of children and adults alike and the casting of the bodies into the street gutters, as one tosses away a useless object? How can one block out the many orgies, the sins against decency? How can one blank out the thousands of people who a few days ago were stable and respectable citizens, to the now hordes of beasts whose only thoughts were the possession and consumption of drugs and other intoxicants which their defeated minds thought they needed to block out their fears of death?

"And it will get worse," droned the voice of Josh Lampish, as his camera scanned landscape.

There at St. Joseph's Church on Elm Street, the Baptist Church on Main and at the synagogue at the Square, all were crowded within and many more thousands were on the lawns in front of each building, kneeling and praying to their god to reassure them that they haven't anything to fear.

Oh, god! Are we strong enough to endure the pains of Hell?

Body and mental strength gone, Jimps was slowly easing into Nature's demands when he was abruptly brought back to reality by John, a John who but a short time ago was a spry young man in the prime of his life, and now a haggard puppet of the unavoidable.

"Get up, Jimps. Let's tie one on. I feel as all of mankind does. The hell with everything. It's time to drink ourselves into oblivion and join the will-nots and have-nots of the world."

An hour later two drunken sots were stretched out unconscious on a concrete bed of imaginary roses. The mixture of Javaline and Gem Juice failed to energize their body or mental powers. The drugs had taken their control for the much needed rest.

May 6-Underwater City to World College

"Henry, I had to contact you again. I still can't believe it. All of the Eastern Hemisphere gone, and no solution. Christ, there has to be an answer or at least a belief in what is possibly happening."

"Jimps, did you ever think about what we are or who we are? Isn't it possible that we are a world within a world? Do you recall reading about the Bermuda Triangle and the unsolved conclusions? What can't we be in the same category? Why can't we be a world that is small comparable to a world so much larger than we are as is our galaxy. Then again, as we are to the lowly ant. Ever consider how long an ant's three weeks of existence is to them? Do you ever think of what happens between an ant's scrambling on a walk and our stamping it out? Think how short its life is. Why not ours? Realistically we may be ants in someone's large world. Then again, we can be dealing with beings far superior to us. I don't believe it, but isn't it a possibility? Perhaps these beings are invisible and perchance they may be amongst us, causing chaotic destruction. Or, is it god's will, if you believe in god?

"Jimps, I only pray that whatever the cause, that it will not come to this Hemisphere. If it does strike us, we will have no time to dear it for it will strike too suddenly and forcefully. There wouldn't be time for anything but a 'god help me'. I'm sorry, Jimps. I only wish that I had a solution or hope. I don't. Goodbye, my friend."

May 6 2155
World College to Underwater City

"Jimps, two hours ago a distress call was forwarded to the Governor's Palace from the countries of Africa. Almost all were simultaneous, jamming out lines. As in Australia and Asia a complete catastophe. No other warning. It was as though all have been sucked into the bowels of the Earth. Our ships circling above report that all but the extreme tip of South Africa is ablaze and the multicolored gases are erupting into mile high gushers. It may be months before the earth cools enough for a landing. It is very doubtful that anyone can survive under the conditions. No one, not one of our scientists can give an inkling to the cause.

"Jimps, in one half hour, I will have a shuttle plane arrive there and transport you here."

For the second time in two days, Jimps stood before the inhabitants of the Underwater City. Upon telling them the news, he marveled at their strength and courage. All seemed to be holding up well in spite of a few tears here and there.

"I am going back to World," said Jimps. "I pray that I can receive some answers. I will return in a few hours, if all goes well. Go about your work. I can't tell you not to dwell on this tragedy as that would be impossible for we have all lost good friends and even family."

As he boarded the shuttle plane, Jimps' thought flashed to Eartha and Olga. For three days, they had no communication. G-d, I pray they are safe, thought Jimps.

CHAPTER XX

Europe-May 7, 2100

"Olga, this can't be. So much destruction in such a short period of time. All is happening so fast that you don't have time to be frightened. Just look out the window. Everyone is going about their business as though these were normal times."

"You know what, Eartha? I believe it's the shock, like waiting for it to happen here and knowing that there isn't anything that could be done about it. It's like accepting the inevitable, when knowing or caring about living isn't important."

"I know. It's exactly the way I feel, just waiting."

"If only Juan was here, my dear little Juan. He wasn't graced with height but he was blessed with love and consideration for all his fellow men, and would have been by women if they only suspected. My goodness, Eartha, I will never forget the first time we went to bed. I could have screamed from fright. That thing is about a foot long and a good two inches in diameter. My only thought was that it would surely kill me. Dear god, I can still feel the throbbing when he was in me. I can almost feel it now. Oh Juan, my love. If only you were here."

"Olga, we have to be psychic, for my thoughts run along the same line. Though Jimps wasn't as long or wide as that, he had the staying power of a wild stag. Upon the slightest provocation he would have an erection, bless his loveable heart. If by chance something does happen fast and we never see our men, what better way is there to meet our Maker than to have our true loves with us to the end, even if it is only in our thoughts."

Both girls, eye to eye, mind to mind, embraced. Peace and contentment had arrived.

Minutes later, Eartha, seemingly composed, tears streaming down her cheeks, eased to her knees and prayed.

"Please god, let me be with him even for a few seconds. Have I been so bad as to cause my abandonment? My love for you has never lessened. Oh, please," head bowed, the flow of tears became a torrent of inner suffering.

"Eartha, you stop it or you will talk yourself into one devil of a state. I, too, feel as you do. I've got to be with Juan, for like you, I also have this feeling of doom, but believe it is caused by our love of men. I think we should start packing right now. Why don't you call and see if you can get us a flight."

Five minutes later the disheartened pair learned that reservations were booked for at least a week and the waiting list far exceeded the slightest hope for a flight from cancellations.

Suddenly all was still, the silence throbbing in their ears, the sweat of fear had taken hold…a slight movement all about them, and then an eruption that must have come from hell exploded. A gigantic opening in the floor emerged.

"Oh, god. Olga, help me…Jimps not this way!"

Another enormous eruption and two of heaven's loveliest creatures were sucked into the bowels of the crater.

May 3, 2125

"Europe and the Governor's Palace, our nerve center," cried Henry in horror, "all gone the way of the others. A warning cry and it's all over. There can't be any suffering. It all happens too fast, or does it? A second can seem like a year. G-d or someone give us strength."

Jimps stared at the communications board in disbelief. Eartha was in Europe and now Europe was destroyed. But Eartha couldn't be dead. It didn't seem possible. *How could I go on without her?*

"Isn't it ironic?" continued Henry, oblivious to Jimps. "In fact, even at this stage of life I would say it's comical. Here a few weeks ago we were worrying about feeding the world and now that we have the food there won't be anyone to feed it to.

"Good bye, my friend. Take a flight to the city. Yours will be the only one as all transportation has been grounded. Jimps, breathe courage into them. We will meet again I promise you. I'm terribly sorry about Eartha. I above all know how much she has meant to you."

Jimps sat on his bed, his head in his hands while speaking into his log tape.

"South America is no more, erased as easily as a child dunking a small toy. Five continents gone in five days! Why are we the last continent to survive? Is it god's will that we suffer longer? Is it because we had become a nation on nonbelievers? Is it because we placed our selfish desires before the teachings of god? Is this god's wrath? Is he going to destroy in six days to mold? Is this really god's doing or is this caused by another power from a world far superior to ours? If only I had an inkling of an answer. How inferior and insignificant we are.

"Lord, help us. Everything has become untied. No police or firemen, no sanitation ties, not even merchants in our federal stores. People just enter and take whatever they choose. Some are even stripping down in the stores and reclothing themselves. One man, who probably had a love of watches, had about ten on each arm. Very humorous, if the conditions would only have warranted it.

"The federal militia has been placed in motion to try to resupply the food needs of the country. Men are attacking women. Let me rephrase that statement. The women are accepting the men right on the streets as though it was the Devil's parlor. Millions are sitting in the streets in groups, seemingly families, all gazing skyward and in a complete stupor, probably caused by fear. G-d help us."

May 8 2055
World College to Underwater City

"RED LIGHT—RED LIGHT—STAND BY—DO NOT LEAVE CITY—RED LIGHT—RED LIGHT—FLORIDA

AND BORDERING ISLANDS ENGULFED—RED LIGHT—
TIDAL WAVES STRIKING BOTH COASTS—STAND BY—
EARTH QUAKING BELOW—STAND BY—DO NOT LEAVE
CITY…"

A fading face on the screen and then the deadly silence of fear ensued, as the forty-six insignificant creatures huddled on the floor, hand in hand, silently prayed for god's help as the buildings about them started to tremble. The Lord was merciful, for by keeping their heads buried in their laps, all were spared the agony of seeing or hearing the cries of the turbulent and erupting waters, as they darkened to a hideous blood brown, circling about looking for prey to devour.

Just as suddenly as the havoc appeared, the calm returned, a calm which by its unexpectedness was more frightening than all of the madness that nature had released moments ago. Having looked Death in the eye and escaped its clutches, the path to death again would be more than the mind could sanely absorb. As the long moments dragged by and Hell didn't return, the forty-six bowed heads began to raise, raise with the hope and belief that all was not over for them. Now, unknowingly, the muttered words of prayer turned to songs of jubilation, for the passage of time had assured them that god had heard their prayers. The destruction had ended.

A pale and sickly Jimps, too shaken to stand on his weak knees was aided by the strong, religious Juan.

"Sit here, brother. I'll see if I can find you something to drink. Come one. Everybody up. The fireworks are over and you can all get your own damn drinks. Come on, get moving. Let's see some action."

The strength of one 5'2" Costa Rican had inserted itself into all of the rest, who only moments ago had given up on life. Now, primed by the spark received from the little fireball, all were crazily jumping about and yelling meaningless words that were somehow understandable. All had arrived.

A back to normal Jimps, sipping a hot drink, was amazed at the drastic change that had come over all. Here before him, and himself included, was a seemingly happy and contented group that short time ago was a segment of the corpses of the dead. Amazing is an understatement if there ever was one.

"Friends," Jimps said. "I believe that the worse is behind us. We were able to survive because of the ingenuity of our scientists and the fact that we were underwater. The all clear green light assures us that there isn't any visible damage to our buildings. Control is what we need now. The time for sorrow is past."

"I don't know anymore about what happened than you do. What I do know is that to survive we will have to work together and make many sacrifices. I know what you are thinking, for your thoughts are the same as mine. What is there to live for, having lost all that is dear to us? Granted, but losing and dying are part of our heritage. Some are destined to go sooner than others, but the survivors do not lose the will to continue, no matter how and when the misfortunes reach us. With the hope that there are other survivors, we nevertheless have to proceed with the belief that only we, this handful exists.

"There are many things to be thankful for. Our atom powered equipment is self contained. We have all the water and food we need. There is recreation enough to keep us mentally active with all of the films, recordings, etc. We have all of the knowhow to exist underwater for years, if need be. Within a week or so, when the sea clears, our scuba crew can check for any possible damage to our outside equipment. Then later with a bit of help from Nature, say in a month or so, we can go topside and check on the clarity of the air. Now, that doesn't sound too bad, does it?"

Walking to his office and in its solitude, a heavy-hearted Jimps, head bowed and mind cloudy, tried to review the past dozen years. Nothing registered, nothing but his longing for Eartha. Even Cindy Joe and the tragedy didn't register. Only the face of Eartha was alive and without her survival would be unimportant.

She can't be gone, he thought. *I won't permit it, I just won't.* Getting up, an aged Jimps walked about aimlessly. *Juan, that's it! I must find Juan. Brothers should be together at times of trouble.*

"Juan, where the hell are you? Goddamn it, where the hell are you?" A very tired and emotional Jimps slumped on his bed and immediately eased into a dreamy sleep.

CHAPTER XXI

June 20

After months of waiting, it was finally the day that had been decided upon to check the purity of the outside air.

"John, Juan, Captain Keely, I summoned you all here so we can freely discuss our next moves. The air test today showed positively that the air is OK for us to breathe. There isn't any doubt that we can survive indefinitely on our present diet of fish, sea greens and our denatured salt water, but I believe for our mental stability and our physical well-being, we need sunlight and other of Nature's gifts.

"I think it is time for us to explore the outer world and then plan our next step."

All nodded in accord.

"Any suggestions when we should try? Captain, it's your ship."

"How about if we set the date for two weeks from today? That should give us all the time we need for preparations."

"O.K. Today is the 20th. We leave July 4, at 8:00 a.m."

June 27-Bulletin Notice

Today between the hours of 1:00 p.m. and 3:00 p.m. each person will be issued a shock pistol. This pistol is capable of rendering a person helpless for a period of approximately one hour. Even our largest animals are susceptible to its power. At 8:00 tonight, for those who are not familiar with the weapon, there will be a demonstration of the workings of the firearm.

July 2 -Bulletin Notice

Seven-day exploration packs have been prepared and will be distributed between 3 and 5 p.m. today in the supply chamber. A meeting will be held in the cafeteria tonight at 8:00 with reference to our trip on the 10th.

0800

"Good evening," Jimps smiled at the people around him. "No doubt you all have your seven day travel pack. The day after tomorrow we will leave this compound and go ashore and survey the area and then decide what course to follow. We will devise a plan whereby if certain conditions arise, there will be a definite route to go. If we are fortunate enough to locate operable equipment and find food of some type, then our excursion will be that much easier, but if we do not find one article that we can use, we are not to be disheartened. We will find a way, no matter what the condition. I promise you, we will survive.

"Relax, try to enjoy the next day and I will see you at 8:00 a.m. on the 4th."

July 4

"Is everyone on board?" asked Jimps. "Fine. Quiet, please. There are four rubber rafts on board and these will be inflated when we leave the sub each carrying twelve passengers. One last note and then we will all be under Captain Keely's command. Captain Codora and his crew will meet us at the south wall's intersection with the shore.

They have gone ahead to get the lay of the land, sort of an advanced guard. Captain, we are in your hands."

One half hour later, the crew stood on the shore looking out over a strange world.

"There she is, Professor," said Captain Keely. "If I didn't know better, I would say that this is a strange world. Everything is leveled."

Juan and his two compatriots left the city funnel and entered the cold, dark brown waters of the Atlantic. All about him everything seemed unreal as they started to swim toward the shore in the direction of the assigned meeting location.

Olga dear, he thought, if we come out of this alive, you are going to be my mate for life and I don't care a goddamn who likes it or not and that includes Papa Codora. Mom will understand. Forgive me good Crista for taking your most Holy Name in vain. Jimps, god love you. You will be with me if by chance we lose our loved ones. How can we go on if we were without each other? One must always have some family. Thank you for that good Lord and protect my little sister who's love of life can never be matched. Men, where the hell are you?

Feeling a tug on his right, Juan spun in that direction and was shocked upon seeing hundreds of the fishmen coming from that direction. Immediately he was surrounded and being pulled into the center of a group.

Get away, you stinking bastards. Let go of the hose. Holy Mother, where are they all coming from. Jimps, Olga, god help me! Please G-d help me...

Like a specter slowly drifting with the tide and fading from view was the dangling face mask, a hose and the body of one of Christianity's most lovable members.

The Captain, upon stepping onto dry land, fell to his knees and as did the explorers of old, bowed his head in prayer and thanked the Lord for safety. As one, all of the followers joined in those prayers. Rising to their feet, the Captain and crew proceeded in the direction of the demolished buildings.

At that moment thoughts of Juan and his crew came into Jimps' troubled mind.

What happened? He should have been at the landing site. Had he ventured ahead? No. That wouldn't be Juan. He would never leave his post. Can this be god's doing? Is there a god? Not likely. If there was, why would he destroy the world and only save a handful of people and most of all me? I am not what one would call a great believer. I don't even know a prayer. So why me? Was it to make me suffer more? Was it because I am the sponsor of those creepy human fish? Or has it all been caused by a superior race from a far off galaxy? Sounds more plausible.

Suddenly, screams of terror came form the rear. Turning the leading Captain and Jimps were shocked beyond reason at the sight that they beheld. The human fish were dragging laggers back in the water. Unsheathing their weapons, they began firing at the hordes of the man creatures.

G-d, the Devil, somebody, anybody, help them! Is that Jane being dragged into the water? Oh Christ, John! You fool! You could never have saved her! Would I have done any differently?

Where the hell are they all coming from? If I can only erase their screaming. I think I'm going mad!

"This way, Captain. There toward that opening. Come on you dirty bastards, go ahead and bite. Go on. Take another bite. It's going to be your last one. How does that hit you? I helped make you, you no good crumbs and I'll be the sonofabitch that will cut you down. Captain, for the love of Christ, get up. This way. Just a few more steps. Oh hell, what's the use?"

Jimps screamed as one of the creatures bit into his leg, tearing the flesh.

Look at that nice, red blood running down my legs. Makes a good-looking striped stocking. I'm so tired. G-d, how tired. There it is, my bed, so soft and clean. I found it just in time. I'm so tired. That hum is so relaxing. I believe I can sleep for a while.

Who the hell are you? G-d, you're ugly. Have I been the cause of another creature? You won't hurt me, will you? Please don't. What's the difference? Eartha's gone. Go ahead and kill me...

"Kill me! Why would I want to live?"

With that painful cry, peaceful oblivion came to the fevered brain.

Hi Mom, Dad...Cindy Joe, baby. Do you miss me...You'll never make a touchdown, buddy. Only over my dead body...Does the knee hurt much...You sure popped your cork...I'm going to the government ten year college...Don't worry we will marry someday...Dr. Hudson, how are you sir...Eartha, if you only knew what you did to me...The damned things are growing like mad...Juan, old pal, did you know that I screwed your sister. I'll bet you did and brothers don't do that to their sister...The stinkers look human...Hell, Cindy, don't be frightened, it's water proof...Jane, you sure are soft and tight. Those are nibbling knockers...I'm sorry, Mrs. Henderson. Please try to understand...Hold my hand, mother...My head feels so good against your breasts...Eartha come here and hold my other hand...John, I believe we have made it. I feel like a god...Cindy, don't ever stop. That sure is some hot box...Yes ma'am I'll take the large trunk on the top shelf...A regular volcano, that's what you are...The crummy bastards bite like hell and look at the size of them...The world is in our hands...Romano, you bastard, I forgive you...How ugly can one get...Please someone help my pretty Eartha... my pretty Eartha...Captain, you are in charge. Only Olga outranks you...You sure are ugly...my Eartha...Eartha.

Keemons, unable to keep the hurt from his beautiful eyes, pointed to the pitiful figure on the transbed and simply announced that the being's mind had joined the body that had expired tiepons ago. Sarsal removed the wired contraption from the head and the body was taken to the disposal and emptied into the ball of flame.

Santee, mindful of the pain about her receptive cove, addressed her light of love. "Keemons, my leader, let's colonize this happyground. It is more than we have expected, the size, the breathable air, the natural resources are far more plentiful here than any of the other happygrounds that we have visited. It would be a simple matter for us to rebuild all that has been destroyed." A long, affectionate look at the ever-beautiful mate before her and a sigh of contentment prompted her to continue.

"The destruction of those things with the four limbs would not be the taking of a native life, for they are only a food developed for the earth beings' consumption. It will be a simple undertaking for us to neutralize their growth and originating factors. Let us settle here. We can call this happyground 'Cindeesia', the bright star, the star of love in Galaxie 4."

Ray guns at their sides, crew after crew diomized to the happyground where they were greeted by a bright awakening sun, a sun that was slowly rising above the dense mournful clouds, a sun that was spewing G-d's breath of love on a new world, a world called Cindeesia.

THE END

Between Worlds: **Nekkel Ace**

Yianna **Yiannacou**

authorHOUSE®

AuthorHouse™
1663 Liberty Drive
Bloomington, IN 47403
www.authorhouse.com
Phone: 1-800-839-8640

First published by AuthorHouse   04/27/2011

ISBN: 978-1-4520-5643-2 (sc)
ISBN: 978-1-4520-5644-9 (hc)
ISBN: 978-1-4520-5645-6 (e)

Library of Congress Control Number: 2011905998

Printed in the United States of America

Preface

I stood there; shock filled every part of my body. I had the phone barely in my hand. I felt my whole body go numb; my fingers went limp and the phone slowly fell out from my hand. It hit the marble ground, pieces flying everywhere. I knew the phone fell, but it made no sound. My heartbeat automatically accelerated as I started to process what just happened. This phone call could not be real. How could this have happened? *Everything was fine five minutes ago, but now I get this message? I have to go back and find out for myself. Things like this don't happen to people like me. Does this mean things are clearer now? Or are they even more difficult than ever. I'm stuck. Should I even go back now? I don't know what to do.*

That's when reality hit me with the force of a thousand ton train. It felt like my heart was clawed out right from the depth of my chest. I finally came to face the truth. The walls and countertops began to blur and spin – nausea and dizziness overpowered me. I didn't have the energy to stand anymore. It became harder to breathe as I slowly started to fall forward. The floor was coming closer to my face faster than ever. That was when everything went black.

Contents

Chapter 1 - The River

I sat there in complete bliss without a care in the world. Sometimes, I wish I could just sit here forever. My eyes were closed but my soul was wide open. Beautiful flowers surrounded me in every direction. There had to be over a thousand different kinds spread around this entire area. Their collective aroma filled the air. I drew in the passing breeze and let the scent overcome me. It filled my lungs and nourished me. It was a smell that can instantly comfort a person. Out of the whole estate, the back garden was my favourite spot. It was quiet and peaceful. The only sound I could hear was the breeze gently touching the flowers and birds chirping above me. I kept to myself mostly so I never had to worry about anyone disturbing me here. This was my sanctuary.

My planet is called Caledonia. It was my home and I loved it. My great grandparents were the first ones to discover Caledonia. It came into orbit with the sun only a few hundred years ago. No one knows how it happened. Its history had been destroyed before I was even born. My parents were now the rulers of Caledonia. If my parents knew the history, they hadn't told me about it and I don't think they ever planned to. Caledonia is hidden from view of Earth. It seems that there is an invisible barrier, protecting it. Humans were unaware of our existence, and the Caledonians intended to keep it that way. I knew very little about Earth. My parents never discussed it. I got the impression that Earth was a taboo subject to bring up in my family.

I have a perfect view of Earth from my house. I would always stare at it and daydream. I had hoped to visit someday. My parents said I was too young. I figured they were afraid for me. Nevertheless, I was determined that when my day came, I would go. No one was going to stop me.

"Sophia!" Mom called from inside. "It's time for lunch."

I guess I *did* have the occasional disturbance. I looked over my shoulder only to see her walking away from the grand entrance at the back of the house. It wasn't an ordinary house. It was an enormous mansion not unlike a castle. The size never frightened me though.

Mom's dress swayed in the breeze as she made her way back into the house. She knew I'd be here. I didn't want to get up. I would have stayed there forever if I could. I stalled for a few moments, but quickly returned to my senses. I knew that if Mom had to call me twice she would have been upset. The last thing I wanted to do was upset her. I rose sluggishly and patted my dress clean. Wearing white was a bad idea for me. Apparently, dirt loves a white dress - especially if I am the one in it. Most of it came off though, just from standing. I checked myself before I started towards the house – I looked decent enough.

I headed inside for lunch. I looked around at the familiar surroundings of my home. The walls and floors were white marble. If this was my first time coming here I would think it was a very elegant house, but I see this everyday so it's nothing special to me. Everything was open. If I looked dead ahead, to the entrance, I could see the - very distant - front yard of my house. It was easily recognizable even from the back. There was not one dark room in my house. There were huge windows everywhere. Lights were unnecessary during the day.

I turned right and headed down the hall. I found my parents waiting for me in the dining room. They weren't alone. I noticed another couple and their son sitting at the table.

I didn't recognize the couple at first, but as I walked closer and got a better look - I realized it was the Carters. I could never mistaken them for anyone else. They both had pitch black hair and were kind of chubby. They were naturally short people. Mrs. Carter was taller than Mr. Carter. She always wore such high heels. It was as if she went to the store and asked for the tallest pair of heels they had - just so she could stand taller than her husband. They were both snobs.

The Carters were very wealthy as well. They were close friends with my parents. They all grew up together. Mrs. Carter's name is Emily and Mr. Carter is Paul. The Carters had their only son with them – Paul Jr. I never understood people that named their child after themselves. It's just plain stupid. Paul Jr. looked like a taller, thinner and more handsome version of his father. I had to admit - even though I didn't want to – I found him very attractive. I think Paul was two years older than I, making him about seventeen years old. I did not know him that well. Now that I think of it, this was the first time I had ever met him. He was always off in boarding school whenever the Carters were over. I heard so much about him, but never had a face to his name. That is, until now.

"Sorry for making you wait," I said, staring at the floor. I couldn't bear to see the look on their faces. If I had known we had guests I never would have taken my time. That was just bad manners and I felt awful.

Mom quickly got to her feet and slammed her hands on the table. "Sophia - look at your dress! How many times do I have to tell you not to sit in the dirt?" She stared at me with her eyes wide open. She shook her head in disappointment as she sat back down.

I didn't bother to respond. My heartbeat accelerated to an abnormal rate. I could feel the blood rushing to my face as I blushed in embarrassment. I felt sick to my stomach. I couldn't eat. Every inch of my body was aching to turn around and run away. I had to force myself to stay. I didn't want to show weakness.

The Carters probably wouldn't have noticed the small spot of dirt on my dress. You could hardly see it! Only Mom would point that out to let everyone know. I wanted to cry. I didn't like to be embarrassed. Any heightened sense of emotion would normally set me off. I managed to hold it together though.

I took a deep breath as I walked up to my seat as one of the servants pulled out the chair for me to sit. I thanked him and sat down. Massimo was my favourite servant. He was much older than I, but I felt like he really understood me. He was more a big brother figure to me.

I sat and waited for another servant to come around and serve us the food. We had mushroom soup for lunch. I picked up the spoon and tried not to sip it too loud. I tried to remember my manners this time. Sometimes I would slurp my soup just to annoy my parents. But we had guests and I didn't want to seem rude. I kind of wanted to make a good impression for Paul Jr. We all sat in silence at the table. I didn't talk to my parents much. I felt like I had nothing in common with them. I never knew what to say to them. I did not react well with guests either. The whole time we ate I could feel the gaze of Paul Jr. burning into my face.

"Sophia," Mom said as I looked over to her, "Emily and Paul came all this so that Paul Jr. could meet you. Isn't that nice?"

"I think they'd be wonderful together!" Emily said as she clasped her hands together in joy.

Ugh, I wanted to puke. I just nodded. I was afraid if I opened my mouth I would have nothing nice to say. I hated whenever people bring their sons over and just assume that I was interested in him. This was the third time that had happened. It seemed like my parents were trying to find me a husband. I was only fifteen years old and they were thinking like *this*? I had no idea what had gotten into them. *Is that normal?* I never asked my parents how old they were when they got married. I realized I'd never really bothered to ask. Whenever my parents would bring random people - some I didn't even know - over just to see me, I would feel so betrayed.

My parents were very good people though - don't get me wrong – but I never felt like I could confide in them. I've talked to the servants more than I talked to my parents. They were a bit overprotective. My parents were tall people. Dad had a deep voice and was a man who you would always catch smiling. He smiled more than my mother did. Dad had brown hair and brown eyes. My mother and I, on the other hand, both had blonde hair and blue eyes. Mom's hair was cut very short because Dad preferred it that way. My hair was very long though. Mom did not want me cutting it. I did not want to cut it either. That was one thing we agreed on.

I quickly finished eating and asked to be excused from the table. My parents knew the only reason I was rushing myself was so I could go back outside. I never liked being indoors- especially when there were people there, trying to set me up with their sons. I only went in to eat and to use the washroom. I also sleep inside - but not by choice. If it were up to me, I would sleep outside every night. We always had great weather. It never went below twenty degrees - even at midnight.

I decided not to go back to the garden. I was going further this time. I didn't want anyone to find me. I quickly walked out the back entrance and started sprint walking down the long pathway.

"Hey Sophia, wait!" I heard someone calling from behind me.

I looked over my shoulder to see Paul Jr. running towards me. He stopped right in front of me. I had to look up at him since he towered over me. I stared at him for a few seconds. His features were just so - perfect. His hair was slicked back; he had pale, smooth skin and very good posture. His eyes were blue like the sky and his lips were a perfect shade of pink.

"Yes?" I asked as my voice cracked. I cleared my throat. I was lost for words. It was as if I had forgotten to speak. I was starting to get flustered. I had never experienced this before! I just stood there and waited for him to say something - anything!

"You're very beautiful, you know." He raised his hand to brush a strand of hair from my face.

I slightly raised my head as he ran his finger under my chin to get a better look at me. I raised my head up a little bit. I still couldn't think straight. All I could do was smile.

"You would be the perfect girl to have my arm and show off to everyone," he said as he dropped his hand. His eyes were fixated on me.

My smile automatically faded.

What did I look like? A damsel in distress, waiting to be rescued by her valiant knight?! I am not a trophy to be put on display! I couldn't believe what I was hearing! And so, there went my perfect impression of Paul Jr. I should have known that the handsome ones were always self-centered.

"No thank-you. You seem very nice but I don't think that's right." I tried to be as polite as possible. I clenched my jaw as I turned around and walked away, for I knew that the next words to come out would be unkind ones. It was hard to keep them in.

"What do you mean? You can't do this to me. Come back here!" He called out to me.

I turned around abruptly and took two steps towards him. "Yes - I can do this, and there is nothing you can do to stop me. You do not own me!" I grunted in disgust and started to run away.

"You'll regret this! No one walks away from me! You will be back! You'll see!" he yelled as I ran faster. I didn't turn back. I just kept running. I ran past my garden and past my lovely pond where many fish swam. I noticed my reflection in the water as I ran. My eyes sparkled in the reflection. They were all watery. Why was I crying? Something inside me just hurt. I don't know if I was crying out of disgust at what had just happened or because I was still in shock that I was running away from this beautiful man.

I don't normally wander this far away from the estate but I was scared if I went back, Paul Jr. would be there waiting for me. I wiped my tears with my arm and stopped running. I was feeling adventurous now. I turned around to look at my house. I tried to forget about what has just happened.

The house stood on a mountain. I decided to walk down - something I had never done before. It wasn't that bad. It was just like a normal walk. There weren't any weeds. My family owned this land and we had someone tend to it every day. There was no danger walking down the mountain, but as soon as it ended, so did my sense of certainty. I found a grass pathway and followed it. I don't know who or what made it, but I just kept walking farther and farther. I went deep into the woods. The grass pathway led me to a small river. It was surrounded by large trees. The sun still shone through the trees so I could see everything around me perfectly. I think I actually remember coming here once with my parents. I was much younger though. My memory was hazy, but I was sure of it. Something seemed familiar. Then again, it could have been a dream. Nobody ever came here. They either stayed in their homes or went to someone else's. There wasn't much to do around here.

I walked as close as I could to the river without actually going in. I knelt down beside the river's edge. I could see my reflection in the blue water. I looked so - sad.

Something splashed up and made ripples in my reflection. It was a fish – a beautiful blue fish with a yellow stripe going across it. I stuck one of my fingers in the water to touch it but it swam away. I thought about how I wished I had real friends – someone I could turn to in a time like this. All the other kids my age were so snobby and I didn't like being around people like that. They all acted like their parents. I did not want to grow up to be like my parents though. Maybe that is why I kept my distance from them.

I sat there as I slowly ran my fingers along the water. I wanted to dip my whole hand in the water. I would be in a lot of trouble if my parents caught me. I looked around and realized my parents were nowhere in sight. They didn't know where I was. They probably weren't even looking for me. I didn't care. I could do whatever I wanted.

A smile rose in the corner of my mouth as I immersed my hand in the water. I rejoiced at the cool feeling it left on my fingertips. The water was so cold, it gave me goose bumps. That did not stop me though. My hand went in deeper. My whole body was leaning over the water now. I placed my other hand in the water as well. Both my arms were elbow deep. The water was shallow. I accidentally touched the mud on the bottom of the river and pulled my fingers up a little bit. I didn't want to get dirt in my nails. I didn't particularly mind it. It was way too much work to clean after. Also, I had upset Mom enough for one day.

I don't know how long I sat there with my arms in the water. I was very relaxed. I didn't want to move. I had never done anything like this in my life. I listened to the water moving past my arms and all the creatures rustling in the grass.

I figured I had enough fun with the unknown water for one day. So I slowly started to pull my arms out.

I heard a loud, startling noise behind me. It sounded like a branch being stepped on and cracked - hard. I quickly looked over my shoulder to see a boy awkwardly standing there. I was completely shaken and quickly got to my feet. That wasn't a good idea because I completely lost my balance. I shrieked as I fell right into the cold water - head first.

Chapter 2 - Mysterious Boy

My hands and feet slowly sunk into the mud where I sat under the frigid water. I never thought I would find myself in this situation. My knees were sticking out just above the water's surface. I stared at this boy as he stared right back at me. I didn't want to move - I couldn't move. I was debating the reason; was it because I was cold or because I was scared? Maybe it was both. The water was cold and I was drenched from head to toe.

This was turning out to be the worst day ever. First, I have these unexpected guests trying to marry me off to their son. Then I end up falling into this stupid river with this odd boy staring at me. His appearance was atrocious. His brown hair was all tangled and dirty and he barely had clothes on. His whole body was covered in dry dirt, wet dirt and any other kind of dirt you could think of. I was willing to bet he didn't smell great either. Underneath all of that grime, he seemed to have an olive complexion. He was fairly tall with broad shoulders. The only thing appealing about him was his blue eyes. He was not alone. He had a little white tiger cub circling his feet the whole time.

I felt something graze my hand under the water and I became startled. I froze for a second. I then screamed as loud as I could and jumped right out of the water without even thinking. I stood on the side of the river looking into the water to see what had touched me. I looked, but I couldn't see anything. My feet felt a bit strange. I looked down at them only to realize that my shoes were gone! They were still in the water, stuck in the mud.

My jaw dropped in utter shock as I looked down at my dress. I screamed again. *My dress! My poor, beautiful shoes!* The boy covered his ears. His little white tiger cub hid behind his legs.

From looking towards the pond, I turned to the boy. "Look at what you've done! I am *completely* soaked! I lost my shoes and I'm completely covered in mud!" I yelled at him as my eyes filled with tears. Now *I* was the mess. I was cold and dirty. My dress was heavy and it stuck to me as I fell to the ground. My dress was already ruined, so I didn't care. I was sobbing uncontrollably. My face was lost in my hands.

Out of nowhere I heard a splash in the river. I sniffled as I looked up to see what was going on. I realized the boy had gone into the water and retrieved my shoes. With complete ease, he submerged his hands into the water and pulled my shoes right out of the sticky mud. The water and dirt did not bother him. I wasn't surprised. He walked over to me. There was a blank expression on his face. He placed my shoes in front of me and then sat down. We sat there for a couple of minutes in silence just staring at each other. I tried to hold in my tears so I could see him better. I dried my eyes with my hand. I had unknowingly smeared dirt all over my face.

This was very awkward. He seemed confused; it was as if I looked familiar to him or something. It was like he had never seen a girl before - let alone a wet one. His little tiger cub jumped onto my dress and was rubbing its face onto my arms. He started purring. I couldn't help but smile. I had never felt anything that soft before.

"Aw, he's so cute. What's his name?" I asked the boy. He didn't answer me. He just stared.

"Does he have a name?" He still didn't respond. "Okay, what is your name then?"

The boy's eyebrows creased even more as he kept staring at me. Why wasn't he answering me? I was getting frustrated. Could he not hear me? Or was he just trying to upset me?

"Hello? Do. You. Understand. Me?" I carefully sounded out each word.

The white tiger cub jumped off my dress and growled playfully at the boy. The boy growled back at him. It was as if they were talking to each other. The boy crouched down to play with the cub. He was rubbing his head on the cub, mimicking the way the cub was rubbing his head onto my arm. I got up awkwardly. I walked over to the boy and reached out my hand. He just stared at me and then rubbed his head onto my hand. I found myself petting him. This was so strange, but it felt normal at the same time.

He started purring and meowing at me. It was as if he was trying to tell me something, but he only knew tiger language. I felt so helpless. What could I do? I didn't know how to communicate with him. He looked so sad and lost. He had probably wandered away from his family. I had decided it was time for me to leave. I didn't want to confuse him even more. I figured if I left, his family would come out and get him.

I bent down and put my shoes on. I took two steps and couldn't stand the squishy noise my shoes were making and it felt pretty disgusting. I bent back down and took them off. I decided just to carry them instead. I looked towards the boy.

"Bye, weird animal boy. I'm going to my home now," I said very slowly. He clearly didn't understand me. I could have said anything. I waved and turned my back to him. I had to tell someone about him. Maybe I would tell Massimo. Maybe he knew something about this boy.

I started to walk away but felt a tug at my dress. I figured I must have snagged it on something. I turned around to free it, only to find that the boy was the one pulling it. The little cub was right beside me the whole time. "I have to go," I said.

I started to leave again. I walked about ten paces. I could hear him behind me. I looked over my shoulder, only to find that we were face to face. I got startled and fell to the floor. The boy reached down and helped me up.

Could I bring him home? I asked myself. He was obviously lost. Maybe he was an orphan. He couldn't speak English and he probably couldn't do much else either. I saw this as an opportunity to do something useful for once. I would be the one to civilise him. Dad would probably say yes, but then Mom would probably say no. In the end Mom would persuade Dad and he would have to give in to whatever she says - that's what normally happened. But I didn't care. I was going to bring him home and that was it.

"Come on!" I gestured with my hand for him to go with me. He face lit up and he followed me. He walked very close to me. I guessed this was a normal thing for him to do. It took me a while to walk back up the mountain because my dress was still drenched and it weighed about ten pounds more than it did when I first put it on. I was debating removing it altogether and walking in my undergarments, but that would have been un-lady like. He probably wouldn't have minded. He was half naked himself. I was surprised he was even wearing anything. Tigers don't wear clothes. I guess he still had some human instincts left in him.

He grabbed my hand and helped me up the hill. I guessed he saw that I was struggling. We passed the pond in my garden. This one I would never fall into because it had exotic fish and a little railing around it. I didn't know how deep it was. I wasn't sure if I knew how to swim. Since I have never been swimming before, I suppose I didn't know how. I was thankful that river was very shallow. I could have drowned!

"That is my pond and this is my garden!" I gave him the tour knowing all too well that he didn't understand me. I felt like I owed him something. Maybe he would learn if I kept talking to him. We were at the back grand entrance. Before we walked in I stopped and turned to the boy. I put my index finger to my mouth and whispered, "Shh. Be quiet."

The boy mimicked me. He put his finger in front of his mouth and said, "Shh," as well.

I smiled and grabbed his hand. I pulled him into the direction of the stairs. We were almost half way up when I heard someone behind us.

"Excuse me missy, but where do you think you are going and who is that with you?"

I stopped dead in my tracks. I closed my eyes tightly and moaned to myself. I was busted. I did not want to turn around, but I had no other choice. I slowly turned around to see Dad walking up the stairs towards me. He had a better look at my appearance from up close. He was only a few steps away before he came to a complete stop.

"I have a better question. What happened to you? You're all wet and muddy. Did he do this to you?" Dad became defensive all of a sudden.

"No! No, I fell into the pond at the bottom of the mountain and -"

Dad interrupted. "What were you doing at the bottom of the mountain? You know you are not allowed down there! We don't have any guards in that area. What if something happened to you? Wait until your mother hears about this!"

"No! Dad! Please don't tell Mom! Please, I'm begging you! Ground me, anything. Just don't tell Mom. I am fine. I just got a little wet."

He raised an eyebrow at me. "A *little* wet?"

"Okay, *a lot* wet - but I just want to help this boy out. He is lost and alone and dirty. I want to clean him up and help him. Please Dad. I have nothing else in the world to do. I have no other friends. You know how all the other kids are." I was pleading. Dad knew how obnoxious the other kids were. He didn't like me talking to them either. Mom didn't know this.

"Alright fine! Just go into your room and clean him up. I will call one of the servants to help you. Don't tell your mother and don't let her see this child like this. Both of you get cleaned and dressed. Go now!" Dad smiled at me when he was finished speaking.

"Thank you Dad." I walked down one step and leaned over to give him a kiss on the cheek. I was going to give him a hug, but I doubt he would have appreciated that – given the dishevelled state I was in.

I ran up the stairs as fast as I could with this boy's hand in mine.

"Can someone clean up this mess?" I could hear my dad yell to one of the servants. I looked down and realized I was leaving a water and mud trail behind me. The servants would easily clean that up.

I ran to my room and locked my door. I went into my washroom and knelt beside the tub. I turned on the water. I held my hand under the water to feel its temperature. I didn't want it too hot or too cold. There was a knock at the door. I gasped and quickly turned my head. I was scared that Mom was at the door. I just listened. I didn't ask who it was. They knocked again.

"Miss Sophia. Your father sent for me to give you a bath," one of the servants said.

"Oh yeah!" I got up and wiped my hands on my dress. It didn't make a difference. I unlocked the door and she walked in. "Okay, I need you to give him a bath first." I pointed to the boy who was standing in the middle of my room straight as a pole. The poor thing looked so scared.

I laughed as I walked over to him. I put both my hands on his shoulders and said, "Everything is going to be alright. You will have a bath now, okay?" I nodded to him and he nodded back to me. I started to wonder if he did understand me. Or was he just mimicking me again? Either way, I didn't care. He just needed a bath and he needed it now!

"Go, go!" I scooted both of them into the washroom and I closed the room door behind me. The little tiger cub crawled out from under my bed. I picked him up and just looked at him. He was actually very beautiful. I have never seen an animal like this up close before. His fur was all white with faint black lines. His eyes were as blue as the ocean, just like the boy's. I was holding him so close to my face. He placed his paw on my cheek. I was so scared he was going to scratch me, but he didn't. He just rested it there, like it was no big deal. He licked my nose. It kind of hurt. His tongue felt rough. I cradled him in my arms and then I brought him to the washroom.

"Don't be alarmed," I said to the servant. I saw her tense up at the sight of the cub. I petted his face to show that it was alright. She was washing the boy's hair with soap with a very disgusted look on her face. He looked uncomfortable sitting in the tub. I laughed as I placed the tiger into the bath. "Wash him as well." I left the room and closed the door behind me.

What was he going to wear? I didn't even think of that. I ran to Dad's room. I went into his dresser and opened it. I found a random shirt and a pair of pants. I grabbed them quickly and shut the door. I ran back to my room but then I remembered he needed underwear. So, I ran back to Dad's room and browsed his drawers for underwear. I found a pair and then headed back to my room.

While I was waiting for him to finish, I took off my dress and lay it over the arm of one of my chairs. I made sure it didn't touch the cushion. My undergarments were still drenched. I left them on until I got into the tub.

The door opened a few minutes later. The boy came out in just a towel. The cub came out shortly after, looking clean as well. His fur was sticking out in every direction. Come to think of it, so did the boy's hair. They both looked flustered. I was sure they had never taken a bath like this before. I guess the servant had given them both a quick and rough towel dry. I started laughing.

"Excuse me, but can you cut hair?" I asked the servant.

"Yes Miss - I can."

I looked at the boy and raised both my eyebrows. She got the hint.

"Yes Miss, of course." She put her arm around the boy. "Come with me again." They went back into the washroom and she shut the door.

A couple minutes passed as I waited patiently. They emerged from the washroom - the servant, the boy and his cub. The boy looked much better now that his hair was cut short. The cub looked the same but of course I didn't expect her to cut his hair as well. He walked over to me and sat down at my feet. He started licking his fur and grooming himself.

"Okay, get dressed, then sit here and wait while I bathe now." I pointed towards the clothes on the bed for him to change into. I then pointed to another one of the chairs in my room for him to sit on. He picked up the clothes I chose for him and just stared at them. He started to dress himself as I made my way into the washroom.

There was clean water waiting for me in the tub. I was so excited to clean myself. I took the rest of my clothes off in the washroom. I walked over to the tub and stepped in. The water quickly warmed my whole body. I didn't realise how cold I was.

I let myself soak up the heat that radiated from the tub as the servant washed me clean. When I was all done I dried myself while the servant went into my room to get me something dry to wear. She came back in no time with some undergarments and another dress. They were all I had. I loved my dresses.

"Who is that boy sitting outside Miss? I have never seen him before but he looks well behaved. He is still sitting on the chair with that baby tiger on his lap. They are both waiting for you to come back out," the servant said as she dressed me.

"Oh, he's just an old friend. He got a little dirty so I offered to bring him home and clean him," I lied.

I was all done and I went back into my room where the boy was still sitting. Dad's clothes were too big for him. I had to roll up his sleeves and pants. Other than that, he actually cleaned up very nice. I couldn't believe what I turned him into. He was very handsome.

All of a sudden I heard high heels coming down the hall way. My heart dropped. I panicked.

"Hurry, take this! Hide it for now! Then wash it and hang it back in my closet!" I grabbed my dress off the chair and I gave it to the servant. She hid it behind her back as she headed for the door. She unlocked it and before she could turn the handle, Mom opened the door and walked right in.

"Why is this door closed? We never close doors in this house." Mom looked at me.

"Madame," the servant said as she bowed her head. She walked by Mom. Mom didn't even look at her. Thank goodness. I was so afraid Mom was going to see my dirty dress hanging in her hands.

My heart was beating steadier now. All I had to worry about now was the fact that there was this boy in my room that Mom had never seen before. Not to mention, there was also a small tiger here. She still looked angry.

"Sophia, who is this boy with you? Where is he from?" Mom looked at him. The angry look on her face had completely disappeared. She now looked shocked.

"This is uh..." I couldn't finish my sentence. I didn't know his name and I couldn't even think to make one up.

"Matteo is my name."

The boy spoke! I didn't know he could speak any language at all, let alone English. This whole time I went on talking to him thinking he had no idea what I was saying! I felt like a fool. I just stared at him. My eyes were probably bulging out of my face.

"Matteo?" Mom whispered under her breath with no emotion on her face. "Well, uh," Mom shook her head to snap out of it. "It's nice to meet you Matteo." Mom turned to me. She was still in shock. "Why don't you two go and play outside or something? I don't like having you playing in your room with the door closed. Do you understand?"

"Yes Mom. I completely understand. We'll go outside now." And that was it. This was not how I would have expected her to handle the situation. I was sure that she was going to be furious with me. She must have been in one of her good moods today.

I grabbed the boy's hand as we walked out of my room. I turned back to look at Mom and I saw her place one of her hands on her chest while the other hand searched blindly for the chair behind her. She sat down abruptly. She looked flustered. I didn't bother going back to ask her what was wrong. I was still in shock from hearing Matteo speak. I just stared at him as we walked down the stairs. He had a lot of explaining to do!

Chapter 3 - The Oak Tree

I couldn't believe what just happened. The boy could speak! All this time he understood me. I had been fooled. I had to find out the truth. I started walking towards my garden since I was going to bring him there to talk, but I changed my mind. I passed the garden and walked the other way to another one of my favourite spots. The whole estate was my playground. I made Dad build me a swing to hang off my favourite tree. It was not just any beautiful tree. My swing was hidden under the *hundred* year old oak tree. The trunk was so wide and the roots stuck out everywhere. It meant a lot to me since this is where I would go and speak my problems aloud when I had no one to talk to. I liked the swing best of all because it was hidden from everything and everyone. The branches and leaves on the tree hung down very low and almost completely covered the area.

The boy followed me the entire time. I walked ahead of him and sat on my swing. I pushed myself back as far as I could and let go. My hair blew in the wind. Even though this felt nice, I was still angry. The cub sat on my right side and watched me swing. I saw his head following me back and forth - back and forth. I had to make sure not to get this dress dirty. I never liked giving the servants more work to do. I just felt bad. The only reason I accepted the help of that one servant earlier was because I was in a rush and in dire need of any help possible.

The boy was sitting on one of the roots sticking out from the ground. I could tell he was looking at me. I didn't bother looking back.

I took a deep breath. "So…you can understand me, can't you?" I said to the boy - or should I say *Matteo*. I looked ahead as I spoke.

I saw him nod from the corner of my eye. I dug my heels into the ground - trying my best not to get them dirty - and stopped swinging. I walked up to the boy so that we were face to face. "Tell me now what you are trying to pull here. Can you understand me? You *definitely* understood my mom when she spoke to you." I put my hands on my hips. I was breathing heavily. The boy's eyes were wide with shock.

He looked down to the ground. "I do understand. I know a little bit on how to speak," he confessed.

He had a very beautiful voice that took me by surprise, so much that I had to take a step back. I guess I expected him to have some sort of an animal-like voice - I don't know. His English was broken, but it was understandable.

"What happened to you? Why were you in the woods? Tell me." I turned my back to him as I walked back to my swing and sat back down. I didn't swing this time - I just sat there holding onto the ropes that held it up. I looked up to make sure it was tied tight enough to the branch. There was no way those knots were going to come loose. I looked back at Matteo and I waited for him to speak.

Matteo began his story. "I had a family one time. I do not know what happened to them. At one time I was with them and then at another time I did not see them anymore. I forgot a little how to speak. So many years ago I have been lost."

Now I felt like a big bully, yelling at him like that. I had to be nicer to him now.

"Oh, I am so sorry. That must be tough. Do you know how old you are?" I asked. This was getting interesting.

"I do not know how old I am. When I got lost I was very little. Maybe I was three years old. I think fourteen years it has been since then. I haven't talked to humans for fourteen years then. When I got lost at first I was found by these tigers. I thought they were going to kill me but they didn't. They saved me and took care of me."

"Okay, so you're seventeen years old then? You're two years older than I am. I'm fifteen years old. Do you know how you got lost?" I was going to ask as many questions as I could. I needed answers. This is normally something you hear about in books or stories. These types of things never happen to normal people in real life. I had to know more. I was getting excited.

"Um, I do not know. I think there was an accident. Something happened and I did not know where my family was. I do not remember what happened. It was a long time ago." His hands were tightly bound to his head which he was shaking. It was as if he were trying to recall memories he had worked so hard to forget.

"I am so sorry to hear that." Now I felt even worse. I was going to change my attitude towards him entirely. He probably didn't know if he could trust me, which is why he didn't speak to me in the beginning. Maybe he was testing me all along. Either way, this boy had a very traumatic life. First his family died or abandoned him, and then he lives the rest of his life in the woods being raised by tigers. Not regular tigers but - white Siberian tigers. They were very rare in our world. There used to be so many, but they were all hunted and killed. After my parents became rulers, hunting the white tigers was banned. Being raised by them must be so exciting - pretty scary, but definitely exciting. I wish I lived with tigers. Anything would be better than living in this place with my normal boring life.

I wanted something more. But at fifteen this was hardly an option. I couldn't travel or find new friends. I still wanted a change. Sometimes I even wondered why I was even brought into existence. What was the reason for my being? I always asked myself that. Now after finding this boy, maybe I do have a reason for life. Maybe I was put on this world to help this boy. Everyone has their destiny and this could be mine.

"The more I listen to you speaking, the more I remember how to speak. It is all coming back to me now. I think I have to learn more." Matteo got up from the tree root and came behind me. I turned my head to the right, half-way and saw him grab the ropes right from under my hands. He pulled me back and let go gracefully. He started pushing me on the swing. This was so much fun! I felt like I could really act like a kid with him. He didn't have the money from *mommy* and *daddy* to spoil him like the other kids I knew. He was poor and living like an animal, but that meant nothing. He didn't have money but he did have one thing. Something I would really admire in a person. He had courage. He lived this long and has this great of a spirit and I respected him for that.

"Do not worry. I will help you. You can stay with me," I whispered with my eyes closed as swung to and fro. I knew he heard me.

This was my time to shine! I normally came here alone. I never realized how lonely it was until this moment. On some occasions I would come here to cry. I would swing while I cried because it dried my tears quicker. I was going to forget those times and think of this one from now on. I would no longer associate the swing with tears. It was now mine and Matteo's swing.

"Wait, hold on for one second!" I said as I just thought of something.

Matteo stopped pushing me and stopped the swing. He came to stand in front of me. "Yes? Is there something wrong?" Matteo asked.

I was just wondering how he even got in the first place. He couldn't have just showed up here at random. "Nothing is wrong. Did you recently get lost from your tiger friends as well?"

"Yes." He looked down at his cub with sad eyes. It seemed like a touchy subject for him. "Kiko ran off one day because he smelled food in the distance and of course I ran after him. I tried to bring him home again but he kept running further and further away from me. He did not understand we were getting lost from everyone. When I did catch him, we looked for our family together but they were gone. For a long time we were wandering the woods. We were going to give up soon, but I knew we could not. Giving up was not an option for me. Family is everything and it was the only thing we had. When we were wandering we found you and we thought that you could help us and you did." He was petting Kiko while avoiding my eyes.

"Oh, I see." I didn't know what else to say.

"We do not normally stay in one place, but here is where we saw a lot of people. We never talk to them. We get scared of humans. They hunted our family. But when we saw you, it was different. You seemed so trust worthy."

"How so?"

"We do not know. You look like a very nice person. Something made me happy to see you. I trust you."

It was weird but I could easily talk to him. There was no awkwardness between us. I could sit here and enjoy myself and not have to worry about anything. My life was on hold while we spoke to each other. I felt like I could tell him my deepest darkest secrets. He listened to everything that I said and took it to heart. I felt like he was my guardian and he was here to protect me. And this time I didn't mind. He wasn't like the guards on my estate who were always around, even when they weren't wanted.

We sat there in silence. Well, I sat there while Matteo went back behind me and continued pushing. I could see Kiko chasing after little bugs crawling on the ground. His head was crouched down low on the ground while his butt wiggled in the air. When the moment was right, he would pounce on them. He kept his paws on the ground and when he felt it was time, he would lift his paw and eat whatever bug was underneath.

Sometimes the bugs were still alive and as soon as he lifted his paw they escaped. Then the hunt would begin all over again.

I could watch Kiko do that all day. He pounced again, but this time he ended up pricking his paw on a sharp root that was sticking out from the ground. He cried out in pain. He sounded more like a cat than he did a tiger. I guess because he was just a baby. Matteo left me and ran over to Kiko. I got up from the the swing and walked over as well.

"Oh no, is he okay?" I asked as I watched Matteo pick Kiko up to examine his paw. I bent down to get a better look.

"Yeah he will be fine. Just a little prick - that's all," Matteo said as he rubbed Kiko's paw.

"You look like you really love him," I said in awe.

"Yes. I do love him. He is my only family right now. I lost everyone. He is all I have," Matteo said as Kiko cuddled up to him. He closed his eyes and purred. I was guessing he felt the same way.

The three of us sat there in silence. We had nothing to say to each other. All we could hear was the wind blowing against the trees. It was a very relaxing sound. It reminded me why I loved nature so much. It was getting darker outside as the sun was slowly setting. It felt as if I was the only kid in this world who appreciates small things like the weather. Most of the kids my age preferred to stay inside and converse about matters that were none of their business. It made me sick to my stomach.

I leaned in to pet Kiko. I heard a tree branch snap behind me. I whisked my head around quickly and gasped. The noise startled me. I saw someone walking towards us, making their way through the long limp branches of the tree.

"Hello Sophia." It was Paul Jr. "My family and I went home but I could not stand being away from you. Every time I closed my eyes I saw your beautiful face. My parents don't know I'm here. If they found out, they would be furious. I don't care though. I just needed to see you." Paul looked over to Matteo. "Who is *that?*" He said in a disgusted voice.

Matteo got up and stood beside me.

Paul took a step towards us. "Get away from her. I don't recognize you and I know everyone here," he said with a cocky tone as he raised his chin. I felt sick to my stomach. "I should call the guards on you - you intruder!" Paul said rudely.

Matteo took a step in front of me. "Sophia, is this a friend?"

"Um, I just met him today." My heartbeat accelerated. This was getting intense. I didn't know what to do or say.

This felt so wrong. I had *never* been in this type of situation. I went from having no boy look at me twice - to having two guys fight over me; if that's what you want to call it. I wanted to cover my ears and close my eyes. I did not want to be there. I preferred being in trouble with my mother at home than standing here listening to this.

"Sophia, you shouldn't be associating yourself with this man. Come with me - where you truly belong." Paul held out his hand for me to grab. I just stared at it.

My jaw dropped and my eyes were watering. My heart was beating so fast I thought it was going to come right out of my chest. It felt like I had one big lump in my throat. I couldn't speak. My throat was burning as I tried to hold in my tears. All I could do was shake my head.

"You see now, she does not want to come with you. She is staying with me - right here," Matteo said.

"Who taught you to speak? Your grammar is horrible. Go back to where you came from." Paul looked over to me. "Do not do this. I know you want to come with me! You can't tell me that you want to stay here." Paul was getting angry now.

"Now you listen to me. My words may not be perfect but I know that Sophia does not want to go with you." Matteo stood strong in front of me. He now was starting to get angry with Paul. I guess Matteo could tell I couldn't speak for myself. He was right in between Paul and me. He took a step forward and was inches from Paul's face. I could hear Kiko growling faintly at Paul.

Paul took a step towards me and grabbed my left arm. Paul squeezed my arm as hard as he could. "You're coming with me!" He bellowed as he pulled me towards him. My whole body flew. My head swung back from the force. I was just this weak and helpless little girl. I had no idea what to do.

Matteo came to my defence and grabbed Paul's wrist. Paul was clearly taken aback by Matteo's strength. "Let. Go. Of. Her." Matteo put great emphasis in each word. I could tell he meant every word. I got scared. I have never seen him like this - even though I only knew him for a short period of time.

I didn't know what was more frightening – Paul's deadly grip or that Matteo looked like he was ready to kill him at any given moment.

They both stared at each other with determination in their eyes. Paul wasn't going to let go of my arm and Matteo was not going to let go of

Paul's wrist. I could see Matteo's grip tighten on Paul's wrist. Matteo was growling along with Kiko.

Paul gave up. He was not used to this type of confrontation. He threw my arm down and as soon as he did Matteo let go of him. Paul looked towards me and spat as he spoke. "Fine, choose this mongrel over me! One day you will realize you made a huge mistake! This is not the end of it!" Paul looked furious. His face was all red and the vein in his head looked like it was about to burst. He then stormed off while holding his wrist and muttering something foul to himself. It was clear his ego was wounded.

I took a deep breath and grabbed my throbbing arm. Matteo turned around to look at me. I could barely see him this time. His body became one big blur. It was as if he turned to me in slow motion. Suddenly I felt light headed. I started to fall over but Matteo caught me before I hit the ground. I leaned on him as I tried to regain my strength and composure.

"Breathe in from your nose and out from your mouth," Matteo said. Kiko came right beside me and started purring. Even Kiko seemed worried for me. That was very sweet.

I did what Matteo told me to do and it actually worked. He waited beside me while I slowly felt my senses coming back. He held my arm gently as I inhaled sharply from the pain. He rubbed my arm with his thumb and shook his head. He looked very disappointed. I wondered what he was thinking.

Through the silence of our surroundings, I heard a low rumbling noise. That noise was very familiar. I realized what it was and I started to laugh. I heard it again and this time Matteo started laughing along with me. He knew exactly what I was laughing at. Each time I heard it, it got louder and louder.

The noise was coming from Matteo's stomach. He hadn't eaten anything all day. I got up, waited for a second just to make sure I was okay, and then started walking away from the tree.

"Follow me!" I said as I ran towards the house. Matteo and Kiko ran after me.

It was pitch black outside but the darkness did not affect me at all. I could run through the estate with my eyes closed. I knew my way around. I could see the lights of my house in the distance. We laughed as we ran. As soon as I got to the house I stopped running. I needed to catch my breath. Matteo on the other hand kept running. He ran right past me, towards the kitchen entrance. When I saw him pass me I went right after him.

He got to the kitchen before me. When I got there I found him raiding the fridge. He grabbed a ham from the fridge and set it onto the island in the middle of the kitchen. When he saw me, he went into the freezer and grabbed a bag of frozen peas and handed it to me. "For your arm so it doesn't darken more." I froze in my spot as I stared at him. I reached out my hand and grabbed the peas without noticing. He walked over to the counter and cut a slice of ham for himself. I watched him devour it.

He noticed my staring. "What?" He said with his mouth full.

I was in complete shock. "How did you know where the kitchen was?"

Matteo stopped chewing and had a confused look on his face - he struggled to swallow. "I…don't know." We both stood there in silence. "I guess I am drawn to food." Matteo started laughing. Kiko put his small paws up on the cupboard under the counter. He was nowhere near able to put his paws on the counter. Matteo cut another piece of ham and gave it to Kiko. He gnawed on it in enjoyment.

I dropped the subject altogether. It didn't seem important for the moment. I jumped up on the counter and took a seat. Then we started to talk. I held the bag of peas on my arm as we spoke. I asked him as many questions as I could. I wanted to know everything about him; from the first thing he remembers to how it was living in the woods by himself. He asked me as many questions as he could think of as well. We spent the whole night talking. No one disturbed us, which was unusual since we made a lot of noise. It was nice to finally have a friend to talk to. I wanted to know as much about Matteo as was humanly possible. I normally don't trust anyone this easily – especially someone I had only just met - but Matteo was different. I wanted him to know everything about me. We talked all night and even into the morning.

Chapter 4 - How to Swim

Years had passed since that eventful day when I met Matteo. It still feels like it was yesterday. We were both older now. I was now twenty years old while Matteo was twenty-two. I still looked the same, only taller and leaner. And of course, I still had my lustrous blonde locks. Matteo had also grown. He was now taller and more muscular. He worked out every day which he had apparently done since he was a young boy. I suppose he had to in order to survive in the wild all those years ago.

Matteo now lived with my family and me. We let him have one of the many spare bedrooms we had. He fit in perfectly with our little family. It was as if he belonged there the whole time. Matteo and I were now the best of friends. We did everything together. I found myself smiling more frequently now and actually laughing out loud. There wasn't a single moment spent with him where I felt nothing but sheer bliss. Matteo lived his whole life alone with no family, yet he seemed like the happiest person in the world. I on the other hand, had everything handed to me on a platter – a good family, a beautiful home, servants waiting on me hand and foot - and yet I wasn't as happy. But that was now behind me. I was now going to live in the present and start thinking about the future.

My parents had gotten close to Matteo. Our family was closer than ever before. Mom and Dad's relationship seemed to grow as well. They were smiling more and altogether enjoying life. Dad would even take days off from his busy schedule to spend more time as a family. Matteo had changed our lives. It was as if he was the bond that brought our family together when we were slowly falling apart.

Today was a day like any other on Caledonia. I had gone for a nice long walk. Matteo was off somewhere doing whatever he normally does. I didn't like to bother him when he wanted to be alone. I liked taking walks by myself. It gave me time to think. I thought about my future and what I was going to do with my life. Was I going to live here forever? Were there places I wanted to go? Would I dare venture to Earth? Why was I alone? Should I have a significant other in my life right now? These questions were just flowing through my head and I had no answers for any of them. I felt like I was stuck in a rut. I couldn't keep living like this. My life was going nowhere. I couldn't stay in my beautiful garden forever.

As I walked along the pathway, I tried to erase these questions from my mind. I felt my skin absorb the warmth of the sun. I was fair skinned and I didn't tan much. My skin just never took to the sun, which is surprising considering Caledonia is warm and sunny all year round. I had heard that on Earth it snows. I read about it in many books my tutor had given me. I still had no idea what it was though. Obviously I had never encountered it before. It seemed lovely - the way it completely covers the ground and shimmers in the sun. Still, I couldn't complain. Caledonia was paradise. I loved how the sun made my fair skin glow.

I swayed my arms as I continued to walk. I noticed a familiar creature in the distance. I smiled - it was Kiko. He was much bigger now. He was a full grown adult tiger. His beautiful white coat still bore the softest fur you could touch. It sparkled in the sun. I brushed it for him every day while he lay there patiently. Kiko was like the pet I never had. Even though he was a wild animal, he was gentle and obedient all the same. I loved him and trusted him and I know he felt the same.

"Kiko!" I called. He didn't even look up. I picked up my dress – I didn't want to trip – and ran over to him.

I finally reached him and I couldn't make out what he was doing. He was staring into the pond. His chin rested on the railing. I stood there for a moment to catch my breath as I wasn't in the habit of running on a regular basis. That was Matteo's pastime, not mine. He lifted his paw and grazed the top of the water. I got down on my knees beside him to see at his level. I looked into the water but I couldn't see a thing. I looked over to Kiko who didn't take his eyes off the water. I looked in again and waited patiently for something to appear – a fish, a frog. Anything. Kiko wouldn't have been standing here for no reason.

I was starting to get impatient, when something suddenly appeared under the water. I couldn't make out what it was, but it was getting bigger and bigger. Without even noticing, my face moved closer to the surface. Before I knew it, something splashed out at me. I shrieked and fell backwards on the hard ground, landing on my butt. At least I didn't fall in the water. I got back up as quick as I could and saw Matteo squirming in the water. *Is he drowning?* I thought to myself. *Oh no, he is drowning! What am I going to do? I can't even swim.* I had never felt so helpless.

"Someone help!" I screamed. I desperately looked around. Of course there was no one in sight!

I looked back to the water. My heartbeat raced and my eyes started to water. *Why are you standing there?* I said to myself. *Do something! Anything!* But I just stood, paralyzed with shock. My best friend was drowning while I watched. Suddenly the splashing stopped and everything went quiet. This whole time Kiko was sitting beside me quiet as ever - just staring. He didn't look concerned in any way. If anything, he seemed more curious than anything else.

I was on all fours staring at the water, eyes bulging out of my head. The hard cement was scraping my hands and knees. But there was no pain worse than the pain I felt in my heart. I bowed my head and my forehead touched the ground. I was sobbing uncontrollably. He was gone and it was my fault.

"Sophia?" A muffled voice called.

I looked up and my jaw dropped - almost all the way to the ground. There Matteo was whirling around in the pond with a fish in his mouth. The fish was flapping its fins, trying to break loose from the prison of Matteo's teeth.

I dried my tears with a fierce movement of my hand. I jumped right up from the ground.

"Matteo! What did I tell you about hunting my fish?" Now that I no longer needed to mourn – I was now very upset with him. I told him so many times that the fish in this pond were not to be eaten! Dad had to keep buying new ones since they were mysteriously disappearing ever since Matteo came to live with us. I caught him red handed!

My eyes filled with tears again. I guess I was still in shock by the thought of losing Matteo.

Matteo's jaw dropped and the fish fell right out, flew back into the water and swam for his life.

"Sophia, why are you crying? I am so sorry. I will not hunt them anymore. I didn't know it upset you this much! I don't always catch your fish. Kiko loves them and I give them to him as a treat. I have given him only two or three - I promise!"

I tried to calm down. I knew I was overreacting. I wasn't going to tell him what I was thinking. I guess I was too embarrassed. I dried my tears for the last time and let out a loud sigh and sat back down.

Kiko nudged his head onto mine. I smiled and brushed my hands through his fur. "Was that fish for you?" I asked Kiko. He just stared at me. I turned to Matteo. "Okay, I guess you can give him one more. But that's it! No more after this one!"

Matteo smiled at me as he did some sort of a back flip in the water. I watched him - or tried to at least - as he swam after the scattered fish. This was the first time I ever seen someone swimming this close to me before. Swimming looked like so much fun! Sometimes he would disappear while other times I could see him clearly. He looked so graceful under the water. I just sat there in wonderment.

Matteo grabbed onto the railing and pulled himself out of the water. He emerged from the pond dripping water everywhere. I screamed in excitement as he purposely sprinkled some water in mine and Kiko's direction. He was holding a fish. It looked like it was about to slip right out of his hands at any minute. He threw the fish up in the air and Kiko jumped up and caught the fish in his mouth. I watched in disgust as he tore into it and devoured every last bit.

I was still kneeling on the ground when I noticed Matteo walking towards me. He shook his hair like he was an animal. Just because he was older now, doesn't mean that he lost his animal instincts. He was wearing only a pair of shorts. I stared at him as he walked towards me.

Matteo looked confused. He looked over his shoulder and then looked at me. "What are you grinning about you silly girl?" he asked.

I didn't realize I was smiling this whole time. I blinked and shook my head. "Oh, it's nothing. I can't believe what a great swimmer you are. You looked so elegant!"

"I swim all the time!" Matteo smiled from ear to ear.

"Yeah, well I never have," I mumbled to myself as I got up from the ground. I looked at him again. He was much taller than I was.

"I'll teach you!" Matteo said with great enthusiasm. His eyes lit up. "Only if you want to learn."

I was hesitant at first but I figured *why not*? I have nothing to lose - besides my life of course - which wasn't that great to begin with. Of course Matteo made it better. I wasn't lonely anymore thanks to him. But there was still a void in me. I knew something was still missing. I knew Matteo wouldn't let anything happen to me.

I agreed to the swimming lessons. I told him that I didn't want to swim in the pond. I asked him if he could teach me in the river down the mountain – the place where we first met.

Matteo stared at me with disapproving eyes. He knew that it was dangerous for me at the bottom of the mountain – so close to the forest. He also knew how mad my parents would be if they ever found out. I assured him everything would be fine. After all, I had a jungle boy with me. I knew I would be safe with him.

Matteo finally gave in to me and we headed down the mountain towards the river. I was almost running down the hill. It's kind of hard to walk down a steep mountain. My stomach was in so many knots and I had a permanent smile on my face. I was ecstatic. This was going to be my first time swimming.

We got to the - oh so familiar - river. All the memories from that day came back. I remembered falling into the water. As soon as I remembered that, my smile faded. I wasn't traumatized or anything like that; I remembered how shallow the water was. It was no more than two feet of water. *How could I have forgotten?* There was no way we could swim in that.

I turned to Matteo to let him know how I felt, but before I could say anything he interrupted me.

"We're not swimming here. Don't worry. If you don't mind, I know a place where I've been swimming before. It is very majestic. It is not that far from here. Would you like to go?"

My body was all for it, but my mind held back. There was that little piece of my mind that kept refusing to proceed. It must have been the years of my parents drilling into my mind how unsafe the forest was and how much they didn't want me going there. They would've been happy to know that the scare tactics worked. The hesitation remained but I was no longer a child. I could take care of myself. And it's not like I was alone.

"Of course," I answered with a nod of my head.

I didn't want to admit that I was scared. My stomach filled with more and more butterflies with every step that I took. I had to grab onto the tree branches to make sure I didn't fall over. The bark of the tree was so rough. It scratched the inside of my palm. It stung a bit but the pain was bearable. The path he took me on wasn't even a real path. I doubt it was ever taken by anyone.

"Here we are!" Matteo said with delight in his voice.

I watched my step the whole time we walked. One wrong move and I was done for. My head was down, but as soon as Matteo stopped walking

I looked up. I guessed this was the beginning of the river. I must have not paid attention to the sounds in the forest because what I was staring at was making an immense amount of noise. There was a huge waterfall to the left of me. Water fell down from high up that mountain and landed in the river. It was absolutely breathtaking. Everything around was so green and lush.

"You're not swimming like *that*, are you?" Matteo stared at my dress. Kiko was already in the water; splashing and swimming around. He didn't wait for us.

I looked down at myself and remembered that I was wearing a dress. I remembered what happens to dresses when they get wet. They stick to you and they get extremely, unbearably heavy. I didn't think twice. I automatically lifted my dress over my head to expose just my undergarments.

"Better?" I asked.

Matteo didn't care much to see me just in my undergarments. It wasn't a big deal and I didn't care either. I guess there was just no embarrassment between us. I just felt comfortable around him.

"Let's swim!" Matteo ran behind me. I didn't ask where he was going - I just turned around and watched him. He started running towards the water at top speed. He jumped right off a rock into the water screaming at the top of his lungs. He made a huge splash. I thought he landed on Kiko but I realized Kiko was a safe distance away from him. That looked like so much fun! As much as I wanted to mimic him, I thought I should stick to the basics for now.

Matteo swam to my right side over to the edge of the river. He told me to follow him. Apparently you could touch the ground there. I listened to him and dipped my foot into the water first. I quickly pulled it back out. "Are you crazy? This water is freezing!" Goosebumps shot up my leg and spread throughout my whole body. This wasn't looking like such a great idea after all.

"It gets warmer, I promise. You just have to get used to it first," Matteo promised as he reached his hand out from the water. I couldn't leave him hanging. I decided to go for it. I didn't grab his hand though. Matteo just nodded his head as he moved his hand back down into the water. I took a deep breath as I slowly but surely jumped right into the water. My head didn't get wet. The water went up to my rib cage. My back stiffened as I stood in the freezing water. I kept my arms above the water. I don't know why but I held my breath as I stood there. I guess I thought that would make me warmer.

Matteo swam backwards away from me. I walked slowly closer to him. Each step that I took the water rose higher on my body - the water was getting deeper. "I can't go any further. It's too deep," I said to Matteo. If I took one more step I wouldn't be able to touch the ground without going under.

Matteo grabbed my hands and brought me deeper in. At this point I wasn't touching the ground. Matteo had a good grip on my arms the whole time. If he let go I knew I would sink right down to the bottom.

"Okay I am going to slowly let go of you now. Just sway your arms and legs, okay?" Matteo said.

"No, no. Please don't let go of me. Please don't!" I pleaded.

"You have to trust me. Just keep moving your legs and your arms. Don't stop moving. Start now and I will move my hands from your arms slowly. You won't even notice. Do you trust me?"

I did trust him. I knew he wouldn't let anything bad happen to me. "Yes, I trust you," I answered.

I moved my arms and my legs. I was doing the best I could. I just kept moving. Matteo had his grip on me the whole time until he felt it was the right time to let go. The water was moving right through my fingertips. I realized I no longer felt cold. Matteo was right - my body did get used to the water.

"You're doing great!" Matteo said to me as he slowly started to loosen his grip on me.

I looked down and saw him moving away. I started to get nervous. *What happens when he lets go? Will I drown?* I didn't know what to do. I started to panic. My heartbeat quickened and I was breathing heavily. I started moving my arms and legs faster than before. Matteo finally let go and as soon as he did, I forgot everything that he taught me. I started splashing everywhere and my head submerged under the water. At the exact same second that happened Matteo pulled me up.

"Whoa! What happened? You have to relax! Don't be afraid just because I let go. Just keep doing what you were doing the first time." Matteo stared at me with his familiar warm blue eyes.

I wanted to quit. I didn't want to swim anymore. *Would it be okay if I just gave up and walked - well, swam - away? I don't know how that would happen because Matteo would probably make me swim back if I wanted to leave.* These were the thoughts running through my mind. So at this moment I pretty much had no choice. I decided to give it one more try. If it didn't work out, I would make Matteo push me back to the edge where I could reach the bottom. He would have to listen to me this time.

This time we went at a slower pace. We took smaller steps and Matteo waited a little bit longer before he let go of me again. I liked this pace better than the first one. I guess in the beginning he didn't know what I was capable of and neither did I. I listened to everything he told me to do - from widening my arms out to pacing my time before each stroke of the water I took.

Hours passed and before I knew it I could swim all by myself! Matteo didn't have to hold onto me. I was really swimming all by myself! It was so easy! I didn't know how I didn't realize this in the beginning. I couldn't swim from one side to another very fast but I could make my way around at my own pace. I also learned how to float on top of the water. It was scary at first but so worth it in the end. I could listen to the waterfall this way. The sound of the water hitting the river was so relaxing. I had never heard such a sound before.

Who knew that learning something new could be so much fun! It was getting late and it seemed it was about time to go home. Matteo agreed with me. We got out of the water and I put my dress back on. I realized that wasn't the greatest idea, but it was too late to take it off now.

As we walked, I took one last look at the water before it disappeared from my view. I couldn't wait to go back! I wondered what surprises tomorrow would bring. For some odd reason I could feel something eerie in the pit of my stomach. At the same time I was so excited for tomorrow to come but I was also dreading it. I couldn't explain why. Something just didn't feel right.

Chapter 5 - Birthday Surprise

I woke up bright and early the next morning. The sun shone directly through my bedroom window right onto my bed. It was beaming directly into my eyes. Normally the sun didn't wake me up in the morning. I would unintentionally sleep under the covers for some odd reason. Then I would wake up in the morning out of breath, only to discover my head was covered and I had been practically suffocating myself the whole night.

I was curious as to why today was different than other days. I sat up and squinted my eyes to protect them from the vivid rays of the sun. I rubbed my eyes to get a clear view and looked around my room. I realized Kiko was sleeping on the end of my bed. This was strange. Kiko wasn't alone - Matteo was right there behind him. Their weight was keeping the covers from reaching my face.

I quietly got up and tip toed to look at myself in the mirror beside my bed. I tried to open my eyes to get a better look. I had perfect bed-head hair and bags under my eyes. It was obvious that I didn't get a good night's rest. *I think a shower ought to do the trick,* I thought. I went straight to my bathroom. I could hear Kiko snoring - or was that Matteo? I couldn't tell which one was which.

I brushed my teeth before I took a shower. When I was done brushing my teeth I adjusted the water until it was perfect, took off my clothes and jumped right in. I savoured the calming sensation of the water cascading onto my back. When I was done I turned off the hot water and just stood there for a second, waiting for the water to turn freezing cold. I wanted to see how long I could stay under there before I couldn't take it anymore. Three seconds was long enough. That definitely woke me up. I got right out and grabbed a change of clothes from one of the many dressers I had in the washroom. I got dressed quickly. My washroom was way too big for a girl my size. There was a shower, a bath, two sinks, three large mirrors and of course, three dressers.

I tried to catch a glimpse of myself in one of the mirrors, but they were all fogged up. That didn't bother me too much. I slowly opened my door, not to wake Matteo or Kiko. I looked towards my bed and realized they were gone.

"Hi Sophia!" Matteo said as he jumped out of nowhere.

I screamed and bashed him on the shoulder. "Don't do that to me! Are you trying to give me a heart attack?" I started laughing.

Matteo laughed along with me. "Ha-ha I am sorry. I didn't mean to scare you - I promise." He shook his head to the side to keep his hair from covering his eyes. Once again his hair was getting way too long for his own comfort. If I didn't see to his regular grooming, his hair would have been down to his ankles by now.

I grabbed a hair tie that was sitting on my dresser. I raised my hands to reach the top of Matteo's head. I had to stand on the tip of my toes just to reach him. I gathered his hair into my hands. He lowered himself even though he didn't know what I was doing. I tied his hair into a ponytail right at the top of his head. His hair stood straight up. I giggled at the finished product. He looked so silly.

Matteo turned to Kiko who looked confused. He just sat there with his head tilted to the side. I moved to the side so Matteo could look in the mirror which wasn't fogged anymore.

"Ah! What have you done to me? I look like a doll! I am no doll!" Matteo yanked the clip out of his hair and threw it at me. "Let's go Kiko!" Matteo stomped towards my bedroom door. He gave me a wink and was gone.

Matteo could never be mad at me. Even if I dressed him up like a girl, and did his hair and makeup! He would only pretend to be upset. I was laughing the whole time he looked at himself in the mirror. That was the reaction I was kind of hoping for.

I grabbed my comb and quickly brushed my hair. I would let the sun dry it for me. It would form into a nice wave. I didn't have to do anything to my hair. It was so easy to manage. It practically styled itself.

I ran down the stairs hoping I would catch Matteo. "Matteo, wait up!" I yelled as I saw them just about to exit the house to go out back.

He waited for me and the three of us walked outside together. We were outside for about two seconds before we heard someone.

"Sophia, Matteo! Hold on one second please!" Mom said as she was walking quickly towards us. She looked extravagant today. Her hair was all done and she was wearing one of her best dresses. I wondered where she was going. *She's probably telling us she and Dad are going to a ball or something*, I said to myself.

"Wow, Mom, you look beautiful. Where are you going?" I asked.

"I'm not going anywhere. Would you two please come with me?" No one moved. "And Kiko of course!" she added, smiling. She loved Kiko - not as much as we did though.

We all followed Mom into the dining hall. I wondered what this was all about. She walked ahead of us and opened the two great hall doors at the same time. We all walked in to see all of the servants surrounding the table screaming, "Surprise! Happy Birthday!"

Matteo and I looked at each other. Today was February 24th. It wasn't my birthday and we didn't know when Matteo's birthday was so... we were confused. Matteo and I stood there in complete shock. We just waited for an explanation. I turned around to make sure no one was behind us. But there was no one there.

The room was decorated to the max! It looked like a party store had exploded in there. Balloons covered every inch of the room. Streamers hung from everywhere - even from extremely high places I never knew could be reached. The table was covered with presents and there was even a big, beautiful cake centre on the table. The cake was outstanding! It was decorated like a tiger. The entire cake was white, but it had black stripes all over it, just like Kiko! We all knew Matteo loved Kiko more than anything in this world. The three tiers of the cake got smaller as it grew. There were three levels with a black bow at the top.

"Oh Matteo, all these years you have been with us we have never celebrated your birthday. You sat there as Sophia had hers and you never complained once. I noticed this and I felt that it is time that we celebrate your birthday. So today is officially your birthday! I hope you don't mind," Mom said looking a little nervous.

I didn't care too much for birthdays. I usually got a cake and some gifts. No one has ever thrown me a surprise birthday party. I was actually kind of jealous. I had never been jealous of anyone in my life but after seeing all the attention Matteo was getting, I felt it growing in me. *I shouldn't be jealous of him! He is like a brother to me!* I thought to myself. *I should be happy for him! He has never celebrated a birthday before - that he can actually remember. He absolutely deserves this birthday more than anyone.*

I only wish Mom had told me about it as well. I would have bought a gift for him.

I looked around and realized someone was missing. Matteo had taken his seat at the head of the table so we could sing 'Happy Birthday' to him. I pulled Mom to the side and asked her, "Where is Dad?" He never missed a birthday. He loves cake!

She told me that he had to leave for a business trip. He has been all over our planet plenty of times for business. I asked Mom where he was this time and she said she didn't know. Mom knew where Dad went every time, when he was leaving, how long he was going to stay, and when he was coming back. She looked nervous. She was hiding something from me. This was unusual. Mom never hid anything from me. Being outrageously direct was one of her specialties.

"Mom - where is Dad?" I said with a serious tone to my voice. I was getting worried.

She tugged at the gorgeous pearl necklace she was wearing as she looked over my head. She was hesitating to answer me! I stayed right where I was. I didn't take my eyes off her for one second. I was determined to get an answer out of her.

Mom exhaled deeply and placed her hands on my shoulders and looked me directly into my eyes for a few seconds before she spoke. "He went to Earth."

My jaw dropped. "What? Are you serious?!" I was furious! My blood was boiling. I didn't really know how that was possible. *How could he go and not take me?* Out of all the places I have ever wanted to go - Earth was first on my list! He was going to get an earful from me when he got back! "How come he can go to Earth, but I can't?" I was acting like an immature child at this moment but I didn't care. When Earth came to topic, and I knew someone went without me – all reason went out the window!

"This is why I didn't want to tell you. It is for business Sophia! He wanted to check out some of their new technology and he'll be back in no time. He's been many times before; we just never told you, for your own safety of course. I don't know all the details but your Dad can take care of himself. He is a grown man. You on the other hand – you're just a young girl. Your father is not a twenty year old girl with only her estate as life experience."

My anger had disappeared and turned into sadness. It was like reality slapped me right across the face. The words Mom spoke actually hurt me in a way. They hurt because she was right. I *was* a twenty year old girl with no life experience. I hadn't been anywhere. I really hadn't gone further than my backyard! Maybe I was exaggerating a bit. I had, after all been past the forest. *But that's not enough!* I thought to myself. *I need more!*

"You're right Mom." I took my eyes off hers and looked to the ground.

Mom kept her hands on my shoulders. She didn't move away from me yet. I looked up again. As soon as I did, she removed her hands and looked at me strangely. She knew something was up. We normally butt heads when it came to my obsession to see Earth. And suddenly, there I was agreeing with her. She didn't bother to question me any further. It was Matteo's day after all.

So we sang to him and he just sat there with a certain glow to his face. Maybe it was the candles but he did look exceptionally happy. I had so many emotions running through me. For one, I was happy for Matteo. Second, I was disappointed that Dad went to Earth without me. And third, I was sad that my life was full of so many restrictions.

Matteo blew out the candles and we all clapped. I scanned the room from left to right. Servants, servants, family friends, Paul Jr., more servants - wait! REWIND! Paul Jr.? *You've got to be kidding me!* I pretended I didn't see him, but he saw me look at him since he was staring at me the whole time. *No, no, no - why now? Go away, go away, go away!* I thought maybe if I said it three times it would happen. If anything, it made things worse. He actually made his way over to me.

"Hello Sophia," Paul Jr. said with a sly tone to his voice.

"Hello, Paul," I said through my teeth as I bit down hard on my inner cheek. I didn't look him in the eye. I didn't have enough courage to do so.

Paul was standing right in front of me. Matteo didn't notice him. He seemed preoccupied with the celebration. So he couldn't save me today. *How am I going to get away from him?* I thought. I looked to Mom who was carrying over a big present for Matteo. She was no help. I looked to my left and stared out the huge window overlooking the backyard. I could see everything from the pond to the oak tree. *I can climb out the window! No, there are too many people around. I can't do that.*

Paul was staring at me the whole time I was contemplating possible escape routes. He stood there patiently. Eventually I decided to turn around and walk away without saying a word. That was a very rude thing of me to do, but I didn't care. Paul would either follow me or stay inside - I hoped he would stay inside.

I walked towards my garden and I heard footsteps behind me. *You've got to be kidding me!* He was unbelievable.

"I was hoping we could talk, please," Paul said from behind me.

I turned around. "What exactly did you want to talk about?" I asked and I started to wonder if this was worth holding a grudge over. I barely knew him. Maybe I was being too hard on him. I decided to hear him out.

I was scared to look at him. My whole body went tense when I just thought about it! I remembered what he looked like when we first met. He was flawless. I squeezed my fists so tightly that my knuckles cracked. That kind of hurt, so I let loose a little bit. I had to look up to him. If I didn't do it now, I would never be able to do it! OK, *here it goes* and I looked up.

Paul Jr. gave me such a warm forgiving smile. It was as if he were a new man. He was a beautiful man. He was even more handsome now than when he was a boy. But he wasn't any wiser. If he *was*, then he would have known better to approach me.

I sighed and asked again, "What could we possibly have to talk about?"

"Well, for one, we could talk about us," Paul said as he shrugged his shoulders.

"Us? There is no 'us'. What are you talking about?" I turned my back and started walking at a slow pace, allowing Paul Jr. walk alongside me. I couldn't stand still - I had to keep moving. I was getting too nervous to stand still at the moment. I wanted Paul Jr. to follow me now.

"We have been avoiding each other all these years for something that happened over five years ago. I have completely forgotten about the whole situation and I was wondering if you could as well." Paul's blue eyes were so forgiving.

Can I forgive and forget? Does he really deserve it? It was all so long ago. Whatever happened no longer seemed like such a big deal. I stopped walking and crossed my arms. The pond was right behind me. I looked him dead in the eye and squinted my face. "I do forgive but I *never* forget."

"Does that mean you actually *will* forgive me? Is my apology accepted?" Paul's face lit up.

"I guess so," I mumbled.

It felt good to forgive him, I suppose. People grow up as they get older right? Who they were five years ago could be the exact opposite of who they are now. Besides, I couldn't hold a grudge against that beautifully chiselled face. Just looking at him felt like there were butterflies flying around in my stomach. His smile made me weak in the knees.

Paul was staring at me. He smiled at me for reasons I really did not know. I stared back at him. The breeze blew my hair into my face. I moved it quickly out of my eyes. I needed them to see everything that was going on at this moment. Paul's stance was strong in front of me. It didn't look like he was going anywhere anytime soon. I didn't know what to say or do. I accepted his apology and I guess we were fine – *so now what?* I said to myself.

My arms were still crossed as Paul lifted one of his hands and placed it on my wrist. I dropped my hands down to my sides. I didn't want him touching me. He let go with such ease. His grip this time was much softer than the last time he grabbed my arm. His hands were so warm and soft. It was as if he were a different person.

I didn't think Paul was done. "Hmm," he said to himself. I don't think I was meant to hear that, but I did. What was he thinking?

He took a step towards me and I took one step backwards.

"It's okay. I just want to do one thing and that's it." Paul leaned in and grabbed my chin. He lifted it to kiss me.

I stood there frozen. I didn't want to kiss him! But I didn't move – I just stood there and let it happen. *Move Sophia! Move your feet and walk away.* Why wasn't I listening to myself? I felt light-headed. I had never kissed a boy before. I know - pathetic right? I was twenty years old and I had never kissed a boy. Paul's lips came closer and closer to mine. I could feel his breath on my face. My eyes slowly closed in this whole process. His lips were a hair away from mine. I felt the slightest touch of his lips to mine - that is when it happened. The electricity I felt made me snap back into it! My eyes shot open as I gasped at what was about to happen!

"No!" I screamed as I pushed him back.

That didn't work out too well because instead of me pushing *him* back, I ended up just pushing myself away from him and losing my balance. Of course with my luck I completely forgot that the pond was an inch behind me.

My heels touched the railing as my legs lost balance. My hands grabbed the empty air in front of me as I tried to reach for Paul. His reaction time was a split second off. Our fingertips grazed as I stared at a shocked Paul who was watching me fall backwards into the pond!

Everything felt like it was happening in slow motion. I hit the cold water hard - very hard. I don't know how long I was submerged at first.

I came back up for my first gasp of air and saw Paul Jr. leaning over the side, reaching his hand out to me. My first instinct was to grab it. My other hand was trying needlessly to keep myself up above the water level in order to breathe. My feet were moving frantically as well. I reached as far as I could but still it was no use. I think I felt the very tip of his finger. I went under again - I held my breath.

I used up more of my energy to get myself back up above the water. "Help me!" I managed to scream out. I begged him to save me. I tried to remember everything that Matteo taught me but I had forgotten it all. I was frantically swimming again. My chest felt tight as my breathing was merely gasps for air that I was barely getting. My lungs felt too tight - they burned and I couldn't handle it anymore. My dress was too heavy. It was weighing me down. I couldn't reach Paul's hand and he couldn't reach mine. His reaching over was useless! Why couldn't he just jump in and save me? It was no use now. I was getting tired - really tired.

"I will be back! Let me get some help!" Paul Jr. screamed.

I barely made out the end of his sentence. I couldn't keep my head above the water anymore. I opened my eyes and looked up to see him running away. I closed them right after. I stopped moving. I couldn't move my arms or legs anymore. I had no energy left in me to care right now. I felt abandoned. The last thing I remember was Paul Jr. running away and the water filling my lungs. I took one last breath. It burned. Suddenly everything went black.

Chapter 6 – The Unexpected Truth

I stood there with my eyes closed. I didn't know where I was and I barely had the energy to lift my lids. I was so dizzy that I was afraid if I did open my eyes I would fall over. I listened to everything around me but there was one problem – I couldn't hear anything. There were no sounds at all. The silence was maddening, yet I stayed focused and relaxed.

I stood there for who knows how long. I was starting to feel a bit better, so I slowly started to open my eyes. Things were blurry at first, but a few blinks fixed that. *Where am I?* I thought to myself. I looked around, only to see pure darkness. I knew my eyes were open, but it didn't feel like it. The room I was in started to become lighter. I noticed someone walking towards me. They had their head down so I couldn't tell who it was right away. They got closer and I got a better look at their face. *How was this possible? This can't be real.* I was staring at a doppelganger of *myself.*

I stood there face to face with her. I stared into her eyes. I didn't move or speak. She was a mirror image of me though something was different. She wasn't a blonde. Her hair was shorter and a dark brown shade. But everything else was the same. I had never seen myself like that before. I kind of liked the change.

I smiled at myself. My dark-haired twin smiled back at me. Her smile then faded. She looked angry - *very* angry. I was terrified. She raised both her hands with both her palms facing me. She stared directly into my eyes. I didn't move. "You're not supposed to die now." With all her force she pushed her palms into my chest. I took a step backwards from the pain. She was really strong. "Sophia it's not your time." Her voice was exactly like mine. She knocked the wind right out of me. I bent down to catch my breath. When I got back up she did it again. My back was now up against a wall that appeared out of nowhere. I couldn't take the pain. It was like a hundred pounds pushing me right in my ribs. They were going to break for sure. She did it again for the third time. My chest was burning as I was gasping for air. I didn't fight back - I couldn't fight back. *What is happening?*

My eyes automatically shot open. The force alone hurt my face. I was lying on my back. I could feel the uncomfortably hard concrete pressed up against my spine. Someone was giving me compressions on my chest. I was gasping for air. Whoever was giving me CPR turned me over so I could cough out the rest of the water from my lungs. It hurt so much. The pain was unbearable. Water even came out from my nose. *How much water did I consume?* I tightly closed my eyes hoping it would ease the pain. My chest hurt, my nose hurt, my lungs hurt, my head hurt - let's just say *everything* felt like it was being torn apart this moment. I started to cry from the pain.

I curled over into a ball and sobbed. It was all coming back to me. I was drowning – I think I actually did drown. Someone saved my life. I couldn't see clearly. My eyes were all watery and my eyelashes were clumped together. Someone was holding me now and rocked me back and forth. It was very calming. They ran their fingers through my wet hair and shushed my crying. I figured it was Matteo since I could hear a male voice. But I wasn't too sure.

I heard a woman screaming in the background. That was most likely Mom. I felt so tired. I took comfort in the warmth of this boy's embrace and from knowing that Mom was worried about me. It felt nice to know that I mattered to people. If no one cared, they would have just let me drown. *Not today though - today I was saved.*

I opened my eyes enough to see Mom running towards me in heels. I could also see Paul Jr. hovering over me. That meant Matteo really was the one who was rocking me. I was right. He pulled back to look at my face.

"Thank goodness you're awake! I was so scared I lost you!" Matteo said. His face was so worried. I had never seen him like this before.

"Let me see her," Mom said and Matteo rose so Mom could hold me.

She was hugging me tightly. I forgot what a mother's hug felt like. The sweet smell of her perfume empowered me. I raised my weak arm and hugged her back. She was sobbing into my shoulder. She was kneeling on the ground, still wearing her heels and her new dress. She didn't seem to care about ruining them. For once it seemed like I was more important than anything else.

"Let's bring you inside," Mom tried to say as she wiped the tears from her face. "Can you stand?" She tried to help me up but I was just too weak.

"Matteo, please help." Mom held my hand as Matteo picked me up. He was cradling me in his arms. I placed my head against his chest and wrapped my arms around his neck.

Paul Jr. stood there the whole time watching, not saying one word. *I hope he is ashamed of himself for leaving me like that. It's probably tearing him up inside knowing that I almost died on his watch. I would be pretty upset with myself if someone I was with almost died because of me.* Matteo started walking to the house. Once we got there, he brought me up to my room and put me to bed. Paul Jr. and Mom were right behind us.

"You should get some rest. Just relax and go to sleep," Matteo said as he pulled the covers up and under my chin.

Moments later, I was fast asleep.

***

I woke up to a warm and comfortable feeling. I could smell the familiar scent of my bedroom. I slowly opened my eyes to see the covers over my head. I still felt very weak. I pulled my covers down from my face to see someone beside me. They were passed out in a chair with half of their body learned over and lying on my bed.

It took me a while, but I was finally able to sit up. I got a better look at the person and realized it was Matteo. I was just staring at him. His clothes were wet. He was wearing the same thing that I last saw him in. *What am I wearing*? I pulled the covers down a bit and realized someone changed me into my pyjamas.

I pulled the covers back up and noticed Matteo was now awake. "How are you feeling?"

"What-" *Ow*! I grabbed my throat. Oh my goodness. My throat was killing me. It felt like someone rubbed sandpaper on the inside of my throat. I couldn't even finish my sentence. I gulped back a bit of saliva as it burned. I tried to speak again, but this time I only whispered.

"What happened?" At least I could whisper.

"I saved your life. Sophia, you almost died!" Matteo sat back in the chair and put his hands on his head. He looked devastated.

"How?" I whispered again.

"I was watching you and Paul Jr. the whole time you guys were walking. I was going to stop you, but you looked like you wanted to talk to him. You even smiled at him. He didn't look like he meant any harm, so I let him. But I never took my eyes off you two – not even once! I saw him about to kiss you. As soon as I saw that I looked away. I figured you forgave him. I felt happy for you. After all these years you forgave him and now you even realized you love him."

"I do *not* love him!" I interrupted, having to grip my throat from the pain.

Matteo just looked at me and I realized it was rude of me to interrupt him. "Sorry," I mouthed. I was going to sit quietly now.

"It's okay. Well, I went back to opening my gifts with a smile on my face. I knew you must be happy so that made me happy. At the same time, something just didn't feel right. I knew it was none of my business but I had to look up one more time. When I did, I literally saw you falling into the water. As soon as I saw that, I automatically dropped what was in my hand, jumped onto the table and ran outside to save you. I realized Paul Jr. was useless when I saw him running towards me. I passed him and he stopped to watch me. I didn't waste any time. I jumped right into the cold water after you. I swam down - you were almost all the way to the bottom of the pond. I don't know why anyone ever needed a pond that deep.

"I pulled you out and lay you on the ground. For one second I just stared at you. Your face was all white and your lips were blue. Paul was behind me, watching intensely. All that was running through my head was, '*She can't be dead. Please don't let it be!*'" Matteo was staring right through me – probably picturing what I looked like when he pulled me out of the water.

"I thought you were dead and I was too late. I put all the blame on myself if you didn't survive. I started giving you CPR. Your lips were like ice to mine. It was very disturbing. It didn't feel right - at all. I was compressing your chest but always in the back of my mind I was preparing for the worst. As soon as you opened your eyes I felt relief flood through my body. I knew you were going to be okay." Matteo was nodding his head.

I felt bad now. I realized my heartbeat was pounding in my chest the whole time Matteo was telling me this. It was scary. *What if I actually did die?* All of Matteo's caring feelings came out right in the open. He really did care for me. It made me happy knowing I had someone there to watch over me. Matteo was like my guardian angel.

Something had just occurred to me! *Where is Kiko?* Those two are inseparable. I straightened my back to look over my bed. Kiko was right there lying down on the ground, listening to everything we were talking about. I sat back down on my bed.

I heard footsteps coming from the hallway. They were getting closer and closer. Matteo and I both looked towards the door and waited for whomever to walk in.

Mom walked through the door. As soon as she saw me sitting up and awake she automatically dashed for my bed. Matteo had to move back to make space for her. She sat on my bed and hugged me. She pulled back to look at me. "I am so glad you are awake. You scared us all!"

"I'm fine Mom." My voice was getting stronger.

More footsteps were coming towards my room. I was hoping it wasn't going to be Paul. Thankfully it wasn't. It was Dad. Paul Jr. was behind him - of course. Dad came and stood beside Mom. He asked me if I was alright. He didn't seem as worried as Mom was. I guess he knew I was a tough cookie. He just smiled at me when he saw me smiling at Mom.

Paul was holding a tea pot in one hand and a cup already filled in the other. He placed it on the table beside my bed. I was actually surprised by that motion. Normally the servants would bring it. I figured Paul Jr. was trying to suck up to me. It was something I definitely expected. I was so furious with him for leaving me to die like that! *We just fixed things between us and then he goes and ruins it all!*

"Sophia," Mom placed her hand on mine. She looked deeply into my eyes. Her eyes looked like they were filled with sorrow. It was as if I could see into the pit of her soul. It didn't look too happy.

I raised my eyebrow at her. "Yes?" I asked as I stretched out the word.

She looked up to Dad. He nodded and she stared back at me. "There is something your father and I would like to tell you."

"Can you give us some privacy?" Dad said, turning to Matteo and Paul. They both started to walk out the door.

"Matteo, wait. You can stay," Mom said before he was out the door.

"How come he gets to stay?" Paul Jr. asked. It sounded like he was complaining. He looked upset.

My parents just stared at him. They never repeated themselves twice.

Paul Jr. caught on stormed out. I could hear him mumbling something to himself as he left. I kept in my laughter.

Matteo came around my bed and sat on my left side. Mom sat on the right side of me while Dad was still standing beside her with his strong posture.

"What is this about?" I asked.

"It is something we have been keeping from you your whole life. We didn't mean to, but we thought it was for the best. Now, I'm not too sure anymore. Your father and I have done wrong by you."

Matteo and I stared at each other in confusion.

Mom was so nervous and her hands started to twitch. It was actually very intimidating. I wasn't too sure if I wanted to know what she was going to say. She was starting to make me nervous.

I knew I wasn't going to get any answers from her so I turned to Dad, "Dad, what is going on?"

"What your mother is trying to say is that… We knew Matteo before you."

"Huh?" I said as I looked to Matteo. He just stared at Dad. He squinted his eyes like he was remembering something.

Mom inhaled deeply. "Sophia. Matteo is your brother!"

My jaw dropped as I looked to Matteo. He was in just as much shock as I was - maybe even more. His eyes were wide open and he stared back at me. We were both astonished. *Matteo is my brother?* A million other questions were running through my mind. *How come I didn't know?* I couldn't comprehend what had just happened. *Why didn't they tell me? How did I not realize?* The only trait we had in common was our blue eyes. No wonder every time I looked into them it left me with a familiar feeling. It was like I was looking into my own eyes.

"It is the truth. Just in case you think I am lying. A long time ago, there was an accident and we were all separated. Our car crashed and everyone flew out." Mom stopped. She covered her face with her hands. She started to sob. I'd never seen Mom cry before. It left a pinching feeling in my throat. I tried to hold it back but it was too painful. I started to tear up as well. It hurt me to see my mother like this.

"Sophia, you were one year old while Matteo was three. We only found you because we could hear you crying. That's what led us to you. We couldn't find Matteo. We looked for hours, days and even weeks. We stopped looking when we found his ripped up clothes. We assumed that one of the wild animals found him and…" Dad stopped talking.

I didn't know what to say. I needed time to process all of this new information. My life was starting to look more exciting after all!

Chapter 7 – Recap

Mom and Dad left Matteo and me alone to talk. We both just learned we were brother and sister and we had no idea! I could see the sadness in Mom's eyes. She felt terrible, keeping this secret from me all my life. She felt even worse keeping it from Matteo all these years as well. I had to admit it was a hard subject to bring up. It is not something one would talk about at the dinner table. *'Can you pass the peas? Oh by the way, Matteo is your brother.'* Now that wouldn't have turned out too well. I think now had to have been to perfect time to tell us.

I wasn't mad at them like they expected both Matteo and I would be. Matteo was the farthest thing from being upset. He looked like the happiest person in the world. When it did finally sink in - after the shock - Matteo turned to me and gave me a huge hug. He whispered 'sister' into my ear.

I couldn't explain how I felt. So many things were going on in my mind. I was trying so hard to remember something, *anything* about Matteo. Nothing came to mind when I thought back that far. I was just a little baby. There was no way I could remember that far back. I had no memory of Matteo.

Matteo broke the silence a couple minutes after our parents left the room. I had no idea what to say. "So you're my sister huh?" Matteo messed up my hair at the top of my head. It broke me out of my concentration.

I grabbed his hand and moved it from my head. I felt a sense of fulfilment in my heart. Just knowing that Matteo was my brother made things fall just the way they were supposed to. It was like the pieces of the puzzle were sitting exactly the way I wanted them to. But of course with me, there was always that one little corner piece missing. It was always either hiding under the rug or long gone, lost somewhere in the couch pillows. I could now rejoice in finding at my long lost brother.

"Sophia, did you ever feel like something was ever missing in your life - like something just wasn't right?" Matteo asked as he looked down at his hands. He was nervously playing with the end of the covers.

I thought about his question and realized my whole life felt like something *was* missing. I didn't fit in anywhere and I always felt like it was my fault for not being part of the crowd. I would never in a million years think that I had a brother. It was like my subconscious self always knew I had a brother. It made me feel that way since I didn't have the brotherly protection from him for all those years.

"It did feel like something was missing," I confessed to him. "I just never knew it was that I once had a brother. After all these years of feeling that way, I now feel better knowing that I will always have you there protecting me like you have been doing." I smiled at him.

He didn't see me smiling. He still had his head down even though he was listening to everything I said. He would nod and the corner of his mouth would rise.

Matteo looked so innocent. I could tell that I wasn't the only person happy to have found a long lost sibling. I only wonder how he feels about having found his little sister! With most of my energy, I pulled my arm back and swung it to hit Matteo right across left his arm.

Matteo looked at me with shock covering his face. His eyes opened wide and his jaw dropped. "Ow, what was that for?" Matteo said laughing. I knew it didn't hurt. It just took him by surprise more than anything.

"I don't know," I replied. "I just felt like I owed you that from all the years of not bugging you when we were children."

Matteo looked at me like I was crazy. I deserved that. His crazy look turned into a devilish one. I didn't like where this was heading.

He jumped and put me in a headlock. I screamed as loud as I could. I tried to pull him off but he was too strong. He was giving me a noogie!

"So that's how you want to play?" he said, but I barely heard him. All I could hear was the scratching noise of my own hair on my scalp under his hard knuckles.

He eventually let go off me. He sat back in the spot where he was sitting before.

My hair was all over the place. I tried to fix it but it was radiating off static electricity. I could hear it crackling as I tried to smooth it back. My hair was getting stuck everywhere. Long blonde hair was hard enough to manage. I didn't need an annoying brother ruining it even more. *Hmm, brother – feels good to say that.*

I tamed my hair a little bit and gave Matteo the evil eye. It didn't bother him.

Matteo was sitting on my bed. "Okay, we're even now!" He said as he squared his shoulders. "Let's figure this out now."

"Figure what out?" I had no idea what he was talking about. My legs were starting to feel hot. I guessed my body was all warmed up now from being frozen from the water. I kicked the covers back and away from me. Matteo helped to pull them back. We pushed them almost all the way down to the end of the bed.

As soon as the covers were pushed all the way back Kiko jumped on the bed. We all heard an odd creaking noise from the weight of all three of us combined. I thought the bed was going to break. We all stopped to look at each other. I could tell we were all thinking the same thing – *please don't break*! A few seconds passed and nothing happened. We all relaxed and I went back to being confused about what Matteo said.

"What were we talking about?" I asked again. I really meant it.

He jokingly shook his head in disappointment. I felt like our relationship grew so much in these past few minutes. We could just relax now knowing we weren't secretly strangers. All along, deep down inside, we both knew there was something else. But neither of us knew what it was. I played off his head shake and waited patiently for him to continue. I knew eventually he would if no one said anything.

"I don't know. I just want to clear things up for my own personal reasons. You have to either agree or disagree with me alright?" Matteo looked at me seriously.

I looked over to Kiko. He was laying there with his head on top of his paws. He looked so sad. He was probably bored from being in my room for so long. I was feeling the same way, but I knew I couldn't leave until we were done talking here. After this I planned to get up. Kiko just looked at me with his eyes filled with sadness. "We will go outside soon, don't worry," I said with a baby tone to my voice and rubbed his head. His eyes filled with delight

I turned to Matteo. "Alright!"

"Well my name is Matteo and yours is Sophia," he started.

I rolled my eyes and tilted my head backwards. I didn't know he was going to go so in depth. I didn't want to do this. I groaned on purpose to let him know I didn't want to listen. I lay back down on my bed pretending

I was dead. I stuck my tongue out and let it hang out of my mouth. My head lay limp to the left side facing Matteo.

He didn't move or make a sound. I peeked open one of my eyes to make sure he was still there. He was still sitting there. And he still was. He just stared at me with one eyebrow raised.

I put my tongue back in my mouth and opened both my eyes. I got up. I figured there was no point in playing dead. He wasn't going to move until he was finished.

"You done?" Matteo asked with an agitated tone in his voice. His eyes could never conceal his true feelings. He was holding back a smile with all his power.

I guess stalling wasn't doing us any good. He wanted to get this over with just as much as I did. He wanted answers while I wanted to go outside. I figured it was time I just stop all of this and give him what he wants. That was the only way I was going to end this.

I exaggerated the whole process of sitting up straight, prim, and proper. I neatly crossed my legs and folded my hands in my lap. "Yes, if you insist." I was all ears.

"Okay, so where were we now? Oh, yeah, we got *our* names down. Our parent's names are Antonio and Susanna. Our last name is Amaro. That is our family. It's just the four of us."

It felt so odd when Matteo said our parents' names. I never addressed them with their first names - even if I was utterly mad at them. I would always call them Mom and Dad - never Susanna and Antonio. Even saying it in my head even sounded weird. Either way, those are their names.

Matteo continued to talk. "I guess there is your *stalker* Paul Jr. to take into consideration as well." As soon as he said that he shielded himself with both arms. He knew I was going to hit him for saying that.

I didn't hit him. I just opened my mouth and laughed out, "He's not my stalker. He is just in love with the fact I don't want him. And I will never want him for that fact." I nodded my head like I made up my mind - which I did.

I realized Matteo was being more carefree with me now. He never made fun of me like this before. It was weird but nice at the same time. I had a brother that I could bug, and he had a little sister he could annoy. *I could get used to this!*

"I know. I am just teasing you. It is just so easy!"

"Alright, alright. You can continue with your lesson or whatever you are giving me. Go on with your little recap." I fanned my hand towards so that he could continue.

He sighed. "Alright. How about our ages? I am twenty-two and you are twenty. Oh, and your lover is the same age as me," Matteo snorted.

I closed my eyes and inhaled deeply through my nose. I thought to myself. *'Relax; he is just doing it to get under your skin.'* I exhaled slowly through my mouth and opened my eyes. I tilted my head slightly to the side and smiled sarcastically.

He continued knowing my patience was slipping. "Let's do birthdays now. Your birthday is…" He waited for me to answer.

"October 4th," I said.

"Yes, and my birthday is February 24th." Matteo stopped and was thinking about something. He looked at me and his eyebrows creased. "Shoot! I don't know our parents' birthdays. I have to find out!" Matteo was shocked at himself.

Come to think of it - I didn't even know my parents birthdays. I suppose they didn't feel the need to celebrate theirs because it just meant they were getting older.

Speaking of my parents - I could actually hear them talking. I couldn't tell if they were in the hallway outside my room, or if they were down the staircase. Voices echoed throughout the house like you wouldn't believe.

"Okay," I yawned.

Kiko yawned as well. Yawns are contagious. Even for animals as well, I guess.

"Forget it. I am done. Let's go outside," Matteo said as he stood up from my bed.

I squealed in excitement as I jumped off the bed. I almost fell over. I had to stop and compose myself. I had the biggest head rush. When I was ready, I walked into the washroom closing the door behind me. I went into one of my drawers and pulled out a simple light dress. I was out in less than two seconds. I changed very quickly. It was quick and simple to slip off my pyjamas and into the dress. I was still a little groggy so I splashed water on my face to wake up.

I opened the washroom door and hurriedly walked out of my room. I skidded to a stop and realized I had no shoes on. I ran back to my room and saw my shoes beside my bed. I slipped them on and automatically ran back to where I was before - out my bedroom door. Kiko jumped off the bed to chase after me. Matteo was right behind. I ran down the stairs –

holding on to the railing of course. I knew if I were to ever fall down these stairs, I could get seriously injured.

I will never forget the first time I fell down these stairs. I think I was about seven years old and I was in such a rush to go somewhere – I don't know where – and I lost my balance as I ran down. Luckily I was about five or six steps up, but I still felt the full effect. I don't exactly know how I lost my balance. There must have been water on the steps that I slipped on, or I could have even tripped on my dress. Either way, my legs flew into the air in front of me while I wiped out backwards. My back hit the marble steps first with a crashing effect. It was like someone threw me into a brick wall.

It felt as if someone sucked all the air out of my lungs. I didn't even have time to scream after I fell down. The wind was completely knocked out of me. I slid all the way down to the end. My eyes and mouth both shot open. My lungs were desperately trying to take in air.

It took me a couple minutes to breathe normally. Nothing was broken but I thought I was going to pass out and never wake up. No one found me since I made no noise. I didn't cry. That was another thing I remember. I just didn't cry. I got up alone and told no one what had happened. I had a bruise, but it was hidden by my dress.

Ever since that day, I always held onto the handrail. I never wanted to go through that again. That was one thing in my life I could do without. It was horrible thinking I was never going to recover from the feeling of not being able to breathe.

I ran all the way outside. The golden rays of the sun were beaming on my skin. I stopped to enjoy it as I tilted my head back. I never realized how cold my house was until I actually came outside to rejoice in the warmth of the sun. I breathed in to fill my lungs with the smell of the outdoors. The smell was a mixture of the fresh cut grass along with the smell of the warm wind. It felt all so refreshing.

Kiko ran past me. I heard his paws hitting the cement ground as he passed me. He was fast. I looked back down and ran after him. I caught up with him and was just jumping around him. He was playing along with me trying to jump as well. He lifted his paws in the air a bit and jumped along. I was laughing uncontrollably. I never knew tigers could actually jump like that.

I loved acting like a kid. I didn't care what age I was. I will always be a little child at heart. Running in the field and playing in the dirt is part of who I am and I will never change that for anything or anyone!

I looked back and realized Matteo was falling behind. I walked up to him and grabbed his hand. I made him twirl me around like a ballerina. He played along with it. We were both laughing and having a good time.

"Uh oh," Matteo said as he stopped spinning me.

"What?" I said out of breath. Twirling and jumping around really took the energy right out of me.

Matteo was looking behind me. I looked over my shoulder. Paul Jr. was walking towards us.

I automatically stopped laughing and my smile faded. I was starting to get creeped out by Paul. He spent *way* too much time wandering the perimeters of my house. Did he not have a house of his own? It was getting kind of annoying now. I couldn't walk peacefully in and out my own house without seeing him somewhere! I just wanted to yell, '*Go Home!*'

He walked up to us. "So, let me guess. You two are a couple now, I suppose?" Paul spoke with a sour tone.

I looked to Matteo; my head filled with confusion and shock. We made eye contact and I wanted to burst out into laughter. I forgot that no one else knew that Matteo was my brother. I could have a little bit of fun with this. I decided to play along with the idea of Matteo as my boyfriend. Maybe if Paul Jr. thought that, he would leave me alone. I linked my arm around Matteo's. He looked at me in surprise, but caught on to my plan. He played along with me and pulled me closer to him.

"It is just so hard to fight the urges towards someone." I was talking extravagantly. I coughed back a laugh. I had to cover my mouth to hide my smile.

Paul bought it. He stared at Matteo with such hate. He always looked at him like that. Ever since the first day he met him under my oak tree, he has loathed the site of Matteo and I together. I wondered what he thought of when he saw Matteo and I arm in arm. Was he mad or jealous?

Would he accept the idea of us together or would he try and break us apart? Something in his eyes told me that he was up to something - something not good.

Paul Jr. had his arms behind his back. He rocked back and forth on his heels. "Well then, if that is how you feel."

"Yup." I almost cut him off. I looked at Matteo and nodded my head. He looked back at me and nodded his head as well. Matteo was a very good actor.

Paul Jr. just stood there staring. Once again we hit another awkward moment. It was as if Paul could not remove his gaze off me. It looked as if he were trying to see into my brain to know my true thoughts. I felt shivers down my spine. I thought of ways to get past this. The perfect idea sprung to my head.

I pulled Matteo's arm down and pushed myself up with my toes. I reached and put my hand on Matteo's cheek to pull it closer to mine. I gently put my lips to his cheek and gave him a sisterly kiss. It was something I had never done before, but it showed the love I had for my elder brother. Matteo didn't seem to mind. He was being such a good sport about all of this. Only because he disliked Paul just as much as I did - maybe even more.

Paul snapped back into reality and blinked his eyes a couple of times. I guess he was trying to erase from his mind what he had just seen. He seemed like a calm guy, but also it seemed like there was something else hidden on the inside that no one could see. It was as if he were hiding his true self behind that composed face.

"I'll leave you two alone then. I must be on my way home anyway," Paul nodded his head and walked away.

Matteo and I watched him walk around the manor until he was completely out of sight. As soon as the coast was clear, we burst into laughter! We were clutching onto our stomachs because when you laugh that hard, it kind of starts to hurt a bit.

"Did you see his face?" Matteo could barely get the words out. But I am pretty sure that's what he said.

"Yeah! Poor thing, I kind of feel bad for him." I was laughing so hard I had to wipe my tears.

Matteo just stopped and looked at me.

"I am just kidding!"

Matteo started to walk as I followed him. Kiko was with us the whole time.

"Sophia!" I heard someone yell. It sounded like Dad.

His voice was very deep. I turned around to see Dad standing at the back entrance of our house. I don't know what he wanted but his posture was telling me he didn't look too happy. He stood there with his legs shoulder width apart and his arms were crossed. I started walking back towards him. I was about to find out what he wanted. Truthfully, I was actually a bit scared.

Chapter 8 – Unsettling Ride

What could Dad be calling me for? I wondered. I kept replaying in my mind what had happened since the last time we talked. Dad told me Matteo was my brother and that was it. He didn't seem mad when he left the room. I didn't do anything bad after that so I couldn't be in trouble at this moment. He couldn't punish me for something I never did. But still, I was so nervous. Parents always find things to punish you for – things that you have long forgotten about. Maybe he saw the whole incident with Paul. Maybe before Paul Jr. left, he went and spoke to Dad, telling him Matteo and I were a couple! *Paul Jr. better be ready for an earful from me if that's the case!* I told myself. Then Dad would tell me that was the wrong thing to do and give me a fatherly lecture which I would have to obediently endure. *I might as well explain myself before he says anything.*

"Dad, listen, what happe-"

Dad took a deep breath. His chest rose. "Sophia, you know what?" Dad completely cut me off which took me by surprise.

I looked up at him. He looked unusually taller today for some reason. I had to tilt my head backwards in order to see his face. I looked down and realized he was standing on the step the whole time. He looked right over my head into the distance. I looked back and realized Matteo and Kiko were gone. They were probably off somewhere wandering.

Dad took a step down and was standing right beside me. He put his arm around my shoulder and we started walking.

"You know what we haven't done in a while?" he asked, looking ahead.

"No?" I was confused. So I guess I wasn't in trouble.

"Horse-back riding!" Dad turned and looked at me. His face was filled with excitement and joy. I guessed he felt free now, knowing he got everything off his chest.

That is why he called me over here? It seemed Paul Jr. didn't talk to him after all. I wasn't in trouble then! What Dad said was true - we really hadn't been horse-back riding in a long time. In fact, I couldn't remember the last time we had been. Maybe when I was ten years old – possibly twelve.

"So, what do you say?" Dad raised his eyebrows in anticipation.

I didn't have any other plans so I accepted his invitation. In fact, I was excited about it. This was a golden opportunity for us to catch up on lost time. I didn't know what we would talk about – besides the obvious, anyway. But I did look forward to spending some father-daughter time together. I wondered where Mom was.

"Sure, sounds like fun!" I said enthusiastically. "Where's Mom, by the way?" I felt like being nosey.

"She went shopping. She said she needed to buy a few things. I never ask. I just let her buy whatever she needs. But in most cases she doesn't need the things she buys. So really; I let her buy whatever she wants." Dad laughed. His charming smile came through. I couldn't help but smile back. Mom *did* love her shopping.

We walked to the stables in silence. Neither one of us spoke. I forgot what the stable even looked like. The barn was always white. It looked as though it had been recently repainted. Dad went straight to his horse while I went to mine. I walked over and peeked into its holding area.

There my horse was – white and beautiful as ever. His coat was so shiny and smooth. His name was Pegasus. He looked at me and started making weird noises. I wondered if he remembered me. I came closer to him and stroked his mane. He lowered his head down so I could pet him properly. The servants took good care of my horse. I had been neglecting him all these years, yet it still seemed like he loved me no matter what. I could see Dad a little further down talking to his horse. His horse was black as night.

Dad told me the story he learned about a horse named Pegasus who could fly. That is where I got the name from. I remember when I was young; I use to wish that Pegasus would have wings. I would fly to any place that I wanted. But no matter how hard I wished, the wings never came.

I opened the door and walked into his holding area. I picked up the saddle to place on Pegasus' back. Dad came over with his horse. He tied it to the railing and came to help me put the saddle on mine. It was much heavier than it looked.

Dad helped me up and we were ready to head onto our riding path. It was just a little pathway that we always took. There was forest beside us on both sides. There was no other way to go, other than straight. We didn't venture into the forest. The trees were too close to each other and you could easily get lost or hurt. The green trees and bushes blossomed in this weather. All my memories of riding came back to me as soon as we started moving. Riding a horse was something I could never forget how to do.

I could see Dad looking at me from the corner of my eye.

"Sophia, I have a confession to make," he said as he took his gaze off me and looked ahead.

I looked at him and my mouth dropped slightly. *What was he going to say? I have* another *long lost brother or sister?*

"Okay?" That was the only thing I could say. "I don't have another brother or sister you're not telling me about, right?" I couldn't keep it in. I had to ask.

Dad's head whisked to my direction. "Oh no, no, no! Not even close!" He even shuddered at the thought.

"Thank goodness," I whispered.

"The thing is..." I could see Dad biting his bottom lip. It looked as if he didn't want to say - whatever it is he was about to say. "We're cowards. Your mother and I are cowards. We have been hiding the truth from you your whole life. The first day your mother saw Matteo she came running to me. I had to calm her down so she could get the words out. She told me what she saw but I needed to make sure for myself. I knew if I saw Matteo, I would be able to know right away if he was indeed my son – no matter how much time had passed. When I ran into him the first time, I knew immediately he was my son. Your mother and I both knew he was ours."

I let Dad speak. I think he wanted to get rid of all the frustration that had built up inside of him all these years. That is something big to keep locked away inside of you. That kind of secret would tear you apart piece by piece. Getting it all out in the open must have been his way of fixing that void.

Dad continued to speak. "For a parent to lose their child... that... that is the worst thing that can happen to anyone in their lifetime. The moment we got into that accident, the first thing I thought of was you and Matteo. I needed to make sure you were okay, but you two were in the back. I grabbed onto your mother and prayed everything would be fine.

We were all thrown in different directions. Your mother and I were only a few feet apart. I will never forget the look on her face as soon as we both got up. Her eyes were in shock, slowly filling with tears. We got up from the ground - covered in dirt and leaves - and looked for the two of you. We couldn't find you. That is when your mother started to panic. She couldn't breathe, stand or even talk. I had to hold her up and search for you at the same time. She fell to the ground sobbing at one point. I tried comforting her. We sat on the ground for no more than a couple of seconds. That is when we heard you cry. Your mother's crying stopped automatically. We stayed completely still, just so we could hear more clearly. We followed your cries and I picked you up from the ground. You were cut on the back of your neck, but other than that, you were fine. You even have a scar on your neck 'til this day on your right side."

I automatically let the reigns go with my right arm and felt the back of my neck. I never noticed anything there before. I couldn't really see the back of my neck in the mirror anyway. "Seriously?" I asked.

"Seriously," Dad answered. "I am only telling you this because I feel like we owe it to you, after keeping this from you all this time."

I nodded.

"The three of us - you, your mother, and I - sat on the cold ground in silence. We waited for another cry. We waited a couple of minutes, but heard nothing. I was the one cradling you in my arms. My heart was beating frantically. Whenever I picked you up, you would instantly stop crying. Your mother would always make me hold you since she could never get you to stop crying. I think it was because you liked me better. I didn't mind holding you. You fit perfectly into my arms. You were just so small. We then got up and started looking for Matteo. We called out his name many, many times but no response. Night came and we knew we had to go home. It wasn't safe to be in the forest at night. Your mother didn't want to leave but I knew we had to. I had to drag her out and bring her home. She cried the whole night." Dad stopped to clear his throat. I knew he was just stalling since this was hard for him to say. "First thing in the morning, as soon as the sun rose, I was out searching in the woods. I searched all day, taking not even one break. Matteo was my first boy, he was so small, and I had so many things to teach him. And just like that, he was gone - gone forever and I knew I would never see him again. In the back of my mind I knew, being lost meant eventually being found, so I didn't give up that easily. Until that one day when I found Matteo's little shirt and pants ripped to shreds." Dad's voice cut out. Clearing his throat wouldn't help this time.

Tears were starting to form in my eyes but I fought them back. Well, I tried my best at least. Seeing Dad in this much pain actually hurt me as well. I have never seen Dad almost cry before - never! The back of my throat burned from holding back the tears. I gripped the reigns as tight as I could to distract myself.

"Anyway, now I know he is fine and that's all that matters." Dad sighed and then looked to me. "Um, is there anything you would like to tell me? How are you handling all of this? I don't mean to overwhelm you sweetie."

I think that's the first time I heard Dad call me sweetie. It was kind of nice. *What should I tell him?* I searched my brain trying to come up with something. "Well it was a lot to take in, but he was already my brother without you telling me that he actually was."

I didn't know what else to say. I wasn't used to opening up to my family. I couldn't think of the right words. *I hope he doesn't ask me any more questions on how I feel. I think it's time to change the subject.*

"Okay -"

"So how was Earth?" It's rude to cut someone off, but I had to.

"Well, I was having trouble with the Portal, but other than -" Dad stopped talking.

My jaw dropped. Not just a little bit this time. I even think my jaw hit all the way to the ground. My eyes shot open as I stared to my right, towards Dad. *There was a portal? I never knew about this! I actually never even thought about how he travelled there. Why didn't I think of this before?* So many questions were running through my mind. I didn't even know where to start.

"Portal? What? Where? How do you use it?" The questions couldn't come out of my mouth fast enough!

"Never mind I said anything!" Dad was biting the inside of his cheeks. He didn't look at me. He straightened his back and tightened his grip on his reigns.

"Wait, how do I use the Portal? Can anyone use it?"

"No! You are never to use it! I mean - there is no portal! Just drop the subject! We have spoken about this already! You are not going to Earth!"

That was the first time I heard Dad yell at me like that. He really didn't want me going to Earth! I was itching to ask more questions but I knew Dad would just get more upset. I couldn't finish the ride without finding out more information about this so called Portal! I was biting on my tongue so hard I think I it was starting to bleed.

We were riding our horses at a slow pace through the pathway. Neither one of us spoke. I knew if I opened my mouth I would just ask a question about the Portal. Dad didn't speak because he was probably kicking himself for even bringing it up!

The ground was worn away and made a visible pathway from being ridden over so many times. Over the years though, the grass started to grow back, since we didn't ride as often as we used to. I hoped we could work the ground in again. Things were going to be different. I could feel it and I knew I could get used to it.

I could tell by now neither of us was going to say anything for the rest of the ride. What was supposed to be an enjoyable ride, took a turn for the worse. We were just enjoying the ride. I expected it to be bumpier, but for some reason it wasn't. It was like Pegasus and I were working as one. My body was moving to the pace of his steps. The clip clop noise on the ground was actually very relaxing. The slight breeze blew back my hair. It was very hot out today and I could feel sweat building up at the back of my neck. Luckily the breeze was taking care of that beautifully. It was very refreshing.

I heard a nearby rustling sound. I couldn't tell if it was in the trees or on the ground. The noise was too quick for me. As soon as Dad and I turned our heads to see what it was, the noise had stopped. Dad gave me a calming, reassuring smile and looked straight ahead.

The moment he did, something quickly came out of nowhere, jumped in front of Dad's horse and ran off. We were startled. I can admit that it actually scared me. I didn't even see what it was. It just looked like a black blur to me, as big as a medium sized dog, but I knew there were no dogs around here.

Dad's horse completely lost his composure. He rose to his hind legs, neighing uncontrollably. Dad tried to get him to relax but he wasn't listening. He darted off. I went to go follow. I kicked my heels with just enough force to command Pegasus to run after them. Dad's horse was much faster than mine was. I was falling behind but I could hear Dad's commanding voice, trying to calm it down.

I yelled out to Dad, but he couldn't hear me over his horse's screams. I had never seen anything like this before. Dad can normally control him but this was getting out of hand. Dad's final attempt to settle him down went terribly wrong.

The horse rose up on his hind legs again, but this time he flung Dad right off his back! Dad fell back with a petrified scream that echoed through our surroundings. I saw the whole thing happen. At first I wasn't scared because I thought he would be fine. But now I wasn't too sure.

I jumped off my horse as soon as I caught up with Dad. As soon as I hit the ground, a sharp pain spread from my foot up to my ankle. I ignored it and fell to the ground beside Dad. He was lying on his side with his back to me. I rolled him over with all my strength and saw he had a huge gash on his forehead. It was so deep I could see his skull. Blood was gushing out of it.

I froze in horror. My hand clasped my mouth. My first instinct was to stop the bleeding. With both of my hands I pressed down on Dad's head as hard as I could. His blood was so warm. It slid through my fingers. I held my breath as I started to feel nauseous.

"Dad? Dad, can you hear me?" He was unresponsive. I had to get him to wake up. Sobs started to fill my chest. I wiped my tears with the back of my blood-stained hand. *What do I do now?*

Chapter 9 – Bad News

I ran back home as fast as I could. I left Dad there alone on the path. As much as I didn't want to leave him there, I had no other choice. I had to get help. I tried to ignore the pain in my ankle as I ran. The pain worsened with every step I took. At first it was a burning sensation just in my foot and ankle. Now the pain was shooting up my leg. I had to put Dad first and think about him rather than myself. I was starting to get dizzy and things were starting to blur. I blinked hard to get rid of the tears in my eyes. I knew I couldn't touch my eyes with my hands since they were filthy.

I looked around as I ran, searching for anyone who could help. I noticed someone kneeling down. I recognized one of the gardeners. It looked as if they were planting something, but I couldn't see clearly. I screamed at the top of my lungs for help.

The gardener turned around and looked at me. She dropped everything and ran over to me. She ran so fast that her hat flew right off her head. As soon as she reached me she grabbed my arms. At that moment my legs gave out. I could no longer stand. I fell to the floor, hands shaking. She came down in front of me and grabbed my face.

I could tell now that it was Romina. She was our favourite gardener. She took a good look at me and started panicking. "Dear Lord, what happened to you sweetie?" She frantically moved the hair from my face. The tears made my hair stick to my cheeks. "Are you alright? Why are your hands bloody?"

I tried to speak, but the words couldn't come out of my mouth. All that was coming out was sobs.

"Sophia!" I heard Matteo call. I looked up past Romina and saw Matteo and Kiko running towards me. They were blurry, but I knew it was them. Who else would be running with a full grown, male tiger beside them?

Matteo dropped to the ground in front of me. He placed both his hands on my face to make me look at him. His grip on my face was so strong. He emphasized his words. "What happened; where is our father?" Matteo saw me leaving with Dad, but didn't see me return with him.

This reminded me of when Matteo and I first met. I spoke very slowly when I thought he couldn't understand me. "The path... he fell... his blood..." I managed to get those words out. I looked down at my hands and showed him the blood.

Matteo automatically rose and ran towards the pathway. Kiko stayed with me. He started licking my hands clean. My heart was pounding. I had to calm down. I felt like I was going to give myself a heart attack if I didn't pace my breathing. I closed my eyes and tried to take in full deep breaths instead of short sharp ones. It started to work. I just kept thinking that Matteo would help him. I knew he would.

Romina helped me up. I needed her to help support my weight since I couldn't stand on my left foot by myself. It felt like someone was stabbing me in the ankle with one hundred sharp needles. It was almost numbing. On top of that, my head was now starting to hurt. This was just too much for my body to handle. I took a couple of steps and heard constant thuds. I guess my headache was worse than I thought.

They were getting louder and I realized it wasn't my head that was making that noise. It was the horses' hooves hitting the ground rapidly. I started to turn but before I could, Pegasus flew right by me. Matteo was on top of Pegasus. "I'll be back!" Matteo yelled. I also noticed Dad lying across the horse's back. Matteo was taking him to the house. I breathed a sigh of relief.

I wanted to run after him but I knew that wasn't going to happen. I slowly took my time as Romina and Kiko helped me back home.

It didn't take me that long to get to the house. Kiko and Romina were a good support team. I made it before Matteo could come get me. We met right at the back where the rear entrance stairs were. Matteo saw me and picked me up. He carried me in his arms. He knew I couldn't walk. He brought me to the living room. I noticed Dad was lying on the couch with his head wrapped in bandages all the way around. Matteo placed me on the other couch beside him. I wanted to get up and see how he was doing but Matteo told me to sit and not to move. Dr. Slike was there. He was the town doctor. Someone must have called him. I guess Matteo asked one of the servants for the number or something. Dr. Slike was quick to get here!

Dr. Slike was hovering over Dad, checking his pulse and doing doctorly things like that. Dr. Slike had been making house calls at our place ever since I was a little girl. Every time I got sick, he would come and make sure I was fine. He was one of the best known doctors on Caledonia.

Clara was there. She was the servant who had washed Matteo the first day I brought him home. I knew I could always count on her. She was there with a washcloth and a large bowl filled with warm water. She washed my face and hands with it. I knew I had to take a shower but this felt amazing for now.

Matteo walked over to Dr. Slike and pointed me out. Dr. Slike was an elderly man. He had white hair and thick glasses with a black rim. He always wore black underneath his white coat. He could tell what was wrong with his patients just by looking at them. As soon as he saw me, he automatically looked down at my foot.

Clara got up and left the living room. "I'll go run you a warm bath," she whispered as she left.

Dr. Slike walked over to the other side of the room and grabbed a chair. He brought it in front of me and sat down. He leaned over and grabbed my left foot. I forgot about the pain if I didn't move it. As soon as he grabbed it I squeezed my fists together from the pain. I let out a little squeal as he lifted it up and placed my foot on his knee.

He put his hand under my heel and took off my shoe. After he removed my shoe, he slipped off my sock. I looked over to see my foot. My ankle was all purple. My stomach started to turn. I started getting nauseous and light headed. My chest tightened up as I wiped my head with my hand. Matteo handed me a glass of water. I drank it and felt a bit better.

Dr. Slike was examining my foot. He turned to Matteo, "Can you pass me my bag please? Oh, and get me some ice as well."

Matteo went over to grab his bag. He handed it to Dr. Slike and walked away – I'm guessing towards the kitchen. Dr. Slike pulled out a tensor bandage and slowly wrapped it around my foot. He got up, still holding my leg, and turned me so now my leg was fully on the couch. He grabbed a pillow and put it behind my back for support. I held back tears from the pain. I knew crying wouldn't ease the pain.

Matteo came back with a bag filled with ice and handed it to Dr. Slike. He put it on my leg and told me to hold it there. It would ease the swelling, but not the pain. My ankle was sprained and I was supposed to stay off it as much as I could. It needed time to heal.

All of a sudden I heard footsteps. They weren't ordinary footsteps. I could tell they were high heels coming my way. The only person in this house who wears heels is Mom. I looked up knowing she would enter the living room any second now.

The noise of her heels became louder and louder as she came closer. "Hello is anyone home? I got surprises!" Mom walked right into the living room with a huge smile on her face. Her white dress flowed beautifully and her hair shone like the sun. She was carrying at least six big bags. She held three bags in each hand. She looked at me first, and then to Dad. Her smile faded automatically. She dropped the bags and ran towards Dad. She looked like her heart had just stopped. She dropped to her knees so she could be more level with Dad.

"What happened?" Mom turned to look at me. "Sophia what happened to you?" Mom's eyes glazed over and she turned back to Dad. She ran her hand over the bandages on his head. She placed one of her hands on Dad's cheek. "Sweetie, wake up." A single tear ran down her face when Dad didn't wake up.

"Patrick, what happened?" She was referring to Dr. Slike – Patrick was his first name.

"It seems that Antonio has suffered from a severe blow to his head. He lost a lot of blood, but he will be fine. As for Sophia, she has sprained her ankle. It is nothing time and a little bit of ice can't heal. She is to stay off it as much as possible." Dr. Slike started packing up his stuff.

Mom turned to me, "I was gone for only a few hours. How did this all happen?" Blood flushed her face. Her face was now a rosy pink and her eyes were filled with tears.

My heart rate accelerated as I thought back to what just happened. It happened so quickly I don't even know if I could remember. It was one big blur to me.

"I don't know what happened," I answered. "Well I do know what happened, but I don't know why or how. It was so quick. One moment we're having a delightful horseback ride and the next I am holding Dad's head making sure he doesn't bleed out." My hands started trembling. I sat on them to make them stop and to make sure no one would see. It was kind of embarrassing.

No one said anything so I guessed they were waiting for me to say more. Mom stared at me with desperation in her eyes. Dr. Slike looked at me like he was jotting down notes in his head as I spoke. Matteo sat on the arm rest beside me on the couch, while Dad lay there not moving and barely even breathing.

"We went for a ride and that was it. We talked about some stuff and out of nowhere something came out of the trees and ran across us. It didn't touch us or anything, but Dad's horse completely lost it. It got so frightened it took off without a command. I thought Dad could handle it himself, but it turned out he couldn't. Dad's horse rose on his two hind hooves sending Dad flying off. I am not too sure if he hit his head on a tree or a rock. Either way, he got a huge cut above his eye and it was bleeding - a lot."

"How did you hurt your foot?" Matteo asked me.

"I jumped off my horse, not thinking about anything else. The impact from hitting the ground so hard affected my foot. All I could think about was that I had to help Dad. I jumped off and ran over to him. I noticed the big gash on his head. My instincts told me to ignore my pain. I immediately knew that I had to apply pressure on Dad's wound to slow down the bleeding, so that's what I did. That's why my hands were covered in blood. I needed to get help. With most of my strength I ripped the bottom of my dress." I pulled up my dress to indicate where it was ripped. "I tied it around Dad's head as tight as I could. I thought of all the possibilities to help him. I knew there was no way of me picking him up and putting him on the horse, so I decided to run for help. I promised him I would be back.

"I tried getting onto Pegasus but it was no use. Dad helped me up the first time. It was even harder now to get up with my foot sprained. I knew it was hopeless." Tears were falling down my face as I recalled the events. It felt worse talking about it than it did actually experiencing it. It just brought back awful flash backs of how everything looked and felt. The back of my throat burnt from keeping in my real tears. The ones that were flowing down my face were the ones that escaped me and I had no choice of keeping them back. My mouth was so dry. I took a sip from the glass that Matteo gave me before.

I continued to speak. "I knew if I stayed there, Dad would have bled to death, so the next best thing to do was run. That is exactly what I did - I ran. Romina saw me and helped me and then Matteo found me as well. Matteo was the one who saved Dad." I looked over to Matteo who was at my side. He really was the one who saved Dad.

Matteo couldn't accept this. He left all the glory for me. Matteo put his hand on my shoulder. "But if it wasn't for you, I wouldn't have known where he was. When I got there, there was only one horse. I don't know where your... where *our* father's horse went. It must have run away after it knocked him over."

Mom was breathing heavily. She looked like she was listening to me, but it also looked like she was thinking of one hundred other things as well. I didn't know what else to say to her.

"That's fine then." Mom turned to Dr. Slike. "Pat, you said he was going to be fine right? You said it before, right?"

Dr. Slike cleared his throat, "Well, I did say he was going to be fine, but..." Dr. Slike started fidgeting with the leather trim on his bag.

"Patrick? But what?" Mom rose from the ground. Her knees were shaking. She took a step towards Dr. Slike.

"Like I said before - he will survive of course, but there is no telling when or *if* he will ever wake up. He is in a deep coma right now. The blow to his head is the main reason. I am so sorry Susanna." Dr. Slike dropped his head.

Mom gasped in horror and covered her mouth. She grabbed onto the edge of the couch for support. Matteo got up in order to catch her if she fell, but she didn't. Mom put her hand up towards Matteo to not go any further. She looked towards Dad and starting wailing. I wanted to get up and comfort her but I couldn't. Mom ran off without saying another word.

I couldn't believe what Dr. Slike just said. Dad had to wake up. He couldn't be in a coma. I didn't cry. I knew he would be okay! *Doctors are wrong sometimes right?* I said to myself. *Dad will just sleep for a day or two - but he will wake up. I know he will.* I looked at him. Blood was starting to seep through the bandage on his head where he was cut. It was spotting.

Dr. Slike sighed as he opened his bag back up to replace the gauze around Dad's head. He told us we had to change the gauze every day in order to keep it clean to quicken the healing process. I didn't mind being the one to do that. It was the least I could do for him.

Dr. Slike also informed us that we had to move Dad to one of the rooms upstairs. We had a special emergency room where all necessary equipment was set up, identical to a hospital room. It had rarely been used, but the room has been there ever since I could remember. It is for the '*just in case*' situation.

I thought back to the incident and realized there was something still bugging me. What was that thing that frightened the horse? Those horses are well trained. Something just didn't seem right.

Chapter 10 – Nekkel Ace

The weeks passed and no one in my family spoke. Well, I wasn't too sure if Matteo and our mother talked while I wasn't there. All I know is that I personally didn't speak to anyone. Every night at dinner we sat in silence. The only noise heard were our forks scraping against our plates which drove me insane, but I tried to ignore it. When we were done eating, we would go our separate ways. I didn't like it like this, but it was the only way I felt comfortable and awkward at the same time. Mom was broken from the thought of never being able to talk to Dad again. It must be hard to suddenly not be able to talk to someone - after talking to them every day of your life. At night when all the lights were off, the hallways darkened and everyone was asleep; I could hear her crying herself to sleep.

I sat beside Dad's bed with every single day that passed. I stared at him thinking about that ill-fated day. *What could I have done differently to have avoided this mess? I should have said no to going for a horse-back ride, even though I knew I would never do that. I shouldn't have asked him about the portal so much, or maybe I should have asked him more about it. Talking about it seemed to have distracted him.*

Was I sitting here, on my Dad's bed, because I was worried about him, or because I was waiting for him to wake up to give me more answers about the portal? *What a stupid question.* I was upset with myself for even thinking about that. I cared about Dad more than I cared about the stupid portal. He looked so pale. I had never seen him look like this before. Even through his dark eyelashes, I could see the bags forming under his eyes from lack of nutrition. He was eating from a tube connected to his arm. *Was that even good for you?*

It was morning now. I sat there all night - just like every other night.

On this night I might have had about an hour of rest. Massimo would come up at least once a day with a tray of food. He knew if he didn't bring it for me, I wouldn't eat. Food was the last thing on my mind. I would pick at the food and nibble on a little piece of bread. *How could I eat while Dad was withering away?*

I couldn't help but feel responsible for everything that happened to Dad. Matteo sat with me most of the time. He couldn't stand my not responding to him. He would do all the talking, and I would just nod my head to answer him. I didn't have the energy to speak. Sometimes he would leave me alone, but he would always come back - always.

How can I wake Dad? I asked myself. *There must be some herb or drink that could wake him up. There is stuff like that to make pain go away, to make you happy, to make you forget things, so why couldn't there be something just to simply make you wake up?* That sounded easy enough. Knowing what it was and actually *getting* it was the problem.

Sitting there and doing nothing wouldn't make him wake up. I had to spring into action and fix this for myself. I got up from the chair and took my first step after many hours of sitting. My legs felt so weak. My ankle wasn't healed properly, but I could walk on it. I thought it would have been much worse but luckily it wasn't as bad as we all thought. It healed much faster than Dr. Slike said it would. Just as I was leaving Dad's room, Matteo came in to check on us. I grabbed his arm and brought him out the door without speaking one word.

"What's going on?" Matteo asked me, whispering.

"I know this might sound crazy, but do you think there is any way we could wake Dad up? Something like an herb or a drink or anything?" I was biting the inside of my lip. I was anxious to get an answer from Matteo.

"Hmm…" Matteo looked down to Kiko who stared back at him. Matteo looked at me again. "I don't think so. I know there are a lot of different plants in the forest that I don't even know about, but I don't think there is anything to make someone wake up from a big blow to the head. Sorry," he was shaking his head.

That wasn't the answer I was hoping for, that was the truth. I wondered who else to ask. I knew I couldn't ask Mom and I didn't want to ask Paul Jr. Just when I thought my search was over I remembered someone! Dr. Slike! *He must know something of the sort that could help my Dad.* I didn't care about the cost. Money was no object. I just wanted Dad to wake up and have things back to normal again. For life to go back to the way it should have been a long time ago. The four of us were one big happy family for about half an hour. Just as things began to look brighter, this happened.

I told Matteo what I wanted to do and he said he wouldn't let me go alone so he and Kiko joined me on my little journey. I had never been to Dr. Slike's house alone like this before. I would normally go with my parents, but right now this was not an option.

We walked there in silence. I was distracted by the sound of the ground under our feet and the steady flow of breaths that Matteo took. Dr. Slike's house was about a ten minute walk away from ours. I swung my arms as we walked down the road. It was a nice walk to go on to stretch my legs out.

Down the length of the road were many, many trees. The trees stood side by side like a long army awaiting us. They closed us off from everything. Their intensity of the green on the leaves made it seem like they were glowing. The leaves hung there, proud to be part of the trees. I knew the trees would eventually lead to an open field. We turned into a little driveway leading into the trees. Dr. Slike's house was just past the trees, secluded on its own in the forest. Not too deep in though. It was right on the edge, hidden from people on the road.

I was nervous to talk to Dr. Slike. Would he think I was crazy for asking these kinds of questions? I am sure I'm not the first one to ask him how to wake someone up from their coma. My heart was racing. It wasn't because I was walking at a quick pace now. It was because I was so nervous. *Should I make Matteo talk? No, I'm going to do this myself.* Matteo was just there for moral support. He gave me the secret courage I needed to talk to Dr. Slike.

We got to Dr. Slike's house in no time. We accidentally got off track and had to walk through a couple of bushes to get to his house. I stepped on a couple of acorns on the way. I twisted my ankle in a way that could have been avoided. I gasped from the pain, but it went away after a few seconds. Matteo was looking at me from the corner of his eye.

We walked up to the front door and I looked at the house. It was much bigger than I remembered. He must have remodelled it because his house was absolutely stunning. The house had many glass windows. The exterior was mostly stone, but there was wood incorporated it in as well. On the far right of his house was a fire pit burning freshly cut pieces of wood. I would have loved a house like this. I could feel the warmth of the fire on my skin. It felt a little bit uncomfortable since I was already hot to begin with. I don't know why he had that fire going. I didn't bother to think much about it.

We reached the glass door. I made a fist and I was about to knock but I stopped.

"Are you alright?" Matteo asked calmly.

"Yeah," I laughed. "I'm just nervous," I whispered hoping that Dr. Slike wasn't secretly listening to us.

I stretched out my fingers to hear them crack and made a fist again - a tighter one this time. I knocked three times. The hard door made my knuckles turn white. I could see right into his house through his massive glass doors. He had a beautiful interior filled with classic antiques and many bookshelves.

Dr. Slike walked into the room. He wore a black t-shirt and black pants, but no lab coat anymore. He looked very curious as to who it was knocking at his door. I wondered if he had many visitors. He grabbed his glasses and pushed them close to his face. He squinted his eyes as he came closer to the door. He suddenly straightened up and smiled when he realized who it was.

Dr. Slike approached and opened the door. "Sophia! What a pleasant surprise." He walked over and gave me a hug. I was taken by surprise. He then turned to Matteo. "Matteo, how are you doing?" He shook his hand. "I see you still have that tiger." Dr. Slike looked down to Kiko and smiled at him. Dr. Slike had a strong accent. I must have gotten used to it from being around him my whole life but for some reason I noticed it more now. It was a thick accent but it was understandable.

I let out a little chuckle. Before I could explain why we were here, Dr. Slike insisted we come in. "Come, come. Sit down. Would you like anything to drink?" He was in such a good mood. *Now I really know that no one visits him.* I said to myself. *He must be a lonely man. But he must like it this way.*

We thanked him and politely declined his drink offer, but he still insisted on bringing us water at least. He said we must have been thirsty from the walk. We agreed. I supposed I could have used a nice cold glass of water.

Matteo and I sat down on the couches while he went to the kitchen.

"Arlene, come out. We have visitors," Dr. Slike called out towards the kitchen as he walked away.

Matteo and I both looked at each other and creased our eyebrows. "Who's Arlene?" Matteo mouthed to me.

I shrugged my shoulders. I had no idea who Arlene was. I had never heard that name before.

I looked around the house from where I sat. The view from this room was very scenic. I could see the wildlife right outside through the window. There were two other rooms and probably another one that I couldn't see. Near the kitchen was another door. It was closed but the frame of it was carved with intricate floral-like designs spread all over the frame with corresponding lines that swirled all over the place. They looked like they were moving.

A minute later Dr. Slike came back with a tray. He placed the tray on the wooden table in front of us. It had three glasses of water and two bowls of water. He picked up the glasses and handed one to Matteo and myself. He then picked up the bowl and placed it in front of Kiko. He picked up his glass and took a seat in front of us on the other side of the table. "Arlene!" he called again.

We heard a bell jingle. Out of the kitchen we saw a small kitten running towards us. It jumped up on the table and meowed at us. It must have been the size of Kiko's paw. Its fur was all black and had a little blue collar with a little bell attached around its neck. Or should I say, her neck. Since its name was Arlene, I assumed she was a female. She was so precious. She took two licks of the water from the bowl which was still on the tray on top of the table. I wanted to pick her up and cradle her in my arms.

"So, to what do I owe the honour of this unexpected visit?" Dr. Slike looked so much happier than he did at our house. I wondered why. Maybe it was Arlene. She jumped from the table onto his lap.

"Well," I began. I took a sip of water and continued. "I wanted to talk about my father."

"Oh, yes. How unfortunate. I wish him all the best," Dr. Slike nodded his head, remembering something.

"Yes," I tried to brush that off and continue. I was stalling. Matteo could tell I was hesitating.

"Sophia came to ask you for some help." Matteo cut in.

Dr. Slike looked to Matteo and then back at me. He was waiting for me to speak.

I shot Matteo a glance and he smiled at me. I couldn't show how I really felt since Dr. Slike's gaze was burning into my forehead. Now my nerves were getting the best of me. My heartbeat accelerated and I knew I had to speak. I started to twitch my feet nervously and I couldn't stop. I started playing with my necklace. That always calmed me down. I've had this necklace my whole life. I've worn it ever since I was a little baby. It was nothing special. It was just sterling silver chain with a long, slim stone wrapped around as a pendant. It was pretty. Normal jewellery didn't appeal to me. This one was kind of cool because it just looked like a piece of stone imitating as a piece of jewellery - which I liked.

I took a deep breath and looked towards Arlene as I spoke. "Well, I was wondering if there was anything we could do to wake up our Dad. Is there something that we could give him? Matteo and I were thinking maybe there was an herb you could make into a drink." I threw my hands in the air. "You know, just throwing some ideas out there." I didn't want to sound stupid. I wanted to take it all back.

By the look on Dr. Slike's face, he didn't think it was such a stupid idea after all. "Hmm…" Dr. Slike said as he picked Arlene up off his lap and placed her gently on the ground. He walked over to his bookshelf and ran his fingers across some of the books as he walked past them. "Ah," he said as he picked out one fairly large, very old and dusty book. He blew off the dust and opened it. He started leafing through its delicate pages. I would be so scared to open that book. It sounded as if it could fall apart any second now. He joined us again and sat back down on his chair.

Dr. Slike started mumbling something as he turned the pages of the book. It seemed like he forgot we were even there.

Matteo cleared his throat.

"Hm?" Dr. Slike looked up to us and shook his head to clear his daze. "Oh, yes of course. Sorry about that. Well I shouldn't be telling you this, but since I am so close with your father, I feel like I should tell you."

I held my breath in preparation for whatever he was going to say. This was so intense. I couldn't believe what was happening. Something he felt like he should tell me, only for the sake of knowing my father? I was so interested. "Okay, go on." That's all I said. It wasn't my turn to talk. This whole moment was for Dr. Slike to say what he had to say.

"Well, I am not too sure but apparently there is something called Nekkel Ace."

"Nekkel Ace?" Matteo and I said in unison. I realized we both interrupted him. I apologized and let him continue.

"Yes. Apparently it heals all. It has special mysterious powers but no one knows how it works. In my books it says that it has the power to heal one hundred men in an instant. I wouldn't underestimate its power just to wake someone up from a coma." Dr. Slike looked towards us.

"Okay, this is good!" The weight on my shoulders was lifted! So there was a way to help my dad, I knew it! I couldn't help but to smile uncontrollably. "So how do we get this Nekkel Ace? Where do we find it? What is it? Is it a flower? A root? A tree?" I was asking too many questions. I was so excited I couldn't keep it in. I wanted to find it as soon as possible.

"That's the problem," Dr. Slike said.

Problem? What problem? He never said anything about a problem. How could there possibly be a problem?

Dr. Slike continued, "Some say that it is impossible to find. It was rumoured that it was made from the very pit of our world - I don't know how that is possible - but that is what they say. It's hidden someplace else, far away from us. The people there can't see it. They don't know it exists. For this reason, it's safe where it is."

My heart was almost broken when he said that, but then I thought - *that's fine.* I would just go look for it. That wouldn't be a big deal right? I had nothing else to do but wait around at home and do nothing. *Think of this as a little adventure,* I said to myself. *It will be fun. Matteo and Kiko would come along with me as well obviously. I couldn't just leave them behind.*

"Okay, where can do I find it? It's not a problem for me to go out of my way to search for it." I smiled at Dr. Slike.

He smiled back, but it faded just as fast as it appeared.

"There might be a little problem for you, my dear. When they say it's far away, what they mean is, it is no longer on this planet. It is on Earth now."

Mine and Matteo's jaw dropped at the same time. Then something immediately occurred to me – the portal!

Chapter 11 – Determination

Shortly after our conversation with Dr. Slike, Matteo and I left. I was curious as to why the people of the region – Earth – couldn't see the Nekkel Ace. Dr. Slike told me that we are very similar to them. We looked like them, acted like them, only our planet was a bit behind technologically. But we were slowly catching up to them. The power from the shield that surrounds Earth has a magical effect on our planet. No one can explain it, but the shield hides things that don't need to be seen. As Caledonians, we have the ability to see what the people of Earth can't. The Nekkel Ace is under some sort of enchantment that keeps it hidden from the people of Earth. *They are not supposed to have it, so why should they be able to see it?* Dr. Slike words echoed through my mind.

I thought about that as I walked a little ahead of Matteo. We paced by the dirt road out of the forest. I didn't talk to Matteo because I had way too much on my mind. First I had to think of where the Portal could be. I lived in the same house my entire life and not once did I see any trace of a portal. I asked Dr. Slike if he knew about Dad's portal and he said no. He looked kind of nervous about it and I didn't want to pester him with any more questions. I got the information I needed and now I knew exactly what I was going to do with it.

On the walk home I skipped each step I took. I was too excited to walk normally, but not excited enough to run. I had to think my actions through before executing them. When I got home, the first thing I wanted to do was see Dad. I would go up to his room to speak with him. *He could be awake for all I know,* I thought to myself.

I told Matteo everything that I knew about the Portal after we left Dr. Slike's house. Matteo, stunned by this revelation, listened intently. I told him how it was always my dream to visit Earth and the portal was Dad's means of getting there. I also let Matteo in on how Dad became upset after spilling the news to me and how he forbade me to even think of it. Matteo agreed with Dad and said I shouldn't look for it either. Matteo knew Dad was a wise man and he knew to never undermine his rules. I ignored him and walked on ahead. I didn't need to hear it from him as well.

Every now and then I would look over my shoulder at Matteo. I had the biggest smile on my face. He was looking down at his feet the entire walk home. He sensed I was looking at him. Matteo would look up and slightly grin. It was more of a forced smile though. He didn't look too happy. I didn't know why. It seemed like he was worried about me. He didn't like the fact that I jumped at the first opportunity on taking the portal. I didn't even know where it was and even if I did find it, I wouldn't know how to use it. Matteo was afraid that I would get hurt in the process. I assured him everything would be fine. *If Dad could use the portal with no problems, then why couldn't I?*

We got home and I went straight upstairs to Dad's room. The railing was just recently polished and it felt smooth under my hand. I quietly entered the silence of his room. The chair I normally sit on was still in the same position I left it. Dad still hadn't woken up. I sat down, explained to him what I found out and what I was going to do about it. I promised him I was going to get the Nekkel Ace and I was going to wake him up. I moved his hair away from his forehead and gave him a kiss on the cheek. His face was so cold. It killed me inside to see him like this. I just wanted to shake him until he woke up, even though I knew that would just hurt him even more.

I went down the stairs and walked towards Dad's office. I was on the hunt to find this Portal. I knew I was alone in searching for it since Matteo was nowhere to be seen. When I did find the portal, I would find him. I wouldn't do anything without his knowing. I would do this, not only out of respect, but also out of fear - though I would never admit the latter to anyone.

So this is where my search begins! I took a deep breath and looked around Dad's office. I knew it was going to be hidden and not out in the open just like that. If it was, I would have seen it by now, but I hadn't. I chose to look in Dad's office first, only because he spends most of his time in it, so I just suspected it would be there. *This is a blind search. It could be anywhere in the house.* I started to feel overwhelmed. Considering the size of the house, there was no telling how many days, weeks or months would pass before I would find this portal. But I refused to give up. I was going to find it no matter what.

Dad's office was fairly large. The walls were half covered with bookshelves. I wasn't too sure if he read all those books or not. Some were old and some were new. Whenever he went to meet people, they would always give him new books to read. Dad recently went to Earth and I think he had some blueprints from there. I walked over to them and took a look. I have never seen anything like this before. The paper was covered with lines and numbers. I didn't even bother to try and figure out what they were meant to resemble.

I looked through his entire room. I looked behind the book shelves; I looked behind the picture frames, behind piles of paper, behind lamps, under the rugs, and even under his desk. I couldn't find anything. I stood right in the middle of the room. With one swift movement I pushed my hair behind my ears. I had no idea what to do. This was going to be harder than I thought.

Maybe the entrance isn't even in this room. That could be too obvious, right? Alright, so time to check the hallways and all the rooms. I vigorously scanned all the hallways and the many rooms we of the house. It took me hours. For the first time I regretted having such a large house. I never realized how enormous my house actually was until I searched every inch of it.

By the end, my hands, knees and feet were filled with dust from the places the cleaners missed. I kind of ended up doing their job for them. I was filthy! My body was engulfed with heat. This was quite a workout. I wiped the sweat from my forehead with the back of my hand. My legs and arms felt sore from having to move heavy things to look behind or under them.

After half a day of searching, I came up empty. Dad was a very good hider. At that moment something occurred to me: The entire time I looked through the house, I didn't once run into Mom. The servants kept asking me what I was looking for, but I didn't tell them. Mom was probably out shopping again. She would do anything to fill the void of not having Dad.

My body was weak and I felt tired. I wanted to lie down for a bit. Continue tomorrow maybe. *What are you doing? Don't stop now!* I could hear my conscious telling me. But, I really was tired. I sluggishly walked back to Dad's office. My feet dragged along the marble floors. I turned on all the lamps and sat down on the chair at Dad's desk. Everything looked brighter now, but not clearer. I rested my arms on the edge of the desk and put my head down. Staring at the ground beneath the desk, I noticed something I had never seen before. There was a bunch of dirt at the bottom of the desk. I guessed the cleaning crew had yet to clean the office.

This also meant that Dad had been outside in the yard. I rarely saw him out there. He hadn't ridden his horse in a while so it didn't make sense. *The dirt must have been here from before. Why would Dad's shoes have this much mud at the bottom of them? He must have been walking around in the garden. Why would he be in the garden? There were stone pathways everywhere to follow. Even if he did wander one day, he would stay on the perfectly placed stone paths.*

I was puzzled. I followed the dirt on the ground. There wasn't that much but it led me to the back door of Dad's office. I pushed the sliding door open and walked outside. The cool air felt refreshing after sweating indoors all day. I walked with my head down the whole time, not taking my gaze off the dried up mud trail. I walked for about a minute when I noticed the path slightly turned left while the mud path disappeared. I look up to my right and the only thing in that direction was a bunch of trees and fairly large bushes. I looked behind me and thought to myself, '*Should I do this? Should I venture into the unknown?*' The only thing I heard in my brain was, '*Uh, duh!*' So I did.

I could see foot imprints in the ground. I placed my feet in them and noticed they were much larger than mine. *They must be Dad's!* I was starting to feel very anxious. My heart was beating heavily. I wasn't too sure if I wanted to find the portal anymore. My nerves were getting the best of me. I knew I was getting close.

Once again I walked with my head down. I didn't want to take my gaze off the foot imprints in the ground. I walked past the first line of trees and was now wandering into places where I had never been.

With my eyes still fixated on the ground, I suddenly saw another set of feet next to mine. I froze with shock and held my breath as I slowly looked up to see who it was. *Please don't be Paul Jr.,* I said to myself. He always turned up at the most inopportune times. But it wasn't him after all. It was Matteo with Kiko by his side. They both looked at me the same way. Matteo looked very sad. His piercing blue eyes stared deeply into mine. I could feel his pain in the pit of my stomach. He was leaning against one of the cement pillars that were all over the grounds of the estate.

"Did you find the portal?" Matteo asked with a raised eyebrow. He wasn't smiling.

"No, not yet. But I think -"

Matteo cut me off. I could see a vein sticking out of his forehead. I knew I wouldn't like what I was about to hear. "*I* think you should stop looking. I have a bad feeling about this. Nothing good can come out of you going to Earth. You have no idea what Earth is like and what if it is more dangerous than you think? Why else do you think Dad would be so against you going? This isn't right. Dad will wake up one day. Just let him be. Everything will be alright."

"Matteo, no matter what you say, I won't stop looking. I'm going to Earth," I said quietly and quickly looked away as I couldn't bear to look into his eyes at this moment. I didn't want to talk back to him but I had no other choice.

"I kind of figured that, so I guess I have no other choice but to join you."

I stopped for a second and looked up at him. My jaw dropped. I wasn't expecting to hear this. He was smiling and I knew everything was going to be fine. I jumped up and hugged him. It's kind of funny how one little smile can change one's emotions so drastically. As soon as I saw both sides of his mouth raise, I had a feeling that everything was starting to go just as planned.

Matteo and I continued walking through the bushes. Dad's footprints were barely visible. I didn't even bother to look down anymore. The footprints were gone, but I still felt like we were going the right way. Matteo and I led each other, the blind leading the blind. We constantly looked at our surroundings. Our guard was up and ready for anything to come up and attack us. We were walking farther and farther from our house. I turned back and I could see just the very top of it.

The bushes made a tall pathway. We followed it thinking it was a maze but there was only one direction to go so we knew it couldn't have been a maze. Thankfully from knowing that, we wouldn't get lost. It was kind of scary because now I couldn't see anything. We couldn't see over the bush walls and I felt claustrophobic, even though I wasn't. I was scared and Matteo could see it on my face.

"Do you want to go back? You know we can stop anytime you want," he said to me in a calm tone.

"No, I don't want to give up. I feel like we're so close!"

We kept walking until the pathway turned slightly. The pathway suddenly came to an end. *What? That's it?* I looked to Matteo for answers. He seemed just as frantic as I was. *We walked all this way only to come to a dead end?* Matteo walked up to the wall and we noticed it wasn't just a normal bush that we could plough through. There was a stone door behind it. Matteo pushed away some of the bush that grew over it and we noticed there was a key hole.

My arms fell to my side in defeat. I didn't have a key and I knew Matteo didn't have one either. He looked up to me and I wanted to cry. I kept it in and tried to see if it was unlocked - I prayed. I went up to it and tried turning the knob. The thing about being able to turn a knob is that there has to be one. There was no knob! *A key hole with no doorknob! Just my luck! How the heck is anyone supposed to go through this door?*

I began pacing around trying to figure something out, but as I did, my foot caught on a root or rock and I fell hard on the ground. Matteo didn't have enough time to grab me. My hands broke my fall as my face was inches from the ground. I hit my knee pretty hard though. I noticed something hidden under the bushes, but I was too preoccupied with the pain in my knee. I sat up and pulled my knee close to me to get a better look. My skin was pushed back. I could peel it off if I wanted to, but I was too chicken. I could see the blood wanting to penetrate through my skin. I ignored it. I've had worse. No blood, no problem.

My thoughts went back to what I saw on the ground hidden in the bush. I pushed the greenery back and noticed something that resembled a button. It was about the size of my fist. I went to push it, but it didn't budge. Matteo saw me doing this and he tried pushing it as well. Nothing happened. Matteo grabbed both my hands and pulled me up. He gently directed me to stand to the side while he looked at the button on the ground. He placed his foot on it and with all his weight he pressed it down. I heard a rumbling noise. I braced myself as Matteo came right beside me and grabbed my shoulder.

The massive door slid open - a bit. It was just enough for the three of us to squeeze through. Of course on the way through, I scraped my arm on one of the branches. This time I wasn't as lucky as before - it pierced my skin. A little bit of blood came to the surface, but I just wiped it away. A little bit of blood wasn't going to stop me now!

We all walked down a set of old, cracked stone steps. They were one with the ground under them. They sloped down quickly, so I had to watch where I placed my foot because at the path I was going, everything wanted to hurt me.

All of this was new to me. None of this looked like it belonged. I couldn't believe this was really happening. I've walked the grounds so many times, yet none of this is familiar. It's unbelievable how I missed all of this. It's like this isn't even part of my property.

We walked through a stone passageway where stone arches were all around. I looked up and noticed how old the stone looked. This must have been here since the beginning days of our planet. We walked for quite some while until we finally stopped at a normal sized door - which had a handle I might add. I walked up first and turned the handle - it was open. I pushed the door back slowly and stepped in. Matteo and Kiko were right behind me the entire time. I could feel Matteo's breath on the back of my neck. It was adding to my nervous goose bumps.

Everything was dark. We walked blindly the deeper we went. The only light we had was the light illuminating from the door we came in from. I took small steps to ensure that I didn't trip over anything. I held my hands out in front of me, making sure I didn't walk into any walls.

I saw something blue glowing in the distance. I didn't back away; I walked closer as it drew me closer to it. The closer I got, the brighter it radiated. I stood there in front of it and I knew right at that moment that I was standing in front of the portal. This was it - this was the portal I had been looking for all this time.

Chapter 12 – Escape

The eerie glow of the portal tickled my skin as my emotions started to overwhelm me. I was still in shock from the realization that I *actually* found the portal. I expected the search to be a little bit harder, but then again, it *did* take me almost an entire day to find it. I had cuts and bruises on my arms and legs to show for the journey. I took another step closer, but the glowing of the portal turned into a bright light. It just kept getting brighter and brighter. I had to cover my eyes because they were starting to burn. It was like staring directly into the sun for a long time, even though I only caught a glimpse of the light.

Matteo automatically pulled me back and the glowing dimmed. Kiko growled the entire time. It was in the pit of his chest, but as soon as the glow of the portal glowed its brightest, Kiko let out a growl of fear. The noise scared me and sent sharp spikes through my nerves. I've never heard him growl like that before. All my feelings of excitement and joy went out the window. What was once happiness had now turned into fear. I wasn't happy to see the portal anymore. I was actually scared to be anywhere near it.

Matteo's grip on my arm was firm as he pulled me towards the door. "Let's get out of here."

We walked outside and my jaw hung low to the ground. My eyes were wide open and watering from being unable to blink – it's as if I forgot how after seeing the portal. I rubbed my eyes and caught my breath.

"Are you alright? Are you hurt?" Matteo was looking into my eyes as if he was expecting a lie from me.

"I'm fine." I guess I was telling the truth. "I didn't expect...*that*!" I blinked a couple of times to get my vision back. No matter how many times I blinked I could see a big blue spot on everything I looked at. Darn that bright light! I knew I had to wait a while before I got my vision back to normal.

Matteo paced back and forth with his hands on his hips. The stern look on his face meant that he was about to say something - something unpleasant. I prepared myself for what he was about to say.

He wiped his face down with his hand and then took in a deep breath. "I knew this was not right. The portal obviously repelled us or something. That light could have blinded us! If I didn't take us out of there, who knew what would have happened. I can't believe I let that happen!" Matteo didn't look at me as he spoke. I could tell that he was struggling with what had just taken place.

He raised his voice. "You see how dangerous it is in there?" Matteo pointed with his whole hand towards the open door.

"Yes." I shyly answered. My voice was barely a whisper.

"And, you want to go back in?" Matteo's eyes widened with anger. *Yes.* "No."

I didn't remember ever getting in trouble this much before. I'd been yelled at - don't get me wrong - but never like this. "I'm sorry," was all I could think to say as my eyes started to water. I looked towards the ground so Matteo wouldn't see my tears. I knew he did. It's easy enough to catch the tears flowing down your face, but hard to hide a trembling lip.

Matteo's head fell to the side as he took in my saddened state. "Aw, Sophia, I'm sorry. Come here." Matteo said as he grabbed me and gave me a hug. His voice went from frightening to calm and soothing in an instant. He realized he had gone too far. "I didn't mean to yell at you like that. I'm your older brother and I have strict responsibilities to protect you. For now I'm the head of the house and I have to make sure everyone is safe, including you. You understand that, right?"

I nodded with my head buried in his chest. I think he got the hint. I wiped my tears on his shirt as punishment for yelling at me. I smiled at the dark blotches they left on his shirt when he let me go. I don't think he minded. He put his arm around my shoulder as we both walked back to the house in silence. I looked over my shoulder one more time to see the closed door that led to the room of the portal.

We entered our house. I would never forget how to get back to the portal. Matteo and I went to Dad's room and I told him what happened. I sat on my chair while Matteo stood behind me. I apologized to Dad for not being able to properly use the portal to get to Earth so I could get the

Nekkel Ace. When I was done talking, I gave Dad a failed attempt at a hug. I placed my ear on his heart for a few seconds just to hear to it beat.

I didn't notice at first, but I thought I felt his hand move! I shot up from his chest and looked at his fingers. I stood there for a few seconds not breathing. Was Dad finally waking up? I didn't even say anything to Matteo who was staring at me with confusion written all over his face. My chest and shoulders were raised high in excitement. "Dad?" I whispered but there was no answer. I shook his hand and there was no response. I guess I must have imagined his fingers twitching. Maybe that was a sign he was getting better. It could also mean that I was losing it.

I walked out of the room not saying a word and headed towards the staircase leading up to the grand towers.

"He will get better you know," Matteo said as I walked away. I didn't bother to turn around. "I know he will." That last sentence was barely a whisper but I could hear and feel the pain in it. I know I was hurt, but I didn't really consider Matteo's feelings in all this. I ignored him and kept on walking. I just wanted to be alone.

I went to the highest tower and walked towards the open window. I sat on the ledge and looked outside. This was probably the best place to come for a view of Earth. I could sit here all day with the breeze tickling my face and Earth just a jump away.

***

I spent all day and every day in the tower for the past five months. Massimo would still bring me food everyday on a trey. Clara would step in when he was busy with something else. I appreciated them dearly. I didn't bother going outside anymore. I felt as if I didn't deserve the luxury of being able to enjoy my time in my garden while my father had to stay cooped up in his room all day. My Mom and Matteo would visit me separately every other day. We didn't have much to speak about. We figured that being in the presence of one another was good enough. We didn't need to speak. We were all miserable. Dad's accident proved to be a hardship on our family.

Every month that passed I promised myself that Dad would wake up. I would give him one more month before I would go back to the portal. It was always the same thing repeating itself. *"If Dad doesn't wake up in March, I will go. Okay now, if Dad doesn't wake up in April I will go. Now, I* promise *if Dad doesn't wake up in May, I will go*". Those were just promises that I kept making to myself which I kept breaking over and over again. It was now the beginning of August, and Dad hadn't woken up, and I hadn't used the portal to help him. I was a coward.

Since all of my time was spent in the tower alone, I slowly realized that I shouldn't just sit there all day doing nothing. I had to figure out something to pass my time. I picked up reading quite easily. I knew how to read obviously from my tutoring classes an hour a day, but I just never enjoyed it. After reading a few of the books in Dad's office, I now couldn't put them down! The book I was reading at the time was called '*Room*.' It was unlike any other book I have read before. The book was written from the perspective of a five year old boy. He, along with his mother, were confined in a place they called 'Room'. After escaping he is released into the world not knowing a thing about 'Outside'. His mother tried to explain things, but there was just too much to take in at once. It wondered if that is how I would be if I ever travelled to Earth. I would be lost and not know anything. I would have to learn their ways. I am always up to learning new things anyway.

Paul Jr. visited me in the tower sometimes but I would completely ignore him. One day I think I pushed one of his buttons because he got upset at me for not talking. I completely lost it on him and told him to leave me alone and I never wanted to see him again. I told him to go find someone else to bother and that I didn't even like him. He was just wasting his time. When I had told him those things, I felt the vein in my forehead rise; just the way Matteo's did, but not as much.

Paul Jr. never visited me again. Instead, every day he would watch me from the garden. He would stand there for about a minute. I never took my gaze off him. I didn't smile nor wave. After the minute was over, he would walk away. I liked that better than having him pester me with questions every day. I suppose it was decent of him to care that much to see me every day, even if he got nothing in return.

Today was like any other quiet afternoon. I sat on the window ledge with the window wide open, clutching one of my books. I enjoyed the sun's rays on my reddening cheeks. Something was off though. I don't know why but I kept reading the same sentence over and over again. It wasn't because I didn't understand it. It was because I didn't pay enough attention to it the first time, or the second time, or the third time. My mind was wandering without my even realizing.

I lay the book down on my lap and closed my eyes. I was probably just thinking too much. Of what you ask? Who knew!

In that exact moment something startled me. Not only did it startle me, it made me lose my balance and I had to grab the window sill quickly in order to make sure I didn't fall to my death. I looked back into the room to realize it was Kiko. He nudged my leg which scared the living daylights out of me. No one disturbed me here anymore so it was totally unexpected. Tigers were such creepers! I didn't even hear him come into the room!

"Kiko you scared me!" I fanned him with my book.

He shook his head and nudged the book out of his way. That was strange. He came closer to me and nudged me a second time. Then a third time, but this time it was harder.

"What's wrong?" It looked as if he wanted me to follow him. I groaned impatiently. He was probably sick and tired of me spending all my time here – alone

I told him I wouldn't follow him, and for him to just leave me alone.

He nudged my leg even harder this time. "Kiko, cut it out! That hurts!" I was yelling at him.

Instantly Kiko jumped up and grabbed my book right out of the grip of my hands. My jaw dropped as Kiko had never done anything like this before!

"Kiko, my book is not a toy. Give it back! You will ruin it!"

I could see his fangs digging deeper into the pages of my book. I didn't want him to ruin it. The book would be ruined forever if I didn't do something - quick. I leaped up from my seat and dove for the book in Kiko's mouth. Obviously, I missed. That wasn't surprising.

He ran away. *If a chase is what he wants, a chase is what he is going to get.* I didn't like dealing with people - or animals ruining my books.

I chased him down the stairs into one of the main room hallways. He stopped in front of one of the rooms. I was right on his tail. I was so close I could almost touch him. As soon as he stopped he turned around and I yanked the book out of his mouth. It was easier than I thought to get it back. "Ha!" I said while I waved it in front of his face. I scanned through the pages to make sure there were no holes. There weren't any holes, but there were a few indents. Those would fade over time.

I heard strange noises coming from one of the rooms. It was the exact room Kiko led me to. It was strange because its door was closed. There were no closed doors in our house. This was definitely something out of the ordinary.

I put my ear up to the door to get a better idea of who was in the room. I was pretty sure this room was one of the many spare bedrooms we have. I heard a woman's voice whispering on the other side. My curiosity was burning through me. I had to know what or who was behind this door.

My fingers twitched as they slowly reached for the door handle. I turned it and slowly opened the door, trying not to make a noise.

What I saw next, would probably stay in my mind for the rest of my life. That is a picture that you could never erase out of your memory, even if you tried your hardest. It was Massimo, our servant, with a woman. She was wearing a lame excuse for a lingerie piece. It left nothing to the imagination. That wasn't even the worst part. Seeing half naked women doesn't bother me. The worst part was that the half-naked woman standing there was my own mother!

Mom slowly turned to me as I looked away not to meet her gaze. Our sight touched for an instant as I turned around to run away. I couldn't stand there and look any longer. Half a second glance was already too much! I heard Mom's shocking gasp through the hallway. As I ran, I heard the door slam shut. I couldn't believe that was happening. I felt nauseous and I was completely sick to my stomach. It was a good thing I hadn't eaten anything yet because if I did, it would have easily come up.

I couldn't believe Mom would do that. All this time I thought she was mourning and hiding from all of us because she wanted to be alone was a lie. Instead she'd been spending time with Massimo- Massimo of all people! I would never forgive them for what they had done to my family; for what they had done to disrespect Dad. It was repulsive!

I ran towards the stairs. I needed to get out of this house and as far away as possible. I didn't know where I was going yet, but I knew I would figure something out. My heart was aching, my eyes were stinging and my chest was burning. With each second that passed, my vision became blurry due to the tears escaping my eyes. As soon as I arrived at the stairs, I reached for the handrail, but missed. I ran down anyways. By the time I reached the middle of the steps, I lost my balance. Memories from when I fell the first time flooded my brain. This time was different. Instead of flying backwards as I previously did, this time I fell forwards.

My body tilted to the left as I collided directly with the steps. My left arm took most of the damage as my body landed on it. I heard a loud crack before I tumbled the rest of the way down. It didn't hurt so I thought nothing of it. I lay on the ground for a couple of seconds, composing myself, before getting back up. I knew exactly at that moment where to go, and how I was going to get there. I fumbled when rising but managed to stand straight. A sharp, agonizing pain shot up my arm. I looked to my left arm and realized it was broken. There was a lump on my forearm that I knew shouldn't be there and it was white under my skin; *yup that's my bone.*

I felt as if there just wasn't enough time to breathe. My breaths were short gasps of air as it felt my world crumbling down on me. I ran out the doors and towards the garden. I knew exactly where I was going.

I ran quickly and caught a glimpse of Matteo in the far distance. I knew it was him even though my eyes were all watery. He came running after me. I could feel the pulse in my arm tighten and become stronger with each step that I took. I ran as fast as I could while cradling my arm with my good hand. I knew my arm was broken for sure. It was as if there was a grip on my arm that became tighter and tighter with every second that passed. The pain was becoming unbearable. The force of my feet hitting the ground with each step wasn't helping the matter.

I reached the first vine covered door and stomped on that button like I've never stomped before. I pushed my way through and kept running. I lost my balance a couple of times, but never fell over.

The door to the portals room was in sight and relief flooded through me. I wasn't going to stop running. Matteo was too far back to catch up to me now. I could hear him screaming my name – but it was easy to ignore as his voice faded in the distance. I didn't stop. My hand grasped the handle of the door and I knew I was free.

Chapter 13 – New Me

All I remember is weightlessness. My body surrounded by nothingness. I felt just like a light breeze flying across a meadow on a warm day. My presence didn't feel real, but I knew I was going somewhere. I could feel the weight of my body floating away. The abyss of my mind was clear and at ease. I couldn't describe what I was feeling. I was no longer upset, or angry or even disappointed. No, now I was feeling… content. I could see a glowing white light through my closed eyelids, but I was too unaware to open them. I could feel the corners of my mouth raised to a smile. I touched myself to feel the warmth of my own body. I had to make sure this was real, I was real.

I floated there, in thin air, thinking of Earth. I kept telling myself that, Earth was where I wanted to be. I wanted to become unrecognizable. I wanted no one to know who I was. Being an unknown person in an unknown world sounded right; sounded so free. I wanted to start a new life on Earth – free of pain. I was in dire need of a new life with no problems or worries. I wanted to become a new person with one purpose. As soon as I found the Nekkel Ace, I would return to my real world and face reality - eventually.

I couldn't tell how long I was in that state. It could have been seconds or it could have even been hours. At that point, time didn't exist; days could feel like hours or hours could feel like seconds. Images of Dad flashed before me. I was doing this for him, not for anyone else. I didn't know what to expect from Earth, but I was ready. *I know I can do this.*

***

I lay there, on my back, with my eyes closed, on what seemed to be a very comfortable surface. It felt like I was lying down on a bed. It was just as comfortable as my bed at home, but I knew I was in a foreign place. The smell of it was off. This wasn't the floral smell of my room or my house. It wasn't a bad smell, it smelled like cleaning products more than anything. It was a minty fresh smell combined with the smell of clean laundry, fresh from the dryer.

I opened my eyes to see a ceiling fan turning right above my head. I got up quickly as the room spun - *head rush*. I closed my eyes and reopened them. I was fine after a few seconds. I used both hands to push myself off the bed onto the ground. I definitely wasn't home. I knew that much for certain.

At that exact moment I examined my left arm. It didn't hurt. The throbbing pain was gone; the bone fragment didn't stick out anymore! I rubbed my hand over my arm and thought to myself, *Am I dreaming?*

I stood in an enormous room with windows that reached from the ceiling all the way to the floor. I walked out of the room to realize I was in an apartment-like house. The size was nothing compared to my house back home but still, this was absolutely beautiful.

"Hello? Is anyone here?" I called out to the big, empty space as I made my way down the stairs. The living room, dining room and kitchen were all one big, open room and the wall was completely covered with one big window. My jaw dropped all the way down to the ground as I took a little tour of the place. I was getting more and more excited and the reality sunk deeper. *Am I on Earth? I think this was Dad's home on Earth!* My chest filled with excitement.

I walked up to the window and looked outside. I could see many, many buildings. I have never seen this many buildings before in my life! I could tell we were up high and my stomach turned a little bit. I wasn't afraid of heights, but this building was higher than any other building I had been in. The highest place I'd been was my tower. And that was nothing compared to this. This must have been the height of five of my towers!

I could see my reflection in the window, but something was off. Shocked, I slowly backed away from the window. I ran back towards the room I first came from and went directly to the washroom. I held my breath before I looked in the huge mirror. My jaw dropped at what I saw staring back at me. *But what happened?* I raised my hand to make sure I was really looking at myself. My mirrored image raised its hand just as I did.

I kept moving around. I touched my hair. I inhaled deeply as my hair was no longer down to my waist *and* it was also no longer blonde. I took a step towards the mirror trying to come to terms with the fact my hair was now a chocolate brown and shoulder length. Also, my favourite dress had been replaced with tight jeans and a loose white blouse. The blouse looked nice, but the jeans were very unappealing. I have never worn pants in my life. Girls weren't supposed to wear pants in general. Not even the men on Caledonia wore jeans. They were always dressed to impress. Only the farmers wore jeans. But the jeans I wore didn't look like farmers' ones. I guess these ones looked a bit nicer. I guess I had to get used to this. *Was this how women on Earth dressed? - Pants?* I didn't like it.

I began to sob but quickly stopped myself. This is what I wanted, wasn't it? *'I wanted to become unrecognizable. I wanted no one to know who I was.'* Everything I thought of in the portal actually came through. I didn't want to feel pain, I wanted to be unrecognizable, and I wanted to go to Earth. The portal doesn't only transport, it also makes your wishes a reality.

I wonder what would happen if I was thinking of another world I didn't even know of. What if it led me somewhere else dangerous? I gulped back the lump in my throat and washed my face with a bit of cold water. I guess I could get used to my hair at this length and colour. This was the new Sophia whether I liked it or not.

I walked back into the bedroom and noticed a wallet on top one of the dressers. I opened it and took out the identification card. It was Dad's. Antonio Amaro, it said. I guess he used the same name here that he does at home. I don't know why it would be different. I just thought he would go by another name.

There was another card in there as well. It said Master Card on it. I didn't know what that was. I folded the wallet back up and put it in my back pocket. I guess the pants did come in handy. None of my dresses had pockets and I didn't have a purse to carry Dad's wallet around in. I guess I would get use to pants eventually. I decided to leave the room and begin my search for this so called Nekkel Ace.

Before I left the room, I looked back to the bed and wondered where the exit for the portal was. I expected to come out of another portal, but I guess it didn't work out that way. *How was I going to get back?* I shrugged my shoulders and told myself I would worry about that afterwards.

I took one last look at myself in the mirror before I left. I noticed the latch to my necklace was at the front. I twisted it and placed it behind my neck. It looked perfect. I walked out the door and into the hallway.

How do I get downstairs? I thought to myself. I saw a couple exiting their room at the same time I exited mine. They looked confused when they saw mw. I don't know why. Did I stand out too much? I expected they would be leaving as well. I followed them without making eye contact.

The man walked up to this wall with two doors and a button on one side. He reached for the button that lit up as soon as he pressed it. He then resumed his place next to his female companion. They stood there waiting, so I did the same thing. I was so nervous!

I heard a 'ding!' noise and the doors automatically slid open to reveal a small room that didn't look like it led anywhere. The couple made their way inside. I stood there not knowing what to do.

"Are you coming in?" The man asked as he held the door open for me. He looked like a kind enough man. He looked about my Dad's age, give or take a few years. He had many wrinkles in his forehead, but a head full of hair. I could see streaks of white peeking out. I looked to the woman. She looked much younger than he did. She was probably in her late thirties. I wondered if they were a couple or maybe they were just friends.

I looked back to the man. His eyebrows were raised as he waited for an answer from me.

"Uh, I-I, y-yeah." I managed to say. I didn't know what else to do. I took a deep breath and went inside with them. I walked straight to the back behind them. It had to be safe if they were doing it.

The doors closed and I felt the pit of my stomach just drop. We started moving and I braced myself against the walls. My arms were spread out and my palms acted as if they were glued to the wall. I looked around with weary eyes. *What was this contraption? Where were we going and how could a room this small be moving?* I was the only one bothered by this. The couple looked completely at ease!

The woman turned around to look at me. "Scared of elevators, are you?" She asked with a smile.

"Huh? Elev-ator?" I could barely speak. I think my throat closed up.

Her eyes were wide and her mouth was the shape of a small O. It looked as if she thought I was crazy. Eh, I wouldn't blame her. I could only imagine what I looked like. We stopped moving and the doors opened again.

The woman went out first and walked towards the entrance while the man stood in the middle where the two doors met into one. "You alright? Do you need some help?" The man stretched out his hand for me to take I guessed. I took his offer and let him help me out of the machine. As soon as I was out, I went directly for the couches in the entrance. I needed to catch my breath. I didn't realize how hard my heart was pumping. I didn't know what to expect from that... that *thing*!

I wiped my face and realized it was covered in a light mist of sweat. *That -what did she call it? Elevator? - really took a lot of out me.*

The man got me a cup of water and said, "It's alright. Sometimes those things need some getting used to." He looked over to the woman who was waiting. "Well, I have to go. See you around." He walked away and caught up with the woman. They both left through the front doors. I couldn't react like that to everything new that I saw. Now I understand why Dad didn't want me coming to Earth.

I got up and threw the cup in the trash can. I could feel the man standing behind the desk staring at me as I walked towards the doors – which had no handles, and were glass. As I walked up to them, they opened by themselves! *This is cool,* I thought. I crossed right through and exited the building.

There were so many people crossing the street. Their cars looked so weird. They were different then the cars we had back home. There were yellow and white lines on the road. *Green, yellow and red lights control the movement of the cars here apparently.* I stood there in a trance watching everything and everyone.

"Sorry." I said to someone as they bumped into me. They didn't even apologize! *How rude!*

I was having second thoughts about this. This was way too much for me to handle. Dad was right. *I should have listened to him.* I didn't know where I was or what I had to do. I figured I might as well walk around and see where my own two feet would take me. *Maybe fate will lead the way for me. Everything happens for a reason right?*

A bunch of people were standing near a pole. They appeared to be waiting for something. On the other side of the road was another pole; attached was this glowing red hand image. A few seconds later the hand disappeared and was replaced by the image of a little white man walking. With that, everyone proceeded to cross the road. So I followed them. I felt relief flood through me as I crossed the street. I was so proud of myself. That sounded kind of stupid, but it seemed like things here were more complicated than at home. We didn't have lights on the streets; we didn't have this many people and cars in one place at the same time. I got a headache just thinking about it.

I walked towards what looked like a park. I found a random bench and sat on it. I had a good view of the park. People were going for walks. I could see parents playing catch with their children and other people playing with their pets.

I sat there with my legs crossed. I was just thinking of my next moves. I shouldn't do this alone. I needed someone to help me. I needed Matteo. I *couldn't* do this alone. My elbows were propped on my knees as my head fell into my hands. *What if I don't know how to get back? What if I can't find the Nekkel Ace?* I thought. I have bad memories of everyone in my life; the memory of my Dad withering away unable to wake up from his coma. The memory of my Mom half naked with Massimo. The memory of Matteo became blurred as my eyes filled with tears. I remember him staring at me as I ran past him and Kiko in pain. I could still hear him calling my name – it echoed in the back of my mind. It sent chills down my spine. Those are not memories that one wishes to keep. As much as I wished they would disappear, I knew they would remain in my mind forever.

The only good memory I have before leaving is Paul Jr. - which I absolutely hate to admit. He was so kind to me those days I spent in my tower. There was something about the way he looked at me from the garden. The peacefulness his eyes portrayed as he stared into mine. I could still picture him now. I guessed that would have to be one memory I would hold onto. I think he really did love me. He didn't really show it too well. It didn't seem like he knew what to do with love. He was slowly learning. I wondered what he would do when he found out what happened with me. I wondered if he would be upset, or sad, or maybe he would try to find me. I really didn't know.

I ran a hand through my new coif. It was nice. I didn't have to worry about it getting tangled or caught in anything. *Maybe when I find the Nekkel Ace and go back home, I will cut it the same length. That's only if it goes back to being long and blonde - I hope it does.*

I caught a glimpse of one of the men playing with his pet. I think it was a dog. It was very small. He ran towards it but was looking at me the same time. He smiled and I couldn't help but smile back. I had no idea who he was.

I heard a loud horn coming from behind me. I jumped up from the sound of a loud crash. Looking over my shoulder, I could see cars backed up at the green light. I wondered what the commotion was about. I saw one car's rear end smashed into, while the car behind it was missing its front bumper, which now lay on the ground in front of it. I think I knew what happened. No one was hurt, but the driver whose car had been rear-ended didn't look too pleased. I could hear them yelling at each other. People on the sidewalk stopped to see what all the commotion was about – just like what I was doing.

"Hey, look out!" I heard someone call from behind me in the park's direction.

I turned around and looked towards the park and realized there was a flying object coming right towards me. Before it registered that I should duck out of the way, it hit me directly in my forehead. I fell back hard onto the bench. I held my head in my hands, sucking in the air, trying not to cry.

Chapter 14 – Friendly Stranger

My head spun as I sat still on the bench. As soon as the spinning stopped, I ducked my head down and buried my face in my hands. I pressed my head down hard on my knees. The pressure eased the pain - sort of. This was my first hour on Earth and I already managed to get hurt! *How am I going to make it out of here in one piece?* I had to be more careful than this! *Come on Sophia! Be more cautious!* I said to myself.

I heard a man's voice repeating *sorry* over and over again to me. Suddenly I felt two paws on my knees. I automatically thought they were Kiko's. Reality kicked in as I could tell - even with my eyes closed - that it couldn't be him. Kiko's paws were much bigger than the ones on me now. It then occurred to me that I didn't know when I would see him again. At that moment I could feel my heart breaking.

"Oh shoot! Are you alright? Let me look at that," the man said. I could feel his hands trying to lift my head from off my knees. I wasn't ready to show my face just yet. My eyes were still tightly shut. I figured keeping them closed would numb the pain – not that it worked.

Just at that moment something hit me - and it wasn't that flying object again. I remembered my dream from a while ago. I knew this was going to happen. I knew I was going to change. *Wait! It wasn't a dream; I was actually drowning. I saw a vision - a vision of myself apparently!* My other self was pushing me to wake up. She has short brown hair. I was predicting what I was going to look like now. *Wow, I guess this portal really digs into your brain.*

I opened my eyes in astonishment and raised my head. The sudden shock of light forced me to squint. The sun was setting, but its rays were still strong. They were coming out from right behind this man. I looked down and saw this adorable puppy, still with his paws on my knees. He saw me staring and immediately jumped to his feet. He was light brown and white. I shoved over to the left so his owner would cast a shadow over me. The man's face was level with mine and I could tell he was checking my forehead. I could feel his cold grip on my head. I stared at him with one eye open.

I touched my head. "Ow!" I moaned. *Aw, I couldn't believe I was hurt. This was so annoying.*

He offered to take me back to his place so we could ice on my forehead which was slowly starting to form a bump. Without saying a word, I got up and walked away. This man I had never seen before in my life was inviting me to his house. I knew that wasn't a good idea. Just because I hit my head, didn't mean I lost all common sense!

I could sense him following behind me. He was talking to me but I didn't pay attention apart from catching a few words here and there.

I walked faster, hoping to get rid of him, but he kept up. I planned to walk back to my own place. Once I got in, he would hopefully go away.

His dog frolicked between us as we crossed the busy street. He had to run to keep up with us. He had a large, round disc thing in its mouth. *So that's what hit me!* I realized

"It's called a Frisbee," the man said, reading my mind. *Frisbee? What a weird name. We don't have Frisbees where I live.*

I finally accepted this man's company as he seemed harmless. I looked around, this time feeling more comfortable in my environment. I was no longer frightened by the bustle of people and cards. I knew about the street lights and I knew I had to obey them. I knew it would end badly if I didn't.

I told the man I didn't want to go back to his place since I was sure my Dad's place had its share of ice in the freezer. He still offered to walk me home. He felt bad for what he did. Apparently, he wasn't in the habit of launching Frisbees at people's heads. He was going to throw it in the opposite direction, but he was startled by the sound of the crash and the Frisbee escaped his grip. Of course with my luck, it found its way right onto my head.

We got to the front of my building. I thanked him for escorting me and insisted I didn't need his service anymore. I entered the lobby and decided not to take that machine again up to my room. I didn't even know what floor I was on. I figured I could easily ask the man at the front desk. He saw me leaving earlier, I was sure he'd remember me. I headed over to the front desk only to discover that my escort and his canine companion had followed me into the building.

"Good evening Mr. Heartwell," the man behind the desk said, slightly bowing his head.

I turned to him with a confused look on my face. "Mr. Heartwell?" I questioned him. His name sounded familiar. I didn't know how that was even possible, seeing as I had never been here before.

"Yup, that's my name, but you can just call me Joshua - no, Josh." He smiled at me. I liked Joshua better than Josh. I liked his smile too. But I wasn't going to let him in on either of those facts.

I quickly but confidently answered back with my full name as well. I was proud to say my name out loud.

"Hm, Sophia? What a beautiful name."

I dropped my head to conceal the fact that I was blushing.

"Your last name – Amaro… You wouldn't by any chance be related to Antonio Amaro, would you?"

I ignored the question at first since it took me by surprise. We now stood at the front desk. I didn't even think to ask the clerk – whose name tag read "Carlos" – what my room number was. That was about the last thing on my mind now. "How do you know my father?" I asked Joshua.

There was that smile again. I couldn't help but smile back. His body was so relaxed. He rested his elbow on the front desk counter. Carlos was listening to our entire conversation, whether he liked to or not. He couldn't go anywhere else I presumed.

"Well he lives here doesn't he? I assume you are visiting him. I live here as well." He started walking towards the elevators. He gestured with his arm. "Come on."

I followed him and we stood in front of the doors of doom. I was breathing heavily, contemplating how I would get around this. I didn't want to show him I was afraid. The doors flew open. I took in a deep breath and I followed him inside. The doors closed and we went up.

"Sophia? Are you okay? Your face is red." Joshua, who towered over me, lowered his head to get a better look at me. "Breathe."

I didn't realize I was holding my breath the entire ride up. As soon as the doors opened, I let out the deep breath that I sucked in prior to entering.

I stumbled out through the doors. Joshua was right behind me. "I'm not too good with, um…uh…" My mind went blank. I scratched my head, trying to remember what I was going to say. I had it just a second ago.

"Elevators?" Joshua asked.

"Yes, yes! I don't like them." I braced myself because I was expecting him to burst out into laughter.

"Oh, why didn't you tell me? My mom was afraid of elevators. We could have taken the stairs. It would have taken us a while – but we could have managed." *Oh, now he tells me! I should have said something before.*

His apartment was on the seventeenth floor. This was the very last floor of the building. No wonder I thought it was so high – it really was! *I really should get used to the elevator. Walking up and down seventeen floors doesn't sound too appealing.*

I recognized the floor as my own. This floor consisted of three penthouse suites according to Joshua. He stopped in front of a door but I kept walking. Joshua came right after me. His little dog was still following with the Frisbee in its mouth. I wanted to grab it from him and throw it down the hall. Not as a nice gesture, but rather out of spite. *That Frisbee deserves to burn.*

I reached my door and turned the handle. It was locked.

"Do you not have your key?" Joshua asked me.

"Uh…" I patted myself down. I didn't have anything with me. I then remembered Dad's wallet. I reached into my back pocket and pulled it out. Maybe the key was in there. I had no other options really. I flipped it open and searched through all the flaps.

Joshua was looking over my shoulder. "There it is!" He pointed to a white card hidden in the back.

I took it out and stared at it for a few seconds. *That's not a key!* Joshua sensed my confusion and took the card out of my hand. He waved it under what looked like a sensor at the bottom of the doorknob. I heard an unlocking noise and I tried the handle again. It opened!

"Hold on one second," Joshua said as he ran back to his room with his dog. He opened the door and led his dog inside. He closed the door behind him and made his way back to my doorway. I walked right in and acted normal. I was still astounded by how beautiful this place was. There were stairs right at the entrance which led to the bedroom. Downstairs was the living room, the kitchen and all that kind of stuff. The neutral colours really did make me feel at home. I didn't mind living here.

"You can have a seat on the couch," I said to Joshua. I figured I might as well be hospitable. I asked him if he wanted anything to drink. He said he was fine.

He sat down comfortably and looked around the interior. His face was impressed. I went straight to the freezer. There were two ice trays. I picked one out and popped a few ice cubes out. I scooped them up with a kitchen towel. I looked at myself in the reflection of the stove. There was a small, dark purple bump on my head with a little cut. *The pain is gone* – I lifted up my hand to touch it – *okay, the pain is not gone!*

I put the ice to my forehead and headed back to the living room. I took a seat on the opposite side of the couch where Joshua sat. I shifted my body so I faced him. He sat there staring at me. I didn't know what to say. I didn't expect him to follow me in. He seemed so at ease; like this wasn't his first time here.

"Antonio changed the place up a bit," Joshua said as he looked around.

"Excuse me?"

"Hm, let me guess; your Dad never mentioned me before?"

I shook my head.

"Alright. Well, as you know my name is Joshua Heartwell. My father, Charles Heartwell, is in fact the primary owner of this building. It was his little masterpiece. He has passed it down to me. My father and your father were pretty close. I've spoken to your Dad a couple of times. He is a really nice guy. He even showed me a picture of you once that he kept in that exact wallet. I guess it's not in there anymore. When I saw you in the park I didn't recognize you at first until I looked into your eyes. You have the most beautiful eyes I have ever seen. They are so out of this world." Joshua scooted a bit closer.

Out of this world, eh? You have no idea, buddy! I laughed out loud. Joshua smiled. He probably thought I was flattered or something. I contemplated whether or not I should tell him. I decided against it. Earth people aren't supposed to know about us. He probably wouldn't have believed me anyway. I had the ice on my forehead the whole time. My forehead was officially numb now.

Joshua looked closely at the big bump on my head. He then shifted his gaze directly into my eyes. But it felt more like he was staring directly into my soul. This was all very strange since I didn't know who he was, but I felt safe at the same time. I didn't mind him looking at me. I even stared back. Our eyes locked from both ends of the couch. I took this time to really study his face. That smile never left his face. Little wrinkles appeared around the outer corners of his eyes. It was cute in an innocent sort of way.

He had the most striking brown eyes I had ever seen. I wasn't use to brown eyes. Almost everyone I knew had blue eyes. I was under a spell and I wasn't able to look anywhere else. I was completely struck by his personality and charm.

"Your beauty is so marvellous. I can't imagine why we didn't meet sooner. Where have you been my entire life?" he said as he examined every inch of my face. I don't normally get close with people this easily but there was just something about Joshua that made me - let me - open up to him. It was just so easy, it felt so natural.

We got talking some more. I wanted to learn more about him. But it seemed like most of the questions were directed to me.

He asked me where I lived. I didn't answer specifically. I just told him I lived far from here in the most beautiful white house. I told him about my delightful garden and how I loved the smell of flowers. Joshua told me he once lived on a farm with many animals, but that was a long time ago. He moved to the city when he was six years old. And that's where he remained.

We talked about our families, birthdays, favourite colours, and favourite foods. Apparently I'd been missing out since I had never eaten Sushi before. I never even heard of it. Joshua told me I *had* to try it. He said he's take me one day.

I sat there all night talking to Joshua, my new friend. I eventually got rid of the cloth and ice. It started dripping all over me so I tossed it in the sink.

It didn't feel weird telling him these things. *Should I be more cautious when talking to Joshua?* I asked myself. *Nothing in life comes this easy.* If I was doing a wrong thing now, I knew I would pay for it later. But at the moment I could have cared less. I knew deep down inside Joshua was a good person. He *had* to be a good person. No one with eyes like that could be bad. They were so warm. His eyes had so many dimensions. They could go on forever. They had so many stories to tell. I would sometimes catch myself getting lost in them. At times I actually had to pretend I was paying attention to what he was saying.

I never felt this way about anyone. But it was getting late and I could barely keep my eyes open. Joshua said he didn't want to keep me up any longer. I walked him to the door.

"Goodnight." He smiled while bowing his head as he bid me farewell. He then turned to walk away.

I was day dreaming as I watched him walk down the hall. He took one last look at me and went to open his door. I turned to my senses and closed the door. I went to the room where I first woke up in and dove onto my bed. There were two other rooms here as well, but I never went in them. It actually felt nice to lie down on a comfortable bed. I hugged my pillow and smiled to myself. *Coming to Earth was the best decision I've ever made!*

Chapter 15 – Disturbed by the Bell

The next morning I woke up feeling lethargic and confused. It must have been around 7:00 a.m. I didn't sleep very well that night. I was too preoccupied with other things running through my mind. As I thought about yesterday's events, a huge smile spread across my face. I wondered when I would see Joshua next. *Should I go and see him? Or do I wait for him to come here?* Then again, I didn't want to sit around and wait for him.

I shook my head in disappointment with myself. *This isn't why I came to Earth. I came here to save Dad. I didn't come here to flirt with his neighbours.*

I wondered what Matteo was doing while I was gone. If he even cared that I was gone. I wondered if he tried using the Portal to find me. *I doubt it*, I said to myself. *I would've found him in the apartment by now, right? I don't know. I only used the portal once. That doesn't make me some kind of expert!*

I had to find this Nekkel Ace and I had to do it alone. As much as I would have loved to see Joshua right now, Dad was my top priority. I got dressed in the same pants as yesterday - since I didn't have anything else - and left the room. I found a t-shirt in one of the dressers. It was a few sizes too big, so I knotted it to the side. I knew it was Dad's. His scent still lingered on it. For a moment I felt like I was back at home.

While in the hallway, I had to pass Joshua's room to get to the elevators. I refused to look at his door as I was tempted to give it a knock. I promised myself I wouldn't get distracted again. A whole day was wasted yesterday with him when I should have been out looking for the Nekkel Ace.

As soon as I reached the elevators I heard a door open. I kept my eyes forward, hoping it was the other couple's door.

"Sophia!" a familiar voice called out.

I knew right away it was Joshua. I could never mistake that new voice anywhere. It was friendly and full of warmth and the way he said my name sent chills up my spine. I rubbed my arms to get rid of the goose bumps. I turned around to see his smiling face beaming at me like a ray of sunlight.

Joshua ran towards me with Milo - his dog – in tow. I got a whiff of Joshua's cologne and it smelled wonderful. I took in a deep breath while he spoke. "What are you doing awake this early? The city normally sleeps in until noon on a Saturday."

I exhaled slowly through my nose. *So it is Saturday today.* I asked Joshua for the date. He informed me that today was August 16th. That sounded about right to me. I left home somewhere in the middle of August that I could remember.

"I was just going for a walk." That was the partial truth of course.

"By yourself? I was going for a walk as well. Milo hates being cooped up inside. I spend most of my time outside anyway. Last night after I left you, Milo was waiting at the door for me. I felt bad for leaving him like that, but I didn't want him roaming around your place. He is house broken, but I wasn't sure if you'd mind. He can be a handful sometimes."

"Yeah, animals can be a handful." My mind went blank as I thought back to the day Kiko stole my book from me and ran away. That was the day I caught Mom with Massimo. I wondered what would have happened if I didn't chase after Kiko. I think he would have made me come after him one way or another. He's very clever and stubborn that way.

"Oh, you know how pets are, eh? Do you have one?" Joshua asked.

I just nodded, eager to get going. I didn't see any point in beating around the bush. We both knew he was going to accompany me. The elevator doors swung open and the three of us went in.

Joshua mentioned taking the stairs instead. I had to get used to the elevator. After all, it *was* faster.

"What kind of pet do you have?"

"I have a cat back home. He actually belongs to my brother, but I guess you could say he's mine as well," I laughed. I was getting used to the elevator. This was only my second time and already I felt like an expert. It was actually starting to remind me of the Portal – sort of.

As soon as we exited the doors, we passed the front desk where Carlos greeted us with a warm 'Good Morning.'

We then headed straight for the park. We talked along the way. Milo would run off ahead, and wait patiently for us to catch up to him. He was a good dog. Besides, his little legs could only take him so anyway.

"Were you planning on going shopping today?" Joshua asked me. "It didn't look like you had any luggage in your place. Well, from what I saw of it at least."

"No I don't have any money on me actually." I didn't know what else to say.

"You don't have a credit card or anything? I swear I saw a MasterCard in your wallet yesterday. Why don't you just use that?"

Joshua was sneaky. I didn't even realize he saw it.

MasterCard, of course! I guess that's what people use to buy things here. I should have learned more about this place before jumping through that portal. There is just so much I don't know! No wonder Dad would come here to study their technology. He was getting tips from Earth to bring back to Caledonia.

I didn't what to think at this point. Joshua knew I had a MasterCard but no luggage. *It could be that he has a keen eye for small details. On the other hand, it does seem a little strange and even suspicious for someone to recognize those details.* Either way, I was thankful to him for bringing the card to my attention.

I didn't know what I was going to do. I couldn't keep wearing Dad's clothes. I decided I would definitely have to plan a shopping trip soon. I had never been shopping alone before. The servants would usually buy me clothes and lay them out for me under my mother's strict supervision of course. As I got older, on the rare occasion when I went shopping with my mother, I would pick out my own clothes.

We continued our talk from last night. Joshua told me that he was an only child and that sometimes he wished he had a younger sister to watch over.

I decided to tell Joshua about how Matteo and I became reunited after all those years.

"For most of my life, I lived thinking I was an only child," I said as I walked. I kept a lookout for any flying objects in the air. I knew I would be alright since the cause of the bump on my head was walking beside me. I was safe – for now.

"Really? What happened?" Joshua said with raised eyebrows. I knew I had his full attention.

I told Joshua about the accident; how Matteo and I met by the river years later and how he came to live with my family and me.

"Five years later, I found out that he was my brother. I never knew those sorts of things happened. I am happy though. I love him very much!"

"That does sound pretty amazing. I'm glad you found your brother. It is never good living in the shadows, not knowing. Right now I only have Milo in my life. I guess I can say I have you as well – if that's alright with you?"

It felt as though Joshua trusted me just as much as I trusted him. *Was there a relationship growing between us?* I don't want to rush into things, or have false hope, but I was developing feelings for him. I didn't have anyone in my life that I could freely be myself with. Of course there was Matteo, but he was my brother and that's not the same, is it? I was so nervous. I didn't even know how to act around someone I liked.

"I don't mind," I smiled.

I was walking with my hands at my sides, casually glancing at the people around me. Everyone looked so happy; like they were enjoying this beautiful, sunny day. Something touched my hand. I looked down and realized Joshua had taken it. I opened my fingers and let Joshua intertwine his fingers in mine. My heart raced as I had never felt so excited and frightened at the same time. *Don't panic Sophia. Act like this is normal*! Coaching myself seemed to work pretty well in this world. I looked up at him and he smiled at me. My innards turned to mush, I completely melted. I could feel the blood rushing to my face from embarrassment. I liked this man and he was showing his affection for me out in the open, in front of everyone to see. This moment was perfect. Neither of us said anything. We walked together holding hands. I didn't have it in me to wipe the silly smile from my face.

After hours of playing in the park, where I learned how to throw a Frisbee, I started to feel hungry. Joshua told me of a place that we could have lunch. I didn't object. He led us to a little café. We sat on the patio where we had a view of the streets. It was a little place but there were many people there. Joshua tied Milo to the rail beside our table.

We spent about three hours there, just enjoying our time together. We had sandwiches and drank iced coffee. I'd never had coffee cold before. *How do we not have this in Caledonia? I have got to tell someone when I get back!*

I told Joshua about my Dad and how he was sick. I don't know where the topic came from. I was thinking about it and before I knew it, the words came out my mouth. I told him I was looking for a way to help him. Joshua seemed very sympathetic. He even offered to help. I could have used his help but then I remembered when Dr. Slike said people from Earth couldn't see the Nekkel Ace.

I had to keep reminding myself that I had to keep this information from Joshua. *They are not supposed to know of our planet. They are not supposed to know it even exists. We are hidden for a reason and I know if I don't shut my mouth now, our whole world could be in jeopardy.*

We eventually left and I invited Joshua over to my place. He said sure. When we got up to the floor Joshua changed his mind and asked if I wanted to see his place instead. I was a little hesitant at first, but I figured it was alright.

Joshua gave me a tour as soon as we got in. It looked like my place only more elegant with all the antique furniture. You wouldn't expect a young bachelor to live in an apartment like this.

"My dad designed this place and I didn't have it in me to change it," Joshua said, reading my mind.

Lastly he showed me his room. It was as big as mine, possibly even bigger. It was painted a dark grey which made it feel like you were in the middle of a storm cloud. His bed had a black headboard with black covers. I didn't really like dark colours, but his room was eerily nice. Milo had a big black pillow on the opposite end of the bed, where he now lay, staring at us the whole time.

Joshua sat on the end of his bed. He watched me as I looked around his room. I glanced at myself in the mirror on top of his dresser. My hair was tied up and I never realized until now, how ugly the t-shirt was that I was wearing. *I was supposed to go shopping today. How does he do it? What is this hold Joshua has on me? I could have gone shopping today – but I didn't. I could have looked for the Nekkel Ace today - but I didn't.* I was annoyed with myself. Then again I was enjoying every moment of this. I could see a clear view of Joshua's bed behind me in the mirror's reflection. Joshua was smiling at me. I wondered what he was thinking. Joshua had some drawings like Dad's on his counter. I asked him what they were and he told me that his company designs buildings for the city. He was an architect and just started designing something new. His company helped design them, and after they are approved, the same company built them. It was a family business. His father, who was also an architect, designed and supervised the creation of this building, so Joshua wanted to create a place of his own. From what I saw on the drawings, it looked pretty big - much bigger than this one. I wondered if he would move out and live there when it is done.

I placed the papers back down and noticed a book on his nightstand.

It was leather bound with a tiny latch. It looked pretty worn out. Before I could even pull the latch, Joshua leapt up and the book right out of my hands.

I stood there, dumbfounded with my hands still open; like I had an invisible book in my hands.

"Hey! Yeah, um, sorry. You can't look at this. It is kind of personal. It was my Dad's journal," Joshua said as he opened one of the drawers and placed it inside. He closed the drawer right after.

"Oh, sorry. I didn't know. I didn't mean to intrude like that." I was embarrassed now. I shouldn't have even touched it. *Who am I, really, to be touching other people's stuff? I really shouldn't have done that. How could I be so meddlesome?*

"It's okay. Don't worry about it." Joshua sat back down on his bed. He looked tired all of a sudden. I on the other hand, I was restless. I suppose coffee will do that to a person.

I looked out the window and saw that it was getting dark. I literally spent the entire day with him. *I guess time really does fly when you're having a nice time.*

"I'm hungry!" Joshua said as he walked over to his phone.

"You are? But we just ate a couple hours ago." I started laughing. I still had that journal in the back of my mind.

"You aren't hungry?" Joshua seemed surprised.

"No," I answered him.

Joshua picked up the phone and I heard him placing an order for pizza. He asked for a whole wheat, thin crust, and well-done pizza with green olives, hot peppers and bacon on it. I was stunned, for I didn't know you could put so many toppings on one pizza. I had eaten pizza once before. But it was just sauce and cheese. It was pretty good. One of the servants made it one day because Dad had asked them to. I guessed he got the idea from Earth. We all thought Dad was crazy for requesting something like that, but after trying the pizza for the first time, we all loved it.

He sat back down on the end of his bed. "It will be here in fifteen minutes, maybe even sooner. I always order from them. I am their favourite customer."

I nodded and looked back to his dresser. I didn't want to drop the whole 'journal' subject. "So how come you have your Dad's journal? Did he leave it here by accident one day or something?" I knew I shouldn't have pushed it further, but I was way too curious.

"Actually, my parents both died a couple years ago in a car accident."

I was shocked as I didn't expect such a response. I also felt guilty for bringing up those sad memories. I should have just kept my mouth shut. I wanted to punch myself in the head. *Stupid, stupid Sophia*! I went and sat beside him on the bed. I put my hand on his shoulder. "I am so sorry. I didn't know. I promise!"

"I know you didn't know. It is just a hard subject for me. I am fine though." He grabbed my hand from his shoulder and slowly brought it up to his face and kissed it.

I stopped breathing. It was so sensual, the way he held my hand. Like it was his most prized possession. His grip was so strong, yet so gentle. His soft lips felt so warm on my hand. Once again he was being very careful. His eyes were closed as he took in the embrace of my hand. I didn't take my eyes off him. I felt like closing my eyes as well. This moment was so personal I felt like I should give him privacy. But it *was* my hand and this was all so new to me.

Joshua moved my hand from his lips and smiled. He still had his eyes closed. He opened his eyes and looked to me. I didn't move, I didn't blink, and I couldn't speak. My eyes just stared deeply into his. *Who is this strange man turning my life upside down?*

Joshua still had my hand in both his hands. He moved one of his hands up and gently placed a strand of my hair behind my ear. He ran his finger down my cheek to my chin. This made my skin tingle.

Joshua's face was slowly coming closer to mine. I could feel his breath on my face. My body went numb as I inhaled deeply. His lips then touched mine. I had never experienced this sensation. His lips were warm. I closed my eyes and felt my other senses go into overdrive. I could feel his grip on my hand tighten. I noticed again the delicious smell of his cologne. It felt like I could hear Joshua's heartbeat, but it could have been mine. My pulse pounded throughout my body. I thought my body would give out at any second.

The kiss lasted about five seconds but it felt like five hours. Joshua moved his lips from mine and pulled his face back enough to look at me. I opened my eyes and stared back at him. I didn't want him to stop. I wanted him to kiss me again.

Joshua sighed with relief. "I've wanted to do that since the first time I laid my eyes on you."

I just smiled. "Hmm," was all that came out. I couldn't say anything else. I guessed he must have been waiting a long time to kiss me, since the first time he saw me was in a picture that Dad showed him. Or maybe he was talking about when he first saw me in the park. I didn't know and I didn't let it bother me.

Joshua closed his eyes again and went in for another kiss. I felt like I could kiss him forever.

I licked my sweet lips as he leaned in and kissed me again. I tasted his soft lips for the second time. Joshua's lips parted, but before he could slip his tongue, the doorbell rang.

Joshua stopped. "The pizza is here!" He kissed my cheek and got up from the bed to open the door. I could hear them pounding on the door. I guessed pizza deliverers were pretty inpatient people.

As soon as Joshua was out of the room, my body gave out and I fell flat onto his bed. I finally took a full deep breath in as I realized my stomach was filled with butterflies. My face felt hot and I knew my cheeks were probably all red. I started giggling to myself. I was so happy he kissed me, but I was also upset that we were interrupted. If this was what kisses felt like, I couldn't wait for the next one to come.

Chapter 16 – Forest Flashback

I lay in my bed wide awake. I'd only gotten a few hours of sleep. The events of last night kept running through my mind. I turned over to check the clock on my nightstand. It glowed in big, bright, red numbers: 6:15 a.m. I kicked the covers off me. I was only wearing underwear since I still didn't have proper clothes, let alone pyjamas. I grabbed a robe that I had purposely placed on the arm chair beside my bed and threw it on. It was white cotton. It felt so soft on my skin. I went to the window and opened the massive curtains. The city was already awake. There were so many cars on the road. The sun was rising steadily in the horizon. I could tell today was going to be a good day.

I left my room and went to the kitchen. I was craving some of that ice coffee from yesterday. I knew they probably weren't open yet, so I decided to make it myself. I first had to figure out how to make normal coffee. I searched for coffee in the cupboards and found a glass jar with a label that read Nescafé and had a picture of a cup of coffee. *Oh, the power of pictures!* I picked it up and looked at the back. It had instructions on how to make instant coffee.

Scoop one round teaspoon (about 5 ml) of coffee into 6 oz (175 ml) boiling water.

Add sugar or cream/milk to liking.

I found a kettle like contraption. It was plugged into the wall. I picked it up and filled it with water and plugged it back in. It had only one button. I pressed it and waited. I could hear the water beginning to boil. I guessed that was the first step. I smiled a bit. *I can boil water!* I was so pathetic. I waited a little while. *How would I know when it was done boiling?* I

112

wondered. *Maybe it will whistle like the kettles back home.* Instead I heard a loud clicking sound as the boiling ceased.

I scooped out some instant coffee and poured it into the cup. I then poured in the hot water like it said. I added sugar and milk. So now I had regular coffee. The next step was to make it cold. I dropped a few ice cubes into the cup. They melted at once, so I added more. When it seemed cold enough, I took a sip and automatically spit it out in the sink. It tasted like a watered down milky coffee. I dumped out the rest, rinsed the cup, and poured myself a glass of milk.

I sat at the kitchen table sipping my milk. This tasted much better than my failed attempt at ice coffee. I had to remind myself never to try that again. I couldn't sit anymore so I got up from the table and walked towards the couches. The sun was beaming in through the window. I let it touch my face. I closed my eyes and last night came flowing back to me.

I remembered Joshua's face as he kissed me. I remembered his touch, his smell, and his words.

But something still didn't feel right. When Joshua first left me to get the pizza, there was no one out there. He returned to the room shrugging his shoulders. I wondered why someone would so frantically knock on someone's door and then leave. He came back to sit down beside me, but as soon as he did, there was a normal knock on the door. Joshua rolled his eyes and sighed as he got up from the bed the second time. This time I joined him. We both sat on the kitchen table together. He ate the whole pizza by himself. I just watched him. I couldn't believe he ate the entire thing!

This is kind of embarrassing to say, but there were times when I would catch him staring at my chest. That made me uncomfortable and I almost left because of it. It was then I realized it was my necklace he was looking at. He said he had never seen anything like it before and asked where I had gotten it. I told him it was a gift from my parents. He just nodded his head.

When I was getting tired, I called it a night and told Joshua that I was going to go back to my place. He walked me to the door and gave me a kiss goodnight. He placed my necklace in his hands and looked directly into my eyes, "This is beautiful, but does not compare to you. Also, I want to give you something." He reached into his back pocket and pulled something out. He grabbed my right hand and placed a key card in it.

I was puzzled. "Oh, I don't need an extra key. I didn't lose mine or anything."

"I know you didn't. This key opens the door to my place, not yours," Joshua laughed.

I was thrilled. I tried to speak, but no words came out. Joshua kissed my forehead and I turned around and walked back to my place with his key in my hand. What a night!

I realized I should stop thinking about last night, and get on with my today. I waited until about eight o'clock to get dressed to leave my place. I knew Joshua got up early to take Milo for a run. I threw on a white t-shirt and a pair of jogging pants that I found in the dresser. I looked awful. I promised myself that I wouldn't look at myself in the mirror before I left. If I did, I would probably cry.

I grabbed Dad's wallet and put it in the front pocket of my ugly grey pants. It made them even baggier. I tightened the drawstring as much as possible. But they were still too big. It felt like they were about to fall at any moment.

Before I left, I looked at the time. It was 8 a.m. on the dot. I opened my door and ran towards the elevators. I pressed the button and waited. I was on pins and needles, hoping I wouldn't run into Joshua again. I wondered if Joshua headed out earlier and was now coming up the elevators – and that was why they were taking so long. I couldn't risk that so I took the stairs instead.

I finally reached the first floor and opened the doors which led to the lobby. I walked casually as I looked towards the front desk. I stopped dead in my tracks and there he was; Joshua talking to Carlos with Milo jumping by his feet, eager to go outside.

I hid behind one of the pillars. My back was pressed up against it so Joshua wouldn't see me. I closed my eyes hoping to become one with the pillar. I listened carefully to their conversation.

Joshua: "Did you see Sophia today?

Carlos: "No, she has not come down yet, sir."

Joshua: "I guess she slept in. Thanks Carlos. Let her know that I am looking for her if you see her."

Carlos: "Will do, sir."

I waited a few seconds before I peeked out from my hiding spot. I was sure that when I did, I would see Joshua standing right before me. I had to relax. I was getting worked up over nothing. I had no reason to be scared of him. I just didn't want to be interrupted again today. Every fibre of my body wanted to see him, but I had to stick to my plan. When I was done doing what I had to do, I would go find him.

When the coast was clear I stepped out and I said good morning to Carlos and he did inform me that Joshua - Mr. Heartwell actually - was looking for me. I thanked him and walked out. I looked behind me and saw Carlos picking up the phone. He was calling Joshua.

Where to first? I asked myself. There was something about the park yesterday that drew me in. I ignored the feeling and enjoyed the day. I knew there was a deep forest further down. I could see it from my place. I couldn't explain it, but I knew I had to go there.

I was embarrassed to be seen in public in this getup. To make matters worse, it was an extremely hot day; I was sweating through my baggy pants. I tried to ignore the people staring as I made my way towards the park. I could see the forest getting closer as I walked. For some reason it was blocked off with a thin wired fence. I could tell people walked over the fence since some parts were flat to the ground. I walked over them and began looking around.

An hour had gone by. The further I walked, the taller the trees grew. I followed a path, but it was beginning to fade as I walked further. I found myself watching my steps more closely. One wrong step and I would end up twisting my ankle again - maybe even breaking it this time!

The heat wasn't helping me one bit. I rolled my pants up to my knees and tied my shirt. I was tired and my mouth was dry. I regretted not packing a bottle of water for this trek. I ignored my thirst and kept walking. The trees were outstanding. Everything was so green and alive around me. Some trees were fallen over, and there was moss growing on them. I could hear birds chirping somewhere in the trees and little animals scurrying on the ground. At this moment I felt like I was wandering the forest near my house on Caledonia. I guessed all forests looked the same.

Another hour passed and I stumbled across large columns. I arched my neck to look to the top. I almost fell backwards. They looked like stone gateways to who knows what. The forest looked the same on both sides. I wondered why these were here. My hand touched the cold hard stone of the supposed gateways. It reminded me of home for some reason. The more I walked, the closer I felt to the Nekkel Ace. I couldn't understand how that was possible, but something inside was telling me, *keep going, you are almost there.*

I walked until my legs were stiff. My back was killing me and I was dehydrated. Just when I was about to give up, something caught my eye. It was a big tree at the top of a mossy, rocky hill. I headed in that direction. My eyes were on the tree the whole time. It looked so old and full of ancient wisdom. I figured this is where the Nekkel Ace was. It was hiding in this tree. I could feel it in my bones. My stomach was rumbling with excitement and hunger. I climbed the rocks, making sure not to fall over. When I got to the tree, I placed both my hands on it.

I closed my eyes. Bright flashes of my home replaced the darkness. I could see the garden, Mom, Matteo, the pond, the portal. I even had a sharp flash back of Dad falling off his horse. I gasped and removed my hands from the tree. I had to catch my breath. I opened my eyes wide in astonishment. *Did the tree just show me all of those?* I wondered. I brought my hand close to the tree one more time, without touching it. I could feel the fibres of the tree reaching for me.

"*Sophia.*"

I turned around. "Hello? Who's there?" I swore I heard someone call my name. *Great, now I'm hearing things.*

I looked back to the tree again but I felt something different this time. Emptiness. What was here a second ago was now gone. *The Nekkel Ace was here, I know it! Someone must have taken it!* I didn't know what else to do. I was so hungry and exhausted. I decided to go home.

My disappointment was getting the better of me. *I was so close – and then nothing.* The walk back seemed so much longer. Of course, I was taking smaller steps. I was in no hurry to go home. Besides, I used up all my energy getting there and now I had nothing left in me for the walk back.

I wondered what time it was. I finally reached that barbed wire I had stepped over all those hours ago. I felt dirty. I felt like all the sweat and dirt from the forest had piled up on my skin. I saw a lady going for a walk and asked her what time it was. She told me it was almost 2:00 p.m. I was gone for a long time. I didn't even realize I spent six hours in the forest. I deserved a nice long shower.

I came to a stop as soon as I reached my building. I could see Carlos staring at me through the glass doors. I thought about going inside, but kept walking. I needed to do some shopping, and fast! These sweaty, dirty jogging pants weren't cutting it for me anymore. I needed to find a store - any store - that sold dresses.

I looked at all the different stores and I had no idea which one to go into. I read the names of the stores as I walked; BCBG, Marciano, Burberry, Coach, Holt Renfrew, Guess, Forever XXI and a Vera Wang. I didn't know what these stores were, but I decided to go into the last one. I saw many pretty dresses in the window so I went in. These were gorgeous gowns. I wanted to buy them all and bring them back to Caledonia with me!

I walked in and embraced the cool air inside this building. I rolled my t-shirt sleeves and my pants back down. People were giving me strange looks as I walked around. They looked disgusted. I ignored them and found a handful of cute, casual dresses in the back. They were exactly what I was looking for.

I looked around to see if anyone would help me. It felt like everyone was avoiding me. I pulled the neck of my shirt away from my body and took a whiff. I didn't smell or anything. *The people in here are just rude.*

I caught the attention of a saleswoman walking past. "Excuse me, can I have some help with these." I said as I handed the dresses over to her.

With a sour tone to her voice she said, "We don't allow people to try on dresses unless they are buying them."

With the same tone I answered, "I never asked to try them on. I just want you to hold them. And as a matter of fact, I *will* be buying them." I gave her an exaggerated smile. She stared back at me in complete shock.

I added two more dresses to the five she already had in her hands. I walked around for another good fifteen minutes, just browsing at some of the beautiful gowns.

"Are you sure you don't want me to start a fitting room for you then?" Her patience was slowly slipping as I could tell she was getting tired of holding my dresses.

"No," I cheerfully said, running my hands over the dresses on the rack.

"I'll just put them by the cash register for you then." Then she left.

I smiled to myself and looked at a few more dresses. I didn't want anything else. I just felt like wasting her time since she was so abruptly rude to me.

I heard her talking to the lady at the cash register.

"Wow, all those dresses? You think she's going to buy them all?" the cashier asked.

"Absolutely not! Look at the way she is dressed; her hair, her clothes - what a disaster she is! There is no way she can afford all these dresses. There is thousands of dollars' worth of dresses on this counter. I'll be surprised if she even buys one."

The cashier didn't respond.

"Well, I'm off to find someone who *will* actually buy something from here."

As soon as she was gone, I walked up to the counter and told the cashier I was ready to cash out. She scanned all the dresses and told me my total. "Was anyone helping you with these dresses today?" she asked.

I looked over my shoulder at the clerk who acted so rudely. She stood there with her jaw slightly dropped as she saw me cashing out. I turned back to the cashier and answered with a sweet, "No."

The cashier raised an eyebrow and smiled at me. She must have been thinking the same thing. *She deserved that!*

I paid with my Dad's black credit card and was on my way back home. Before I knew it, I was in the shower, washing off today's adventure. It felt so nice to clean up after that!

I put on one of my dresses and hung up the rest of them. I checked myself in the mirror and was out the door. I was satisfied with the shopping I did today. My dress flowed beautifully and fit my body the way I liked.

I headed down the hall towards Joshua's place. I stood outside his door. I brought the key with me. I was going to knock, but thought, *why should I if I had the key?* He gave it to me for a reason. I stood outside the door contemplating what to do. *Aw heck!* I closed my eyes and swiped the card. The door opened and I walked right in. Milo was there at the door as if he were waiting for me.

I called Joshua's name but he didn't answer. I went closer to his room and called out his name a little louder. He called back saying he was in the shower and he would be out in five minutes.

I considered going back to my place and waiting there, but I felt like staying. I grabbed a bottle of water from the refrigerator and threw myself on the couch. I placed my water on the coffee table and that was when I saw it. My fingers twitched. There it was - Joshua's Dad's journal! Right there in front of me.

Chapter 17 – The Journal

I closed my eyes tightly and clenched my fists as tight as I could. *You can't do this. He trusts you*, I said to myself. I tried to distract myself from thinking about it. With my eyes closed I took in the atmosphere of the place. It smelled of old cedar and oak wood. The wood smell was probably coming from all the antique furniture he had. It was actually a very homey sort of smell.

The journal crept back into my mind. *Distract yourself.* I listened carefully. I listened to Joshua showering. I could hear the sound of the water hitting the tiled floor. Hearing the sound of it splashing on his skin made me want to take another shower, or even join him. *Oh dear! I didn't just think that! I can't believe I just thought that! Moving on -* I could hear something else. It sounded like humming. *Is he singing? Alright, that's it! I can't take it anymore!* My curiosity got the best of me. It was eating away at my insides. *Besides Joshua only has himself to blame. If he hadn't made such a big deal about it in the first place, this wouldn't be happening. So it's really his fault that I want to read it so badly.* I opened my eyes and there it lay staring back at me from the coffee table, waiting for me to discover it. I didn't think twice this time. I grabbed it and rose to my feet.

I took a deep breath and opened the front page - it read: Charles Heartwell. I didn't think I had much time, so I read through the short entries only.

Saturday January 7th 1989

We have a new tenant in the building. He is younger and better built than I. I do have to take into consideration that I am no longer in my prime. He seems like a decent enough man. But there is something about him. I can't quite put my finger on it.

In the evening, I was carrying some paper work to the office downstairs when I was bumped into and accidentally dropped all my things. It was a clumsy move on my behalf. Frustrated, I bent down to pick up the papers on the ground.

The person who bumped into me was none other than the new tenant from upstairs. He was generous enough as he offered to help me pick up my belongings. I thanked him and he went off not saying one word to me. He doesn't look like a rich man. I know that those rooms don't come at a cheap price. How can he afford to live here? I am a good judge of character and that man is hiding something; whoever he was. I have to know more.

I knew right then that he was writing about my father. I read on.

Wednesday January 11th 1989

The new tenant looks frustrated every time we cross paths. Today in the lobby I stopped him for a quick chat to see what was wrong. After introducing ourselves I asked him if everything was alright. He hurriedly responded and told me he was having a difficult time looking for something that was left behind for him. He searched and searched and could not find it. I asked him if he needed help and he responded with a blunt 'No.'

Thursday January 12th 1989

I got home from a long day at work and Vivian and Joshua were waiting for me at the table with a birthday cake. They both love throwing parties. Joshua was just as excited as Vivian. She easily rubbed off on him. It was mine and Joshua's birthday today. Vivian looked beautiful as usual. I feel like the luckiest man in the world to be wed to her. I completely forgot it was my birthday today. It was definitely a memorable day. I loved my family. They are all I have left.

Friday January 13th 1989

Vivian and I were going to tell Joshua today but just couldn't. We have decided to not tell him after all. He won't know the difference. I wish that we could have another child but it is impossible. Vivian and I have been trying for years and we have had no luck. One child is enough. Joshua seems content with being an only child.

Thursday January 26th 1989

Joshua has told me that when he grows up he wants to be an architect just like his father. He is only five but he has a great mind. I am very proud of him. I couldn't ask for anything more. I know he will carry on the family business very well.

The shower stopped running. Joshua was finished. I froze and looked towards the bathroom. My hearing zoned in on the tiniest movements he was making. I knew he still had to dry off and get dressed. That bought me at least five minutes. I listened carefully, praying that he wouldn't peek out here and see me. My heart was beating so fast. I was on the verge of getting caught with his Dad's forbidden journal in my hands. My palms were getting sweaty with each page that I turned. I didn't have time to read full entries. I quickly scanned through each page in search of my father's name.

The journal was hard to read at times since some of the entries were written in pencil. I could tell this was an old book, so the pencil markings were slowly starting to smudge and fade:

Antonio and I have become good friends. Antonio even invited me out one night for a couple of drinks. We had a little bit one too many scotches and he told me things; things that one stranger would never tell another stranger while sober. Where did he come from? He knew how to cure things instantly, but how is that possible?

I haven't seen Antonio in three weeks. He tends to go away for great periods of times. It makes me wonder if he has a home somewhere other than here. I must know more about him and his research.

Antonio ran past me without even a glance. He was holding something and had a big smile on his face.

Antonio doesn't seem to have it in his possession anymore. I know what it looks like. It is in the form of a –

It? What was *it*? He was talking about the Nekkel Ace, I knew it! "Sophia!"

My heart skipped a beat – or stopped – and I dropped the book. I looked up and Joshua wasn't there. I picked it up with shaking hands and placed it back where I found it. I was so close to finding out what the Nekkel Ace was. At the same time, I realized my search was over. I was too late to find the Nekkel Ace. Dad had beaten me to it. *Why wouldn't he tell any of us that he had it?* I wondered. *It must be back on Caledonia. Or maybe it doesn't work. Maybe it's just a funny hoax.* Well it didn't seem that funny to me. I was actually kind of upset.

Joshua came into the living room, shirtless with a towel around his waist. He was rubbing his head with a smaller towel. I couldn't see his face. I looked down a little shy and smiled. I noticed there was a piece of paper on the ground. It must have fallen out from the journal. I quickly put my foot on it and casually slid it under the couch. Joshua then pulled the towel off his head and walked towards me. He gave me a sweet 'hello' followed by a sensual kiss on the lips. I could feel the blood rush to my face which turned to an instant blush.

I didn't want him to stop there and I knew he didn't want to stop either. I closed my eyes as I took a step closer to him and went in for another kiss. I had never made out with a guy before. I didn't know what to do. Part of me was so nervous, but the other part knew this was right. I would just let it come naturally. Joshua kissed me with so much passion it was almost overwhelming. I put my arms around his neck. I ran my hands through his wet hair. It felt kind of nice to feel his wet hair against my skin.

Our lips parted and the feeling of Joshua's tongue caught me by surprise. It was new and exciting. He placed both his hands on my hips and then moved them to my lower back. He brought my body close to his. Our bodies were so close together, it was like we were one person. The heat from his body went through my dress and warmed up my torso. Joshua never loosened his grip on me. I didn't want him to.

I don't know how it happened – I guess from our bodies being so close and tight together – his towel fell. I realized that the front of the towel still stood in place since my body was keeping it there. I couldn't concentrate on kissing Joshua anymore. I wrapped my arms around him as tight as I could to keep our bodies pressed together. I dug my face into his chest and started laughing. I didn't want to move. I knew if I moved, the towel would fall completely! I was laughing uncontrollably. Tears were forming in my eyes. I couldn't remember the last time I laughed like that. I couldn't even move.

"Don't move," Joshua said as he slowly moved his hands and grabbed the top of his towel.

As soon as Joshua grabbed the towel, I was free. I wiped away the tears of laughter and sighed. I fell back on the couch and watched Joshua go back to his room. The back of his towel wasn't covering everything. The top of his butt was showing. I didn't say anything. I watched as he disappeared into his room.

At that moment I thought about the circumstances I found myself in. *The one reason I came to Earth was to find the Nekkel Ace for Dad. I went looking for it and couldn't find it. Dad had already brought it back to Caledonia. All this time and effort I spent looking for it and I find out it's not even here.*

Mom probably knows where the Nekkel Ace is and avoided using it so she could continue her affair with Massimo. I wonder how many years this was going on for. Wait! Maybe she felt guilty for what happened and decided to use the Nekkel Ace after all. Yeah, she must have used it by now so I am sure Dad is perfectly fine. I would now have to find a way to get back through the portal and go home.

Joshua came back from his room with pants on this time. He still didn't have a shirt on. His muscular chest still had a red glow from his hot shower. His body was so sculpted. His broad shoulders and the v-line of his pelvic bone made palms sweaty. I really wanted to touch him. He came and sat down beside me on the couch. "Sorry about that," he said.

"It's alright." I smiled as I placed my head on his shoulder and closed my eyes. His skin was so smooth.

Joshua sighed. "Sophia, there is something I have to tell you. Something I have been meaning to tell you for a while," it came out barely as a whisper.

I lifted my head off his shoulder and looked deeply into his eyes. They almost looked sad. I didn't know what to expect. I sat up and positioned my body to face his. "Yes? What's wrong?" I started to get nervous.

Joshua stared at me. I was wondering what he was thinking. Looking deep into his eyes it seemed as though he was struggling with something. He wanted to tell me something but at the same time he didn't know how to say it. I waited for him to speak.

His facial expression changed from sorrow to happiness in less than a minute. I don't know what kind of internal struggle he went through right then, but he seemed to push it aside. He shook his head and smiled a pure, sensitive smile.

He grabbed my face with both of his hands. His hands were so warm; it made the hairs on my arms stand up. He waited a few seconds to look deeply into my eyes, as if he were trying to find something. The corner of his mouth rose as he said those three words that would take any girl by surprise, "I love you."

"I love you too." I didn't let a second pass for me to even think about it. I knew right away I was in love with him. I wouldn't be thinking about someone, spending so much time with someone and even kissing them unless I knew that I had strong feelings for them. Joshua just broke the seal on the love barrier. He was in love with me and I was in love with him.

Joshua kissed me as I made up my mind. Since I was in love with him, I would stay here with him. I thought back about my home. I would miss Matteo and Kiko. I would miss them greatly. But until now I felt so alone. I didn't think I'd ever fill that void in my heart. But now it was gone. I had been waiting for Joshua my entire life. He was my missing puzzle piece.

I would miss Dad the most I think. Even though we didn't have the best relationship, I knew deep down inside he would always love me and nothing would change that. Dad loved Matteo and me. When he told me the story of our accident I felt so much sorrow in my heart. I can only imagine how Mom and Dad felt on that fateful day. The one thing Dad wanted most in the world was to have his family back together. *I am tearing our family apart, but this is for the best. I will be happy. They would understand if they knew. They can always come and visit. That would be easy since they had the portal. For now I had to put their memories behind me and move on with my new life with Joshua.*

So it was settled. I would forget about Caledonia and start a new life on Earth.

Chapter 18 – Fast Forward

Joshua and I now shared his condo. We were already down the hall from one another so it just made sense to live together. We could have stayed at mine, but Joshua's place was way more equipped. Most of my clothes remained at my place. I didn't have much closet space at Joshua's. So my condo had been transformed into one massive closet. I couldn't have been happier!

I didn't know I was capable of feeling this kind of love. Every second spent with Joshua felt like heaven on Earth. I hated being apart from him, but it made the reunion that much sweeter. The months just flew by...

October

I awoke from a dream world I couldn't recall. I looked to my side and there he was; the man I loved, sound asleep.

He had a long day at work and I didn't want to disturb him. I got up from the bed and saw that even Milo was still asleep. I left the room as quietly as I could. I went to the kitchen and made myself some coffee. Joshua had a handy dandy coffee machine. He prepared it for me every night so all I had to do in the morning was press a button and wait for the java (that's what he called it) to brew.

I looked out the kitchen window and gasped in horror at what I saw! I ran back to Joshua's room screaming his name. Joshua jumped up from his sleep. "Huh? What is going on? Sophia! What's wrong?" Joshua said. His eyes were still closed.

I couldn't help but let out a chuckle. I jumped onto the bed and grabbed his hand. "Something is wrong! Look! Look outside!" I pulled him - no, dragged him – out of bed and to the kitchen. I opened the drapes in one swift movement. I pointed to the trees in the park; once so vibrant and full of life. Now their leaves were changing colour and falling to the ground. Something was wrong.

"The trees are dying!" I cried.

Joshua gazed at me with a blank expression. "You're kidding me right? You are really funny some days you know that? You act like you're from another planet or something. I'm going back to bed." He left and I followed him back to the bedroom.

He still didn't know where I came from. I wasn't planning on telling him either. It would have been too much for him to handle.

I sat on the bed, dumb struck staring at the bump that was Joshua's body hidden underneath the covers. He didn't even answer my question!

As if reading my mind, Joshua suddenly peeked his head out of the covers and said, "Welcome to the first day of autumn."

Oh, right! I remembered. *They have seasons here! The leaves are supposed to fall and then comes winter.* I was excited for winter. I couldn't wait for snow.

***

I woke up to the smell of freshly brewed coffee. I was usually the one who makes it, but I guessed Joshua had an early day ahead of him. I got up, threw on my robe and groggily walked over to the kitchen.

"I need you to do me a favour today," Joshua said, planting a kiss on my forehead and handing me a cup of coffee.

"Is that so? What can I do for you?" I asked as I sipped the hot - but delicious - cup of coffee. Double milk, double sugar - just the way I like it!

"Could you go to the shops and get me some new clothes? I am sick of the ones I have now." He smiled, handing over his credit card. I gladly accepted it. Joshua's warm eyes invited me in. Waking up to those every morning - and coffee - was something I never grew tired of. At this point in our relationship, there were still things we didn't know about each other, but it seemed we were both alright with this. We were here, living together, happy and in love. *What else was there to know?*

Joshua asked me to get him a new pair of shoes, a dress shirt, dress pants and a jacket. He even said I could get something special for myself. I was glad to go as I had become quite the shopper. I was then reminded of my mother and how much she loved to shop. *Am I turning into her? No! Never!*

I asked Joshua if he wanted to come along with me, but he rejected my offer and said he had some important plans to finalize at work. I was disappointed but shopping time alone didn't sound too bad.

***

I spent a good three hours shopping. I bought a little lunch for myself as well. I sat down at my favourite café and relaxed a little bit. My heels were hurting my feet from standing up all day. It was definitely worth it.

When I was all shopped out, I went home. I wondered if Joshua was back yet from work. I had four bags in each hand. I purposely put the key in my bra so it was easily accessible. No one could see it through my shirt. With the many bags I had in my right arm, I raised it - I felt like a weight lifter – and swiped the card in the door.

I opened the door but something was in the way. There were streamers covering the entrance way. I looked up in astonishment and noticed the ceiling was covered in pink balloons! I wormed my way through the door, carrying these big bags. I never took my eyes off the ceiling. *What's going on?* I wondered.

"Joshua?" I called. *He must be here. Who else would have blown up all these balloons?*

The streamers tickled my face as I made my way through.

"In here!"

The living room was filled with balloons as well. There weren't as many here as there were at the entrance. By the time I reached the kitchen all the balloons were gone. I found Joshua standing behind the counter, waiting for me. I was dumbstruck. He noticed. *Am I missing something?* I dropped the bags on the ground and stared at them for a few seconds. When I came to my senses I looked back up to where Joshua was standing, but he was gone!

I walked closer to the counter and Joshua jumped up and screamed, "Happy Birthday!"

I screamed from the surprise and realization of what was going on. I covered my shocked, gaping mouth with my hands. My eyes started watering.

All this is for me, I thought to myself.

127

Today was my birthday. I *completely* forgot!

Joshua brought up a cake with icing that read, '*Happy Birthday Sophia.*' It was a light coffee colour with dark brown icing swirls. It was perfect.

All this brought back memories of home. It reminded me of Matteo's birthday; all the people who were there to celebrate, his beautiful cake, his many gifts. The memory of my jealousy surfaced. There was no need to feel jealous now. I had this perfect man who remembered my birthday from when I told him the first time we met. He came around the counter and smiled. He put his arms around my waist and I put my arms around his shoulders.

"What? You think I would forget a day like this?" Joshua said as his eyes sparkled with delight.

I bit my bottom lip as I nodded, ashamed. I would never expect him to remember my own birthday when I didn't even remember it. A flood of memory hit me as I remembered Joshua's father's journal. In it he wrote '*They both love throwing parties. Joshua gets as excited as Vivian does.*'

Joshua gave me a small kiss on the lips as he let me go. He walked over to the bags on the ground and started to go through them.

"So what did you buy me to wear tonight?"

"Tonight?" I asked.

"Yes, tonight. You bought us outfits to wear when I take you out for a celebratory birthday dinner."

November

It was the second week of November when Joshua informed me that we were expecting a huge snow storm. I have never been more excited for anything in my life. Maybe I was exaggerating, but this was definitely one of the top three!

I had waited all week for this day. Joshua explained to me that meteorologist said that it was going to be the first snow storm of the season. Apparently there was going to be fifteen centimetres of snow. I wanted to be outside when it all happened but Joshua said I would get sick. He also told me that the storm was going to hit at 2:00 a.m. and that I should go to sleep and see all the snow in the morning.

We were both in bed. Joshua was fast asleep. The heat was on, but I was still cold. I didn't think I would ever get used to this cold weather. I could hear the wind shaking the foundation of the whole building. It was actually pretty scary. I pulled the covers over my head so I couldn't hear anything. I scooted closer to Joshua and put my ear to his chest. The rhythmic beat of his heart soothed me to sleep.

It was morning before I knew it. My eyes opened to see Milo lying on the pillow beside me. He was staring directly at me. He was so close; I could smell his dog breath. Disgusted, I turned to the other side and tried to go back to sleep but I couldn't.

I automatically sat up and rubbed my eyes. The brightness of the day shone through the blinds. I looked over and Joshua was still sleeping. I crept over to the window. I grabbed the end of the curtains and embraced myself. I slid them open as wide as they could go. I let out a loud scream! Milo barked at me, or maybe it was with me - I couldn't tell the difference. Joshua sat up scared and looked at the ecstatic expression on my face from the realization that this is my first time seeing snow. He smiled at me and I think he even laughed a little bit. "Yup, I have come to the conclusion that you *really* are weird. I would never change a thing about you though," he said as he plopped back into bed, pulling the covers over his head.

December

I struggled to pull out my key as I opened the condo door. I forgot this time to put it in my bra. As soon as the door opened I felt a warm sensation tickle my face. It felt very comforting. I guessed Joshua blasted the heat and had the furnace on at the same time – even though I told him to turn it off whenever he wasn't home. Today had to be one of the coldest days since I had been here. I walked towards the kitchen and dropped my purse off on the counter. I draped my jacket over one of the chairs to thaw out.

"Joshua?" I called, but I heard no response.

I was right. He wasn't home. He was either still at work or he went for a walk with Milo. I couldn't believe poor Milo wanted to walk in the snow with those small paws. What a trooper he was!

I walked into our room. It was nice and clean. The bed was fixed nicely. Joshua was a very clean and neat kind of guy and I loved that about him. I dropped all my shopping bags beside our bed and went to take a shower. It was so cold outside. It felt like I had frost bite on some parts of my body. But I regretted nothing. After all, I couldn't stay inside all day. I could bare a little cold to shop!

I headed to the washroom and removed all my clothing. I had so many layers on, so it took me a while. I turned the water on from the outside and waited for it to heat up. I opened the door and popped in. I jumped in a bit too early and realized the water was still frigid. I quickly turned the knobs to make it warmer. As soon as I changed it, I could feel my body defrost. All the cold was melting away. It felt so nice.

I turned the hot water way up and let it burn my skin. It massaged my head, neck and back. I don't know how long I stood like that for. It felt like forever. I wondered if Joshua was home yet. Just thinking of him made me excited. Seeing his charming smile would make my day. He had the cutest dimple on the one side of his cheek and his teeth were perfectly straight.

I stepped out and dried myself in the bathroom. I wiped the foggy mirror and attempted to look at myself. It was a failed attempt since the mirror just fogged over immediately. I wrapped the towel around my shivering body and stepped outside the washroom.

I made no noise as I walked to our room. I listened carefully and realized Joshua still wasn't home yet. I didn't even know what time it was. I looked to the clock and realized it was only three o'clock. He would normally come home around four o'clock. On rare occasions he would surprise me at noon and we go out for lunch. Today wasn't one of those days.

I removed my towel and put it on my head. I went to my drawer and grabbed a boy-cut pair of underwear. I put them on and opened the drapes to our oversized bedroom window. This was probably the biggest window I had seen. It was three normal sized windows made into one big one. As soon as I opened the drapes, the sun rushed in. It made our bed glow. For a day this cold, it was surprising to see the sun shine so brightly!

I grabbed one of my favourite books from the bookshelf and lay down on my bed to enjoy it. I lay on my back just in my underwear. I held the book over my face and started reading - even though I read this book many times before. To me, love stories could never get old.

The sun felt so good on my skin. It felt like I was getting a tan just from lying there on the bed. I decided to stop reading and just enjoy the sun. I lay the book open on my face. I didn't want my face to burn. My legs were hanging off the bed and before I knew it I passed out.

I don't know how long I was out for but I felt cold all a sudden. *How long have I been out for?* I removed the book from my face and saw a silhouette of a man standing right in front of me. I got startled and quickly sat up. My eyes focused and I realized it was Joshua.

I looked at myself and realized I was half naked. I playfully screamed and covered my body. I completely forgot that all I was wearing was my underwear. I wrapped my arms around my body trying to cover myself.

Joshua came on top of me and we started kissing. I guess he got the hint that I was uncomfortable so he got up and grabbed my robe and tossed it to me as I turned around to put it on. I was blushing.

Joshua lay down beside me. He lifted up his arm so I could lie down close to him. I thought about how far our relationship was going. Joshua and I have made out a lot but we never had sex. I didn't know what to expect. Joshua was such a sweet guy and he had never pressured me into anything. He hadn't even brought it up. I didn't want to be the one to bring it up. I always told myself that I would wait until marriage to have sex, and I assumed Joshua felt the same way.

I nuzzled my face closer into his chest. I could hear his heart beating quickly. I thought about maybe one day marrying Joshua. We would be a family.

Family. That word brought back images of my own family back home. My smile automatically faded as I was on the verge of crying when I thought back to my planet and all my loved ones.

The feeling was impossible to ignore. As much as I tried, I could not erase my family out of my memory. This wasn't right. What I was doing wasn't the right thing to do. I should have realized this earlier. I *did* realize this earlier, but didn't want to listen to my conscience. My emotions got the best of me. *What was I thinking?* Going back home would come with the repercussions for leaving unexpectedly. But deep down inside, that was what I wanted. A part of me wanted to go home. I don't know how to tell Joshua. Going home also meant leaving him. I didn't want to hurt his feelings, I loved him too much. *What am I going to do?* At the same time though, I knew Joshua was keeping something from me, and I couldn't figure out what.

Chapter 19 – True Struggle

It had been four months since my very first day on Earth. I thought I could move on with my life and start a new one here, away, with Joshua, but I was wrong. I missed my family too much. My chest ached for them. I could no longer ignore the burning sensation in the back of my throat every time I thought of them.

I missed the feeling of being able to freely and safely roam outside my house and sit in my garden. I missed closing my eyes and embracing what nature had to offer me. Sitting in my garden for hours, not thinking, talking or even seeing – this was what I needed. I couldn't do that on Earth. Even if I did want to go sit in the park, I would hear people talking, children playing or crying and worst of all, I would hear cars driving by and honking their horns. While I had learned to drown those noises out, sometimes they did get the best of me.

How could I have just abandoned my family like that? I wondered. *I left Matteo without a proper goodbye. He didn't deserve that and I am an evil person for leaving him in that state. He probably wonders why I left. Why I didn't say goodbye. What if he blames himself? He always said he was responsible for my wellbeing. What if he thinks he has failed his duties in keeping me safe? What have I done?*

I couldn't keep living this lie. I had to tell Joshua everything. Okay, not *everything*. Joshua and I couldn't be together. I couldn't bring him to my planet, and I could no longer stay on Earth. I felt like I was even lying to myself. I was telling myself that I could start a new life far away from my loved ones. But who was I kidding? *Maybe I can bring Joshua back with me. Or maybe my family could move to Earth. That would be so bad. Oh, I don't know anymore.* There were so many things running through my mind, I knew that if I didn't relax, I would soon have a meltdown.

When Joshua comes home from work, I will tell him that I have to leave, I promised myself.

I waited a few hours for Joshua to come home. I spent the entire time sitting quietly on the couch. Milo slept on the couch beside me. I was no fun for him today. I played out every potential scenario in my mind. I pictured myself telling Joshua that I had to leave and not come back. I saw him shrug his shoulders and go on about his evening. But then I also pictured tears falling from his deep brown eyes, begging me to stay. Lastly I pictured his hands balling into fists as his temper rose out of control. This was a particularly frightening thought.

It was my entire fault for allowing this to go on as long as it had.

I heard the door open. I knew it was Joshua. He walked through the door and I could hear him whistling. I guessed he had a good day and now I had to be the one to ruin it. I sat curled up in a ball. I had my arms wrapped around my knees. I waited for Joshua to come and sit beside me.

"Hey sweetie," he said when he saw me sitting on the couch. "I'm home. Miss me?" Joshua took off his shoes and walked towards me. He placed his jacket on top of the chair. It still had snow on it from outside.

I didn't answer him.

"Sophia? Hey, what's wrong?"

I closed my eyes. I could feel Joshua's gaze burning into the side of my face. I couldn't do it. My chest tightened and the words were stuck in my throat. My mouth was open, but there was no sound.

I grabbed my necklace. I held onto it as tight as I could. I had to keep reminding myself I had to do this; not only for me, but for my family as well. My necklace was the only thing that reminded me of home. I had nothing else in my possession that I could have brought over from Caledonia. Dad gave it to me all those years ago and every time I held it, it reminded me of him. It reminded me that I had to go back and that I had no choice. *Strength, Sophia.*

"We can't do this anymore." I looked deep into his eyes as I said those dreaded words.

Joshua's eyebrows creased. He didn't seem to understand what he was hearing.

"Me," I pointed to myself, "and you," I pointed to Joshua's chest, "we cannot be together anymore. I have to go back home. I don't think I can ever come back. I had an amazing time with you but some beautiful things have to come to an end, even though we don't want them to. Please understand." My head hurt as I heard the words come out of my mouth.

"You're leaving me? Why would I ever understand that? You're joking right?" Joshua's smile was forced. I could sense his heart being ripped in half. "We're in love and happy together. How could you possibly ever want to leave?" Joshua took my hand and held it between his own. He was making this so much harder that I thought.

"I *have* to go home," I blurted out.

"Okay, I will come with you. I can meet your family!" His face eased up a little but didn't lose all tension.

"No, you can't come. You just can't." I shook my head.

"Why not?"

"Because I said so!" I broke free from his grip with a force that shocked us both. "You cannot come. We cannot be together. I am leaving here. I can't stay with you. I can't keep doing this. I don't want to hurt you, but I have to go. And you have to let me go!" My hands clenched up into fists. "You just don't understand!" I yelled. Anger was building up inside and I let it out. I wasn't mad at him, I was mad at myself for the trouble I had caused.

"No! I think you are the one who doesn't understand!" Joshua shot up from the couch and was standing directly in front of me as I sat there. "I've given up everything to be with you! Nothing matters to me except you! Don't you get it? Don't you see? Nothing else matters!"

I was struck with his sudden fierceness. *What did he give up?* I didn't understand. I sat there confused and shocked. Joshua never yelled at me before. It brought back memories when Matteo yelled at me. They both had the anger part bang on.

Joshua walked out from the living room and stormed into his room. I caught up with my breathing as he was gone. My heart was skipping beats and it was almost as if I forgot how to breathe. The back of my throat burned with sadness and I tried to hold back the tears until I was alone. I had to keep it together. I had to show Joshua I was strong.

I heard his dresser open and then abruptly close. He returned with anger written all over his face and painted over his body. I knew this wasn't going to end well.

Joshua came and stood in front of me again. I noticed he had his Dad's journal in his hand. "This," he waved it in front of my face, "doesn't matter! Nothing matters anymore! From now on, I will listen to myself and not listen to what anyone else says! I am breaking life promises, but it means nothing to me now that I've met you!"

I stared at him with bewildered eyes. What did his Dad's journal have to do with anything? I felt like I opened up a chest of internal struggles that Joshua was going through that I had absolutely no idea about!

He opened up the leather latch and ran his fingers through the pages, shaking his head. His eyebrows creased as he grabbed a handful of pages and ripped them out. He did it again, and again, and again, until all the pages were out of the book, crumpled up and on the ground.

I sat there with my mouth wide open in shock. *Um, what do I do now?*

"There!" Joshua said and he threw the page-less book to the ground. It lay there right beside the crumpled up pages.

He grabbed his jacket off the chair and stormed out, slammed the door behind him.

As soon as the door closed, I couldn't keep it together anymore. Sobs poured out violently. I hurt him and I hurt myself. Tears flowed down my face. I didn't know it was going to hurt this badly. I should leave now, but there was nowhere to go. I forgot that I didn't know where the exit portal was. I would have to sleep on it and in the morning I will go back to the forest. *There is something in that place that can bring me home. There must be a portal there that I missed. I will go back and find it. When I do find it, I will go through and never look back.*

I wiped my tears with the back of my hand and looked towards the ground. I got up from the couch. My muscles were stiff from sitting there all day, not moving. I started walking towards my room but turned back and walked up to the papers to pick them up. I couldn't just leave them there on the ground. He completely tore them apart. This was so sad. After collecting them all I placed them back inside the spine of the book. I closed the latch so the pages would not escape. I ran my hand over the leather cover. I wondered what could have driven him to rip the journal apart.

Just as I was about to get up I noticed there was a piece of paper sticking out from underneath the couch. It must have flown under when Joshua was ripping the journal apart. I placed my hand on top of the paper to slide it from under the couch.

At that moment I remembered all those months ago when I came to see Joshua. I was looking through his journal and realized something had fallen out. I slid it under the couch so Joshua wouldn't see it. I didn't even remember to look at what it was. I was about to find out.

It was still face down when I picked it up. I sat on the ground and turned it over. What I saw made my hairs stand on end. *How could he have this?* I wondered. I was looking at a picture of myself. It was a small picture, but I knew it was me. Someone circled around me with a blue pen. Beside the circle was an exclamation mark. *This fell out of his Dad's journal, but why would it be there?*

I got up from the ground and ran to my purse. I pulled out Dad's wallet and placed the picture inside the clear slot. It was a perfect fit. This picture belonged to Dad. Why did Joshua or his father have it?

My head was swarmed with questions and I couldn't think straight. I was exhausted. I walked to my room, got changed and went into bed. I would question Joshua in the morning. At this point I didn't have the energy to even keep my eyes open. I was sound asleep before I knew it.

***

I woke up startled. I looked over to the clock and it said 4:12 a.m. I then looked over my shoulder and realized Joshua wasn't in bed. I wondered if he was even home.

As soon as I lay my head back on my pillow, I heard the door open. Joshua was home. I pretended to be asleep as he came into the room. I heard him change and slip into bed.

I wanted nothing more in the world than to turn over and hug him. Our backs were to each other with one big space in the middle. I wanted to feel him and see if he was alright. Every bone in my body told me not to, but I couldn't help it. I wanted one last embrace before I left. I would see him tomorrow morning. I would have to make him believe I wasn't going to leave anymore. He would have to think I took back everything I said. In the morning I would tell him I was going shopping. Then I would leave, never to return again.

I rolled over and placed my hands around Joshua's back. I closed my eyes and rested my cheek against his ear. I didn't say anything and neither did he. I took in a deep breath. Joshua's body was tense. Either he was trying to prove his strength or he was just unsure of what to do. After a few seconds Joshua let his guard down. I knew he was slowly drifting into his dream world and that was all he would have left of me – dreams. This would be the last time he smelled or even felt me.

I didn't sleep at all that night after Joshua came home. I was so worried when he stormed out and even more worried when he came home and didn't say a word to me as he got into bed. It was late so I suppose he didn't want to wake me. He didn't appear to mind the little hug I gave him. That definitely eased the tension a bit.

I heard him get in the morning. I was afraid to get up right after him. *Should I say good morning, or just ignore him completely?* I wanted nothing more than to run into his arms and say that I was sorry for everything. That, I knew I couldn't do. I had to stick to my words. They were all I had left. I thought that maybe having him upset would make leaving that much easier. But deep down I knew that leaving would be just as difficult – if not more so.

I decided I couldn't stay in bed any longer. The door was cracked open and I could hear Joshua in the kitchen. The smell of coffee filled the room even though the door was barely open. I wondered if he heard me get up. I went around to the window and peeked through the curtains. I placed my hand on the window and felt the cold merge through my hand. I removed my hand and the window fogged up from the heat that was left behind. Just seeing that sent tingles down my spine.

With a sigh, I grabbed my robe and dared myself to walk into the kitchen. I figured Joshua was waiting for me in there.

I opened the door and Milo was right at my feet within seconds. With each step that I took, he followed me. I was pretty sure if I took a step backwards he would come back as well. I sat down at the counter and didn't say a word. Joshua placed a hot cup of coffee in front of me and said, "Good Morning," in a monotone voice without even looking at me.

"Good morning," I whispered back as I brought the hot cup up to my lips. I didn't look at him either. My eyes were locked on the steam that was rising from the cup.

As Joshua walked back to his room, he said, "When you are done with your coffee, get dressed, we're going somewhere."

No, I couldn't go. I would say no, but part of me wanted to know where he was planning on taking me. "Where are we going?" I asked without even thinking. *You can't go Sophia. You're leaving, remember?* I was quick to my senses. Before he answered me I said, "I can't go. I have other plans." I was looking at Milo down at my feet. It was like I was talking to him. Milo cranked his head to the side in confusion. I tried to smile but it didn't work. I was still very sad and upset.

With a cold and stern voice Joshua said, "Cancel them!" His door slammed closed. Well that was a great answer! I didn't want to get dressed. I wanted to just leave now and not come back. The door was in clear view from me. I can easily walk out and not turn back, as hard as that may be.

But, I *was* in my pyjamas and it looked about minus twenty-five degrees Celsius outside, so that was out of the question. I guess I had to oblige with Joshua's demands this time. I would leave right after! I promised myself that!

I took my dear time drinking the coffee. Every drop counted. I had my back to the living room so I didn't really see what was going on behind me. I could hear Joshua walking in and out of our room - doing what, you ask? - I have no idea. I could hear his footsteps pacing in and out. I didn't bother to turn around.

When I finished my coffee and was done stalling, I got dressed and Joshua and I left. We walked to his car. It was parked on the street so we didn't have to walk all the way to the underground parking lot. It was already running and warmed up for us.

As soon as I stepped outside, a chilly breeze made its way up my jacket. It really was freezing outside. I had a big sweater on, a nice down feather jacket with a big hood and thick black boots. I pulled on my black gloves and lifted my hood over my head.

I had never been in Joshua's car before. It was actually very nice. It was nothing like the cars we had back home. His car was black and shiny. There were four silvery metal circles overlapping each other on both sides (front and back) of the car. I had no idea what that meant. I walked to the passenger side and sat quietly. Neither of us talked the entire car ride. I didn't have anything to say. It was a good thing I had my hood on since I didn't want to see if he was looking at me or not. I kept my eyes to the passenger seat window. It made me sad to see everything covered in snow. I missed the sun and the flourishing flowers.

We drove for a while and ended up on the coast. I stepped out and looked over to what seemed to be a little lake. It was completely frozen solid. All the trees around were covered in snow and I could see icicles forming on their branches. Another breeze caught me by surprise and I felt even colder. I wrapped my arms around myself in an attempt to keep warm.

I walked up to the frozen water, and touched it with the tip of my boot. I looked back to Joshua who was grabbing something out of the trunk of his car. He held two boxes. He walked towards me and dropped one of the boxes in front of my feet. "I hope they fit," was all he said as he walked over a couple paces to a log that had fallen over. He used it as a bench as he took off his shoes.

I lifted the box and opened it. Inside I found white lace up boots with blades on the bottom. *What are these?* I held one up and raised an eyebrow to Joshua.

"They're yours. I got them for you yesterday."

I was still confused.

"I got you your very own skates. You know, to skate with."

"But, I don't know how to," I said mostly to myself. This was going to be bad.

Joshua finished putting his on as he trotted towards me. He didn't say anything as he grabbed the box and my hand. He brought me over to the fallen tree and made me sit. I sighed deeply as Joshua took off my shoes and replaced them with the skates. He tied them very tight. He helped me stand up. I suppressed a smile as they looked funny. *I shouldn't – no, couldn't– be doing this!*

Joshua held my hand the entire time I tried balancing myself. I caught on pretty quick. Skating came naturally to me even though I had never done this before. It was amazing. Eventually I was skating on my own. Joshua watched me with a sense of pride as I skated around him. He never took his eyes off me once.

We skated all day. I was exhausted, but by the end, I didn't want to stop. I skated farther and farther into the lake. Joshua was unsure about going that far, but it seemed fine. He decided we eventually went too far and that we should really go back. Apparently the farther we go into the deep, the thinner the ice would get. He told me to be careful since we could fall through if we weren't cautious. I got scared so I agreed with him. We started to skate back hand in hand. To leave this, to leave him, was almost a sin.

Suddenly, we both heard a big crack! I stopped and squeezed his hand. I gasped in shock as I thought I heard the ice begin to separate near us.

Joshua shook his head and looked upset. "Don't be worried," he said. "Skate lightly and we will be fine. Don't put too much pressure on your feet at one time." His grip tightened.

I gulped back the fear that was lodged in my throat and nodded in agreement. I trusted Joshua. I knew nothing would happen if I was with him. We skated side by side.

"Sophia, before we go back to the shore, I want to tell you something. I am completely serious and this is something I must tell you before anything else." Joshua looked straight ahead as he spoke. He couldn't look me in the eye.

I spoke before he could say anything else. "I know, I know, you love me. I love you too. You don't have to keep repeating it. I can feel it. But my leaving is something I must do, no matter what. The argument we got into last night was intense. I didn't mean for that to happen, but it did and I'm sorry. But I still have to go." I looked down as I spoke, paying attention to the slippery ice under my skates.

Joshua let go of my hand as he skated a bit ahead. He abruptly turned to me again. "No, I *do* love you but that is not what I had to tell you. This is more important and I should have told you the day we met, but I was such a coward and I apologize." Joshua looked to the ice under his feet.

"I don't understand what you are talking about. You know you can tell me anything. I wanted to ask you about the journal last night. What did you mean when you said you will not listen to what anyone else says? Why did you rip the book apart? And why did you have my picture in your Dad's journal?" I attempted to skate closer to him but of course with my clumsiness, I tripped. Not only did I trip, my knees hit the ice *hard* and I landed on all fours. I then heard an even louder crack. I tightly closed my eyes to ease the sharp noise.

I looked down at my hands. "Joshua," I said unsteadily. My voice filled with fear.

He skated closer and his eyes bulged with panic as he realized what I was looking at. He dropped down onto the ice with me. My hands were drenched in water. The ice was cracking around us.

"Crap, Sophia!" Joshua panicked.

Pain flushed through me. It wasn't because I was cold or wet. This was a different pain - a weird pain. It shot through my body. I felt nauseous and I didn't know how to control it. At that moment everything went blank. A blinding white light flashed before my eyes. It was just as bright as the light the portal emitted. I looked up to Joshua to see if he saw it as well.

Joshua was blinking his eyes, wiping them with his sleeve. We looked at each other. The nauseous feeling worsened. I took deep breaths to steady the feeling. It didn't work. I looked down to my hands and clenched them into fists. As I looked back down, my long blonde hair touched the water. Wait. *My long blonde hair?*

I lifted my head and looked up to Joshua. His face was distorted with fear and shock. "Sophia?" he asked.

The white light came back but this time it circled me. My gloves, skates, and jacket - everything disappeared. I tried standing. As soon as I did, I realized I was wearing the dress I left Caledonia in all those months ago. Something was gently pulling me upwards. "Joshua, I - I," was all I could get out. The look on his face erased anything I had in my mind. His jaw was wide open; he was on all fours on the ice just as I had been not long before. I could sense his heart breaking.

The ice under my feet gave out and before I could fall completely, I disappeared. I closed my eyes. That strange feeling of travelling through the portal took over me. It was the same feeling I had when I first went through.

I opened my eyes as I saw Earth falling farther from me. It was a remarkable sight. The first time I took the portal, my eyes were closed the entire time. This felt like I was flying through space, heading back home. This is how it was meant to end. *"Goodbye Joshua."*

Chapter 20 – Portal Trouble

I lay in bed and I fell in and out of consciousness as the warm air tickled my face. The fresh breeze of the morning burst through my open window. I took a deep breath and smiled at how wonderful it made me feel. The smell of the breeze felt like a drug that took over my body. I lazily opened my eyes and lifted my head to look towards the window. I could see the vines from outside trying to come through. I had to get someone to take care of that. A stray blue bird sat on the windowsill and sung me a pleasing song.

I relaxed, lying back down. As soon as my head hit the pillow, my eyes widened in horror. I gasped in shock at my current location. Everything about Earth came back to me in a burst of memories. My head ached. *How could I possibly forget? Where am I?* I looked around and realized I was in my bed back in Caledonia. That must have meant that I did take a portal when I was with Joshua. I didn't even know how that happened. I pushed the covers off me as I jumped out of bed. My feet hit the cold marble floor as I ran out of my bedroom.

I ran down the stairs. I slowed down as a feeling of nausea engulfed me. I had to stop in the middle of the steps, I couldn't walk anymore. I placed my hand on my chest as I closed my eyes and took in a deep breath to steady myself. The nausea was partly due to a head rush and partly due to the memory of falling and breaking my arm. The image of my bone broken under my skin was sickening. I still couldn't believe that the portal healed my broken arm.

I shook my head and continued down the stairs. I passed the doors that led outside. My bare feet were almost burning from the hot stone that covered the ground. I figured the faster I ran, the less it would burn. So I ran.

"Miss. Sophia, you are back! We all missed you dearly! But why are you in your pyjamas?" Romina called from a behind a bush. Her head turned at the exact time I passed her.

I looked down at myself and what she spoke was correct. I *was* in my pyjamas. I didn't have time to go back and change. I had to go back to the portal. I had to go back to Earth and find out what Joshua had to tell me. I needed to make sure he was alright. From what I remembered, I was almost falling right through the ice, but the portal must have saved me. *What if Joshua fell through?* I worried. We were still so far out on the ice. There was no way he could have made it back to shore. No one was there to save him. My eyes watered as I ran faster. *I can save him if I go back now!*

My feet were practically bleeding by the time I reached the portal's doors. I couldn't stop running now. I smashed right into the door before I had time to turn the handle. I opened it and as soon as I did I ran up to the portal, thinking the same thing would happen; the light would flash and I would run right through.

That is not what happened this time. I ran up to the portal and there was no light. The only light in the room was coming from the door behind me. I walked up to the black mirror of the portal and saw only my reflection. I touched my reflection in the mirror. *Why isn't it glowing?* I needed to go through. I was overcome with sorrow as I realized I didn't even know how to use this darn thing. I covered my face with my hands as I felt like a helpless child.

From behind me I heard footsteps. They were faint, but I could still hear them. I removed my hands from my face and looked into the portal. If anyone was to come into this room, I could see them this way without facing them directly.

First I saw a foot, then a leg and then the torso. All my muscles tightened in my body. I stared at Matteo in the doorway. Of course Kiko was right there beside him. He looked much bigger from that I remembered. His coat shone in the sun. I wanted to run my hands over his fur. I missed him.

I turned around. I knew I had some explaining to do. "Matteo, I am so sorry," I whispered.

Matteo stared at me. Just by the look on his face I could tell he felt betrayed and alone. I know how he felt. I was alone for most of my life. He probably didn't think I would ever come back.

Matteo sighed as he stared into what felt like my soul; silently searching for an answer to the question he didn't want to ask. *'How could you leave me without saying why?'*

Before I could speak again, Matteo turned his back. He didn't say one word. He just shook his head and walked away. He kept walking until I couldn't see him anymore.

Kiko still stood there staring at me. His blue eyes were the colour of the sky on a clear, sunny day.

I bent down on one knee, "Kiko," I whispered with affection as I opened my arms to him.

Kiko made a faint sad growling noise in the pit of his chest but then walked away exactly as Matteo did. They were turning their backs on me just as I had done to them.

I stood up, bit my bottom lip and kept repeating to myself, *don't cry, don't cry, don't cry!*

I turned around back to the portal. I was angry at it. I couldn't really recall why I was angry at the portal but my chest filled with rage as I looked at it. I lifted up both my hands and made them into fists. With one swift movement I hit the portal with the bottom of both my fists as hard as I could. It did nothing. It didn't even move. It looked like glass, but it didn't really feel like it. It was much smoother than glass. There was some life form underneath that reflective surface. It was like it could talk to you at any moment and have many, many things to say. I knew this wasn't possible.

I turned my head to the left, arched it to look at the top and then brought it back down to look at the right side of the portal. There was stone all around it except on the bottom. The stone had beautiful designs on it. I ran my fingers over the different curves and lines it made. This stone felt just like the stone I felt in the forest on Earth.

These designs felt familiar somehow - like I had seen them before. Not here and not on Earth. I tried to think from where else I could have seen them but I couldn't remember.

I turned my back to the portal and walked towards the door. I grabbed the doorknob and took one last look at the portal before I closed the door to it.

I decided it was time to see Dad. I needed to see how he was doing. I walked back to the house. I walked past my garden. Seeing it, after all this time, gave me goose bumps. As much as I wanted to stay there, I knew this wasn't the time. I went in the house and walked up to Dad's room and thought; if he was awake, I knew he wouldn't want to see my dirty bare feet and pyjamas. I ran quickly to my room and changed in less than four minutes. I wiped a wet cloth over my feet to clean them and slipped on shoes.

I walked to Dad's room again. I closed my eyes and listened carefully as I turned and walked through the doorframe. I hoped to not see him there. I hoped he was out hunting, or shopping, or anything else, but no, he was there. He was still in bed, wasting away. The machines were hooked up to him like they always were.

Mom was sitting on the couch beside his bed. She was sleeping, covered with a light blanket. She looked peaceful as she slept. Her hair was a mess but nothing could change the way she looked. We had the same clear, ivory skin.

I didn't even realize the way my body reacted to seeing her. I wanted to run up to her and yell at her, scream at her, cry to her for doing what she did. I was too much of a coward to confront her now. I came to see Dad and that was it.

I slowly walked to his bed, making sure my shoes didn't make any noise on the marble floor. I even held my breath. I didn't want to wake up Mom. Dad looked the same as when I left him; pale skin and dark circles under his eyes. His cheeks used to have a touch of rose in them but that was gone.

I sat beside him on his bed. I sat ever so gently to minimize the noise the bed made when you sat on it. I grabbed Dad's hand and placed it in mine. His fingers were so cold and skinny. He was wearing a long blue sweater to keep him warm. I placed both his hands on his stomach. I then lay my head on top of his hands. I closed my eyes and pictured him on those steps, inviting me to go horseback riding with him, all those months ago. His strong body towered over me as he was filled with joy at the idea alone. I almost smiled myself, thinking of that.

I tried to empty my head as I lay there. It was peaceful to be home in my comfort zone. I relaxed a little bit and that's when it hit me! The designs on the portal! That was no deja-vu! I *did* see those designs somewhere. I couldn't believe I forgot. I first saw them all those months ago when Matteo and I visited Dr. Slike. When we first entered his house, I noticed the designs on the wooden door in his house. I guessed Dr. Slike had a portal as well! I would use it to go back to Earth and make sure Joshua made it back safely. If he did, I would make amends with him, and then have a proper goodbye.

It is kind of ironic how when I was on Earth, I was looking for a portal to come back to Caledonia, but now I was looking for a portal to go back to Earth. *I can never win!*

I heard Mom groan and stretch. "Sophia?" She groggily asked. "Sophia! You're here!" I heard her automatically jump up from the couch.

My eyes shot open and I lifted my head to get up and get away. I lifted my head a little bit but it fell back down. I realized that my necklace was stuck to Dad's sleeve.

"Sophia! We missed you! Why did you go? We all tried using the portal to get you back but it wouldn't let us! I was worried sick. I had your Dad sick and you missing. I wanted you back. It was as if my soul were ripped from me. I felt so helpless! But you are back and none of that matters. Oh I am so glad to have you back, my sweet daughter." Mom's eyes glazed over.

I groaned, "Stupid thing! Let go of my necklace!" I wasn't even paying attention to what Mom said.

Mom walked over to try and help me free. "Don't pull it sweetie, you will break it. Here, let me help you."

"No! Don't touch me. Don't come near me. I don't want your help!" It wasn't budging. My hands were shaking and I couldn't get it out. My current state got the best of my nerves. My hands started to shake as a result. I gave up and undid the clasp. I then backed away from Dad's bed. I didn't take my eyes off Mom the entire time.

"Sweetie? What is wrong? What has happened to you? It's me, your mother. Do you not remember me or something?" Mom outstretched her hand to me.

I looked at her hand and then back to her. "How could you do that to Dad? How could you do that to your *family*? You sicken me. And you obviously know what I am talking about! Why don't you just leave us alone and go back to *Massimo*!" I uncontrollably spat out as I spoke.

"Sophia! I have no idea where you got this nonsense from! You are ridiculously mistaken!" Mom started walking towards me. I pushed the chair beside me in her direction. It stopped her path. Her face was frozen in horror. I ran out as fast as I could.

I knew where I was going. I had to go to Dr. Slike's house and ask him to use his portal. He would let me use it without a doubt - I hoped!

I ran without a break in between. I could feel my sweat escaping my pores. I had to constantly wipe my forehead with the back of my arm. It was such a hot day compared to the freezing temperatures on Earth. I imagined wearing all the clothing necessary on Earth, but wearing it now? I would die of heat!

I finally got to Dr. Slike's house. It took much less time than it did the first time coming here with Matteo. I grabbed the back of my neck. It throbbed. It was a feeling that I had never felt before. I ran my finger over the large scar I had there. It was from my accident so long ago and now it decided to hurt. It probably throbbed since I ran so much. I don't think I've ever ran that much in my life - maybe that was why.

I collapsed purposely on the stairs in front of his house. I needed to catch my breath. It wasn't coming. I needed to calm my breathing in order to calm my heart.

I knocked on the door, but opened it myself anyway. I didn't have time to wait. I called Dr. Slike's name, but he didn't respond. Maybe he wasn't home. I saw Arlene sleeping on the couch. As soon as she heard me call his name, she woke up. She arched her back and ran over to me. She brushed her body against my legs. "Hi Arlene," I whispered as I bent down to scratch under her chin.

Inside, I looked towards the door frame that had the design on it and as soon as I lay my eyes upon it, I knew instantly that the designs matched. The door was open. I walked up to it when I heard someone call.

"In here, child," a voice said.

I placed a hand on the designed door frame and peeked my head through. Dr. Slike stood there with his back to me.

"Dr. Slike?" I asked.

He turned around and I saw his face. He was still the same doctor I left a while ago. He smiled at me.

I couldn't help but smile back. "What are you doing?" I asked him.

"I would have to say that I am doing nothing. I am an old man. I can get away with things like that. It was nice when I used to have my portal - which I am sure you know all about since your mother called me the day you disappeared."

"*Used* to have a portal? What, you don't have one anymore?" I looked to the wall and noticed it was empty. Dr. Slike was staring at a big empty space where something once stood. The walls around were faded but that one spot looked like it was brand new. That must have been where the portal was.

Dr. Slike doesn't have his portal anymore? Oh, come on! Someone up there is really pissed off at me to play these sorts of games with my body and soul! "What happened to your portal?"

"I shouldn't be telling you this, but I don't really care anymore. A few years back Paul Jr. Carter came to my house seeking a portal of his own. He said that he knew I had a portal. He also insisted that I give it to him without any questions asked. Obviously at first I refused. Paul gave me two options: he would take it by force with no pay, or he would pay me a great amount to buy it off me. At my age, I don't have the energy to argue. I knew I didn't have the strength to stop him if I said no. Strength is something I lost many years ago when my bones started to become weak. I can get from point A to point B, but I tire easily. I have been around for many years and sometimes all I want is peace and quiet. So, I took Paul's offer. He offered me a great lump sum of cash for the portal. I didn't expect so much, but I didn't say anything after receiving the amount of money. They had to knock down a wall in order to retrieve the portal. I figured I might as well redecorate my entire house while I was at it. I had nothing else to spend the money on, and I thought remodelling my house was a good start. I also bought Arlene over here off one of my friends who had a litter of kittens. She cost close to nothing, but I still spent the money Paul gave me on her. She's a cutie isn't she?"

Arlene meowed as she could tell Dr. Slike was talking about her. She was circling his feet now. He picked her up and nudged his face into hers. He rubbed her fur on his wrinkly skin. He looked happy with his life. I didn't want to interfere anymore.

"Well, I better be on my way then. It is getting late. Thank you for that information. You were always a very informative man." I ducked my head and turned to walk away.

"Oh!" Dr. Slike said. "Did you ever find the Nekkel Ace?"

I turned around and smiled at him. "No." Little did he know what I went through. I would tell him, but right now just didn't seem like the right time.

"I see. Well good luck with that, and I hope your father recovers." He pet Arlene's head. I could hear her purring from where I was standing.

"Thank you," was all I said as I walked away from him and went outside.

I could see the sun setting as it descended in the sky. I knew it would be nightfall by the time I got to Paul's house.

So I would go home and rest. When it was bright and early in the morning, I would venture to Paul's house. I wondered what he would say about my disappearing. I wondered if anyone told him I went to Earth. I would find out tomorrow. Tomorrow was definitely going to be an exciting day! I could feel it.

Chapter 21 - The Truth

It was early morning and I had my daily tasks already planned out. I planned to visit Paul Jr. immediately, but then I had a change of heart. I decided to push that back a bit and find Matteo. I convinced myself that Joshua would be fine for a few more hours. Something inside told me that he was alright and that I shouldn't worry about him. He was a strong and determined man. He is probably out and about in the cold, taking Milo for a walk.

First, I had to make things right with Matteo. I wanted to tell him everything that happened to me and I wanted to tell him about Mom - as much as I dreaded it.

I took a detour to my tower. I climbed up and remembered the months I spent there, sitting, all alone.

I went to the window to take in the fresh breeze that passed through. I missed this smell from being on Earth for so long. *I've taken the littlest things for granted.* A sudden gust of wind burst through the window and it made my hair fly all over the place. My hair covered my face and I had to grab it strand by strand and remove it from my view. It even stuck to my lips. I was staring out the window the whole time. I noticed someone in my garden. At first I thought it was Paul Jr., but then I looked again and noticed it was Matteo. He sat crossed legged with his hands on his knees. His back was perfectly straight, the exact same way I sat whenever I dozed off while sitting there. He looked so peaceful sitting there with his eyes closed.

Sadness and joy overwhelmed me. It was sweet to know someone was picking up my good habits instead of my bad ones. The bad thing was that, from up here, I could tell Matteo was wearing all white. He wore a white buttoned down shirt and white pants. If Mom were to see him sitting in the garden like that - I stopped that thought - *who cares about what Mom thinks?*

I turned my back to the window and went down the stairs to see Matteo. There was no better time than now to talk to him.

I stood on the stone pathway staring in his direction. I was a few feet away, but he didn't hear me approach. I walked over quietly. I knew once I stepped onto the grass and into the flower patch, he would hear me and open his eyes.

Here I go. My first step didn't disturb him and neither did the second. On the third step, Kiko lifted up his head and looked at me. He still lay there beside Matteo. As soon as Kiko lifted up his head, Matteo slowly opened his eyes. I had to take another step to make sure they were actually open.

When I reached him, I knelt down in front of him. I placed both my hands on top of his, which were still on his knees. I looked deep into his eyes. A strand of my hair blew in front of my eyes but this time I didn't bother to remove it. I had to make sure he wouldn't get up and walk away. I needed to keep my eyes locked onto Matteo's. Looking at him was like looking into a mirror. We had the same blue eyes and long eyelashes.

Matteo relaxed his back as he exhaled in defeat. He was upset with me, but I could tell he was on the verge of forgiveness. I relaxed as well and finally moved the strand of hair from my face.

"First, let me start off with saying I am truly and dearly sorry. I didn't leave to hurt you. I didn't leave to upset you. I did nothing of the sort! Let me start off with *why* I left in a hurry like that - into the portal without you." I inhaled as I prepared to tell him the story of Mom. He listened and hung on to every word I said. His jaw even dropped when I got to the climax of the story - the part with Massimo and Mom. "And so you see, I didn't have time to talk, time to think or even time to breathe. I had to leave far away from her. I saw her yesterday and I started yelling at her. I couldn't believe it. I will never forgive her." I looked down to my hands. I choked up and couldn't talk anymore.

"I... I can't believe it. Are you sure? Are you sure it was Mom? It can't be. But..."

I nodded with my eyes closed. It cut him off. His jaw was open like he had to say something to defend her but he could tell I wasn't lying. I would never lie about something as serious as that.

"Huh, right?" I said.

Matteo looked down to Kiko who looked right back at him. "Sophia… I wanted to say sorry about yesterday. I saw you running from the house so I followed you to the portal. I wanted to talk to you but as soon as I saw you, I lost all words. I couldn't speak, so the only thing I thought of was to walk away. I expected you to disappear, like last time."

"Don't worry about it. I understand. I deserved that."

Matteo looked at me. "I know, but still. I saw you standing there and I looked to the portal and it looked exactly the way I saw it last."

"What do you mean?"

"That day in August when you ran for the portal, I knew something bad happened, but I didn't know what exactly. I caught a glimpse of your face and it was drenched with tears. My heart dropped when I saw you like that. I then saw you cradling your arm as you ran and I knew you were badly hurt. I tried catching up with you, but you had a bigger head start. I ran as fast as I could but it was no use. I was in view of the portal doors and I saw that same bright light. I ran faster. I got to the room, it was dark and worst of all, it was empty. I tried going through the portal but it just mirrored my expressions on the glass."

I thought back to when I went yesterday and it just reflected my image. Matteo saw the exact same thing that I did. I know what that felt like. Pure and miserable failure to help the one you love.

Matteo continued. "Going back every day did nothing. Each time I went, it was the same thing; a black mirror laughing at me. I think you broke it." He smiled to lighten the mood.

"Yeah, ha, I think I did. It wouldn't even let me through when I tried yesterday."

"I know, I saw." Matteo looked past me. His eyes were looking into the empty space behind me. I knew he wasn't really looking at anything. He snapped out of it and looked back at me.

"You know, I missed home while I was on Earth. I missed everyone greatly!" I went to grab my necklace. It normally comforted me whenever I thought of home. I came up empty. I spread my hand across my chest as my heart skipped a beat. I gasped.

"What's wrong?" Matteo asked as he clearly noticed my shock.

At first I thought I lost my necklace, but remembered I left it with Dad. I completely forgot about it. How shameful. I knew it was safe so it didn't really matter to me right now.

"Oh it's nothing, never mind. I thought I lost my necklace, but Dad has it. It got caught on his shirt when I went to see him and I didn't have the time to take it out. I couldn't talk to Mom so I left it there." I calmed down and fell down on my side and lay on the ground. I didn't have the energy to sit up anymore. The blades of grass tickled my face. I had to squint to look at Matteo since the sun shone directly in my eyes. I could barely see anything since the sun was right behind Matteo. He was a mere shadow.

I was happy that Matteo and I were talking again yet I was so sad about the unreal departure with Joshua. I also feared that I failed Dad when I told him I would make him better. I even promised him. I had broken that promise. I had to see Paul Jr. immediately. Tears filled up in my eyes. I couldn't tell from which cause, since I was one big emotional wreck.

I closed my eyes hoping that would stop the tears from flowing, but it didn't.

"Sophia, please don't cry. What's the matter now? You are so emotional you know!" Matteo stayed sitting on the grass as he grabbed my arm and tried lifting me up. I used none of my power to make myself get up. I wanted to stay lying on the grass, but Matteo wouldn't let me. "Get up." My head fell back as he pulled me up. "Come here. Everything will be fine. I don't know what is going on in your head right now, but it will all turn out for the best. I promise."

Matteo pulled me close to him and gave me a hug. It was very comforting. Matteo was always there for me. *What a great brother.* I loved how he loved me so much and wanted the best for me. I hugged him back and wiped my eyes with the back of my hand. Through my blurred vision I saw two people walking my way. I couldn't tell who they were since once again, the sun blinded my sight. One of the people walking towards me was holding something that clashed with the intensity of the sun. It looked like they were carrying a miniature sun in their grasp, tied to a string. It swung back and forth in this person's hand.

I pushed back from Matteo as I looked behind him and wiped my eyes again to get a clearer view. I hated being blind like this. Matteo looked over his shoulder and squinted his eyes as well. We both sat on our knees and at the same time we lifted our hand to shelter our eyes from the sun.

"No way! You have got to be kidding me! It's a miracle!" Kiko and Matteo got up from the ground immediately.

"What? Who is it?" I got up and noticed who it was as they walked closer to us. I dropped my hand and at the same time I stood up slowly as my mouth was wide open in awe. I screamed at the top of my lungs and ran towards one of the persons walking my way. I jumped and wrapped my arms around him. I hugged him as tight as I could. He swung me around as I looked behind him and saw Mom and Matteo staring at us. Mom had the biggest smile on her face as I could tell her eyes were all red from tears of joy. I knew exactly how she felt as tears of joy ran down my cheeks.

I looked up to this man and smiled. "Dad, you're awake!" I was in shock. I guess time did help all.

"Thank you Sophia. Thank you so much!" Dad said as he wiped the tears from my face with both his thumbs.

I shook my head. "Thank you for what? Dad, I didn't do anything. You're awake now and that's all that matters." I jumped a little.

"Oh, my child, but I have *you* to thank for being awake. I guess you don't even know the power you hold."

I didn't say anything as Dad lifted up his hand. At a closer view I saw the shimmering object that I noticed from afar. It was my necklace. He undid the clasp and tied the necklace around my neck.

"This necklace has great powers - powers that woke me from my coma. It has the power to heal all sicknesses. You mustn't tell anyone about it. Many people claim it is there's but it belongs to our family. I went through a lot to get this into my possession."

"Nekkel Ace," I whispered.

"Sweetie, it's your necklace, not Nekkel Ace," Dad said with a weary look on his face.

"I thought it was Nekkel Ace that would wake you up. I guess I was told wrong." I shrugged my shoulders.

"You went to talk to Dr. Slike didn't you? He has told me that name as well but no one really knows the true name of it. Nekkel Ace does sound fitting, so that is what we shall call it. But remember, you cannot tell anyone about it. If people were to know you had it in your possession, they would try to take it away from you. Let's keep that our little family secret alright?" He said as he nudged my chin with his finger.

"I won't tell a soul," I said back to him with complete seriousness.

"This is so wonderful! We're finally together again!" Mom tried putting her arm around my shoulder but I backed away from her.

"Sophia!" Dad said with a disapproving tone. I flinched.

"It's okay Antonio." Mom put her hand on Dad's shoulder.

"Sophia, sweetie, listen, it was one big misunderstanding. I don't recall *any* of it. I had no idea what you were talking about. I told your father what happened between you and me when you came into your father's room and was livid with me. I knew you wouldn't give me an answer, so

I had to think of the next best option. We went straight for Massimo and asked what you could be talking about. Massimo explained everything that happened that day. He said he walked into the wrong room at the wrong time. We unfortunately had to let him go. What happened was not my fault and I promise you that." Mom stared deeply into my eyes. She tried convincing me. I guess Dad knew about it as well. *He believed her, so why shouldn't I?* Maybe it was a misunderstanding. I only saw a split second. My eyes could have been deceiving me. But then I knew what I saw and my eyes don't lie. She wasn't telling me the entire story. I could feel it deep inside. *What if Massimo lied to her and didn't tell her the whole truth?* Maybe he made something up in front of Dad. I didn't want to ask any more questions so I took a step forward. I would find Massimo and ask for myself. For now, I accepted her apology, but I would find out more eventually.

Mom put her arms around Matteo, Dad and I. We all huddled into one big hug. I had no choice but to smile in everyone's embrace. Laughter roared from all of us. It was heart-warming to hear everyone happy and laughing again.

"So what were you up to as I was uh, sleeping, you could say." Dad took a deep breath of fresh air. Something he hadn't done in quite some time.

"Nothing." It came out too quick it sounded like a lie - only because it *was* a lie. I didn't want to tell him I went through the portal. He would be so cross with me! Matteo and Mom remained tight lipped. Some things are best kept to ourselves. I mostly didn't want to tell Dad I went through the portal, since I had to go back again. If I told him I went already he would see that I was fine but forbid me to go again. So if I didn't tell him I went in the first place, he couldn't say anything.

As happy as I was to get my family back together again, I needed to get to Paul Jr.'s house.

"Well then," Dad said as he placed both hands on his stomach and rubbed, "I am starving!"

"We'll fetch you something to eat my darling. Let's go inside." Mom turned to Matteo and me. "Are you two hungry as well?"

"No." I answered. I was actually starving, but I had no time to eat. "I think I will go for a walk."

Matteo looked at me with his eyes slightly closed.

"Matteo?" Mom asked.

"No, I am not hungry either."

I thought I heard Matteo's stomach growl, but I knew he wouldn't let me out of his sight again.

"Alright then, we will see you later then at dinner. Don't be late!" Mom said shaking her finger at the both of us. I was looking forward to our first family dinner in a long time!

I gave Dad a hug before they walked away. I watched them as they both went inside. Mom had to support Dad since he was still weak.

I pretended to walk around the house, but as soon as they were out of sight and in the kitchen, I walked inside. It was much faster to cross right through instead of going all the way around. I didn't want my parents to see where I was going.

I turned around to see Matteo following me as I took my first step inside the house. "Not hungry I see? But you're always hungry," I whispered to Matteo.

"I know, but I had to see what you were up to. You had that mischievous look on your face that I know *too* well, darling sister." Matteo grabbed the back of my neck and squeezed it. It hurt and tickled at the same time. I couldn't help but laugh.

At that moment, we heard the phone ring. Normally someone would answer it right away, but it kept ringing and ringing and ringing. I told Matteo to answer it, but he kept telling me to answer it. We argued, *"You answer it, no you answer it!"*

Matteo pushed me and I gave in, annoyed. He and Kiko left me and started walking towards the front. I looked at the phone. I picked it up and put it to my ear. "Hello, Amaro residence," I said. There was no voice on the other end. "Hello?" I said again, but this time with more emphasis.

"Hello," a man's voice on the other side finally spoke.

"May I ask who's speaking?" I asked. The voice sounded familiar. No answer. I waited.

"Is this Sophia?" he said.

"Yes," I answered. "Who are you?"

"I have some news for you," he spoke in a deep voice, "Joshua, the one you love, is dead."

"How do you know me? How do you know about Joshua? Why are you calling me?" The phone shook in my hand.

"I only speak of the truth. You should go and see for yourself. I am sorry for your loss." *Click.* A low, steady tone followed.

"Hello? Hello!" I guessed he hung up.

I stood there; shock filled every part of my body. I had the phone barely in my hand. I felt my whole body go numb; my fingers went limp and the phone slowly fell out from my hand. It hit the marble ground, pieces flying everywhere. I knew the phone fell, but it made no sound. My heartbeat automatically accelerated as I started to process what just happened. This phone call could not be real. How could this have happened? *Everything was fine five minutes ago, but now I get this message? I have to go back and find out for myself. Things like this don't happen to people like me. Does this mean things are clearer now? Or are they even more difficult than ever. I'm stuck. Should I even go back now? I don't know what to do.*

That's when reality hit me with the force of a thousand ton train. It felt like my heart was clawed out right from the depth of my chest. I finally came to face the truth. The walls and countertops began to blur and spin – nausea and dizziness overpowered me. I didn't have the energy to stand anymore. It became harder to breathe as I slowly started to fall forward. The floor was coming closer to my face faster than ever. That was when everything went black.

Chapter 22 – Heart on Fire

I knew I passed out. This was something I had become accustomed to recently. Whether it was flying through a portal or falling down steps, I knew when I was entering another reality. It is weightlessness that you cannot control. It is pure happiness without a care in the world. I flew high above the clouds, running my fingers through their fluffiness. When you are flying, it is kind of obvious you are unconscious. I am thankful that I can realize this. The bad part is that you don't know when you will awaken.

I was now flying over Earth. The clouds aren't as nice on Earth as they are on Caledonia. I slowly landed on the ground in the park. I had a white dress on and my hair was back to being short and brown. I looked towards a tree that seemed out of place. There was a little orange cat on it. It looked like it was stuck. I stared at it hoping maybe it would jump down to safety.

The cat was meowing and it sounded so sad. It sounded like it was crying. I stood there waiting, hoping the cat would stop. It stared at me with its green, eerie eyes. It felt like it was trying to tell me something. I then thought of Joshua. He was scared to tell me something. I was determined to find out what that something was. With a blink of my eye, the cat transformed into a man. It wasn't just *any* man, it was Joshua. Joshua now sat in this tree. He sat on the lonely branch. He opened his mouth to speak, but I couldn't hear anything.

I shook my head and opened my mouth to tell him I couldn't hear him, but the words came out from my lips in a soundless motion. I then grabbed my throat in shock. I was overcome with frustration. I felt so useless.

I tried speaking to myself, but it was no use. I looked to Joshua and he looked so sad. He was telling me something important, but I couldn't hear him. I tried telling him to stop or to speak louder but he didn't listen. The only words I understood from reading his lips were 'I am sorry.'

"Sophia." Joshua said over and over again. But this time I heard him. A voice came with the movement of his lips. "Sophia. Sophia. Sophia, wake up!"

My eyes shot open and I found myself lying on the ground with Matteo's big head hovering over me. I grabbed my nose with one hand and my head with the other. "Ow!" It came out muffled.

"Gosh, woman! I leave you for two seconds and you pass out on me! What is the matter with you?" Matteo yelled as he sat on the ground beside me. With his back pressed up against the house, he closed his eyes and leaned his head back against the wall.

I propped myself up on my elbows and removed my hands from my face. I wrinkled my face to erase the pain. My nose was killing me. I tried not to move it. The more I moved it, the more it hurt. I noticed we were in the front of the house now. We were hidden in the shade of one of the large bushes.

"What happened?" I asked.

Matteo opened his eyes and looked at me. "I could ask you the same question! Who was that on the phone?"

"The phone call! Someone called for me! Joshua! They said he is dead! We must hurry. We have to go find out, quick!" I got up swiftly and balanced myself.

"Where are we going? And what's the hurry? Who called? Who's Joshua?"

"Stop with all the questions! We have to go! Come on!" I grabbed Matteo's hand and dragged him away from the house. He pulled his hand back and followed me willingly.

We walked in silence at a fast pace for about five minutes. "So, where are we going?" Matteo asked finally.

I hesitated at first, but he was going to follow me so I figured I might as well tell him. He deserved to know after all. I slowed down to catch my breath. "I have to go to Paul's house. Strictly business," I said, trying to sound serious.

Matteo started laughing. "Why on Caledonia would you want to go to see Paul Jr.?"

"Well turns out that Dr. Slike had a portal. I figured that out all by myself," I said matter of factly. "I went to his house yesterday, but he told me that Paul bought it off him. I needed to go back to Earth and fix some things with Joshua, but now after that phone call I need to go back to Earth to see if he is…" I didn't want to say it, "dead. I don't feel it. I don't feel like he is dead. I won't believe it until I see it. So I have to find him."

"Who is Joshua?" Matteo asked for the second time.

I felt my face heat up and my chest felt warm. I wrapped my arms around my torso as we walked.

Matteo noticed my reaction to his question. "So… who is this new guy?" He nudged me with his elbow. He is such a weirdo.

I shook my head and smiled from ear to ear. I told Matteo about Joshua and how I fell in love with him. I told him exactly how we met. As I did, I reached up to touch my forehead. The bump was completely gone. The first day we met was nothing but a memory now. I had no scars to prove it. I told Matteo about my shopping sprees, how we moved in together, and also how he remembered my birthday.

Matteo listened intently the whole time. He stared at me with a big grin on his face. It was as if he wanted to say something.

"What?" I asked. I smiled with each step that I took.

"Nothing."

"Tell me!" I pushed Matteo. He almost bumped into Kiko.

"It's nothing I said. It's just nice to see you this happy. I can tell this Joshua guy means a lot to you. I will meet him. I will be the one to see if he's good enough for you or not." Matteo stuck out his chest, trying to be all macho.

"Easy there tough guy!" I couldn't help but laugh out loud. "I am sure you will love him. He is sweet, and kind, and gentle, and beautiful." I sighed.

We both walked down one long road to get to Paul's house. We walked near the shore. We could see it in the distance. His house was huge, almost as big as mine. His house seemed much darker than mine was. The exterior was a mix of dark greys and blacks. It was eerie. It gave the illusion that it was floating on the water. I could hear the water splashing against the rocks. Fear overcame me as I imagined myself falling into that water. It looked so dangerous.

After a long walk of carefully averting the shore, we finally reached Paul Jr.'s house. Matteo, Kiko and I walked over the bridge to get to the grand doors at the front entrance. I went to knock on the door, but my knocks were weak and pitiful.

"Uh, a little help?" I stepped aside and let Matteo knock. His knocks were much stronger and I felt like whoever was inside, heard them clearly.

"And *that* is how you properly knock on a door." Matteo pulled my hair. I just stuck my tongue out at him.

The door opened and an old wrinkly man answered. He looked like a depressed, old bell boy. The bags under his eyes had bags of their own and he had many chins despite the fact that he was very skinny. The loose skin jiggled as he greeted us. I didn't know whether to throw up or laugh in this poor man's face. I figured I might as well say something.

I looked at this man and said, "Hi, we're here looking for Paul Jr." I couldn't look at him in the eye anymore without smiling, so I looked behind him, instead. "Is he home? I am Sophia and this is Matteo."

"One moment please," The man sighed as he closed the door.

I looked to Matteo and he hung his hand under his chin to mimick the old man. With every word he said, he shook his hand to show the wiggling flesh. "One moment please." Jiggle, jiggle. "One moment please." Jiggle.

I was laughing as the door opened again. It was the same old man. "Right this way please." He bowed and motioned with his hand for us to enter.

"Thank you," I said as I walked by him.

Matteo was right behind me.

"Not you." The old man blocked Matteo's way.

"But he is with me. We are both here to see Paul Jr."

"Master's orders. I am sorry Miss, but he is not allowed in." He stared at Matteo while speaking to me. His back was to me. *How rude.*

I looked to Matteo with helpless eyes. He wouldn't let Matteo in, but I needed to continue on and speak with Paul.

"It is alright. I will be out here. If anything happens, remember, I'll be right outside!"

I nodded my head as the man closed the door on Matteo's face. "Follow me please," he said as he led me into an enormous room with a huge lit fireplace. I stayed away from it, considering how hot I already was. Shortly after the man bowed and left me alone in this room, Paul entered the room holding a glass of liquor. The moment Paul walked in; I knew he was drinking brandy. I could smell it. It was one of Dad's favourites when guests were over.

"Sophia! What a pleasant surprise to see you here!" Paul said with his arms wide open - almost spilling his brandy in the process.

"I need to see your portal. I have to go through it!" I spoke before my mind could even process what he said.

He arched his eyebrow. "Now how did you know that I had a portal? No one knew about that." Paul took a step towards me.

I stood my ground. "I have my sources," I said with my head held high.

"Dr. Slike told you, didn't he?" Paul said as he nodded his head.

"Yeah." Nice one Sophia.

"Alright. Well how are you anyway? How rude of me for not asking." Paul smiled seductively.

"Sorry, hi, I am fine. I just have this dilemma, you see. I got this phone call and someone told me that this man I know has died. So I need to see for myself that this is not true."

"Really? Well that is pretty disturbing." Paul Jr. turned around to walk away. "I will take you to it. Come."

That was easy, I thought. I followed him and we walked down a tall hallway. The walls went up very high and were covered with beautiful paintings. I knew this was an old house, but it was very well cared for. It was like a castle in here. Everything was dark. It was nothing like my house, which was all white and bright and open. This was more secluded and intimate. The darkness was concealing something; I could feel it.

We walked towards a room and I knew instantly that was the room with the portal. The door leading to it had the designs. I stopped in front of the door and I asked Paul why the trimming of the outside had all those designs. He told me that he didn't really know why. He thought it just looked nice. He said he was kidding and really told me that the designs enhanced the portal's powers. It makes it become one with its surroundings.

I thought back and noticed that my portal didn't have that on the door outside. I shrugged my shoulders. It didn't seem like that big a deal.

Paul opened the door for me to. Just as I was about to go in, he blocked the entrance with his arm. His hand was inches away from my stomach. "Before you go in, you must clear your mind okay? Do not let your emotions overwhelm you or else the portal will read on that and go crazy. Just clear your mind and all will be well. Okay?"

I nodded my head and gulped loudly. *Why was I so scared?* I wondered. Paul removed his hand and I walked in as he followed right beside me. My heartbeat quickened as I stepped inside. His portal looked exactly like mine. I calmed myself down and cleared my mind. I thought of Earth and nothing else.

There was definitely a difference from my portal compared to Paul's. There was no blinding light and no darkened mirrored reflection of myself. The edges of the glass glowed white, while the rest of it showed me a picture of Earth. I then thought about the park outside my condo. As soon as I changed thoughts, the portal showed me the park.

Astonished, I asked Paul Jr. how the portal could show me what I was thinking.

"It knows what you think and feel. The portal becomes one with you. I wouldn't mind coming with you and making sure you are safe. I am not too sure if more than one person can enter the portal at one time. We can try it out together if you like. I can come with you." He swirled the brandy in his glass as he spoke.

"No. I need to do this alone."

"Very well then." Paul Jr. bowed and took a step back.

I closed my eyes and thought of Joshua's place. I thought of the bed we shared so many nights together. I opened my eyes and there it was – his room, his bed, it was all there. I pushed back tears as I took a step forward. I closed my eyes and walked through the portal.

I was conscious the entire time and I even woke up in the place I wanted to be. I didn't wake up passed out in Joshua's bed. It was like I entered the apartment through the front door. I looked around his room and it looked the same. Nothing was different. I felt his presence still in the room. *Is it because he is dead and his spirit still lives on, or is it because he was here not too long ago? How can I really tell if he's dead?*

I opened his drawers and they were empty. The first two drawers had nothing in them, but the bottom two still had clothes. That's when it struck me. Someone started clearing out his things. I made a beeline to the closet, I pulled open the door. It was empty. I don't know who, but someone was here to clear the apartment of Joshua's belongings. Soon enough they will be back to clear out the rest of his things since Joshua is not coming back – ever. My breathing got heavier and I took a few steps backwards to sit on the bed. I held my hand on my heart. I could feel it pounding away.

On the dresser, I noticed a picture lying face down in the frame. I got up and grabbed the picture of us which was taken not too long ago. It was that night we went out for dinner for my birthday. We asked the waitress to take a picture with Joshua's camera. It was remarkable. It was far different from the cameras we have back home. Anyway, I held the picture frame with both my hands as I went back and sat on the edge of what used to be mine and Joshua's bed. All the happy memories from that day came flooding back. I remembered when he surprised me by remembering my birthday when even I had forgotten.

We sat across each other at a small table in the middle of the room. It was as if all eyes were on us but at the same time it felt like we were the only two people in the entire restaurant. We held hands as the picture was taken. The candle in the middle of the table glowed with our love for one other. The love radiated in the depths of our eyes and souls. We were completely devoted.

Tears rolled down my cheeks and splashed onto the glass covering of the picture frame. It was heart breaking to realize I would never see him again. I would never be able to feel his touch, or even hear his voice. I would miss the way he held me tightly every time we embraced each other, as if he never wanted to let me go. I took his touch for granted as if I knew nothing could tear us apart. I was wrong. He was gone and I was alone.

I crawled to the top of his bed and curled up into the fetal position. I hugged the picture frame as if I was hugging Joshua himself. I shook my head in disbelief that he was actually gone. The sobs of the truth that I kept locked up inside burst out. I cursed the world for taking him from me. My eyes burned with each tear that fell from my face and sunk deep into his pillow. My chest stung as my heart ached for Joshua to come back.

The nauseous feeling came over me again. It was much worse this time; I even gagged from the impact. Less than a second passed as I felt myself slipping from Earth and back to Caledonia. I ended up back in Paul's portal room. I was on the floor crouching on my knees, still holding onto the picture frame. I brought it back with me from Earth. I didn't even know that was possible.

Paul lifted me up from under my arms and helped me walk to his couch. We sat there together. My head was buried in his chest as I cried. Paul hushed me gently and ran his hand over my hair to comfort me. It hurt so much. With each breath that I took, it felt like someone tore a little piece of my heart and lit it on fire. Each piece that was torn belonged to Joshua. *Sooner or later there will be nothing left of my heart; it will be one big ball of ash. The fire will consume it entirely eventually. I lost the one I loved. He took a part of me in his departure. I have lost him forever.*

Chapter 23 - The Whole Truth

How can I continue on with my life if Joshua is not part of it? I kept thinking. I knew I planned to leave him all along, but at least I knew he was alive on Earth. But now to find out that I had lost him forever was torture.

Paul Jr. sat by my side for almost an hour not saying a word. He switched from gently rocking me to caressing my hair which felt comforting. Every so often he would hand me a new tissue which wouldn't last three seconds in my hands. It would already be drenched right after he handed it to me.

When I finally got enough strength to speak, I leaned away from Paul's shoulder and sat up straight. I looked forward; I didn't want to look at Paul since I knew my eyes were all red and swollen. It would have been such an embarrassment to be seen like this. Paul was a handsome man and would probably be disgusted see me in this state.

He sat closer to get a better look at my face. Looking away, I turned by body to face him. With my eyes averted I could feel him staring directly at me as he stroked my hair. He ran his fingers through my hair to remove the strands that were stuck to my face, damp from the tears. Paul leaned close to me and kissed my forehead. I looked directly at him - red eyes and all. "What are you doing?" I quickly moved away. With both hands I wiped away at my tears and looked at him with creased brows.

"You look so helpless, so vulnerable. I don't like seeing you in such pain." He tilted his head to look more closely at me. "I have taken you for granted and I apologize. I missed you while you were gone all those months on Earth, you know."

"How did you know I was on Earth?"

"Well, you were gone and I figured you couldn't be anywhere else.

165

Also, you confirmed it when you showed up here today and said you needed to use the portal."

"Right," I said as I tried blowing my nose. It was so un-lady like, but I could not care less. I wasn't here to impress Paul Jr.

Paul Jr. scooted closer to me. I stared at his knees as they were an inch away from mine. He placed his hand on my knees. He rubbed them in a circular motion. I wondered what he was doing. Both my hands were placed on my lap. Paul Jr. moved his hands from my knees, up my leg, to my hands, up my arm and to my neck. He grasped the back of my neck and started massaging it. My eyes closed from how good it felt. I had so much tension there and it felt very relieving. With both his hands he grasped each side of my neck. I opened my eyes to look at him.

Once again, I was taken by how striking he was. His black hair shone even without sunlight in the room. I wanted nothing more than to run my hands through it, or even grab a fistful and pull. His blue eyes were menacing yet inviting at the same time. If looks could really kill, I would have to go blindfolded all over the place.

I tried figuring out what Paul Jr. wanted from me. With both his hands he clenched and unclenched the skin on the side of my neck. It felt good, but I didn't close my eyes this time. I wanted to know what he was up to. Our eyes were locked for quite some time. Neither of us was going to give in and look away or close our eyes. I don't even think we blinked during this.

Paul Jr. smiled and dropped his gaze. *I win.* He pulled my face closer with both his hands still on my neck as he leaned in to whisper in my ear. I closed my eyes since he was in such close proximity with my face. I flinched from his breath tickling my ear and neck. It sent chills down my arms.

"I love you Sophia," he said. My eyes shot open! "I love you so much. You're perfect! I need you. Have you not noticed?" He stayed there, breathing in the scent of my neck.

I pulled my head back and placed both my hands on his chest to ease him away from me. I could feel his muscular body under his clothes. I wondered what his body looked like. "I am sorry Paul, but I don't feel the same way. I like you, yes, but I am nowhere close to being *in love* with you. I am in love with someone else and that will never change." I shook my head. "My heart belongs to him."

"But, the one you love is dead. How can you love someone who no longer exists?"

Stab, right in the heart. I literally felt my heart skip a beat as he said those words. *'But the one you love is dead.'*

"I know, but, I-I… d-don't love you." I stammered out the words. My chest became so tight; I couldn't even speak.

"Ah, see, but you do. You just don't know it. We were meant to be. Every obstacle that came our way, we surpassed it, and in the end, we ended up together - the way we were destined to be."

"N-no."

"Don't fight destiny. I know you love me, even though you haven't figured it out yet." Paul Jr. leaned in for a kiss.

"But…" He was doing a real good job in convincing me. But I wasn't going to be tricked that easily.

"Sh…" His lips stopped my rebuttal.

It was one little peck but it shocked every muscle in my body, taking me by surprise. I pushed Paul Jr. away and stood up. My hand quickly went up to cover my lips. Joshua was the only man I had ever kissed. He sat there staring at me; willing me to come back with his eyes. I wouldn't. "I can't do this. What are you trying to do to me? I just lost the one I love and you expect me to move on so fast? I don't think so! I am sorry. I have to go now." I was disgusted as I looked around for a way out. I knew Matteo would be right outside. Matteo would wait outside for however long it took. I knew he would not leave.

I took a step in the direction of the doorway as Paul rose but grabbed my hand before I could take another step. He sat back down. I remained standing. He stared up at me with a calm face. Both his hands grasped my one hand.

"You are absolutely impossible Sophia. Can you not tell that I am madly in love with you? I have been ever since the first time I met you at your house all those years ago. That fiery attitude you had. The day you turned me down when I asked for you to be mine. I was angry and upset with you, but at the same time I kept telling myself, *'I have to have her.'* I would do anything for you - you name it and I will do it. What do I have to do to make you mine?"

I sighed hard. Paul looked so sad. I couldn't just walk away from him. *He just poured his heart out to me, and how do I repay him, I walk away?* I couldn't do that to him. I knew I would regret this later.

With my hand still in his, I sat down beside him and looked at our hands which were now intertwined. His hands were much bigger than mine were. He was much taller as well.

"There is something I must tell you. I wasn't going to, but you leave me with no choice."

"What is it?" I looked at Paul, but his gaze was still on our hands.

Paul hesitated at first but then ended up telling me. "The entire time you were on Earth I was spying on you."

"What? Excuse me? Why? How?" I pulled my head back.

"I knew you went to Earth. I got the portal from Dr. Slike a while ago because I wanted something to use to get away from my parents and boarding school. I wasn't gone long, but it did its job. I had even more reason to use it once I realized you had gone to Earth. I had to keep an eye out for you. I saw you met that Joshua guy. I wanted to protect you from him. I was there that one day when I saw you kiss him. I watched you through my portal. All I had to do was think of the place I thought you were, and it would show me you. Just like when you thought of the park before, it showed you the park. I went through and knocked on the door to interrupt you two."

"That was you? I thought that was the pizza guy!" That was so uncalled for. My stomach was turning.

"You shouldn't be grieving for this man you know. He used you. He was using you for your necklace!"

I clutched my necklace in shock. "Why would he ever want my necklace?" I had to play dumb. No one was supposed to know about the Nekkel Ace.

"No need to play dumb, my sweet. One day while you two were out, I went through Joshua's things. I found his Dad's journal. I went through it and found out about the Nekkel Ace. I read how your Dad found it and how it was in the form of a necklace. Joshua must have known this as well and tried getting close to you so he could take it from you. There was a picture of you in the journal. When I saw that I was furious. Your necklace was circled, which confirmed that you did have it in your possession. I knew that guy was no good. If he tried to hurt you, I would come there and beat the living crap out of him."

A lump filled my throat. I opened my mouth but no words came out. My ears rang at the words Paul just spoke.

"You ended up falling in love with him. I couldn't have that. I watched when you two went skating. I knew it was dangerous so I kept an eye out for you through my portal. As soon as I saw you about to fall through, I ordered the portal to bring you back home safe in your bed. So that's how you found yourself back here."

My head was spinning. This couldn't be possible. This was not true. Paul was lying, but then why did it all make sense? Why did I believe him? I thought back to my time with Joshua. The time I thought he was looking at my chest, he was really looking at my necklace. Probably trying to figure out how he was going to take it off me. Joshua was lying to me all along. He used me. He tricked me into falling in love with hi m so that he could take the necklace and abandon me. I felt like I was going to throw up. I wrapped both my arms around my stomach. I placed my head between my knees and took in deep breaths. The air couldn't fill my lungs fast enough.

"Sophia, Sophia." Paul raised my chin so that we were face to face. I was panting still. This was too much. I looked to my left and realized the picture I brought back from Earth was still sitting there. I grabbed it and threw it across the room.

Paul smiled at this action. He tried speaking to me. His voice sounded so gentle. "Joshua is gone and you don't have to worry about him anymore. He got what he deserved. You are alone now Sophia. Even you know this. You said yourself Joshua was dead. You even went to his place to confirm it for yourself. I will also admit I have been with my share of women before I met you and none of them come even close to you. I couldn't even enjoy the company of other woman after meeting you. Being with another woman was meaningless to me if the woman wasn't you. But now I am alone, and I need you. We need each other." Paul moved in for another kiss – slower this time. His face was right in front of mine. His breath tickled my lips as he whispered, "It is time to move on."

I *was* alone. Joshua left me alone. I would miss the touch and taste of Joshua's lips on mine. I would miss waking up every morning knowing he was right there beside me, madly in love. But something in me was saying Paul Jr. was right. It *was* all a lie. All the kisses from Joshua meant nothing now. I closed my eyes and gave in to Paul.

I kissed Paul Jr. I couldn't believe it. I was kissing Paul Jr.! Or was he kissing me? He grabbed my face with both his hands. He was treating me as if I were so fragile, which I was. Our bodies were sitting, facing each other. Paul Jr.'s warm lips tasted like desire. It was as if his lips waited so long to touch mine and now that he was kissing me, he never wanted to stop. I allowed myself to be pulled into the moment. Paul Jr.'s hands moved to my hips as I wrapped my arms around his neck.

Paul Jr. slowly descended our bodies to lie on the couch. As soon as my back touched the pillow behind me, I opened my eyes. I looked into

Paul Jr.'s eyes, but they were no longer his, they were Joshua's. I saw Joshua kissing me. I stopped kissing Paul Jr. and gasped in shock.

Paul Jr. pulled his face back from mine. "What's wrong?" He stared at me in confusion.

I shook my head. Paul could never replace Joshua. Something in me still loved Joshua even after finding out all those things about him. Yet I still wanted Paul at this moment. "It's nothing. Never mind. Ignore me."

Paul did exactly that. He ignored that even happened as he leaned in again and kissed me. As soon as Paul was on top of me and had the upper hand, his kissing became more aggressive. I tried stopping him but he kept kissing me. His hard lips on mine felt wrong.

Paul's right hand moved from my face and went down, over my breast, down to my waist and then around my thigh. It made me feel uncomfortable so I stopped kissing him and looked down to his wandering hand. He kept kissing my neck even though I moved my face away from his.

As soon as I looked away from Paul, something caught my eye. What was that? I was shocked. "Paul, stop! What was that? I saw something in the corner of my eye. It was something dark and quick. It moved from one side of the room to the other. Who else is here?" Was it Matteo spying on us?

"It's nothing, ignore it." Paul pushed my face back to his.

"No, Paul, get up. Get off me!" With my arms and my legs, I pushed Paul off me and I sat up.

"What is the matter with you?" Paul said as he grabbed a pillow and put it on his lap.

"What was that?" I got up from my seat and started walking towards the other couch which was directly across from us, on the other side of the room. I knew I saw something hide behind the couch – I was sure of it!

Before I took my second step I heard a growling noise. I stopped walking and noticed a black tiger walking towards me. My eyes opened wide in fear. That wasn't a black tiger, it was a black panther. It was about the same size as Kiko. I had never seen one before. I knew they lived in the forest, but I would have never thought that Paul Jr. would have one. It growled even louder and it took slow steps in my direction. Its eyes were on me the whole time.

"Easy there, Kioné. It's okay," Paul Jr. said from behind me.

Wait one moment. It was black. It was quick - just one big blur. It came out of nowhere. My back straightened as I turned back to Paul Jr. "Paul, is this your animal?"

"Yes," He answered as he walked over to the animal to pet its head.

"Where did you find him?"

"He was in front of my house one day. He was wandering. I wanted to catch him, but he led me on a wild goose chase to the forest near your house."

My palms were sweaty as I balled them into fists. I knew I would regret this later but I had to. "You were there that day my father got into the accident with his horse. You were chasing this animal, and it got in the way of our paths and freaked out my father's horse."

"I know." Paul Jr. dropped his head.

Oh dear. I grabbed my chest as it tightened up. I felt for the couch and dropped down onto it. Dad's accident was Paul's fault! My heart pounded against my necklace, or Nekkel Ace. I couldn't believe it. It was all coming together now. That black blur that I saw was nothing more than Paul's new pet. It was unusual to have a wild animal as a pet, but after seeing Kiko and Matteo, nothing is unusual anymore.

"It was you," My voice went deep. "All of this was your fault!" I said it in complete disgust. I don't think I have ever been so disgusted and put off in my entire life.

"No, I know Sophia!" Paul came and knelt down in front of me on the ground. He grabbed my hands. "It wasn't my fault though! You have to believe me. It was one big accident and I was terrified to tell you. I thought it would be better if I just didn't." Paul was pleading with me.

I looked at him through narrow eyes. Something still wasn't right. I couldn't trust Paul. He gave off an eerie vibe. It felt like he was responsible for everything that went wrong for me in these few months. He knew a lot more than he was letting on. I was determined to find out what else he was hiding from me. "I talked to Massimo," I lied. "He told me everything that happened with him and my Mom."

Paul jumped up from the floor and slammed his hand onto the wooden table in the middle of the room. The loud noise echoed in the hallway. I jumped from the sound. Paul Jr. was furious. "Damn him! He came here and told me he made up some lie when your parents confronted him. He told them that he accidentally walked in on her changing. They forgave him but fired him, and that's why he came to me. I told him not to speak of this to anyone else – especially you! When I find him-" Paul cut himself off. "If you knew, then why are you still here? I am surprised you even came here at all. Oh that's right; you just used me for my Portal."

Work with the lies, Sophia. Don't get caught. "I wanted to see you since

I wanted to know the truth as well as use your portal." I had no idea what I was talking about. I couldn't let him realize that I didn't really talk to Massimo. "I want to hear it straight from you."

"What Massimo told you is the truth. I went over to your house that day to see your mother. She was in a fragile state with your Dad being in a coma. She welcomed the company since you had secluded yourself in that tower. I offered to pour her a drink. She accepted. I then asked her if I could see you but she wouldn't allow it. She got all defensive. I poured her another drink. This time I laced it with something. I just wanted her to sleep while I went to see you. When she woke up she wouldn't remember a thing. Instead of putting her to sleep, it made her aggressive. I couldn't control her. I told Massimo to find a way to distract her, if you know what I mean. He lusted for your mother all these years and told no one, but I could see it in his eyes every time he looked at her. Massimo failed what I set him out to do. He couldn't even go through with it."

I took in short, sharp breaths. *Keep it together Sophia*, I kept telling myself. My hands gripped the couch where I sat. *From what Paul knows, you already heard this information. Don't make it seem like this is the first time hearing it!* "That is what he told me." *Be strong.* "Why would you ever do that to my mother? Why would you do that to my family?" I had to keep it together for a little while longer so I could find out more. I wanted nothing more than to slap him hard across his face and run out of here, but I still needed more answers.

"With your Dad out of the picture, it seemed like you and I got along better. You allowed me to visit you every day. I felt my feelings for you grow stronger every time I saw you. It seemed like you slowly grew to love me as well."

I put up my hand to stop him. "We never got along Paul. I let you visit me because you were more than ten feet away from me and I didn't have to talk to you. I wasn't going to go to the lengths to get you removed from my property every time you showed up in my garden. And I never grew to love you."

"Well, then I assumed that if I got rid of your Mom, you would come to me for comfort and be all mine." Paul Jr. smiled an evil, devilish smile.

Anger boiled inside of me. I couldn't keep it in anymore. Something just snapped. "You monster! You fool! How could you? You sicken me!" I got up from the couch and ran towards Paul, raising my arm to slap him. He grabbed my hand midway through. He squeezed my wrist.

"Ow, let go of me!" I tried pulling free, but he was much stronger than I was. Memories of the day Paul Jr. first met Matteo under my tree came back to me. Paul tried pulling me away from Matteo, but ended up hurting my arm in the process. This time he had my wrist and his grip got tighter and tighter.

"Oh, I am sorry love. I cannot let go of you now. You will have to stay here with me. You *want* to stay here with me because you love me. You can never go back to your family."

"No!" I yelled. Paul was crazy! "Matteo!" I screamed at the top of my lungs.

Paul twirled me around so my back was tight to his chest. His right hand still had a good grip on my wrist while his left hand clasped my mouth muffling my screams.

"Sh. Quiet, my dear Sophia. Everything will be alright now. Sh." Paul's lips were to my ear. I wanted to punch him in the face.

I heard the front door smash open. "Sophia!" Matteo called out.

Paul's panther Kioné started growling and crouched down to pounce.

As soon as I saw Matteo I elbowed Paul Jr. in the stomach and stomped on his foot. He let go of me. I ran towards Matteo.

"Duck!" Matteo yelled as he grabbed something off a side table.

I dropped to the floor a few feet in front of Matteo to see him throw something behind me. I think it was a thick glass ashtray. He came down to grab my hands and pull me up to get away. We ran away together. I took one last glimpse over my shoulder and saw Paul Jr. lying on the floor. There was a gash on his forehead from where the object hit him. His panther was right beside him licking the wound.

I had to run back home and tell my parents everything!

Chapter 24 – Fix the Past

I ran as fast as I could with Matteo and Kiko right beside me. Matteo kept telling me to slow down but I couldn't get my legs to stop running. I wanted to get as far as possible from Paul Jr. and his malevolent ways. If I had to run all day, I would. The more my legs hurt the better; anything to lessen the pain I felt in my heart. Two men had deceived me in such a short time. I couldn't believe I let this happen.

Matteo didn't mind running with me, but he knew it was taking a toll on my body. The heat was making me pant and sweat. I felt like I was running endlessly through a dessert of no hope of returning home.

"Sophia, you can stop running now!" Matteo said as he tried pulling the back of my dress. It just made me push harder.

Matteo was a faster runner and stopped right in front of me. It surprised me and I didn't have enough time to stop. I ended up colliding with Matteo and we both fell straight for the ground. As soon as we were on the ground, I rolled off Matteo. He was holding his head with both hands.

"Fu… Shoot, my head!" Matteo sat up and rubbed the back of his head. That looked like it hurt.

"It's your fault for jumping in front of me like that." I mumbled under my breath as I sat in the dirt.

Matteo shot me an icy look. "Would you like to explain to me what happened in there?"

My hands flew in the air. "Where do I begin?!"

"Uh, the beginning?" Matteo answered.

"It was a rhetorical question," I said, irritated. I pushed myself off him to get up from the ground. I lent him my hand, he grabbed it and I pulled him up.

We walked back home. It was getting late and I knew Mom wanted us to be home before dinner was ready. *Mom*. I felt so guilty for thinking those cruel thoughts about her. I shouldn't have thought those things. She was oblivious to the entire situation and I only made her feel worse over something she had no control over.

"Alright. Well. Um. Uh. I don't know." I really didn't know where to begin.

"How about you tell me what you did first. Don't hurt yourself while you think of it. I think I see steam coming out of your ears." Matteo laughed at his own stupid joke.

"This really isn't a laughing matter Matteo. Let's be serious for once. Please."

Matteo noticed I was distraught. He could sense the pain and sadness in my voice. It hurt to even speak but I knew I had to tell him everything. Matteo's smile instantly faded and he was more mature about the situation. He nodded to let me speak.

"When I got there, the first thing I did was ask to use the portal. His portal was different than ours. It was better. His portal works on our emotions while our portal does whatever the heck it wants. I wanted to go to Earth, it showed me Earth. I wanted to go to the park, it showed me the park. I controlled the portal. I wanted to go to mine and Joshua's room, and it took me there. Turns out I was right." I had to clear my throat since I could feel a lump forming. "Joshua is dead."

"I am sorry Sophia." I could tell he really was sincere. "Did you find out how he died? How come you're not crying? Aren't you upset?"

"I did enough crying. I am mourning my loss, but I also found out something about him." I paused to look at Matteo. He looked confused. I looked back to the ground and continued. "Turns out that Joshua knew all about my necklace and was planning on taking it from me. He was just using me."

"No way! That's impossible! Really? Wow!" Matteo was in shock.

"It makes sense. I believe Paul." I shrugged my shoulders.

"You believe stuff that comes out of his filthy mouth?" Matteo was disgusted.

"Yes. He also told me something else. Well he so much as I got the truth out of him." I laughed a bit. "You will never believe this."

"Try me."

I told Matteo everything that happened. He was furious and was ready to go back to Paul's house and deal with him himself if I hadn't stopped him. I had to take a couple of second of silence to make sure Matteo calmed down before I began speaking again.

We stared at our feet the whole time we talked. We were accustomed to doing this while walking. We rarely made eye contact. We never took our eyes off our shoes. No apparent reason. It was just a habit that we both seemed to pick up. At one point I looked at our surroundings and realized we were almost home.

The closer we got to the house, the darker it got. Mine and Matteo's stomachs were growling. I was starving and Matteo must have been as well. Eating nothing all day inevitably does that to you.

"I need something to eat before I pass out," Matteo said.

I agreed with him. We were almost home. The closer I got, the safer I felt to be near home, but my stomach was in a knot, knowing what I had to tell my parents was not going to be pleasant. I decided that I would tell them after dinner. It wasn't because I was selfish or anything since I was hungry, but because I knew Mom was excited for dinner with the family and I didn't want to ruin it.

Before I knew it, we were all sitting at the dinner table waiting to be served. First came the mushroom soup as an appetizer and then for our main course we had a huge buffet. The servants kept going into the kitchen and returning with more plates. There was so much food just for the four of us. I thought Mom overdid it this time. On the table there was regular salad, pear salad, balsamic vinaigrette salad, veal cutlets, chicken cutlets, steaks, pork chops, corn, beans, peas, mashed potatoes, roasted potatoes, and baked potatoes. Those were the things that I could see. There were still more dishes on the other side of the table that were hidden from my view. I stared at Mom the entire time during dinner. Matteo and I didn't say one word. He was waiting for me to tell them. He didn't know exactly when I was going to do it. Mom had a smile on her face the entire time we ate.

After dessert, chocolate soufflé, which I didn't touch, we all went straight for the family room to relax. Matteo helped Dad sit in his usual chair while Mom sat beside him. Dad didn't have all his strength back yet. I knew he would be back to normal in a few days. Now that he was awake, time would help him recover quickly. Dad grabbed a carving knife from the table beside him and started chipping away at a piece of wood. Matteo and I both sat together on the couch. Matteo could tell my nerves were getting the best of me. I couldn't stop fidgeting with my hands. Matteo had to place his hands on mine to stop the twitching.

It felt like a chilly night. A newly lit fire was burning, but not warming me up. The logs were recently placed and the fire grew fairly large. I sat the closest to it since I had the chills. I didn't know if I was actually cold or if I was just going crazy.

Mom slumped her head to the side as she stared at me. "Sophia, what's wrong?" she asked. She was the first one to comment on my behaviour. I knew Matteo noticed before her, but didn't say anything.

I cleared my throat. I turned to Matteo who gave me a comforting nod, letting me know I was doing the right thing. I turned back to Mom. Dad now had my attention as well. "Well, I went over to Paul Jr.'s house today."

"Oh, Sophia, that's so nice of you." Mom cut me off before I could continue with the rest of my story. "How is he doing? Is he well? He was worried about you."

"Yeah, he's fine." I thought back to him passed out on the ground with a gash on his forehead. "I went to his house and he told me some... things."

"What kind of things?" Mom looked concerned. Dad brought both his hands to his lap and lost all interest in the piece of wood he was carving. He still held the wood and knife tightly in his hands. His eyes were stuck on me like glue, even though I looked at Mom the entire time.

"Well, I learned the truth behind Dad's accident." I turned to Dad, "Do you remember anything before you fell off your horse? Anything at all?"

Dad tried remembering. He sighed as he thought about it. "It was so long ago. All I remember is hearing something in the bushes, then something black jumped out of nowhere and scared my horse. I didn't see what it was and I don't remember what happened after that. My mind went blank." Dad shook his head.

"Exactly. Well I just found out what scared your horse. It was a black panther."

My parents' eyes widened. "Here, at our house?" Mom looked scared.

"How is that possible? They live deep in the woods. No one has seen a panther around here, ever. They never come out of the woods," Dad said. It was as if they didn't believe me.

"I don't know why or how, but that is what scared your horse. Also, Paul Jr. now has this panther as a pet. Paul chased it that day to capture it. That exact moment it ran by you, it scared your horse and that's how you fell off. It was an accident; an accident with bad timing."

Mom gasped in shock and covered her mouth with her hand. She turned to Dad to see his reaction. In fact, we were all staring at him at this moment; wondering how he would react.

"Well," Dad said as he picked up the piece of wood and knife again. His gaze went down to the wood as he started picking at it to think about what he was going to say. "Accidents happen. I am not one to get upset with someone over something that was unintentional."

We were all taken back by his calmness. *Okay, that was easy,* I thought. It was now time to tell them the worst part. "Also, when I was there, I found out the truth about Massimo."

Dad's head was down as I spoke, but as soon as I said 'the truth about Massimo,' he kept his head down but his eyes shot up. I saw his knuckles turn white as his grip on the knife tightened.

Oh gosh, oh gosh, oh gosh. "Massimo lied to you." I closed my eyes tightly. I couldn't look at my parents as I said this. "He told you that he accidentally walked in on Mom changing. This was not true. Mom remembers nothing right?" I opened my eyes to see Mom nodding. "Do you remember Paul coming over for drinks?" I saw Mom's eyes widen in fear. "He slipped something into your drink. He drugged you and told Massimo he could have his way with you."

"WHAT?!" Dad roared as he stood up. With the knife clenched tightly in his right hand, it looked like he was about to stab someone.

Mom's eyes started to water. "No, he didn't... But... I must have known." Mom's hands were trembling as she shook her head.

I stood up. "No, Mom, don't worry. Massimo didn't do anything. Paul told me that Massimo had a change of heart and couldn't go through with it."

I sat back down beside Matteo. "Paul orchestrated all of this so he could get closer to me. He wanted *me.*" I felt disgusted saying those words.

Out of anger Dad stabbed the desk that was beside him. "You are to never see that boy ever again! You hear me Sophia?!" Dad yelled and pointed a finger at me.

I shot back up for my rebuttal. "Me? You don't have to worry about that! Dad, I hate him! I hate Paul Jr.! He disgusts me and I will never go see him again! You can't pay me enough money to go back to his house. If he ever shows up here again he will have to pay the price for messing with us!"

Dad's breathing became heavier. Matteo got up and ran towards Dad before he could fall over. Dad needed to rest and by bringing this up to him didn't help his condition. Matteo carefully helped him sit back in his chair.

"I need to speak with Paul. This behaviour is unacceptable!" Mom got up from her seat and bent down in front of Dad. "Is that alright with you, sweetie? I need to talk to him and clear my mind. Hearing it from him will only convince me." She placed both hands on Dad's knees. Dad's breath was still coming out heavily.

"I am coming with you," Dad said.

Mom shook her head. "You are much too weak. I will only be gone for an hour or two. I promise."

Dad didn't want to let her go alone.

Matteo interfered. "I will go with Mom. I will make sure she is safe. Kiko will come along with us. He will be our protection against his panther." Matteo and Dad's eyes locked for a few moments; as if Dad was contemplating on whether or not this was a good idea. In the end Dad nodded in agreement.

Mom gave Dad a kiss and said she would be back soon. They left.

I took Mom's seat next to Dad. I felt horribly about everything. It was my fault entirely for allowing this to go on as long as it had. Since I was on a truth telling spree, I thought that I might as well tell Dad about his portal.

"Dad, there is something else I have to tell you. "

Dad sighed, "There is always more. Alright, let me hear it."

"I used your portal." I flinched expecting Dad to be upset and yell at me.

He chuckled a bit. I got even more worried. *Had he lost it?* "I thought what you were about to tell me was going to be much worse. I know you used my portal. That is not something new to me."

"How did you know?" I asked.

"I know many things, child."

"Well then, did you know now that it is broken? I didn't break it though! I swear! At least, not intentionally."

"It is not your fault. There's an imbalance. In order for it to work again, something has to be set in balance before it lets anyone else go through. You have to fix whatever you have done on Earth before you can use it again. See, going against my rules of forbidding you to go to Earth only ended up in me having a broken portal. Whatever you did on Earth, you must undo it. You don't have to tell me what you did. All you have to do now is settle this business and all will be well."

"Oh."

"Now, with that being said, can you please help me to my room? I am exhausted and I have had a very eventful day. Even in my normal and healthy state, this would be too much for me to handle. I hope you don't mind my leaving. You must understand how tired I am."

I knew Dad worried for Mom and Matteo. He intentionally didn't want me to notice. I smiled and helped Dad up to his feet.

After helping him into bed, and bidding him goodnight, I thought I might as well go to my room. As much as I would have rather been outside, I knew it was too late to be outside alone. I didn't feel safe anymore. I sat in the middle of my bed with my back straight and my legs crossed. The lights were off and the window was slightly open. There was an eerie silence. I wondered what was going on at Paul's house. Dad's words echoed in my mind.

"You have to fix whatever you have done on Earth before you can use it again."

How can I fix what I did? I wondered. I met Joshua. I fell in love and now he is dead. He betrayed me and I fell for it. *How do I undo the past? How do I bring someone back from the dead?* I couldn't fix it. The portal would be broken forever. I lay back on my bed and stared at the ceiling. I thought back to Earth and the many memories I had there. The sharp pain of realization reminded me that it was all a sham. Joshua was an imposter, a fake and I trusted him with my life.

I had to live with that on my conscience now. There were only two men in my life I could trust now. Dad and Matteo. Tomorrow I would figure out how to fix that darn portal. I knew that I would never hear the end of it until I did. *Tomorrow is another day. When will this all end?*

Chapter 25 - Determination

PAUL

I lay on the ground not able to move. It felt as if someone was squeezing my head as tight as they could. My forehead felt as if sandpaper were being dragged against it. I realized my body was numb and I couldn't feel my limbs. My brain was telling me to get up, but my body refused to. I couldn't control my movements. I was going in and out of consciousness.

I don't know how long I was out for, but eventually I got the strength to open my eyes. Everything was blurry as I turned my head slightly and realized Kioné was licking my forehead. I sluggishly lifted my hand and placed it on Kioné's face. I was slowly regaining feeling in my limbs. It took a lot out of me, just to lift my arms. It was as if I were holding invisible weights. Kioné took one step back from me as I touched him. That would explain the rough texture against my forehead. I don't know how, but cats have the roughest tongues. *Why is he licking my head?* I wondered.

What happened? Where am I, and why am I lying on the floor? It all came back to me at once - the confrontation with Sophia! I quickly stood up. Blood rushed to my head, causing a massive head rush. I fell down onto one knee while I used my hands on the floor to balance myself. I lowered my head as my vision went black. I closed my eyes, and slowly reopened them. My vision came back in dotted pieces. I blinked a few times to get my vision back to normal. I shouldn't have gotten up that fast. My head was pounding. I walked over to the couch to sit down and pull myself together. I touched my forehead where it hurt and brought my fingers back in front of my face. My forehead was wet. I assumed it was just from Kioné, but I was wrong. When I looked back at my fingers, I realized they were spotted with blood. I groaned in disappointment. *Blood?* Oh yes,

Matteo surprised us both and threw that stupid ashtray at my head at the last minute before he and Sophia got away from me. I must have passed out from the effect of it.

I took in a deep breath to calm myself and with all of my strength, I stood up. I went to the table behind the couch to make myself a hard drink on the rocks. I felt I deserved it. I dropped two ice cubes into the glass and filled it three quarters of the way. I normally fill my glass only half the way, but I think I needed a little bit more this time. Not only did I have the pain from the cut, but I also had a throbbing headache that I could tell was going to hang around for a while. I needed something to numb the pain.

Kioné stared at me from the other side of the couch. I stared back at him, contemplating what I would do next. It looked like Kioné was trying to read my mind. He was always mysterious like that. I couldn't believe Sophia knew the truth about everything. She knew about the accident with her father, and how it was my fault. I will admit that it was, but I will *not* admit that I did it on purpose. On the other hand, the situation with her mother was my fault. I will not deny it, but I am definitely not ashamed. I don't regret anything in my life and I am not going to start now. I stand by my decisions.

I was wrong, in a sense, for what I did with her mother, but it was my only move; I had to get closer to Sophia. When Antonio went into his coma, she secluded herself in her tower and didn't talk to anyone - not even Matteo - which was very surprising. I remember those days so vividly. I had waited by her side every day, trying to talk to her. I spoke as she sat there, listening – or so I thought. I was wrong. I would ask her questions and she wouldn't answer. At that point I knew she was not listening to me. Her body was there, but her mind was millions of miles away, lost in space somewhere.

One day, months ago, I felt like I had to tell her how I felt. I was taught in boarding school to go after what I want. There was no failure in life. You were a winner or you were a loser, no '*in between*'. My teachers taught me to stay strong and not to give up on things I want in life. Giving up is for the weak. I may be a lot of things but weak is not one of them!

I had to let Sophia know I was in love with her. Keeping those feelings inside was never good for the body or soul. She let me visit her every day, so I assumed she felt something for me as well. Maybe she was one of those shy girls who keep those things to themselves. There was only one way to find out. I stood behind her and she sat on her window sill at an angle. I could see half her face. She didn't turn to me as I stood there, but she did know I was there.

I had hoped she would listen to me this time, "Sophia, I came here today to tell you that I am in love with you." I straightened my back and stuck out my chest. It made me feel stronger. "These feelings I have for you, I tried to ignore them, but with every day they grew stronger and I knew they were true. I think you are the most beautiful woman I have seen in my life. There is something that draws me to you. You have a hold on me that would be unbearable if you chose to break it. I hope you choose not to. Do you feel the same as I do? Do you have any feelings whatsoever towards me? You must, right? You *do* like me?"

I stood there in complete silence, waiting. A breeze then blew in from the window. Sophia closed her eyes and took in a deep breath of the fresh air. Her hair flew backwards and away from her face. Her pale skin glowed from the sun. I got a whiff of her perfume - or shampoo - that got mixed up in the breeze. It made the hairs on my arms stand up.

"Sophia?" I asked, more calm, hoping to get an answer this time. I took a step forward and spoke with a more powerful tone to my voice. "Your feelings are mutual I assume?"

She didn't even look at me. I wondered how she could sit there and ignore me like that.

"Sophia, are you even listening to me? I poured my heart out to you and you don't even say anything? I can't stand here like a lost puppy and expect you to say something! It is a losing battle. Answer me, woman!"

She turned and looked directly at me. I couldn't tell what she was thinking. At that moment I could see the pain in her eyes. She stared directly into my anger ridden eyes. I couldn't think of any words to describe the sadness in her eyes. I was no longer mad. I stood there panting. My heart raced for some kind of answer from her. It was as if the situation just dawned on her and her eyes went from empty to angry – very angry. She slammed the open book on her lap shut - which she wasn't even reading - stood up, and slammed it onto the ledge she was once sitting on. She then lost it with me.

"Now, *why* are you so upset? What are you doing? Who *are* you? Why are you even here? I am just sitting here, trying to think and I have you babbling in my ear about who knows what! *News Flash*, I am not listening to you! Have you not realized this? Just leave me alone, please! I don't want to see you again. Go find someone else to bother because, seriously, I don't like you and I think you are wasting your time by coming here every day. I am sorry."

And just like that, she sat back down to stare out her window like I wasn't even there. I stormed out of her tower and went home. I didn't need her – I didn't need this. To be treated like that was unacceptable! I would forget about her. No girl with that radiating beauty, that strength and endurance deserves my time. She is too hard headed and determined and rude and… and… absolutely amazing. *Darn her!*

I went home that day and thought of ways to get over her. I thought taking a trip. I had the portal; I could go anywhere. But I knew in the end I would just end up in the same place; Sophia's house.

I came to the conclusion that I would wean myself from seeing her. Instead of going up and talking to her pointlessly for hours, I would just visit every day and watch her from the garden. I stood there for a minute each time. This way I knew I would get over her. It was a surreal feeling to see her up there, staring down at me. She looked like she was in complete bliss, but was being eaten away on the inside, and it was my fault. I didn't know how to make it better, but I felt like we were getting somewhere. The more I went to visit her, the happier she seemed.

I normally visited her at the same time every day. One day I was running late but when I finally got there, I noticed the look in her eyes – she missed me. Her face lit up and her beautiful smile emerged. I couldn't help but smile back at her. She had a gift of making people smile, just by smiling herself. My plan to get over her had failed miserably.

I knew right then and there that I had to come up with a plan to get her back to normal and in love with me. Incapacitating her father was the first – unplanned – step. I figured getting rid of her mother would be the next. It backfired on me. It did the exact opposite of what I expected. Finding her mother and Massimo together made her run away in the opposite direction. It made her turn to the portal for an escape. I should have seen that coming, but it was too late.

Now I was stuck in this predicament. She knows everything about me. She thinks I'm crazy, but I am not. She just doesn't understand my need for love. All my life I had never felt loved. My parents, at their first chance, sent me away to boarding school. The teachers didn't love me; my friends didn't love me. I am pretty sure many girls lusted over me, but that is about it. Now I find myself being shunned by the one person who *could* love me.

I failed to make Sophia realize what she truly means to me. I failed to make her love me back. I don't take failure lightly and by having her despise me is failure in my eyes.

I will not be satisfied until I have her. I don't know how to fix the relationship between us. I wish I had a relationship as strong as Sophia and Matteo's. For once I am jealous of that petty excuse of a man – Matteo. Sophia loves him. How can I be jealous of their relationship? They are brother and sister for crying out loud. Of course they love each other, but the love I seek from Sophia is love of a different nature.

Damn that Matteo. I have to get rid of him some way or another if I want to spend the rest of my life with Sophia. I know with him in the picture, I will never have her. He is much too protective of her. In a way I don't mind it since I know Sophia will always be safe around him, but he should not be protecting her from me.

Drastic measures must be taken. I am glad Sophia is over that Earth human Joshua. He was just a waste of her time and I am glad she didn't find out the total truth about him. For now he is gone and she will never see him again. He was not worth her time. I would never use Sophia the way he did.

I will never forget the first time he kissed her. I watched from my portal. Not because I was spying on them, well maybe just a little, but I needed to see that he wouldn't harm her. I would never forgive myself if he hurt her and I had the power to protect her by just watching through the portal.

I watched them sit on his bed together; I watched them stare into each other's eyes. I knew exactly what he was thinking; staring at her lips, imagining what they felt like, what they tasted like. Her red lips would drive any man crazy! I couldn't let him kiss her. The closer they got, the more my blood boiled. I felt nauseous just watching them. I kept repeating in my mind, *'I have to stop them, I have to stop them!'* I couldn't hold it back anymore. I almost ran straight into their room, but how would I explain myself to Joshua? Earth people are to not know about our world under *any* circumstances.

At the last moment, before I walked into the portal, I told it to take me to their front door. Curiosity got the best of me as I pushed a button which made a ringing sound on the other side of the door. I heard Joshua's voice. I punched the door with an angry fist as hard as I could; then about six more times after that. It wasn't a knock; I literally almost punched a hole through the door. I think I hurt my hands more than I hurt the door. I realized that once a door is knocked, someone would answer it. I panicked and told the portal to bring me back. By the time the door handle was turned, I was already on my way back to Caledonia. It was a close one but I hoped it prevented them from kissing.

The portal shut down as soon as I got back. I was dizzy from going to Earth and back so quickly. I was too angry to concentrate on anything else. He was going to kiss Sophia and feel her soft lips on his. I couldn't stand it. I wanted to kiss her. I was the one who was *supposed* to kiss her, not him. I ordered the portal to show me Sophia one more time. As soon as the picture showed, she and Joshua were sitting at his table together, gazes locked in lust. Sophia's cheeks were flushed and her lips looked redder. He kissed her, I know he did. *Damn it!* Joshua stared at her like she was a piece of meat! I know what he wanted; what any guy would want from a beautiful woman like Sophia. I was bursting with outrage. Without even thinking I went to punch the image of Joshua's face. But his image disappeared before I got the chance. I wondered if I could have punched him through the portal like that. I didn't want to try. It is a good thing it disappeared before anything. Of course Joshua didn't feel the punch. I was the one who ended up getting hurt. Punching a door multiple times and punching a portal can do some serious damage to one's knuckles.

After bandaging my bloody knuckles, I told myself that I would no longer look in on Sophia and that she has moved on without me. I had to accept that. At this point I had no choice. She has chosen who she wants to be with.

Of course it wasn't that easy. I looked in on her one day. I noticed she was running through the forest. I had no idea what she was doing. It wasn't until she approached the tree that I realized what she was doing. She was looking for the Nekkel Ace which meant she had no idea it was around her neck the entire time. I called out her name. It came out almost as a sad whisper. I felt sympathy towards her for everything she was going through. At that moment, as I said her name, she turned around and asked, *'Hello? Who's there?'* I straightened my back as I stared into the portal. *She couldn't possibly have heard me, could she?*

After that I tried for months to get her out of my mind. One day I fell ill. I threw up and thought it was because it was something I ate. I had never felt like that before. My stomach was in knots and something was telling me to go see Sophia. That little voice in my head kept telling me to go and see her all those months, but I ignored it. That time though I knew something was off. I ran as fast as I could to my portal. I told it to show me Sophia and I saw her on hands and knees on the ice. Water flowed on top of the ice quickly around her hands and legs. I could see the fear in her eyes. That Joshua boy looked scared out of his wits as well. I knew this wouldn't end well. I could hear the loud cracks of the ice getting louder. I knew I had to act fast.

I told the portal, *"Bring her back. Safe in bed."* And just like that, a bright light took her away from Earth as the ice underneath her gave way. I felt like my heart was going to explode out of my chest. If I didn't give into the urge to see her one more time, I never would have been able to save her life.

After those two experiences I knew I had no choice. Not only did I physically want to be with her, but my heart, body and soul knew that we had to be together. I knew she could never go back to Earth. As much as I didn't want to call her and tell her Joshua was dead, I had no choice. I disguised my voice so she wouldn't recognize it. She fell for it. She didn't have a clue it was me. I could hear the sadness in her voice, but it was for her own good. It brought her to me.

I realized thinking about the past wasn't going to change the future. I walked over to the window and looked outside. The moon was out and it was full. It glowed a bright orange as it hung so low in the sky. It looked as if I could almost reach out and touch it. I took a sip of my drink as the pain slowly started to subside.

I looked down and realized that beside my foot was the picture and frame that Sophia brought back from Earth. I looked at it. It was a picture of her and Joshua. I don't know what she saw in him. He was a waste of air and a waste of Sophia's time.

I walked over to the fireplace and threw the picture, along with the frame into the fire. I watched it as it burned to a crisp.

I went and sat down on what used to be my Dad's master chair. I lifted the icy glass in my hand and placed it on my pounding forehead. It was cold, but it felt good. The shock of the coldness woke me up a little.

The house was quiet tonight, just like every other night I spent here all alone. The only sound I heard was the crackling of the fire from behind me, devouring every last piece of the picture frame, erasing it from existence. Kioné lay down on the ground half asleep. My parents were both gone. As soon as I got the portal, and they found out, they decided they didn't want to stay on this planet any longer. I was grateful I didn't have to convince them to leave. They did it on their own. I got used to not seeing my parents so having them gone didn't affect me one bit. I have Kioné and my butler, Corrado at my side.

Corrado was old and spent most of his time alone in his room. He had a wife at one point. She was our head chef. I didn't know her too well. Corrado didn't always used to be a grumpy old man. After his wife died from a massive heart attack all those years ago, he has never been the same man. Love can change a man in many ways. Sometimes it looks as if he is just waiting to die so he can reunite with his beloved.

I want to experience that one day, as weird as that sounds. I don't want death to separate me from my loved one, but I like the idea of spending eternity with someone. Whether if I go first or she does, I know we will wait for each other.

This late at night, Corrado didn't bother me and I didn't bother him. I only see him during the day when he brings my meals and when he has to tell me someone was at the door. Other than that, we were oblivious to one another.

I realized that being sweet to Sophia didn't work. It only pushed her into the arms of another man, so I have made up my mind. *I will not sit here and hope for her to fall in love with me. I will make her love me whether she wants to or not. Right now, it is not her choice anymore. I gave her time to consider it, but I cannot wait any longer. Tomorrow I will go over to her house. She will most likely be in her garden, sitting, meditating, and doing whatever she does. I know Matteo will be around somewhere watching her from a distance, hidden in a bush or somewhere. I have to make sure he is not around when my plan is in motion. I will make a distraction first to get rid of him. When the time is right, I will capture Sophia. I will bring her here. I will tie her up and keep her in one of my rooms. I will make her love me, I will!*

I finished my drink it one last gulp. I was beginning to feel a little dizzy. I heard slight pounding and assumed it was my head telling me that was enough alcohol for one night. I wasn't sure if the dizziness was because of the injury to my head or if it was from the alcohol. Actually, it could have been a combination of both. I placed both my hands on the armrest as I prepared myself to get up. Before I did, Corrado sluggishly walked into the room. *Ugh, what did he want now?*

With a deeper voice than he normally has, Corrado spoke, "Master, Mrs. Susanna Amaro and her son with his pet are here to see you. Shall I let only Mrs. Susanna in?" The time of day seemed to be taking a toll of Corrado's body. The later it got, the more his back slumped. It seemed as if there were just too many hours in the day for this old man. I wondered what time it was anyway. *It must be at least 10:00 p.m.* I guessed.

I waved my hand at Corrado. "No, no. Let's see what they both have to say. Let them both in. I am curious as why they are here at this hour. For sure this will be most interesting!"

Chapter 26 – And Nothing but the Truth

SOPHIA

I woke up early morning and didn't know what to do with myself. I found out yesterday that Paul Jr. has lost his mind over me and will do just about everything and anything to have me. As much as I regret to say this- or even think it – part of me was willing to give Paul Jr. a chance. But this was before everything; before going to Earth and meeting Joshua. After what I went through yesterday, that idea is out the window and thrown into the sun; burned into a smouldering crisp. I don't even want to be on the same planet as him!

As much as yesterday's confrontation bothered me, there was something else that irritated me more. I still loved Joshua. When I first found out that he was just using me, I was furious. But the more I thought about it, the sadder I became. He had plenty of chances to take the Nekkel Ace from me and he didn't. What was he waiting for? But it really seemed like he was in love with me. I replayed our first and last fight over and over in my mind. I dreamt last night about the last moments we spent together. It was more like a nightmare than a dream actually. The terrified expression in his eyes as he feared for my life was something I could never forget. The bright light blinded his eyes before I disappeared. I figured he probably went through the ice that same instant and froze to death. My hands shook and my heartbeat accelerated as I thought about him struggling to swim in that cold water. I dreamt of seeing him struggle for his life as his limbs froze and he couldn't swim anymore. He gave up as his frozen body slowly descended into the dark, cold water. He hung there in the weightless gravity of the icy water, slowly sinking. *Why did we have to go skating that day?* It was my entire fault! He brought me there to show me something new and to make me happy again. He wanted to make up for our fight the night before. I was the one who tripped and fell hard on the ice, even after he told me to skate lightly as we headed back to shore. So technically, in the end, I killed him. My actions are what made him die.

I loved him but now he's gone. I didn't have the energy in me to be happy today. I couldn't smile and lie to myself anymore. I knew when I ran into Matteo he would probably try to cheer me up. I would smile to make him happy, but deep down inside I would always feel the torn pieces of my broken heart failing to mend itself back together; that feeling would never disappear, even if I wanted it to. Pain didn't come. Sadness didn't come. It was just an awkward numbness.

I lay on my side with my legs curled up to my chest. I opened my eyes slightly to see if I was, in fact, still in my bed and this wasn't all just a horrible, horrible dream. I didn't realize it at first, but my pillow was damp. I didn't think I cried last night. My pillow told a different story. My pillow was still cold from the tears that soaked it. I didn't want to cry anymore. I couldn't cry anymore. Tears weren't going to fix anything.

My body was in shock and didn't know what to do with itself. Feeling numb was the only thing that felt right. If I blocked out all my feelings and emotions then I don't have to worry or think of them. I stretched out my arms and legs and accidentally kicked something at the end of my bed. I was scared at first, but my first instinct was to sit straight up and see what it was. It was Matteo's arm. He lay on the end of my bed. He slept the exact same way I did. His hands covered his face as his knees were crouched into his chest. As Matteo slept, his face always looked calm like the sea on a windless day.

I thought back to all those years ago when Matteo used to sleep in my bed when he first moved here. Or when I first found him, I should say. Matteo didn't like going from the rocky ground outside in the forest, to an oversized bed with down covers and pillows. It took Matteo and Kiko almost a year to get used to their own bed and room. If I was correct, Kiko would be on the ground beside the bed right now. I arched my head to look over, and of course, there he was, snoring like a tiger - whatever that was supposed to sound like.

It was a little bit weird. On any other day if I kicked Matteo, he would have automatically woken up. His wild instincts don't let him sleep in like this. The only explanation is that he must be really tired. I must have been tired as well to not even notice him sleeping there the whole night. I wonder what time he and Mom came home. I would ask him, but I didn't want to disturb him. I got out of bed and quickly got dressed. As soon as I walked out of my room, I looked over my shoulder and saw Kiko looking at me. He barely had his eyes open. I motioned with my index finger in front of my lips and whispered, "Sh." Kiko's head went back into his paws in front of him and he went back to sleep. I didn't know how this was possible possible, but Kiko looked exhausted as well.

I was going to go to my garden, but I didn't deserve that beauty today. I decided to go to my oak tree and hide in the shade; away from humanity. I didn't want to be seen by anyone. I wanted to be hidden from the world. As soon as I got to my tree, I parted its branches so I could walk through. I went directly for my swing. I needed to think. I needed to relax. I swung back and forth a couple of times, filling my lungs with clean crisp air. When I didn't feel like swinging anymore, I stopped.

I sat on my swing sulking with a sickening pain in my stomach as I inevitably thought of Joshua. I knew I would never get over him. At least I knew he would live on in my memories. But that provided very little comfort.

I didn't have the energy to even sit anymore. I let go of the ropes on the swing and crawled to the ground. I turned over on my back and stared up at my tree. I loved my perfect, beautiful tree with its huge round trunk. The blades of grass were tickling my ears, but this time I felt no emotion. Tears streamed down my face. I couldn't control them! They came without any notice whatsoever. Even if I wanted to, I don't think I would have been able to stop them. The numbness was still there as tears came streaming down. I could hear each drop hit the blades of grass. I felt sorry for the grass. This was the second time I had tainted it with my salty tears. I wished to be a tree right now. I wished to not have to feel this way. Trees have no feelings, no worries, and no sorrow. If I were a tree, I would not feel like this.

I heard two sets of footsteps coming up from behind me. I sat up and wiped my eyes. I knew already who they were. It was Matteo and Kiko of course. I was looking down at first because I didn't want Matteo to see my red eyes, but he stood there without saying anything so I looked up to him first.

As soon as I saw his face, I bolted upright. "Matteo! What happened to your eye!?" I didn't realize when I first saw him sleeping on my bed since he was covering his face with his hands. I raised my hand to gently touch his right eye. My touch made him wince.

He laughed. "Well, Paul Jr. has a better punch than I thought." Matteo's right eye was all purple and blue all around.

I gasped in shock. *Paul Jr. did this?* "What happened last night?" I asked.

"Well, I learned something new about Mom." He paused. "She has much more courage and bravery than we give her credit for. That's for sure!" He laughed awkwardly.

I waited for him to continue. I needed to hear what he was going to say.

"So we went to Paul's house. Get this; he actually let me in this time. We sat down, Mom was being all nice, but when she got down to the point, she took me by surprise. She stood up and got right in Paul's face. They stood with their faces inches apart. Paul was even taken back by this. She forced him back into his seat – she pushed him down actually – and made him tell her everything. He wouldn't. He refused to! He stood back up and Mom had to take a couple steps back from him. He raised his voice to her. Paul was fuming. I loved the sight. When he raised his arm to Mom, that's when I cut in. I grabbed his arm and he pulled it back. Some nasty words were exchanged, but you don't need all the details. Paul went to punch me, but I ducked. I went to take a step backwards, but his stupid pet was behind me and I tripped and fell flat on my back! Paul came on top of me and started punching me in the face. He got two good punches before I rolled him over and started punching him in the face. Mom ran to the wall and pulled off one of Mr. Carter's collective swords, pulled off the sheath and placed it over Paul's neck! I stopped punching as I held his arms down while Mom held his neck down with the sword. I couldn't believe it! She was actually digging it into his skin! There was blood, I'll tell you that, not a lot, but there was. He refused to tell us exactly what happened with you, so Mom decided to shed a little more blood to make him speak.

"In the end, he told us *everything*! Even things you had no idea about. I guess threatening someone with their life really pays off! Oh, and don't worry. You won't be seeing Paul Jr. from now on. He is long gone."

"What? Mom didn't... did she?"

"No. no! Hell no! You think I would let her kill him? Now *that* is taking it too far. You don't have to ever worry about Paul Jr. again."

I was frozen the entire time Matteo spoke. I couldn't believe it. *Mom is amazing. She is such a strong woman and when I see her I will thank her for everything she has done for me.* "Thank you," I whispered as I took a little step towards Matteo and hugged him. He hugged me tightly back.

"Anything for you, little sis. I am your big brother remember? It is my

193

job to protect you. I can't tell you this enough times." Matteo pulled back from the hug. "There is also one more thing I have to tell you."

More? I didn't think I could handle anymore news. I was out of breath from doing nothing and my hands were shaking.

After hearing all of that, I wanted nothing more than to just sit down and be alone.

"Someone is here to see you. You have a visitor," Matteo said as he sounded a little too happy.

Matteo covered my eyes since he said he wanted to surprise me. "Matteo what are you doing? I don't like surprises. Just tell me who it is. Stop." I tried pulling his hands off but he didn't move them. Of course Matteo didn't want to make things easy for me so he insisted on covering my eyes for the full effect of the surprise. "Matteo, I am not in the mood for this! Please just tell whoever is here that I will see them another day!" I hated complaining, but I *really* didn't want to see anyone. Matteo's hands were warm against my face.

I sighed and gave in.

He led me away from the tree. I had my hands in front of me to push the branches away. Matteo turned me around so the front of my body was now facing my tree and my back was to my house. The sun warmed up my back. Matteo removed his hands from my eyes and he told me to keep them closed. I didn't know why I was going along with this, but I did anyway.

Matteo took two steps to the side of me. "Okay, ready? Sophia, open your eyes and turn around."

I couldn't. My legs froze. I forgot how to walk or even open my eyes. I couldn't move. I got so nervous all of a sudden. I couldn't explain it. I didn't turn. I just stood there with my hands clenched. I didn't want to play along anymore.

"Sophia," A voice said. It wasn't Matteo's. "Please turn." The voice was so calm and charming.

I took a deep breath and held it in for a few seconds as I turned around. When I turned around completely, I saw something that didn't seem real to me; but I had to believe this moment was real, even if it wasn't. My heart pounded hard in my chest, and made me believe it was real. In these few moments everything was fine. The hole in my heart was fixed and my life was complete. Grass was growing and flowers were blooming again. I was weightless. It was as if I was flying and he was with me again and things were perfect. His face was so familiar, his eyes beamed with happiness, his smile - breathtaking.

He ran up to me and lifted me in his arms. This was real. He really was here! As soon as his body touched mine, things were back to normal. I exhaled and my thoughts fell back into place. I remembered how to breathe; I remembered his scent like it was never gone. How was this possible after believing this whole time he was dead? I believed he was selfishly taken away from me; ripped directly from my heart.

Our beating hearts pounded against one other as he held me as tight as he could. I didn't have it in me to release my grip. I was afraid if I let go, he would be forever gone. I wouldn't be able to bear it, not again, just like that.

"You're here. I'm here. It's really you, but you're blonde. I thought you were dead," he whispered softly into my ear. My body tensed as his sweet whispers left tingles down my spine.

My body relaxed as I slowly moved back to take in his face. I wasn't dreaming. No one can dream their lover's touch, presence and scent like this. I still didn't understand how he was here, on my planet. How did he ever manage to find me and get here? It was impossible. "Joshua," I said finally as tears escaped my eyes once again.

I looked around and saw Mom covering her mouth. She was about thirty feet behind him. Her eyes were red, filled with tears - tears of joy I'm sure. Dad was right beside her. They were talking – about us of course. I could just tell. I couldn't wait to introduce Joshua to my parents.

Before I introduced them, I had to ask the question I've been wondering this entire time. "What happened to you? I went back to your place and your things were gone. Who was cleaning out your room?"

"What? You came back to my place?!" Joshua seemed to be out of breath as well. We were both filled with adrenaline just to be in one another's presence. "No one cleaned out my room. I did that! I packed my things and left. I tried to remember what you told me about where you live. You told me it was a big white house on top of a mountain with an amazing pond and a beautiful tree that you loved to swing on. It was always sunny and your garden was your favourite place to be."

He remembered. The tears flowed endlessly and I felt like something was caught in my throat.

"I went searching for you! Milo and I went on a little journey and looked all over the place for a description that matched what you told me. I couldn't explain what happened on the ice - you disappearing and all - so I figured if I found your home, I could ask your parents or a family member what happened. Your family found me before I could find them. I knew you lived somewhere mysterious, but I would never think you lived on a different planet! You're a little alien!" Joshua smiled my favourite, eye wrinkling smile.

Alien? What the heck was that?

Joshua turned around to look back at Mom and Dad who were still standing in the background. Joshua looked to his right. I followed his gaze and saw Matteo, Kiko and Milo all playing together. Milo and Kiko were rolling on the ground together.

It all came back to me as I grabbed my necklace. I didn't have the courage to confront him. I loved him so much and I didn't want to ruin the moment, but I knew I had to. I would regret it if I didn't. "I have another thing to ask you."

"Anything, my sweet Sophia!" Joshua grabbed a strand of my hair and gently placed it behind my ear. He then ran his finger down my jaw. I almost lost my train of thought. I had to pull it together for this one.

"My necklace. You knew about it. You didn't tell me. You wanted to take it from me, didn't you?" I looked to the ground. My eyes were fixed on my shoes. I couldn't bear to look at him. I could sense Joshua's body stiffen from my words. *Busted. I knew it.*

"It's true," Joshua said.

I closed my eyes and clenched my fists tight. I couldn't believe it. Straight from the horse's mouth. My nails dug into my palms.

"Sophia," Joshua said as he lifted my gaze up by cupping my chin and lifting it. "Do you not remember the fight that we had?"

I nodded even though I wanted to forget all about our one and only fight. It's what got us into this mess in the first place.

"Do you remember what I said to you?" Joshua's voice came out softly. There was no fear in his voice, no regret. It was pure satisfaction. It was as if I was in a dream and I was making this up. I knew I wasn't dreaming. I could never make this stuff up.

I shook my head. I did remember him talking about his Dad's journal and saying it didn't matter anymore and then ripping it up. "Not really. Sorry."

"I said, '*Nothing matters anymore! From now on, I will listen to myself and not listen to what anyone else says! I am breaking life promises but it means nothing to me now that I have met you!*' Do you remember now?"

It sounded familiar. "Yes, but I don't get it."

Joshua exhaled. "My father… his journal… he made me promise him one thing in life, that I would find the object Antonio Amaro found. He told me this object, a necklace, yours, had great healing powers. My Dad was a greedy man and wanted this object more than anything in the world! I promised him I would continue to look for it. My Dad stole the picture of you from your Dad's wallet to show me who you were and what the object looked like. It was weird since Dad could only see the chain on the necklace. I kept telling him there was a rock attached to it, but he didn't believe me. I thought he was playing games on me. I got annoyed and ignored the situation completely. After seeing the picture of you, I was blown away at your beauty, but nothing compared to the first time I actually laid my own bare eyes on you. The whole Frisbee thing was an accident, but I knew immediately it was you when you looked up at me for the first time. Your clear blue eyes cast me in a trance. Your hair was a different colour, brown, but I knew it was you. My heart skipped a beat. I knew right then and there I could never do that to you. I knew the instant our eyes locked that I could never hurt anyone as lovely and innocent as you. I decided not to go through with my Dad's last wishes. I told myself to forget it and to just be happy with you. I broke the promise and I couldn't be happier. I regretted nothing!

"The necklace meant nothing to me since I was able to hold you in my arms at night. Watching you smile and hearing you laugh is more valuable to me than a piece of rock. I was never going to go through with it. That's why I ripped up the journal. The journal was filled with plots on how to get the necklace. After I met you, and read those things, it made me sick to my stomach to even think of it! I wanted us to spend the rest of our lives together, forever. I don't care if you had a billion dollar diamond necklace hanging around your neck. Nothing would ever come close to the purity and gentleness of your face and those kind lips that I have been longing to kiss for so long now." Joshua ran his thumb over my bottom lip. I parted my mouth gently. I could feel my pulse in my fingertips. I don't think my circulation was working properly. Joshua stopped my blood dead in its tracks.

Everything made sense now. From now on, I will not believe what anyone says until I get facts. Jumping to conclusions will get you nowhere in life. Asking questions and finding out from the person is the only way to get the true answer. I am glad I asked Joshua.

Joshua took a step towards me and inched his face closer to mine. He brought his body as close as he could to me without touching me. It was such a tease since I wanted to feel his body against mine. He leaned in, licked his lips and gently placed his soft, wet lips against mine. I inhaled deeply through my nose as I pushed for a harder kiss with my lips.

I heard throats cleaning and I backed away from Joshua. It was my parents. I didn't even hear them approach! Matteo and the animals were walking towards us as well. Out of pure embarrassment I hid behind Joshua. They all saw us kissing! Joshua and my parents started laughing. My circulation started up again and it felt like all of it went directly to my face.

I linked arm to Joshua's and came out from behind him. I still covered half my face. When I felt my face start to become normal again, I spoke, "Mom, Dad, Matteo, and Kiko, I would like to introduce you to my boyfriend, Joshua. I actually thought he was dead, but he proved me wrong. It is a long story, but we are together now and that is all that matters." I tightened my grip on his arm as I gently placed my head on it. I would have put it on his shoulder, but he is too tall for me to do that.

"Yes, we know. We introduced ourselves already. I was the one who found him actually." Mom smiled at Joshua. He smiled back.

Good. First step done - getting approval from the parents. That took a lot of weight off my shoulders. I was surprised Mom approved since Joshua is from Earth. This is the first time a person from Earth has laid a foot on this planet. He would never be able to go back!

Mom continued, "I got Paul Jr. to tell me everything that happened with you. I was very kind about it too," she lied. "Paul told me that you were in love with a boy from Earth named Joshua and that you thought he was dead. Paul Jr. saw Joshua leave the frozen lake unharmed that day and go searching for you. Paul intentionally let you go through the portal to see his room and closet empty. After Paul filled me in on those details, I told Matteo to return home and ice his face, which looks much better than it did yesterday, and I went into the portal after Joshua. When I found him I told him who I was and what I was doing. After giving him the ultimatum of choosing life on Earth or you - I didn't even have to finish my sentence - he obviously chose you.

"I fully understand and I couldn't ask for anything else." Joshua nodded his head as if going back to Earth was the last thing on his mind. He didn't even seem to care.

"What about your business, your plans, your house?" I asked.

"I made a few phone calls and passed them along. The business was moved to my partner but my place will always be there. I didn't have it in me to sell it. I would rather have it deserted rather than strangers living in it." He squeezed my arm. "It has some precious memories that I don't want others tainting."

"Oh," was all I could think of to say.

Mom interrupted. "Sophia, there is also something else I have to tell you and I need to tell you now before anything. It is a confusing story, but please keep up with me. What I am about to tell you was a secret that Paul's parents, the Carters, have told your father and me." Mom turned to Dad. "Remember what happened all those years ago when they went to Earth?"

"Oh…. I do remember, but what does that have to do with anything now?"

Mom looked to Joshua then back to me.

"Mom, I am lost," I said.

"One moment Sophia. Let me just put the pieces together." Mom was concentrating on something. We were all anxiously waiting for her to continue. "Okay, let me try that again."

She cleared her throat and began. "The Carters, before they were married, came to us and asked if they could use our portal. They wanted to leave Caledonia and start a new life on Earth. Their parents didn't approve of their relationship, so they wanted to run away together. Don't get any ideas though." Mom gave us 'the look.' "Anyway, so they went to Earth and started a life there. One problem though - they got pregnant. They were about to have a child out of wedlock and that was something neither of them were ready for. When the time came, they had the child, named him and gave him up for adoption in the first week he was born. A young and in-love couple adopted him right away, no questions asked. It was a hard time for the Carters and they decided they couldn't live on Earth anymore. They came back to Caledonia, got married and had their *second* son, Paul Jr., and sent him to boarding school. They couldn't bear looking at Paul Jr., knowing that they abandoned their first child. They came to us and told us their secret and we promised not to tell anyone." Mom took another deep breath. "Every year they went back to Earth to check on their son. No one knew about this except us. The adoptive parents didn't even know. The Carters just wanted to make sure he was being taken care of properly. They would bring back pictures of him to show us every year."

I shrugged my shoulders. "Okay. So what does that have to do with me? Why are you telling me this now? I didn't really ask." I didn't want to sound rude, but when the topic turned to Paul Jr., I didn't really care.

Mom linked her arms with Dad, just as Joshua and I were doing. "It's because, Sophia, the Carters first son, Paul Jr.'s older brother…" She paused to look at Dad. "You know him."

"How could I possibly know him? I don't know too many people, you know that."

"Yes you do because his name… is Joshua."

All of our jaws dropped. Mine, Joshua's, Matteo's and I'm pretty sure Kiko's dropped as well.

"I…I didn't know I was adopted," Joshua whispered. He looked into my eyes, shaking his head.

My shock-filled eyes turned to Mom. "Mom, this can't be true. It can't."

"Yes, it *can* be true Sophia. Look." Mom held out a little piece of tattered paper for me. It was a picture of Joshua but he was about fifteen or sixteen. He was playing baseball. He had a blue uniform and a cap on.

Joshua picked up the picture and positively identified it as himself. He used to play baseball on a team when he was much younger. Earth parents would bring their children to play ball and while their child was on the field, they would normally take pictures of them. No one thought it was weird when a parent took pictures of their own child so that's why, he guessed, no one thought it was weird to see a couple taking a picture of him. He couldn't believe it.

I turned to Joshua and spoke with a sour tone. "You and Paul are *brothers*?" I was disgusted.

Joshua grabbed my hands in a panic. "I don't know! I swear! I never even heard of the guy in my life! My parents didn't have any other children." His face was filled with shock. He had no idea what was going on. I couldn't blame him. It wasn't his fault he's related to that piece of scum.

Mom spoke. "Joshua, your parents weren't able to have children. This is why they adopted you. I am sorry."

At that moment, I remembered the journal entry on how his parents were going to tell Joshua something about not being able to have children. They weren't going to tell him that they couldn't have kids; they didn't want to tell him he was adopted!

Friday January 13th 1989

Vivian and I were going to tell Joshua today but we didn't have it in us. We have decided to not tell him after all. He won't even know the difference. Vivian and I are Joshua's only family and I wish that we could have another child but it is impossible. Vivian and I have been trying for years and we have

200

had no luck. One child is enough. Joshua seems content with being an only child.

"It is alright though. You don't have to worry about Paul. None of us do. He will never find out. Everything is well," Matteo reminded us.

"Well, I've got something to do," Mom turned to Dad, "You were going to help me, right sweetie?"

"Huh? I mean, yes of course, things to do, right on it." Dad had no idea what Mom was talking about. I think she just wanted to give us some time together. Dad caught on later. Just like that, they left to go back inside.

Now it was down to three humans and two animals. Matteo smiled at us both, nodded his head a bit and then walked away. Kiko and Milo followed.

Joshua and I walked towards my garden. "It's just the two of us now. Alone, together," I said.

We lay down in my garden on our backs staring up at the blue sky in complete serenity together. I turned my head towards him, "Do you really not care about going home?"

He turned to look at me. "Sophia, wherever you are *is* home to me. Starting a new life with the one I love was all I wanted my entire life." Joshua propped himself up with his elbow and leaned his face closer to mine. He kissed me once more. It was the second time he kissed me since our reunion on Caledonia.

It was time for mine and Joshua's relationship to start over again. I couldn't ask for anyone other than him. We would live a 'happily ever after' life on Caledonia together. Paul still lurked in the back of my mind, but Matteo told me I would never have to worry about him. For now, I will think positive and be happy with my new love. Who knows, maybe one day we will get married and have kids of our own. The future is definitely something to look forward to, but for now we are taking things one step at a time and I couldn't be happier. You find love in the most random places. I found mine on a different planet, but no matter what, you will know right then and there who the right one is for you. I am glad I found mine before it was too late. The paths in life are set out for you already; it is up to you to choose which path you are willing to take. Choose wisely; choose from your heart.